The Checklist

The Checklist

Addie Woolridge

 Montlake

Published by Montlake, Seattle

www.apub.com

Amazon, the Amazon logo, and Montlake are trademarks of Amazon.com, Inc., or its affiliates.

ISBN-13: 9781542029278
ISBN-10: 1542029279

Cover design and illustration by Liz Casal

Printed in the United States of America

To the wolves who raised me, thank you.

CHAPTER ONE

"Sorry about the death sentence."

Dylan looked up from the document she was scanning, a little startled to find Kahn MacElroy, notorious Kaplan and Associates office gossip, looking down at her from over her beige cubicle wall.

"I'm sorry?"

"Oh. You haven't seen the email?" Kahn asked, pity dripping from his lips.

If there was an email with bad news in it, especially bad news for her, it must have been sent in the last five minutes. Dylan was religious about checking her email.

"Nope. Just here reading these briefs. Prepping for the Les Enfants project." She kept her smile neat.

"You'll want to read this email." He shrugged.

Dylan hated the fact that Kahn knew something she didn't. But she couldn't look with him there.

"I will, eventually," she said, turning her attention back to the document and summoning all her willpower to wait Kahn out.

"I'll leave you to it." Kahn's tone was less sympathetic once he realized he wouldn't get the inside scoop.

Dylan waited until the olive green of his sweater rounded the corner before furiously wheeling her chair over to her screen.

To: All Associates

From: Jared Gilroy

Subject: Congratulations, Dylan Delacroix!

In light of Dylan's unplanned leadership on the Davis Communications project, it is with great excitement that I announce her placement with me on the Technocore team. Her quick thinking and willingness to step in when the Davis project was off-track produced one of the best corporate turn-arounds Kaplan saw last year. I'm confident Dylan has what it takes to turn Technocore around. Be sure to stop by her desk before Friday and wish her good luck on this next assignment.

Jared Gilroy
Junior Partner
Kaplan & Associates—Helping your company get results!

Dylan stared at the email, then checked her pulse. No, she wasn't dead or hallucinating. She swallowed hard and reread the email. Kaplan didn't usually send out placement announcements before notifying the employee. Surely this was a mistake. She'd saved Jared's job on the Davis Communications project. There was no way she should have been assigned anything less than Les Enfants in Paris. Everyone at Kaplan knew the further you climbed, the better the assignment. She had been practicing with a French tutor for weeks.

A muffled *thunk thunk* on her cubicle wall made Dylan jump, interrupting her third reading of the email. Barb Maisewell stood in the entrance, looking genuinely perplexed. Her suits were always frumpy, and her insistence on wearing maroon didn't help, but Dylan liked Barb. She was one part office mother, one part gossip mill. You'd think that as head assistant to the elusive Mrs. Kaplan, she'd be discreet, but Barb was the exact opposite. If she liked you, Barb would tell you whatever she heard about you from the top brass. She was half the reason Dylan had bought that stupid, expensive French Rosetta Stone subscription.

Barb opened her mouth, sympathy puckering her face. "Technocore, huh?" Dylan didn't say anything, so she plowed on. "Jared must be really bitter about you making him look bad with the Davis thing. I heard rumors about you and Paris just last week. Wonder what changed?"

"I'm sure there is a mix-up. In fact, I was on my way to meet with Jared now." Dylan tried to appear as if talking to her weasel-faced boss had always been her plan.

Barb looked at her as if she were a tad delusional, ignoring Dylan's attempt to salvage the situation. "Honey, if I don't see you, have a great time in Seattle. Technocore is . . . well, it's a challenge. But I know you can do it."

After giving her a quick hug, Barb scuttled toward the kitchen, probably to gossip with someone else about Dylan's assignment. Dylan stood up, then took a moment to straighten her untwisted hem and check for any flyaway hairs, carefully smoothing her center part, before walking toward Jared's office. It wouldn't do to appear unprofessional. If there was any trait Kaplan and Associates could count on, it was that Dylan was always professional.

Taking a controlled breath, she knocked on the office door. After a few heartbeats, Jared's familiar nasal invited her in.

"Hi, Jared. I saw the announcement. Did I miss something?" Dylan kept the anger out of her voice as she sat down, uninvited. Across from her was the biggest pastel-wearing asshole she knew. Unfortunately, Jared was also her direct supervisor and the one person standing between her and a chance to make junior partner before the end of the year. She waited for him to answer, registering a boost in his uncomfortably healthy glow. It was the kind of tan some white people got from playing lots of tennis in the sun. Only, Jared acquired his through a tanning booth.

"Right. The partners suggested I go, but I really feel Technocore is perfect for you." He smiled, his teeth the same unnerving shade of white as the walls, as if he were handing her a compliment and not the career death sentence Technocore was. In the last six months, the company's hapless founder had made every unforgivable management gaffe known to man and even a few new ones that had surprised both Dylan and the press. Technocore had gone from a groundbreaking start-up to a profit-sinking black hole in record time, losing employees, money, and public opinion faster than a politician in an infidelity scandal. They didn't need Kaplan and Associates. They needed a miracle. Or, Dylan thought, they at least needed their founder to get a clue and stop wearing hoodies.

Jared continued, shifting uncomfortably in his chair under her fixed gaze. "The firm has been brought in as a personal favor to Mr. Kaplan. I'm sure you saw the article in *Management Today*. Anyway, we need a quick intervention on this one. Share prices have been down for the last two quarters. As you may know, Technocore's board of directors is looking for a new productivity consultant to get their image cleaned up and their leadership in line by the end of Q3."

"I'm sorry." Dylan's mind instinctively jumped over the condescending sections of his speech and homed in on the important details. "The third quarter? Of this year? That timeline is overly ambitious. We are already midway through April."

"That's why you'll be stationed in Seattle for the duration of the project. There is really no time for back-and-forth here."

"Jared, I don't mean to question anyone's judgment; you certainly know more than I do about the project, but I'm sure I could commute and—"

"Look, Dylan. I'm going to need you to be a team player on this one," Jared said, dropping the encouraging-manager persona and doubling down on the jargon-riddled belittling she was familiar with. "The cowboy antics may have worked well with Davis, but Technocore is the real deal. Not the big-fish-small-pond stuff you are used to. We need to be rowing in the same direction on this, got it?"

Dylan did her best to bite back a sarcastic remark about not being able to hear him over the volume of his sherbet sweater. "Yes, of course. I understand. But won't the senior partners notice that I'm there and not you? I mean, we don't look alike or anything."

"You'll be handling research and first steps. I'll have ultimate approval of the analysis and produce the final report. Besides, you're from Seattle, correct? You have a better grasp of the culture. After the whole Davis Communications"—Jared paused to find the right word— "*ordeal,* I want to make sure we have our best and brightest on the ground."

Dylan thought her boss should have used the word *fiasco*, but that would have been an indictment of his own work and a possible admission that she'd saved his job. An act she was steadily growing to regret.

"I see." Taking a deep breath, Dylan tried a change in tactics. "The thing is, Nicolas and I are looking at moving into a condo soon . . ." Dylan smoothed the hemline of her pencil skirt and started praying. Unless God was wearing noise-canceling headphones, he would hear her begging to stay in Houston. If she couldn't have Paris, at least he could leave her in the humidity.

"That's great. Do this successfully, and your condo budget increases exponentially." What Jared didn't add was that if she failed—and anyone would—she wouldn't have a job, let alone a condo budget. His simpering grin expanded. "Besides, don't you have family there? It'll be like a nice, long vacation. Save the company money too."

Dylan's heart plummeted to her stomach. She could think of about 1,422 other things she would rather do than see her family.

Taking her silence for consent, Jared added, "I'll have accounting send over your travel details. See you in Seattle!" He gave a jaunty, dismissive wave, effectively telling Dylan to get out.

"Merde!" she whispered as she left Jared's office. She had to hand it to him. The man was an evil genius. Jared was going to torpedo her career, and he was going to make her stay in the house of bedlam while he did it. Shaking her head, Dylan collected her handbag, computer case, and blazer before power walking toward the door.

~

Dylan continued her march to the car, moving as fast as her Manolos would allow, which was faster than most people could move in flats. Since leaving Seattle, she had gotten good at moving quickly in an ankle-breaking shoe. She had also figured out how to flat iron her curls into oblivion. The Houston humidity was no match for her skill and salon-quality hair products. All these talents would be useless in Seattle. Sloshing through the tireless drizzle in extreme heels was a dangerous impracticality, and wielding an umbrella was something no self-respecting local would tolerate.

After pressing the unlock button, Dylan crawled into her car and glanced around the parking lot to make sure none of her coworkers were there to witness her cutting loose. Then she laughed, the sound bordering on hysterics. She had managed to avoid going back to Seattle for years, and now she'd be making up for lost time.

Holding her breath, she slowly counted to ten. She was meeting Nicolas at the gym soon, and if she didn't get it together, he would start his workout without her. Exhaling loudly, she eased out of the parking lot, using the voice-recognition feature on her phone to start an *Unfortunately, I'm Going Home* checklist. To-do listing was a technique she'd developed while living in her parents' structureless madhouse, and it always helped. Sure, nearly everyone but Nicolas, including three-quarters of her coworkers, six of her closest friends, and her butcher, thought her listing was ridiculous. But those people didn't know what it was to unironically wear pajamas to school because your parents lost track of the laundry one too many times . . .

Dylan cut the memory off, redirecting her focus to the list. First, her standard appointments would be canceled: eyebrow threading, manicures, blowouts, and waxing. Easy enough to manage while she waited to board the plane on Friday. Also, dry cleaning, prescheduled workouts, and her ballet tickets needed to be handled. And, of course, she had to call her parents. Her thumb hovered over the call button on the steering wheel as mental recordings of every bizarre conversation she'd had with them in the last six months replayed in her head. If her father went on another tangent about his favorite disco queen, she was pretty sure she'd be forced to slam her car into a brick wall. Noticing the panic creeping up inside her, she decided to wait until after her workout, which she was officially late for.

Dylan grabbed her gym bag and jogged through the door, inspecting a chip in her nail polish as she stepped into the familiar smell of sweat and sanitizer. Waving hello to the tiny-T-shirt-loving man at the front desk, she streaked into the locker room and threw on a pair of running capris and a matching top. She took just enough time in the mirror to work her thick hair into a smooth high ponytail before blending a nearly imperceptible smudge of sepia foundation into the reddish-brown skin near the edge of her jaw and swiping away a stray spot of mascara. Giving herself a nod of approval, she bolted out of the locker room and took the stairs two at a time to find Nicolas mid–bicep extension. Her shoulders relaxed as she released the tension in her chest. There was a familiar comfort that accompanied seeing Nicolas, his blond hair stuck to his forehead with sweat, wearing the autopilot look he got when he was exercising. Or having sex.

Dylan felt instantly guilty. Thinking her boyfriend had an autopilot for sex didn't sound great. And autopilot or not, Dylan was glad to have someone stable in her life. Someone who knew her well enough that she could vent about her forced family vacation, manipulative boss, and possible loss of employment without sounding whiny. Nicolas loved routines and a job well done even more than she did. After years of hit-and-miss parenting, meeting him had been a godsend. No matter how messy her family seemed, he was always consistent. Dylan knew what she was getting with him, and although robotic at times, Nicolas's response to her was always reliable.

"Hey, sorry. Work was a bear," Dylan said, bouncing to a stop in front of him and rocking back on her heels as he took out one earbud.

"No worries, I figured as much."

"Today was possibly the worst day ever."

"Listen, I already did the lat pull downs and the leg press. You can come back for those later." Nicolas pushed the strands of sweaty hair out of his eyes, his ivory skin red from exertion.

"Right. Sure." Dylan nodded, feeling her ponytail bounce against the back of her head. "So guess where they're sending me? And let me eliminate the fun possibilities now. It isn't Paris."

Nicolas resumed his repetitions, answering her query with a grunt.

"Seattle. Two months. Technocore. Can you believe it?"

"Not great," Nicolas grunted, his eyes sliding toward himself in the gym's mirrored wall.

"Not great at all! I think Jared is trying to get me fired over the Davis Communications thing. It isn't my fault he thought giving people company tchotchkes as they were being laid off was a good idea. Of course it backfired. No one feels better when handed a Rubik's Cube and a pink slip."

"If you ask me, Jared is the one who needs a fidget spinner and a pink slip," Nicolas grunt-laughed, the joke encouraging Dylan.

"What was he thinking? *Here. Now you have an activity to do while you wait in the unemployment line.*" Dylan's arms windmilled around the gym, getting more animated as she gathered steam. "You know what really bothers Jared?" Dylan propped a fist on her hip and pointed a finger at nothing. "That stupid article. As if anyone cares about press in *Management Today*. It's a trade journal. It isn't the Bible or anything."

"Right." Nicolas nodded, the sound of metal plates clicking on the machine.

"If they hadn't called me the Davis Communications Savior, none of this would be happening. Severance packages for minimum wage employees isn't rocket science. Besides, *savior* is a—"

"Hey, babe, can we talk about it at home? I'm in the zone right now." Extending his designer earbud toward her, Nicolas explained, "It's Skrillex," before putting it back in his ear.

"Yeah, sure," Dylan said, then nodded her agreement, realizing he couldn't hear her answer.

Nicolas was right. She'd probably vented enough. After all, complaining wasn't really productive. Ambling over to the ab-crunch machine, she selected her settings and gritted her teeth. Giving the padded seat a look of disdain, Dylan resigned herself to taking her frustration out on the gym equipment.

~

Dylan stood over the contents of her underwear drawer, trying to find the matching panties to her favorite bra as her throat burned. She wanted to cry, but Nicolas needed to make some calls, so she decided to pack while he shouted over *SportsCenter* at a first-year associate.

"Where the hell are they?" Dylan asked her dirty-laundry hamper, clutching the bra as disappointment set in. All her bras had matching panties. If Dylan was rushed to the emergency room, she didn't want the paramedics wondering why she had leopard on top and pink lace on the bottom. She looked at her suitcase and back down at the bra. It wasn't like she needed lingerie. After three years of living together, Nicolas was more likely to give his attention to email than her underwear.

Bringing her mind back to the task at hand, Dylan gave the bra a hard look. She should leave it behind or throw it out, but she really didn't want to. Placing the bra with the other sets, she reasoned that she'd pick up replacement panties when she got to Seattle.

Putting a check mark next to *suitcase* on her list, she cringed. She had stalled all week, and now there was no way around it. She had packed, answered her email, confirmed her travel arrangements, and even tracked down the strongest antifrizz product the salon carried to accompany her industrial-grade flat iron. If the product didn't work against the rain, nothing would. The only item left was calling her family.

Gingerly picking up the phone, she took a steeling breath before pressing *Mom* and listening to it ring, half praying for voice mail.

"Hello, sister," Neale's voice singsonged through her mother's phone, crushing her voice mail hopes. Her younger sister still lived with their parents. She was purportedly pursuing a performance art career, but as far as Dylan could tell, she was mostly waitressing and watching her father's collection of obscure German films.

"Hi, Neale. Is Mom there?"

Dylan felt Neale's dreamlike thought process floating through the line before she spoke. "Not sure. I think she and Dad are installing something in the front yard."

"So she's in the front yard." Dylan had learned to appreciate that her younger sister consistently sounded high. Half the time she was, but that was beside the point.

"Yeah, she is. Did you want to talk to her?"

Dylan fought the urge to say no and leave a message with Neale. But there was a good chance Neale would forget. And if she didn't give the message directly to her mother, there was a shot she wouldn't be able to get into the house without setting off an alarm. Her father regularly left the door unlocked because he didn't like carrying keys on his walks, which had prompted her mother to install a keypad lock.

Unfortunately, her father still didn't lock the door most of the time, and every resident of the house habitually forgot the code. It meant her mother constantly changed the door code, resulting in a lot of false alarms and angry police officers.

"Yeah, if you wouldn't mind grabbing her for me."

"Mkay," Neale said, setting the phone down with an audible clunk.

A few seconds later, Dylan heard her mother shout something at her father, then pick up the phone.

"Prodigal daughter, is that you?" Dry humor and a slight accent dripped through the receiver.

"You have two of those, Mom."

"I know it's you, Dylan. Billie would have called collect." Bernice Delacroix was always direct, which was painfully off putting to most people. She was also brooding, artistic, and the exact opposite of a Canadian stereotype. Sometimes Dylan wondered if her mother fed the image so she wouldn't have to speak with her collectors. Then again, she even treated the dog with direct disdain, so Dylan was pretty sure it was just her temperament.

"Good point."

"So what can I do for you? I know you like to call with a purpose."

Ignoring the jab, Dylan began, "I've been assigned—"

"Hang on. Henry, do not put that there! I want it front and center." Dylan held the phone away from her ear as her mother shouted instructions to her father. Sighing heavily, Bernice continued, "Your father, I swear. You were saying?"

"I've been assigned to Technocore, and I was hoping to stay with you and Dad. You know, not waste company dollars and such. I arrive Friday morning." Dylan said this as quickly as possible. Announcing her intentions tasted like cough syrup. She was beginning to regret letting Nicolas talk her out of renting a place in Seattle. It was easy for him to say their condo budget wasn't worth the price of city rent. He wasn't the one who had to live with her family.

"Technocore, huh? You're working for those corporate fascists now?" Bernice labeled any company large enough to need an HR department "fascists."

"Yup. And I want to stay under your roof while I screw over the little man."

"Very funny. Of course you can stay. Your room is always here when you need it. I'll text you the door code so you can let yourself in. See you soon, sweetheart." As gruff as she was, her mother always used endearments when getting off the phone. It was as if she wanted to tell her children she loved them but despised the sentiment too much to say it, so she stuck with pet names.

"Thanks, Mom." Setting the phone down, Dylan looked at her suitcase with less trepidation. As far as Delacroix family communications went, that phone call had been downright pleasant. She pulled on her pajamas and shut off the lights, deciding not to wait up for Nicolas, who from the sound of it was going to continue berating his associate for a while.

CHAPTER TWO

Dylan got out of the rental car and wondered, again, if she should have leased a place. The house was completely different and exactly the same. Glaring at her from the dead center of the yard was an eight-foot-tall tiger clutching a beach ball. Her father liked to let each piece "live in its space" before installing it at its final home, either in a collector's sculpture garden or in some corporate lobby. When she was young, her father had sold a massive replica of the Marty McFly shoe to developers, who'd placed it in front of the football stadium in honor of the team's new digs. Once someone like Paul Allen or his representative purchased a piece, a lot of other people wanted one, and her father had no problem taking advantage of that. Dylan secretly hoped the Tiger was for an investment banking firm.

"Welcome home," Dylan whispered, pulling her suitcase toward the house and trying not to get her heels caught in the weeds growing between the paving stones that led to the front steps. She could hear the dog's whines through the bright-teal front door as she tapped the new code into the panel. She had just enough time to pull her suitcase through the door before being pummeled by excited leaps and licks from the perro de presa, whose mass shoved her into the corner, effectively knocking her over.

"Okay, Milo, down. I love you too. No. Stop. I'm covered in dog hair and—oh God, you licked my teeth!" Dylan said, shoving the dog away and toeing off her heels before trying to stand. Milo happily slurped at her slacks and hands, leaving a big wet imprint on the side of her leg as she surveyed the interior of the house. The inside of her former home had the same neglected feel as the exterior. Dylan was conscious of how little dog hair she had on her in comparison to the designer mismatched furniture and expensive carpets. In her childhood, her father had not been able to resist buying beautiful things, but neither of her parents could be bothered to clean or maintain them. So the beautiful things had been broken, either by the girls tap-dancing in the halls or by the tails of overeager family pets. There was dirt and dust everywhere, including on the hallway table, which Neale had helpfully signed and dated last August.

"Hello?" Dylan called to what she figured was an empty house. Her parents were never quiet. Thanking God for a moment of peace, she hauled her suitcase up to her bedroom while Milo raced happily up and down the stairs. Collapsing into her attic room, she surveyed the damage. It looked like her mother had been using the room as a storage space for her work. She had clearly taken pieces off the bed, but a few easels still stood with glossy coats, drying. Peeping around the easels, she could see Billie's attempt at self-expression still written on her bedroom walls, along with the Langston Hughes poetry she had painted on the ceiling.

Casting a sideways glance at the twin bed, Dylan started a *Things to Clean* checklist. Wincing, she watched Milo settle into the armchair by the picture window and made a note to wash the cushion cover along with her sheets. Her aspirational list making was interrupted by her mother's alto barreling through the wooden beams of the old house.

"Henry, it won't stand. I'll go over and tell them myself."

"Honey, I don't think you're wrong. I just don't think we need to deal with it while they're at work. Let the Robinsons come home first."

"No. This is the last straw. Installing a motion light? It shines right in our window whenever some squirrel runs by." Bernice spoke at an impressive decibel, unfazed by being indoors.

"Where's Milo?" her father asked as Dylan quietly padded down the dark-wood staircase. The beauty of a third-floor room was that it gave her plenty of time to prepare herself for her parents.

"I hope he's digging a hole in their front yard," Bernice spat.

Dylan took in her mother from the top of the second staircase. Ever sturdy, Bernice was largely unchanged in a pair of hiking pants a few inches too short for her tall frame and a winter fleece. Her graying curls were pulled up in a messy bun held by a purple scrunchie. Small spatters of paint ran down the brown skin on her neck where she'd forgotten to wipe her hands before she scratched an itch.

"I'm sure he's not doing that. Is Neale at work right now?" Henry answered, completely missing Bernice's sarcasm.

Taking a deep breath, Dylan descended the stairs and answered his earlier question. "Milo's with me. Passed out on my chair, to be exact."

"Dylan! You're home." Her father still wore his self-proclaimed uniform—a pair of light-blue jeans, a black T-shirt, and tennis shoes. His dark skin made it difficult for anyone except other Black people to determine his age, a trait that supported the general feeling that he had as much energy and enthusiasm as a twenty-five-year-old. His signature large glasses were perched on his nose, amplifying his eyes in line with the "Coke bottle" tradition. He considered them to be the height of fashion, and nothing could convince him otherwise. After pulling her into an effusive bear hug, her father released her directly into her mother's stern embrace.

"Hello, sweetheart. It's good to have you home. Your father and I were just discussing the latest Robinson travesty. Those women—"

"Are you thirsty? Tea? Something stronger?" Her father spoke over her mother's burgeoning rant.

"It's ten fifteen a.m."

"That's one fifteen p.m. in New York."

"Still not acceptable for drinking," her mother shot over her shoulder as she wandered toward the kitchen. "Let me finish. She can deal with them, and then she can have a drink. By then it will be five p.m. or later in all American time zones."

Dylan started, "Mom, the thing with the neighbors—"

"Not in Hawaii," her father added.

"Not helpful," her mother countered.

Dylan felt like her head was on fire. Her parents were already speaking at light speed over one another, and Neale wasn't even home yet.

"In Guam it'll be ten a.m.; then we're back where we started." Her father was downright giddy over this.

"Are we considering unincorporated US territories?" her mother asked, temporarily distracted. "If so, then it appears there is never a good time to drink."

"Mom, I'm not going over to the neighbors'. I'm almost—"

"Or it's always a good time to drink. Glass half-full!"

"Of tea."

"Or whiskey."

"How about both?" Dylan asked, her voice ricocheting through their airy butter-yellow kitchen.

"Like a hot toddy. I like where you're going with this." Henry beamed at her as if she had solved a pressing family issue.

"Tell me what the Robinsons have done." Dylan held up her hands, halting her mother's interjection. "That doesn't mean I'm going over there. Neale said she put her foot down on this ages ago. I plan to invoke the same right."

"Neale is a household contributor, so she can do that," Bernice answered with her usual haughty tone. "You are a visitor."

"Mom, Neale doesn't pay rent. She's technically been visiting for the last six years."

"Be that as it may, she lives here. You do not." As usual Bernice's logic was questionable, but her argument was airtight.

"Just tell me what they've done. Then I'll decide." Dylan sagged onto a barstool and tried to swat the dog hair and dust off her wool trousers. As far as she could discern, their neighbors across the street had a new motion-sensor light that shone high-powered beams directly into her parents' bedroom with the movement of every nocturnal critter in the neighborhood. It was Bernice's singular wish that Dylan communicate a cease-and-desist order to the couple immediately.

Most normal people would assume this was a mistake made by their otherwise pleasant, tidy, churchgoing neighbors. Most normal people had never endured the longest-standing family feud since the Hatfields versus the McCoys. The light was probably retribution for the tiger statue. Even for her parents, it was an unusual eyesore.

"So you'll go over there tonight and tell them to get rid of those insidious things?" Henry wrapped up her mother's raging tale with equal fervor.

"Dad. Mom. You know I love you and have for years participated in the Robinson loathing. But honestly, this is too much. I'm over thirty. I can't go over there like I'm ten. I doubt Linda and Patricia will do anything I ask anymore."

"Your room faces their house too. You act all high and mighty, but it'll upset your sleep pattern, and then you'll get off your high horse and go over there."

"Mom, please. You're being dramatic," Dylan said as her mother picked up her mug of cold tea and ambled toward her studio.

"Just wait. You'll see what I mean."

CHAPTER THREE

"Dear God. Are they trying to signal someone in outer space?" Dylan asked Milo, squinting out of her bedroom window. As if in agreement, Milo grunted, slowly moving off the window seat and onto her freshly made bed. So much for clean sheets. Setting her book down, she unpretzeled herself from the armchair she'd been installed in. Quietly, she opened her bedroom door to survey the rest of the house's response.

"I told you so! Now, do what you must." Bernice's mocking voice floated up three stories. Dylan marveled at her having heard the bedroom door open over her dad's experimental Ghanaian drum-circle music.

"I'm on it," Dylan called back before slinking down the stairs and grabbing her heels from over by the door. "'Do what you must.' Who says that?" she mumbled as she reached for the door handle, already regretting how quickly she'd caved. What had she said to her mother? Something about her age and independence? Obviously, that wasn't true.

Cursing herself, she closed her parents' door and began the slog across the street to the Robinsons' house. Although modestly painted and well landscaped, the house wasn't entirely dissimilar to her parents' home. However, it was scientifically impossible for the family living inside of the house to have less in common with her own. Linda and Patricia Robinson were both tech-industry big shots in their own right. Linda was a patent attorney and the recent recipient of the Latina Bar Association's Trailblazer Award, a fact she never failed to mention. Patricia was an accomplished programmer and volunteer youth-cheerleading coach who'd even made the cover of *American Cheerleader* magazine when her all-Black squad had pulled a real-life *Bring It On*–style competition victory. Both had come through the tech boom when the industry had still employed few women, and they took absolutely no shit from anyone—including Dylan's parents. Dylan believed her parents objected more to the Robinson women's love of golf than their jobs. As far as Bernice was concerned, golf was like standing for hours in a glorified front lawn.

The Robinsons had two boys around Dylan's age, and she had been jealous of the entire family while growing up. They'd gone to church and played organized sports, their clothes had always matched, and their mothers had joined the PTA. Dylan's dad had endured a short stint with the PTA, but the Delacroix didn't do organized anything. If Dylan had left the house wearing something that matched, it was by accident.

Distracted by the past, Dylan had stopped paying attention to where she was walking until her foot sank into the divot near a storm drain, filling her heel with water. She cursed, her heart thwapping in her chest. Visions of her father toilet papering the neighbors' house ran unchecked through her head. As did the memory of her mother nailing the police citation to the Robinsons' door when it had arrived in the mail a week later. Dylan thought this was a tame response where Bernice was concerned, but it led to the Robinsons sending boxes of craft-store glitter to the house. The Robinsons had lost that round, and the joke was on them, because her mother loved glitter. It had appeared in several of her most lauded collages that year, which she'd named for Linda and Patricia Robinson when she'd taken out an ad in the *Seattle Times* to feature the work.

Ignoring the panic sweat forming on her palms, Dylan knocked on the door, then frowned, looking down at her soaked woolen pant leg. If she didn't dry-clean those ASAP, they were going to reek.

"One minute." She had barely registered a man's voice when the door swung open. "Hello."

"Uh. Hi." Dylan's voice cracked.

Mike was, if possible, better looking than the last time she had seen him. His thick hair had been cut short, highlighting his high cheekbones and the ambient glow of his golden-brown skin. Time had turned him into the sort of made-for-TV manly pretty that seemed unfair for one person to achieve. The vaguely chiseled features and broad-shouldered Latino archetype that beer commercials aspired to.

Aware that she needed to state her purpose, Dylan said the first thing she thought—"You still live here?"—and instantly regretted her decision.

"No, I'm visiting. Do you still live here?" Mike asked with an incredulous laugh. The Robinsons' younger son filled up what felt like the entire doorframe, with one arm on the handle and the other resting comfortably on the jamb, as if being the J.Crew catalog guy were no big deal.

"I'm staying with my parents while I'm here for a work assignment. How are you?" Dylan smoothed a hand over the hem of her blouse and collected herself.

"Great. I live in Capitol Hill. I'm finishing my PhD at the U-Dub. I basically come here to bum dinner off my parents." He smiled, and Dylan wished he still had braces. Braces had made him just above-average looking in high school. Now, hazel eyes and straight teeth made him uncomfortable to be around. Or maybe it was the vast amount of water in her shoe.

"I'm sorry. My dad's drum circle carries all the way over here. I forgot how loud it is." Dylan gestured around the front door with a nervous laugh.

"We've gotten used to it. Do you want to come in?" He stopped leaning on the frame and took a step back to let her in.

"Thank you. I . . ." Dylan nodded, then paused as her shoe squelched. Panic left the little corner of her brain and seeped all the way to its outer edges as she tried to find a graceful retreat. If she walked in, she would track muddy water into the Robinsons' otherwise spotless home, further cementing her place in the Worst Neighbor Hall of Fame. "Actually, I really shouldn't."

Mike must have sensed her guilt, because his face relaxed into an easy smile. "No worries; I wouldn't want to be seen entering the home of the enemy either."

"Oh no. It's not that." Dylan rushed to explain herself before she was firmly entrenched in Camp Dreadful Delacroix. "It's just, my shoe is full of storm drain water, and your house is always spotless, and I don't want to track it in." She pointed erratically at her heel, which seemed more absurd now that she was drawing attention to it. What kind of Seattleite wore expensive shoes in this weather? "I promise I'm still significantly less strange than the rest of my family. Shoe thing aside." She let her hands drop helplessly to her thighs.

To her horror, Mike started laughing, his face cracking into a lopsided grin. "Why don't you dump your shoe out and come in? My parents are picking up dinner, so we don't have to tell them about the averted carpet disaster."

"That is probably the most reasonable option," she admitted, adopting a woman-as-flamingo pose as she tried to take off one heel while still wearing the other.

Wobbling precariously close to a fall, Dylan threw her hand out to catch the front of the house, but instead she caught the lean muscle of Mike's bicep as he grabbed her forearm to keep her from toppling over. Appreciating the feel of muscle under the cotton dress shirt he wore, Dylan grabbed her heel and pulled. *He likes the gym,* she thought, smiling. *Those don't just happen overnight; it took Nicolas how many months of lifting?* Thinking about Nicolas, Dylan cut herself off. How Mike Robinson got his arm muscles—or what they looked like without a dress shirt over them—was 100 percent none of her business.

"Thank you," Dylan said, clearing her throat.

"Do you want to try to dry it or something?" Mike asked as a sizable amount of water fell from her shoe.

"I'll just leave it by the door for now." Dylan felt a small twinge of regret, which she refused to acknowledge, as she let go of his arm. It wasn't like she didn't have her own set of nice arms in Texas. Why should she notice someone else's? Especially anyone related to the Robinsons.

Following Mike into the gently lit living room, Dylan experienced an overwhelming urge to point out that all of Patricia and Linda's furniture was unstained and that the drapes matched. Instinctively, she reached out to touch a lumpy clay statue covered in Crayola paints. Picking up the dust-free object, she turned to face Mike, who'd been watching her with curiosity as she wandered around the shelves. Conscious of her overly familiar behavior, Dylan set the object down and put her hands firmly in her pockets.

"Sorry, I was noticing how many of these y'all have."

"They come from the children's museum where I work. Mom's company sponsors a table at our fundraising gala every year, so she gets little things made by the kids. I keep telling her she doesn't have to save them, but she does anyway." Sensing the question Dylan was too polite to ask, he added, "Linda's company."

"That's sweet," Dylan said, noticing the different flecks of brown in his eyes. Trying not to stare, she turned back to the shelves, adding, "So you work at a museum? I thought you were getting a PhD?"

"I am. My dissertation explores early-childhood development and experiential education, hence the children's museum." Mike said this with the easy confidence of an academic, as if everyone knew what he was talking about.

"This is the point where I confess that I have no idea what experiential education is." Dylan laughed over her shoulder, then moved to look at the framed pictures next to the shelves.

"Basically, learning through activity and reflection. Students who learn to discuss their thoughts and feelings are better equipped to handle peer-to-peer or peer-to-adult relationships. My interest is in finding ways to provide those experiences outside of the traditional school setting."

Mike smiled as if he had been waiting months for someone new to ask him about teaching methods for children. Dylan hadn't even known toddlers could be socialized. Kids, she thought, were wild, sweaty, and unpredictable. Their singular purpose was to make her nervous. Mike did not share her fear. Intriguing.

"So how do you create that in a museum setting?" she asked and watched as his smile widened.

"In roughly one thousand different ways. However, my dream is a high-tech sensory room."

Dylan cocked her head and arched an eyebrow, prompting another explanation.

"For example, I can use lights, sounds, and images to create a jungle. The kids can listen to jungle sounds, see animals . . . and maybe I add a mister so they can feel humidity." He ran a hand down the back of his head, stopped at the base of his neck, and then continued. "The idea isn't new. But the community around the museum needs something like this. Anyway, I'm developing one that can transition into a number of experiences using technology so children can feel a desert or a frozen tundra or a crowded city all in one place."

"When does it open?" Dylan was pretty sure she had never met anyone with more enthusiasm for developing well-socialized children.

"Sometime between never and when I win the lotto." He laughed at her expression. "Prior to my mom's company getting involved in the museum, the place was almost completely underwater. Things are improving, but a new sensory room, especially the kind I want, is expensive."

"Oh," Dylan offered awkwardly. She had run out of knickknacks to examine and was forced to look Mike in his unusually symmetrical face again.

"Enough about me. How are you? How are your sisters? Sometimes I see Neale driving out of the neighborhood, but I haven't really talked to any of the Delacroix in months."

After picking her way over to the adjacent love seat, Dylan sat down, tucking her feet under her, instantly more comfortable in the Robinson home than in her own. "Oh, you know . . . Billie is still in New York working on her variety show, which I'm pretty sure means waitressing. And Neale is . . . well, Neale is just Neale." Dylan sighed. In Texas, she usually said her sisters were waitresses, but she couldn't lie to Mike, who, through the unfortunate proximity of their houses, had been forced to observe her entire family history.

"It's good they're pursuing their dreams."

Mike was being nice. She could have said her sisters were mutants, and she was positive the pleasant smile on his face would still be there.

"What about you? I'm sure whatever you are doing is super impressive. You were always a good-looking go-getter. What's new?"

Dylan's face felt hot. Did he think she was good looking? The expression was as old as the hills and too goofy by a mile. He couldn't mean it like *that*. Clearly, he was just channeling some old Hollywood charisma to go with his looks. The charm just rolled off him and messed with her head in the process. She cleared her throat and said, "I'm still the family oddball. I work for Kaplan; it's a corporate-productivity consulting firm. I'm starting with Technocore on Monday, helping—"

"Wait. Technocore? As in Tim Gunderson, the activist guy who hacked the mayor's office and exposed all that city fraud?"

"The one and only."

"Didn't he just lay off an entire department, then buy a Tesla?"

"That's him." Dylan cringed as she said this. The infamous candy apple–red Founders Series custom Roadster wasn't half as bad as his memo instructing all departments to give out T-shirts instead of holiday bonuses. Gunderson prided himself on being frugal when it came to business but was completely extravagant in his personal life. As a result, Technocore was hemorrhaging key employees who wanted to be paid well and treated to more than a doughnut at the annual Employee Appreciation Day.

"What are you doing for them?"

"For starters, getting rid of the Tesla." Dylan's smile was more of a flinch. Technocore was nothing short of a career death sentence. Four of the last consulting firms had either been fired or had quit within weeks of attempting to work with Gunderson. She just hoped she lasted long enough for a stay of execution.

"Hello? Mike? Whose shoes are these?" Patricia's crisp voice floated down the hallway.

"In here," Mike called over his shoulder.

Dylan suddenly became aware of her legs tucked under her, the wet hem of her wool pants soaking into the couch. Feeling guilty, she pulled her legs to the ground just as Patricia and Linda rounded the corner.

"Oh, hi, Dylan." Patricia looked surprised the shoes belonged to her but recovered quickly enough. After walking over in her ultrawhite and well-pressed sweater set, she stood in front of Dylan with her arms open. It took a moment for her to realize that Patricia Robinson actually wanted to hug her. A Delacroix. Stooping to embrace the petite woman, she wondered what alternate universe she'd stumbled into. Since when did the Robinsons unlace enough to hug?

"You look so grown! I haven't seen you in forever."

"I haven't been home in a few years," Dylan said as Patricia released her to Linda, who was equally well put together. Dylan spotted pearls under Linda's black fleece jacket. Her hair was pulled into a tight bun and covered in enough hair spray to make sure each strand stayed in place into eternity. "How are you?"

"Same old, same old. Are you here about the lights?" Linda asked without preamble.

"I'm sorry. It's killing my mother," Dylan said with an uncomfortable shrug.

"I heard her tell Henry last night. I thought they would send Milo with a note again. You're a pleasant surprise," Linda said happily, holding up the take-out bag. "Join us in the kitchen?"

"Mom, if you knew it was bugging them, why didn't you fix it?" Mike had the decency to look confused. Patricia wore the same contrite expression her father wore whenever her mother did something ridiculous.

Ignoring Mike's question, Linda shook the bag of food at Dylan. "Stay for egg rolls?" she said, looking entirely unrepentant.

"Oh no, I didn't mean to interrupt your dinner. I was only stopping by to see if maybe you could angle the lights a little more toward your driveway?"

"Come have something to eat. You have to be starving," Patricia answered, disregarding the stubborn set in Linda's jaw. Whenever Dylan had been sent to negotiate peace as a kid, the Robinsons had fed her. Patricia and Linda were convinced that two people as strange as her parents could not possibly feed their children. This wasn't true. In point of fact, Bernice was obsessed with family meals, just not at regular meal intervals. Dylan had never bothered to correct the Robinsons' assumption, mostly because it got her a lot of cookies.

"No, really, it's okay. I'm sure you want to eat with your son." Dylan's stomach chose that moment to rumble at the smell of fried vegetable goodness.

"You sure sound hungry," Patricia added, her voice tight with disapproval.

"Nope, I'm leaving them all for you."

"Let's compromise. You take one for the road," Linda said, her litigator skills showing. She popped open the container and held it out to Dylan. "Also, honey . . . one of your shoes is dripping all over the hall. You may want to look into that."

~

Dylan's cheeks burned as she crossed the street in her dripping heels, munching on the last of her egg roll. When she shoved open the front door, she found her dad following along with an old *Darrin's Dance Grooves* video. At one time her father's impromptu dance marathons might have seemed normal to her. She would just have to pretend she didn't know better now.

Filling her lungs to drown out the tape, she called, "Mom, what's this about sending Milo to the Robinsons?"

Her dad was so in the zone he didn't notice her shouting over the tape. Bernice popped her head around the corner of the kitchen and grinned. "Genius, isn't it? I usually flag down their son and make him deliver the message, but he was on vacation, and I really couldn't wait, so I sent Milo. Damn dog nearly went to the wrong house." Her mother appeared genuinely dismayed at the dog's inability to deliver angry letters to the neighbors. "So was I right? Did they agree to remove the lights?"

"Not in so many words, but I think their son is going to work on it."

"Ha. What did I tell you? And you were over here all, *Mom, that won't work because I am an adult. I'm above everything,*" Bernice said in a terrible, nasal approximation of Dylan, complete with a robot voice and stiff movements that managed to be as inaccurate as they were patronizing.

"Good impression, Mom. You are a great actress."

"What? You sound just like that," Bernice said, waving off her complaint, then adding, "Since you're here, we may as well push for another victory. I don't want to stretch our luck, but maybe next week you can talk to them about the hideous speedboat they park in their driveway every summer." Bernice turned back toward the kitchen. Her change in location made absolutely no difference to her speaking volume. "Talk about an eyesore. And they have the nerve to think the Tiger is tacky."

"Right," Dylan said, shaking her head and wandering up the stairs. When she opened her bedroom door, she found that Milo had pulled the blanket off her bed and was lounging on the floor with it. "Gross," she mumbled, trying to pull her now-dirty comforter out from under his hulking frame. Begrudgingly, Milo rolled over, giving it up. Dylan stood in the middle of her room, debating what to do with it. On the one hand, she wanted her comforter. On the other, it smelled like Milo, whose bathing schedule was more than a little suspect. She decided to risk it and wash the thing in the morning with the rest of the sheets Milo had rolled in.

Exchanging her soaked slacks for her favorite pair of menswear-inspired pajama bottoms, Dylan picked up her phone and toyed with the idea of checking her email. It was part of her and Nicolas's nighttime ritual: email, dinner, more email, then bed. It felt strange checking email in her childhood room without him there, and Dylan decided she'd live dangerously and skip the ritual.

She texted Nicolas a quick update, since it wasn't a scheduled call night, then pitched the phone on the paper-strewed desk before staring at the massive patch of fluorescent light coming through her bedroom window. She stepped over Milo and closed the curtains. Sinking back into the chair, now only slightly bathed in glaring white light, Dylan wondered exactly how much a fancy sensory room cost and made a mental note to ask Mike if she saw him again.

CHAPTER FOUR

Dylan finished applying an extra coat of antifrizz serum and gave her favorite tan pencil dress a once-over, proud she'd managed to successfully keep Milo from shedding all over it. Pulling up the exposed gold zipper, she stepped into a matching pair of patent leather pumps and then shrugged on a heavy trench. Dylan decided today was going to be a good day. Sure, she was starting at Technocore, but it was only misting, and that boded well for her hair if nothing else.

Cruising toward downtown, she went over her list of things she wanted to accomplish today. Her contact at Technocore should have arranged a vital sit-down with Gunderson and interviews with four senior managers from various departments to keep her on schedule. Dylan hoped the interviews would support the action plan and timeline she had developed on the plane. The faster she could get Gunderson to commit to her ideas, the easier the transition would be. If she could score a few early wins to gain the founder's confidence, she would buy herself more time to solve the big problems before the finicky tech genius—or his board of directors—fired her.

Putting the car in park, she threw a small prayer to the workplace gods and then walked up to the sleepy-looking security guard. She glanced down at her watch and smiled. After years of missing doctors' appointments and chasing planes with her parents, Dylan thoroughly enjoyed being early. When she cleared her throat, the young security guard looked up from the book review section of the *Seattle Times*.

"Hello. I'm here for Marta Woods. I'm Dylan Delacroix, with Kaplan and Associates." She was never sure what information had been given to security about her, so she said everything to be safe. The guard looked up at her blankly. "I'm early."

"Let me, uh . . . let me check and see if she . . . uh, Marta . . . ," the guard stammered, furiously typing on the screen in front of him. "Uh . . . I don't see you on the manifest." He looked at her apologetically.

"You know, it may be under my boss's name. Jared Gilroy." Dylan drew a deep breath and smiled in what she hoped was a reassuring way. It wasn't the guard's fault Jared was incompetent. She should have double-checked this before she arrived.

"Nope." The guard shook his head but didn't offer any suggestions.

Dylan felt a twinge of irritation kick in. She would add customer-service training for security personnel to the list of processes to be reviewed. "You could call Marta. She'd con—"

"Marta quit last Friday," the baby-faced guard sputtered.

"Oh."

"Yeah. So . . ."

Dylan racked her brain, trying to come up with the name of another contact in the office. She pulled out her phone and began scanning through emails. "I'm sure there's someone in the office who can vouch for me. I was hired to help sort through some of Technocore's recent"—Dylan tried to phrase the next part carefully. People got squirrelly when they found out consultants were being brought in to evaluate them—"staffing trouble."

"The thing is, I can't let you up there without clearance."

"Perhaps Mr. Gunderson knows I'm coming? Why don't you give him a call?"

"I'm sorry; I can't disturb him. We get a lot of phonies trying to reach him. Press, stalkers, you know."

"I just told you. I'm a consultant," Dylan said, giving up the fruitless email search. "Do I look like a stalker?"

The kid shrugged, indifference written all over his fawn-colored, freckled face. "Stalkers come in all kinds. I'm sorry, but if you don't have someone to vouch for you, I'll have to ask you to leave."

"Look, there has to be someone you can call." Dylan's voice went up a few notes with her mounting desperation. Jared's email last night had made it clear he wasn't to be disturbed. She didn't want to call Kaplan and explain that she had been kicked off the Technocore campus for seeming like a stalker. It wouldn't go over great with the partners.

The guard's indifferent expression stared back at her as heat began to radiate from under her collar and up her neck. Glancing down at his golden nameplate, she tried again. "Charlie, I'm making an effort. Will you please work with me?"

"Ma'am, really—"

"Good morning, Charlie." A rumpled man in a sweater breezed past the security desk.

Dylan noticed the badge clipped to his belt loop. Taking a few quick steps sideways, she knew what she needed to do. It was better to risk the guard calling the police than be the inept subject of Kaplan office gossip. Gritting her teeth, she dashed past the security guard toward the elevator. Sliding into the elevator with the startled man, she felt a small sense of pride as she watched the shocked guard jolt out of his chair.

"Hello," she said to her elevator companion. "I was trying to reach Marta Woods, who has, apparently, left the company. Would you know who I should contact in her place?"

The man gaped at her for a minute as the doors began to close. Dylan tried to smile, as if being chased by a security guard were normal. Pressing a hand to a wrinkle on her coat, she jumped from the entrance, squeaking, as Charlie's right arm shot between the sliding doors, his hand wiggling. The man jolted, knocking his glasses sideways and stifling a screech.

"Ma'am, I'm going to need you to step out of the elevator, please," Charlie said, straightening his jacket with his free hand as the doors retracted. Dylan debated swatting him and trying to make a run for the stairs. They were probably unlocked in case of an emergency. Sidestepping Charlie's arm, Dylan bumped into the man, who seemed to recover from the shock of witnessing a campus break-in.

"Hang on, Charlie. You're here for Marta? Are you with Kaplan?" Dylan watched as Charlie's face went slack with surprise, his hand dropping like deadweight.

"Yes. I'm scheduled to start today," Dylan said, flattening the sleeve of her coat, where Charlie's fist had been moments before.

"Hell. I remember her mentioning that. Charlie, she is okay to come with me." The man leveled his glasses and pushed his graying hair around his head. Dylan wasn't sure if the gesture was meant to make his hair lie flat, but it had the exact opposite effect.

"Oh. Okay." The poor guard looked completely deflated.

"I'm sorry for the confusion, Charlie," Dylan said as the doors began to close again. He looked so distraught that she felt a smidgen bad about the whole thing. She turned to face her savior, who was busy staring at her shoes.

"You move very quickly in those things."

"Thank you. I'm Dylan Delacroix." She held out her hand and did her best to look dignified after a near brush with trespassing charges.

"Steve Hammond, COO. I'm taking care of Marta's responsibilities until we find someone new. Her departure was rather sudden, and unfortunately I dropped the ball on this," he said with a slight frown.

The doors opened, and he stepped out, continuing to speak as he walked. "I don't believe Marta had a space prepared for you before she left, so we'll stick you in her office for now. I'll have an intern come by to help you get set up," he said, expertly navigating the maze of cubicles and hallways. "I have a nine a.m. meeting with Tim." He glanced down at his watch, frowning again. Dylan was starting to marvel that the frown had not become a permanent fixture on his stubble-covered face when he stopped in front of a bland office door. "I'll be back after my meeting to check on you and get things going."

"Sounds good to me. When can I expect you?" Dylan said, shifting her satchel from one hand to the next.

"Whenever Tim decides we are done." The corners of Steve's mouth sank deeper.

"All right. I'll get the lay of the land until then," Dylan said, trying to keep her disappointment at bay.

"Take care." Steve turned and marched back down the hallway.

"Right," Dylan said to his back. Sighing, she turned to her office. Marta was clearly not a sentimental woman. Papers and trinkets still covered her desk. Pulling open a drawer, she found a series of take-out menus, pen caps, and an assortment of detritus that she decided was better boxed than analyzed. As if on cue, a timid knock drew her attention. Glancing up from the crush of papers, Dylan found a pale young man slouching in her doorway, holding a brown moving box as if it were a shield.

"Hello," Dylan said, watching the pink splotches in his cheeks creep toward his white-blond hairline.

"Are you Ms. Delacroix?"

"Yes. Can I help you?"

"I'm Brandt Fenner. I'm your intern."

Dylan was concerned for the guy. Was he afraid of her? Or just painfully shy? He was practically hiding in his flannel shirt, which was strategically worn under a fleece jacket to make him look bulkier.

"Hi, Brandt. You can call me Dylan," she said, holding out her hand. Brandt looked as though he were being asked to walk under a ladder holding a black cat. He shifted the box to one arm and took her hand with a surprisingly firm grip for someone who seemed like he might be sick.

Brandt's skinny jeans were baggy on his tall frame, and he had the standard Nordic features some longtime northwesterners had. If Dylan had one guess, she would probably say he had about ten generations of distinctly blond relatives living fifteen minutes from here.

"So should I start clearing out Marta's stuff for you?"

"I'll take care of it. How about you come by in an hour to cart the box off to wherever former-employee paperwork goes?"

"Will it count against me if I don't help?" Brandt practically shuddered as he asked this.

"Count against you how?"

"You know . . . since you're"—he looked at the corner of her office as if it would help him find the right words to complete his sentence— "picking who to fire."

If he hadn't looked so terrified, Dylan would have laughed. She wasn't going to suggest anyone be let go. But if she did, it would be an expensive middle manager, certainly not a minimum wage graduate student intern. Dylan gestured at the door. "Does everyone here think I'm going to fire them?"

"Maybe? That's what the last consultant did."

"If anything, I'm more likely to suggest you be rearranged. In truth, I can't fire anyone. That is all up to Tim, Steve, and the rest of the brass. I'm here to observe and make suggestions."

"Oh," Brandt said, uncoiling. "Well, I have a few things to wrap up from my last assignment. Would it be okay if I come back in an hour?"

Dylan decided he was simply one of those people who appeared to be afraid all the time. "Of course. When you come back, maybe you can give me the grand tour. I haven't even found the restroom yet, let alone the coffee maker."

"Bathroom is down the second set of cubicles to the left, past the green emergency-exit door. The coffee stand is on the top floor as close to Tim's office as our clearance badges will get us," Brandt answered in a factual manner.

"Great. See you in an hour." She took the box from his outstretched hand.

"I'm in the basement with the other interns if you need anything. Have a good morning," Brandt said, defaulting to the standard polite greeting that all Seattleites used with strangers. Dylan chuckled to herself as she started placing files in the box. You could be terrified of someone in this town, and it was still mandatory to wish them a good day.

~

She wasn't sure how long it took to clean out Marta's desk. All Dylan could say for certain was that Marta was a pack rat and that she was behind schedule. At some point Brandt had shown up to take away the box and bring her a few more, along with a cup of coffee in a ridiculously shaped brontosaurus mug, mumbling something about the office being a "green campus."

Taking a sip from the dinosaur, Dylan pulled out her laptop and began spreading out her Technocore paperwork. Looking at her schedule, she started identifying places where she could shorten meetings to make up for lost time, until a subtle tapping on the narrow glass window of her door pulled her attention away from the screen. Waving at Steve, Dylan tried to hide the mug behind her computer and appear professional. The last thing she needed was for Jared to get a call about her brontosaurus obsession in addition to her penchant for skirting security protocol.

"I see you're settling in nicely." Steve gestured to her computer, and Dylan got the sense that he was referencing the mug behind it.

"Yes. Thank you for sending Brandt; he's been really helpful." She nudged her mug more toward the center of her screen.

"Is Brandt the intern they sent you? Good," Steve said without waiting for confirmation. Pushing his hands through his salt-and-pepper hair, he continued, "So I'm here because it doesn't look like you're going to get the chance to speak with Tim today." He exhaled in a way that conveyed more than exasperation. "I've asked that he make it a top priority for this week."

Dylan blinked at Steve for a minute, regrouping. "I don't need more than twenty minutes. Is there any way that I could schedule a call with him?" She thought back to Jared's incomplete notes in his initial project brief and cringed. She really needed about three hours.

"I'm sorry. Tim made it clear that his day is packed. But I have you on the docket for first thing Thursday." This time Steve didn't wait for her to ask another question. Turning toward the door, he said, "Please let me know if you need anything else to get settled in. Enjoy your coffee. You can always get more upstairs."

"Thanks." Dylan's tone was as lukewarm as her beverage. Glancing at her coffee, she tried to silence her anxiety alarm. There was no way that she could waste a week waiting for Tim. Even if she couldn't meet with him for a full three hours, she absolutely needed him to send out a company-wide memo letting people know she was here in a friendly capacity. Given Brandt's initial reaction, if she tried to interview employees without it, they might run screaming at the sight of her.

The question was how to get to him. Dylan was almost positive she couldn't just walk through Tim's door without some kind of security card. Frowning down at her coffee, she felt her mind reaching for the thread of an idea. Pushing her hair back, she toyed with the handle of her mug for a moment before it came to her. Brandt had mentioned that the coffee cart was close to Tim's office. If she waited by the coffee cart long enough, surely he'd have to come out.

After snatching up the dinosaur and cramming a few papers into her bag, Dylan hooked the three free fingers not dedicated to the mug around the door handle and pulled it shut. Her head began to spin as she looked for the elevator hidden in the sea of cubicles. Finally, she marched to the first occupied desk she found, read the nameplate, and cleared her throat. "Excuse me, Deep. Could you direct me to the elevator?"

The woman's pixie cut shot up, a look of horror stuck to her face. The nail file she had been using moments before hung limp in her hand. "You scared me! Just because I'm in a cube doesn't mean you shouldn't knock." Deep's expression went from shocked to offended in the span of five seconds.

"I'm sorry. You're right—I like people to knock on my padded walls as well," Dylan said with more spunk than she meant to. Deep stared, her bright-pink lips parted in surprise. Arching an eyebrow, she tilted her head back and started laughing, shaking her bangs off her forehead. When she finally opened her dark eyes, Dylan got the sense that she was being appraised. After a moment Deep smiled.

"I like you. You're secretly saucy under that beige corporate attire. Follow me."

So much for people fearing her. Apparently, Deep found her so unintimidating that she was willing to insult what Dylan considered one of her more flattering professional outfits. Walking behind Deep, she noticed a small bar code tattoo on the base of her neck and smiled at another local custom. In Seattle you could be tattooed, pierced, and pixied and still have a desk job.

"Are you the replacement for Marta or the person they're bringing in to fire me?" Deep asked casually.

"The latter. Except I don't have plans to fire anyone. Just make the company run better."

"Sure. I'd totally buy that if I hadn't seen *Office Space*. You are a productivity consultant, correct? Should I call you Bob?" Deep laughed. Dylan didn't think she could be more surprised. *Office Space* jokes were part of the productivity consultant territory, but it was unusual for people to make them in front of her.

"You could call me Bob, but Dylan would be better."

Deep looked at her and sputtered. "Bob Dylan. Ha! Good one."

"Actually, Dylan is my first name." Deep's face froze midgiggle. She figured Deep could take a little heckling, so she waited until they reached the elevators before adding, "I was named for him, though, so it isn't a bad guess."

Deep smirked. "You are secretly sassy. Where're you trying to go? Or should I ask who you're trying to fire?"

"I need to get to the coffee cart," Dylan said, wiggling her empty mug.

"Don't we all?" Deep sighed, leaning in with her badge and punching a floor. Dylan smiled as the doors closed. Secretly sassy was something she had been accused of exactly never in her life. Anal retentive, yes. Sassy, no.

As the doors opened, she saw exactly what Brandt had meant when he'd said the coffee cart was as close to Tim's office as it could be. A quick scan of the floor yielded only a coffee cart, a few tables, a restroom, and a massive door labeled **TIM GUNDERSON, FOUNDER**. That was it. Dylan looked over at the barista, who was rapt, tuned in to a romance novel complete with a shirtless pirate on the cover. She thought she'd be embarrassed to be reading that in front of one of America's wealthiest CEOs, but then again, she couldn't really be embarrassed by her literary choices in front of a man who drove an aggressively red Roadster.

Dylan took a step toward the cart, shifted her dinosaur mug onto the counter, and asked for another coffee, please. Sooner or later, Tim would come out to use the restroom, and she'd be ready for him.

~

Three cups of coffee and two hours later, Dylan was starting to wonder if Tim was a camel. She had begun her waiting process by reviewing Jared's spotty notes and addressing her timeline problems, but by her third cup, Dylan began to feel the unfortunate combination of caffeine jitters and short attention span kicking in. After fifteen minutes of her tapping on the coffee table and staring into space, the barista had given her the pirate romance, which Dylan had begun to read against her better judgment. She'd concluded that as long as she left the book open on the table, no one would even know it was a pirate romance. Besides, she would only read it until Tim appeared, at which point she would politely return it to the barista.

All this had been about fifty pages and one daring rescue ago. Dylan had reached the part where the captive duchess began bandaging the wounded, misunderstood pirate captain when the sound of Tim's door smashing into the wall behind it made her jump. She looked up in time to see the vestiges of his hoodie heading into the bathroom. Shaking off the caffeine jitters, Dylan stuffed everything back into her bag and hustled over to wait outside the bathroom door.

She had enough time to straighten her skirt before the door opened with a similar force and she came nose to nose with Tim Gunderson.

"Holy shit!" He clutched his throat as if he were wearing pearls.

"Gah!" Dylan jumped, more in response to his surprise than her own, dropping her satchel in the process. The bag hit the ground with a nauseating crunch that could only have been her laptop before exploding papers, pens, hair ties, and a romance novel everywhere. Dylan watched in semihorror as the frizzy crown of Gunderson's head bowed toward the floor and began picking up the book.

"Sorry, you scared the hell out of me."

"It's my fault. I shouldn't have been standing so close to the door," Dylan said, diving toward the mass of paperwork and a breath-mint container. "I was hoping to catch you before you went in." The moment she said it, Dylan realized it was the wrong thing to say. Panic spread across his freckles.

"Layla, would you mind calling security?" he stage-whispered to the barista, dropping the novel and inching away from her. "Look, if you've been recently let go, Steve handles all that now. I don't know how you got in here or what you want, but I can assure you that I don't keep large sums of cash on my person."

Dylan had to wonder if Gunderson was really as brilliant as everyone said he was. If she were going to rob or otherwise maim him, did he think she would come dressed in heels and a pencil skirt?

She sighed. "No. You haven't fired me. In fact, you hired me. Look, Mr. Gunderson, I'm desperate for twenty minutes of your time. Time you agreed to give me." She crossed her arms as he sputtered to a halt, then added, "As I'm sure Steve reminded you this morning." She watched as recognition slowly spread across his face, his shoulders retracting from his ears a quarter of an inch.

"Are you the consultant?"

"Yes. And given the time limitations imposed by your board of directors and our mutually agreed-upon contract, I believe it's best we get started right away. I understand you're busy, but I must insist we meet, at least briefly, today. The rest of our discussion can be put off for another time." She nodded authoritatively as his shoulders dropped another fraction.

"Steve mentioned you were a little unorthodox," he mumbled, adjusting his hoodie. "I guess I have a few minutes before my next meeting."

"I'm only unorthodox when dealing with Technocore. Would you like to step into your office, or do you prefer conducting business outside of the restroom?" Dylan asked, instantly regretting her off-the-cuff remark. She sounded like her mother.

Tim bent down and picked up the novel, drawing his eyebrows together before letting out a bark, which doubled as a laugh. "You're funny. In a bizarre, bathroom-stalker kind of way." Handing her the novel and her emergency deodorant, he continued, "What's your name, again?"

She stuffed the pirate book and the deodorant back in her satchel before standing up and rearranging the busted bag under her arm. Squaring her shoulders, she extended a hand toward Tim. "Dylan Delacroix."

Tim shook her hand, recovering his swagger. "I guess you already know who I am."

Before she could stop herself, she added, "Mr. Gunderson, I think you should come up with a code to ask Layla for security. *Could you please call security* is a surefire way to cause both the intruder and the employee to panic."

"You can call me Tim," he said, ignoring her criticism.

"Okay, Tim. Shall we get going?" Dylan said, appraising his Dockers and obnoxious neon-orange high-tops as he started toward the office door with a curt nod at Layla. Biting back frustration, she continued, "I'm here because of a board of directors mandate to right this ship. I know it is hard to run a company. It was easier when you were a small team of white-hat hackers in a basement, but now you have thousands of people counting on you and scrutinizing your every move. Not to mention countless investors wanting more out of you. Sound right?"

Tim gaped at her, his mouth slightly open so she could see the wire retainer glued to his bottom teeth. He nodded, taking a seat in the swivel chair behind his desk.

"Good. I know it's tough, and I want to help you. But I need you to do a couple of things for me. First, your employees are terrified that I'm here to fire them. Will you please send out a company-wide email letting everyone know that I'll be asking to speak with some of them? Explain that I am not here to fire them but to assess the culture of Technocore and make improvements."

"Can't Steve do that?" Tim seemed to be regaining some of his pluck. Apparently, a stern talking-to only silenced him for so long.

"No, because Steve's in charge of firing people. Think about how that looks to the staff," Dylan commanded, trying to withhold some of her exasperation.

Tim grabbed a stress ball off his desk and nodded as if he understood her logic, blessedly shutting his mouth so she didn't have to see his charming retainer anymore.

"Also, I need to get on your calendar for a full discussion of your company goals and director expectations ASAP. This will take about three hours. If that means I stay until ten p.m. to meet with you, fine."

"I've made time on Thursday. Anything else?"

"Yes." Dylan drew a deep breath. Since she was already making guaranteed-to-get-her-fired requests, she continued, "Enough with the red Roadster. It's killing you in the court of public opinion and makes recruiting quality people near impossible."

Tim's mouth dropped back open, encouraging the eggplant color creeping toward his hairline.

"But I like—" Gunderson jumped as his phone rang. Glancing over at the caller ID, he switched gears and put on a headset. "Fine. This is my next appointment. I'll think about the car."

"That was all I needed." Dylan couldn't hide her smile as she stood.

"Any other pressing business before Thursday?" He adopted an ultraprofessional tone that Dylan assumed was more for the benefit of the people listening on the other end of the line than for her. She shook her head.

"Great, I'll get the memo out this afternoon and make sure that you're cc'd." Without missing a beat, he switched back to the line. "Tim here."

Dylan could hear the phone line wah-wahing like Charlie Brown characters as she walked toward the door.

"Hang on."

She turned to face him, resting one hand on the door.

Covering the receiver with his hand, Tim leaned forward. "Is that book any good?" Dylan looked at him quizzically. "The one with the shirtless dude on the cover?" he asked, pointing to her overflowing bag.

She felt the same shade of eggplant he had worn minutes before trying to appear on her own face as she struggled for some clever way to disavow ownership of the novel. Gunderson grinned as if he had won a small victory. That could not happen. Consuming her pride, Dylan shrugged. "So far. I can lend it to you when I'm done."

Tim shifted his hand away from the phone, his smile steadily working its way back toward his ears, and returned to his call.

~

Dylan rushed back to Marta's office as fast as she could without breaking into a sprint. To say her meeting with Tim had gone well would have been an overstatement. At least she hadn't set his ridiculous oversize desk on fire. Pressing the power button on her laptop, she held her breath. The last thing she needed was to have to call Kaplan's IT department on top of everything else. After what felt like an eon, the thing booted up, and the usual pinging sound of incoming emails began, followed by the ding of a chat message. There were roughly twenty Kaplan emails about the state of the office kitchen, as well as an email from Jared marked *URGENT*. Dylan decided to deal with the chat first.

Stacy Castello's name blinked at her, drawing an unexpected smile from Dylan's memory. She and Stacy had been best friends through high school, surviving braces and frizzy hair together. Of the three Delacroix sisters at Roosevelt High School, Dylan had been the least likely to get invited to anything other than a student council meeting. Stacy was also the odd one out in her family, making the two of them fast friends. At exactly five feet two inches, she was a Filipina made up of all curves and bleached-blonde hair, a holdover from her family's move from Everett in the seventh grade. The Castellos owned a series of car-part-recovery locations that made them the unusual combination of blue collar and wealthy in a neighborhood dominated by white-collar tech professionals. Everyone had wanted to hang out with Stacy; they just hadn't wanted to deal with her truck-driving, BB gun–loving, ATV-worshipping brothers, who referred to themselves as the Trailer Park Mafia.

Still smiling, Dylan clicked on the icon.

I hear you're back in town. True or False?

Dylan felt guilt clawing its way to the front of her mind. She avoided coming home as much as possible, and when she did get here, she made it a short trip. Not seeing Stacy was a byproduct of the unintentional time constraint.

True! I'm here for the next couple months.

Good, then you have plenty of time to come to Lenny's tonight.

Lenny's was where everyone who'd graduated from Roosevelt and never left town spent their evenings. Dylan could think of about a million reasons why she didn't want to go there but very few good excuses not to. The bar was literally within walking distance of her house and divey enough that she could wear her pajamas and be considered "dressed to kill." She wanted to see Stacy; she just didn't want to see her at Lenny's surrounded by the ghosts of high school football stars past. Her fingers were hovering over the keyboard, searching for an excuse, when a second urgent email from Jared came in. The subject line was *Anyone Home?* Grumbling, Dylan flipped back to her chat with Stacy, deciding that Jared's email was the perfect excuse to avoid an evening at Lenny's.

Sorry. My boss just sent the email from hell. Looks like I'm gonna be working late. Maybe this weekend?

Of course! I ran into Neale today. She says you have some huge account or something.

It's becoming more intense by the minute. Remind me to tell you about the romance novel and the bathroom ... oof

Dylan felt bad putting off Stacy, but there was too much to do, and social time just wasn't carved into her calendar. Pressing send on a response to Jared, she watched as another email hit her inbox, this one from Tim. She opened it with smug satisfaction, knowing Tim had bent to her will.

To: Technocore All

From: Tim Gunderson

Subject: New Consultant

All,

I would like to welcome our new consultant Dylan Delacroix of Kaplan & Associates. Previous consultants have been hired to assist in restructuring and occasionally downsizing our workforce, which is not her role. I ask that you please cooperate with Ms. Delacroix as she asses our work.

Tim

Asses our work. Blinking rapidly, she read it again.

Nope. Dylan was still assing things. Tim hadn't noticed the typo; maybe the rest of Technocore wouldn't either? She dropped her head into her hands, only to have someone knock on the door. Jerking her head up, she watched Deep pop her head into the office.

"Hey, so what time did you want to ass me?" Deep didn't linger in the doorway to see if Dylan was laughing. Grinning, she turned to a man walking by and said, "So you're being assed first, then?"

Cringing, Dylan looked from Deep to the people giggling in the hallway and said, "How about we do your assessment tomorrow?"

"I see. Too much assing for you to do tonight, then?" Deep cackled.

Dragging her attention back to the screen, Dylan clicked on Stacy's chat.

I can't wait to hear all about it. Brunch on Sunday?

Actually, I could do with a drink. Lenny's at 7:30?

A martini was the least her Kaplan expense card could do for her after the day she'd just had.

CHAPTER FIVE

Dylan barreled into Lenny's, feeling the curl return to her hair as the Seattle mist sank through the layers of strategically placed hair product. So much for the salon's promise. Stopping to let her eyes adjust to the grimy lighting, she felt her pumps stick to the dingy green-and-white checkered floors. Formica countertops and an unfriendly-looking bartender with a beard to rival Santa Claus's greeted her. The martini glasses would be passably clean, but that was about it. Scanning the room for Stacy, her eyes fell on the sad remnants of what used to be a pool table, now doubling as a beer stand in the corner. Dylan wasn't sure how long Lenny's had been around, but she was convinced the table and the layer of dirt that covered it were even older. Finally, she spotted Stacy's familiar bob frantically waving at her from a semirevolting brownish-maroon booth.

"Look at you!" Stacy shouted as she came hurtling toward Dylan, her teddy bear scrubs blurring in the dim light. "You are the exact same! Seriously, how have you not aged?"

"Me? Look at you! You're fabulous. I'm loving the hair color." Dylan's words were muffled by a hug.

Releasing her bone-crushing grip on Dylan's neck, Stacy stepped back and appraised her. Dylan was a solid five ten, without the heels. In them, she was nearly a foot taller than her friend. "Neale was right: you are like a megaprofessional now."

"Oh, please. I like how you've seen Neale and I haven't." Dylan smiled. This was typical of Neale.

"Shall we grab a drink?" Stacy said, not waiting for an answer before finding a home on a barstool. "Dyl, what do you want?"

Doing her best to sit delicately on the stool, she started fishing around in her purse for cash as she spat out her usual. "Hendrick's martini, with extra olives, please." She continued to dig around in her purse for a beat before feeling eyes on her. Glancing up, Dylan made eye contact with Santa the Bartender, who was staring at her in disbelief.

"We don't carry Hendrick's. We aren't exactly your standard martini joint." Santa's gravel-packed laugh filled the gloomy space, catching the attention of the patrons sitting next to her.

Suppressing the urge to give Father Christmas a dirty look, she cast a desperate glance around the bar, trying to pick up on what the locals were drinking these days. The guy in a black knit cap next to her held a beer glass full of something that looked like a promising gin-based drink. Attempting to sound casual, Dylan tilted her head toward Knit Cap. "I'll have one of those."

Kriss Kringle's eyebrows shot toward his hairline, but he didn't say anything; instead he picked up a bottle and began pouring. "And you?"

"Pink Lady, please," Stacy answered without missing a beat.

"One Pink Lady and a Beast." He handed Stacy a pink concoction in a highball glass, then passed Dylan the Beast. "Cheers, ladies," he said, wandering away with a slimy-looking rag to wipe down the bar.

"Cheers!" Stacy shouted, knocking her dainty drink into Dylan's.

Dylan took a sip and did her best not to gag. To say the Beast tasted like whiskey fortified in a shoe would have been generous. No wonder Santa had looked shocked. To go from high-end gin to moonshine was a far fall from grace. Trying not to think about the drink in her hand, Dylan shifted her focus back to her old friend. "So clearly Neale filled you in on me. Tell me, what have you been up to?"

"Oh gosh. What's new?" Stacy said, wrinkling her nose and taking another sip of her drink. "Ack! I can't believe I didn't mention this to you. I saw the evil spawn of Andrea Curtis this week. That demon baby tried to eat my hand as I was showing him how to floss." Dylan's skeptical laugh in response was punctuated by her gagging as she tried to swallow another sip of shoe drink. "Don't look at me like that. Andrea was always the worst. You can't possibly think she would give birth to anything other than a cannibal."

"I didn't say anything. She was always a—"

"Total a-hole."

Dylan's smile spread. Stacy worked as a hygienist in a children's dental clinic, and it showed. Not only was she dressed in kid-friendly scrubs, but curse words were generally off the table. *A-hole* was probably the strongest language she would use all night, and Dylan suspected Stacy felt guilty about it.

"I find it hard to believe that a six-year-old consciously tried to eat you."

"Well, he did. Because his mother is Satan's Barbie Bride," Stacy said, shaking her hair out of her face and taking another sip.

As Stacy carried on about the different kids she saw every day, former classmates, and bad boyfriends, Dylan felt lulled by the easy rhythm of an old friendship. It would have been more convenient to blame the warm, nostalgic feeling on her drink, but as they wove in and out of topics without preamble or backstory, she had to admit that in avoiding her family, she'd missed at least one person back home.

~

Dylan was glad she'd had the foresight to park the car and walk to the bar as she fell through the front door of her parents' house, slightly sweaty from both the alcohol in the Beast and her brisk walking pace. After pulling her trench and heels off in one motion, she wandered into the living room. She had expected to find her father doing Tae Bo or something. Instead she found Neale thrown sideways in a chair, reading what appeared to be her mother's battered copy of *Either/Or*.

"There you are. I was wondering when we'd run into each other," Neale shouted, launching a hug at her sister.

"Hey, sister. How you been?" Dylan said, giving her sister a squeeze before carefully folding her coat over her arm.

Neale sat back down airily and looked around the room, as if she were surprised to be there. "So good. I'm sure Mom told you—I'm working on my next manifesto. I think it's going to get a good response."

"It sounds promising," Dylan answered, knowing the vagueness wouldn't prompt a response from space's reigning queen, then made a mental note to ask her mother about the manifesto. She didn't have the heart to tell her no one had so much as emailed her about it. Not even Grandmama, who was a relentless cheerleader for her grandbaby's art.

"How's the active pursuit of claiming souls?" Neale said, picking up Kierkegaard again.

"Oh, you know. I met the devil's quota when I took the Technocore gig, so overall I'd say it was a pretty good day."

Neale snorted into her book and looked up as Dylan shifted her heels to her other hand so they couldn't drip mud onto her coat. "Good to have something you are good at, big sister." She giggled, picking up her coffee mug, then fixed Dylan with one of her rare I-am-present-on-Earth stares. "God, Dyl, everything in your wardrobe is so neutral I want to fall asleep looking at you."

"Thanks. I believe it is called *professional*. If I wanna look like a hobo, I'll visit your closet."

"It's a miracle you manage turnarounds. I feel like you are more likely to achieve a narcoleptic takeover in that getup." Neale laughed, chucking one mud-covered sneaker over the arm of the chair she was curled up in. Dylan cringed at the mud, then remembered that in her parents' home, mud was probably cleaner than the cushions anyway.

"Well, if you ever have trouble falling asleep, feel free to peek in my closet. I have an entire wardrobe full of corporate attire."

"Oh, I know. I went in there to find something to wear today and came back empty handed. I dare you to buy something in a color other than beige, black, or navy."

"I think I have a gray dress somewhere," Dylan shot back, reminding herself that nothing in this house was strictly hers as long as her sister was around.

"You would have an inventory of the colors in your closet. I'm guessing you have an itemized list too?"

"Yes." Dylan rolled her eyes as if they were back in school. "Just so I can track exactly what you've stolen out of there."

"Oh, goody. I've missed your lists." Neale snickered. "I noticed the spotlight is gone. Seeing as the Robinsons' house isn't on fire, I'm guessing I should say thank you," she said, not batting an eyelash at the abrupt turn.

"You're welcome. Honestly, Mom and Dad bring it upon themselves."

"False. Linda and Patricia are sociopaths under all that hair spray."

"I very much doubt that. They raised two perfectly normal children without any homicidal tendencies."

"To your knowledge." Neale shook her mass of curls toward the neighbors' house. She could not be bothered to comb out her hair, which had grown into something resembling Yoko Ono's coiffure during the Lennon years, only dyed blonde. The whole copper-skinned, lion-maned goddess-of-space vibe worked for her.

"Well, I ran into Mike last night, and he didn't try to strangle me, so I think you're probably safe from the Merry Murderers Robinson."

"Oh, you saw Sexy Robinson?" Neale asked, excitement tingeing her voice. "No wonder you think Patricia and Linda are normal. He's so good looking I wouldn't care if he was an ax murderer either."

"Neale." Dylan rolled her eyes.

"Please. You could be blindfolded, and you'd still notice he was good looking. Don't feel bad; everyone has a crush on him, even Mom, in that weird-old-lady-who-is-married way," Neale nettled, shaking an unintentional dreadlock out of her face.

"That's gross."

"I think he's way nicer than the other brother," Neale carried on, pointedly ignoring her. "Maybe Mike is the exception to the serial-killing rule? You could totally date him once the rest of the family goes to jail."

"I live with Nicolas."

"Who we've never met. Are you sure he's real?" Neale's gaze started to go fuzzy, following her thought process.

This was too much family time for Dylan. If she let Neale keep going, they would soon be discussing the aliens who tended bar at Lenny's. "Okay, Neale. You win. Nicolas is a figment of my imagination that I've photoshopped into all my social media posts. The Robinsons are totally mass-murdering maniacs, and I'll marry Mike when they are all safely locked away."

"That's my girl. Never let homicide stand in the way of what you want."

"Good night." Dylan smiled over her shoulder, making her way up the stairs.

"FYI—last I checked, Milo was sleeping in your bed. You may need to move him or something . . ." Neale's voice trailed off into her book.

Dylan walked up the stairs, trying not to let the weight of talking to Neale bear down on her. She loved her sister so much it hurt, but Neale refused to grow up. She couldn't stick to one idea for long, and unlike Billie, Neale was not cut out for the starving-artist schtick—hence what she was doing living with their parents at twenty-seven. The thought of an untethered Neale made Dylan nervous.

Sighing, she pushed open her bedroom door to find Milo deeply ensconced in her sheets. Dylan wondered whether it was worth it to shower tonight, knowing she would have to get up and rinse Milo's fur off in the morning. She had just decided to skip the shower when her phone buzzed, startling her. Glancing at the phone, she watched *Nicolas* scroll across the screen. She had completely lost track of time and their scheduled call. Picking up the phone, she made her way to the bed and pushed on Milo's backside.

"Hi, honey," she said, prompting Milo to groan and slink off the bed.

"Babe! How was your first day?" Dylan could hear the smile in his voice. Everything must have gone well with the divorce settlement.

"I'm concerned about this one," she sighed and started to sink into her bed, only to jump back, praying she hadn't gotten dog hair all over her dress. "The woman I should've been working with left the company. They didn't even remember I was coming." She reached around her back and let down the zipper. Pushing one sleeve off her shoulder, she started chuckling and added, "I practically stalked Tim Gunderson to get a meeting. It's kind of funny—"

"Oh! Guess what? Sorry, I'll let you finish in a minute, but this is awesome, and I don't want to forget."

"What?"

"Totally got that woman to back down on the health care stipulation. I should have the Wilson divorce done in a week or two, tops."

"That's great. You didn't even need your lucky tie," Dylan mumbled, stepping carefully out of her dress.

"Still haven't found that. Are you sure you don't know where it is?"

She immediately regretted mentioning it. Dylan loved a good luck charm as much as the next girl, but Nicolas had been going on about the thing for weeks. The guy had a place for every one of his possessions and was convinced he'd never lose an expensive Thom Browne tie. Dylan was pretty sure it was still somewhere in the gym's locker room, despite how many times he tried to convince her otherwise. She opened her mouth to say something rude about his tie obsession, but Milo chose that exact moment to howl at nothing, cutting her off completely. *That's probably for the best,* she thought. When had she ever cared if Nicolas obsessed over something as trivial as a tie? She usually just tuned that side of him out.

"What's that? Are you outside?" Nicolas shouted into the phone as if she were standing next to a fire truck and a jackhammer.

Holding the phone away from her ear, Dylan called out, "Sorry. It's our dog—Milo, knock it off." Milo stopped and lay down on the floor with a self-satisfied thud, the metal of his collar ringing as it hit the wood. "Good boy—anyway, no. I have no idea where your tie is," Dylan said, shrugging her pajama top over her head. Thinking back to what Neale had said about him, she chimed in before Nicolas could bring up the case again.

"Hey, I've been thinking—I'm not sure how long I'll be assigned to Technocore." *Or anywhere,* she thought. "So, we should take advantage of the free companion ticket Kaplan offers. You could come up here, meet my folks. Show my sister you're not made up." Dylan laughed as she pulled the drawstring on her pajama pants. "Maybe next weekend? Since the divorce is wrapping up, you could take Friday and Monday off and make it a long weekend."

"I don't know, Dyl. We hadn't really planned for me to take a vacation right now."

"True. But we hadn't planned on me being assigned to Seattle either. You could just use the time you set aside for a trip to Paris."

"But that's in August. You'll be back by then."

"I know. But you do have the vacation time. And who doesn't love a spontaneous weekend away?" Dylan joked, trying to ease some of the tension that had crept in over the line. These long placements were always tough on their relationship. She had to remember that.

"You don't," Nicolas laughed. "Our last weekend away was on our calendars six months in advance."

"Thought we could try something new. Spice it up," Dylan said, a hint of sarcasm poking through her otherwise jovial tone.

"That's kind of a lot of time away from the office right now."

Dylan tried not to be offended. Early in their living together, she'd made the mistake of having a phone call with her mother on speakerphone so she could fold their laundry, and Nicolas had caught an all-too-real glimpse of her parents' life, complete with petty struggles between them and a gallery. To say Nicolas had left the call disinterested in her parents and concerned about their self-employment would be downplaying his reaction. The following week, he'd thoughtfully scheduled a meeting for her with his financial planner to explain the pitfalls of feast-or-famine income and the impact it could have on her retirement savings. Nicolas's heart was in the right place, even if the meeting had been entirely unnecessary. Giving her head a shake to clear the memory, she tried again. "It's no more than the time you took off for the comp tickets to New York."

"Yeah, but things are pretty busy around here."

"We've been together for years, and you still haven't met my family. The last two times they came to Texas, you were out of town. I figured now would be a perfect opportunity." She shrugged, put the phone on speaker, and picked up her scarf to wrap her hair. Hearing Nicolas's exasperation, she tried a softer tone. "It doesn't have to be a long weekend. You could always fly up late Friday and leave Sunday. Whatever works for you."

"I'll think about it, okay?"

"Just let me know so I can send the details over to the office."

"All right, babe. I've got to be up early tomorrow. Talk to you later?"

"Of course," Dylan said, trying to match his casual manner.

"Night."

"Love you."

Nicolas hung up the phone before Dylan realized she'd never finished telling him about her day.

"We were tired anyway, weren't we, Milo?" After tying off her head wrap, she sank into bed and pulled her comforter around her.

~

Dylan woke up to Milo crushing her legs and a steely determination to make the Technocore assignment work. As far as she was concerned, things could only go up from yesterday.

"It's not like Tim could announce my assing the company twice," she said, stealing bites of her mother's soggy peanut butter toast.

Bernice quirked an eyebrow. "At least you'll be getting a lot of ass."

"Yuck, Mom." Dylan rolled her eyes as her mother snickered. A small corner of her brain wanted to laugh along, and she quickly squashed that instinct, annoyed at herself for even thinking it was funny. If Dylan laughed, her mother would make more inappropriate jokes, and the next time they'd be in public. Best to nip that instinct in the bud before it got them kicked out of a Fred Meyer or something.

She snagged the rest of the toast and hopped into the car, where she called items to Siri and tried to navigate the growing traffic snarl that was Broadway. She waved as a driver let her merge into a crowded lane, and her optimism picked up when she found a metered spot right in front of a popular coffee shop. Ordering her favorite skinny vanilla latte, she picked up coffees for Brandt and Charlie, hoping to buy herself a little goodwill and a lot of luck on her second day at the office.

After dispensing the coffees and begging the pair to spread the word that her assessment was not a Hunger Games–style selection of employees to fire (or ass), she got started on the interviews.

Several hours and six interviews later, Dylan wondered how Tim Gunderson had managed to go from principled hacker and computer genius to resident doofus without anyone stopping him. She was having a hard time reconciling the young man who had lovingly hired Frank—the now-tearful seventysomething head of admin from his old elementary school—with the man Frank was currently describing as having "callously dismissed half of the administrative team with no notice or severance."

Deep's pixie cut popped through a crack in the door. "Hey, Frank. Sorry, but I have to speak with Ms. Delacroix here before my three-thirty meeting." She didn't look the least bit sorry, but Frank seemed to buy it. Standing slowly, he prepared to go.

"Of course. I lost track of time. Ms. Delacroix—"

"Please, call me Dylan."

"Dylan. Thank you for your time. I hope you get things turned around here. I mean, it's so frustrating to put—"

"All right, Frank, I think she's got it handled," Deep said, wrapping an arm around his shoulders and steering him toward the door. As soon as Frank crossed the threshold, Deep closed the door, letting out a little laugh, then sank into the chair across from Dylan as if she owned it.

Glancing down at the schedule in front of her, Dylan scowled.

"I'm not on it today. Or at all, I don't think. I could hear Frank crying at you for, like, the last forty-five minutes, and I couldn't take it anymore. I had to save you," Deep said, a you're-welcome look running circles on her face. "Frank is a big crier. You should see him when we do a charity event. Waterworks for days over the garden Technocore planted for a preschool."

"Thank you." Dylan sighed.

"So. What are our problems?" Deep said, examining her perfectly polished fingernails.

"I'm really not certain I should be discussing them with you before talking my findings over with Tim," Dylan said, her back stiffening.

"Relax. First, I can hear everything because I'm right outside your door. Second, Tim's office is like a sieve. Layla at the coffee cart tells everyone everything. And finally," Deep said, ticking off reasons on her long fingers, "you need help. And God knows Brandt and Charlie are only going to get you so far."

"Be that as it may, I still have quite a few interviews to get through before I can even start to come to anything conclusive."

"Please. You must have some inklings," Deep said, leaning forward as if she were about to hear state secrets.

"Fine. But do me a favor and keep them under your hat until I talk with Tim. Cool?"

"As if I tell these scrubs anything." Deep grinned conspiratorially. "Now spill."

"First, let me call Brandt."

~

"We're like a dysfunctional crime-fighting team," Deep shouted at Brandt, who had become so pale as to be translucent. In the time she'd spent going over issues, Dylan had recognized two important facts. The first was that both Deep and Brandt had a knack for spotting behavioral patterns and tracing them to specific company policies or events. The other was that Deep, despite her many skills, could not under any circumstances whisper. Half the floor heard Deep shout every time she got excited.

"I think this is more of a loose affiliation, really," Brandt actually whispered.

Deep shook her head. "Nope. This, right here, is a team. I don't know what they taught you clowns at Lakeside, but when people work together and are clearly killing it, that is a team."

"I didn't go to Lakeside." To Brandt's credit, he was holding his own against Deep. An accusation that he'd attended Seattle's most elite private school wasn't going to stand with him. Dylan smiled despite herself. The idea of a team united against crappy corporate culture tugged at a corner of her brain, and she let it rotate in her mind a few times.

"Well, you act like—"

"All right." Dylan cut Deep off before another volley of insults was fired. "Deep, as much as I like having you here, I have to ask—what is it that you do?"

Deep extended one finger and flung her bangs from her face so Dylan could see her pouting, then sat back in her chair. "Front-end developer. Well, I would be, if anyone in the new app group would stick around long enough to code anything worthy of a front end."

"So I've heard." Dylan sighed. Technocore wouldn't have to fire nearly as many people if they could retain the good employees they had. Unfortunately, the mountain of issues in front of her made it clear that saving the development department would take a lot more than a few bonuses.

The crime-fighting-trio idea turned over in her mind again, then clicked. Dylan grinned. Tapping the page in front of her, she said, "I'm taking these issues to Tim. Assuming I get his okay, I have an idea I want to run by you both."

"Which is?" Brandt asked, his usually cautious tone carried away by Deep's enthusiasm.

"What if you two chaired a staff-appreciation committee?" Deep snorted before Dylan had finished the sentence. Brandt leaned back in his chair, like her idea was contagious. Shaking her head, Dylan rushed on: "Hear me out. You're both good at pinpointing where the morale sinkholes are. It makes perfect sense that you use your powers to fix them."

The skeptical lines on Deep's face slackened ever so slightly at the flattery. Brandt still looked like he would rather jump over a canyon, but Dylan suspected that when push came to shove, he would probably do it. "Come on, you're both in here because you care about where you work, and you actually want to do your jobs, which is unusual. *Please* help me out and chair the committee. Then I can tell Tim it's already happening, and you can add it to your résumé or your LinkedIn or whatever."

By the time she had finished drawing the *e* sound out in *please*, she could tell she had hooked Deep, who sighed. "Fine. I'm good at this kind of thing. Besides, I don't have anything better to do. And contrary to popular belief, I like to be useful and actually earn my paycheck."

Brandt nodded vigorously, pushing up his glasses. "There's no structure for interns. I can either work with you or try to act like I'm not reading under my desk."

"Done. I'll send you both an email once I have 'the conversation' with Tim. It's getting late." Dylan glanced at her watch. "I should let you go. Thank you both for your help."

"No problem," Deep said, with way more pluck than anyone who had been working all day should have. "See you tomorrow, Captain!" She grinned and gave a mock salute, then marched out the door.

"Do you need anything else?" Brandt asked, standing up and pushing Deep's chair in.

"Nope. Head out, Brandt. You don't need to put in fourteen-hour days with me. I need you fresh and ready for tomorrow."

"All right," Brandt said. Dylan turned her attention back to the firestorm on her desk as Brandt reached the door. "Hey, Dylan. You sure you have all this under control? It's kind of overwhelming."

Overwhelming didn't begin to cover it, in her opinion. But she didn't need to scare Brandt with that. After all, she was here to help. Fixing was her specialty. "No worries, Brandt. I got this."

"Well, Captain, if you need help, I'm here. I mean, no one ever asked me to lead anything before now." Brandt said this mostly to his feet.

"I have a feeling your leadership will make this place better. Get home safe."

Brandt smiled, his shoulders falling away from his ears. "Don't stay too late."

"Night," Dylan said, wondering if she could capture even a quarter of the confidence she acted like she had.

As she looked around her desk, her stomach grumbled at her. Given the time, it had probably been grumbling for a while; she just hadn't been able to hear it over Deep's whisper-shouts. After taking a moment to carefully pack her bag, she shut off her light. She might as well head home and work over dinner.

CHAPTER SIX

Working at the house was a poor choice, Dylan thought over the sound of Neale and Bernice howling to a Motown classic. She stared down at the notes in front of her, then rolled her eyes and heaved herself out of the well-worn armchair she had been using as a desk. It was no longer sprinkling out. Maybe she'd indulge in a walk to the coffee shop around the corner. On balance, working in overused and comfortable coffee-house chairs was a rite of passage in Seattle, not a cliché. After packing up her computer and notes, she bounded down the stairs.

"Going out?" Bernice hollered over Neale. That woman's hearing was the stuff of myth, Dylan was sure.

"I'm going over to Cruise. Trying to get a little more planning in before tomorrow."

Bernice ambled toward the door and appraised Dylan over the rims of her glasses. "You doing okay? You just got home a few hours ago, and you are already working again. The soulless aren't getting you down, are they?" First Brandt, now her mother. Shifting her bag, Dylan wondered if the stress was aging her already. She couldn't remember the last time her mother had checked in on her physical welfare, let alone her mental health.

"I'm all right. And on the plus side, the employees of Technocore would like their souls back, so who knows?"

"Devil drives a red Tesla, and he doesn't like to bargain, darlin'."
Bernice grinned, which made Dylan smile against her better judgment.

"Perhaps Mephistopheles is feeling generous?"

"Don't bet on it," Bernice said, turning back to the kitchen, where
Neale's braying had come down in volume, probably so she could
listen in.

Dylan stood alone in the hallway, marveling at her mother's sudden
interest in her well-being. It felt oddly comforting, like the memories
of her mother drawing hearts on the Band-Aids Dylan had put on her
own skinned knees as a kid. For a second, she considered wandering
into the kitchen and telling the yelping women inside about her day.
Asking them for guidance might not be as traumatic as she remembered
it being. Then again, if their guidance was anything like their singing
voices . . .

Dylan smirked, and the impulse passed almost as quickly as it had
come. She was not in the mood to listen to suggestions ranging from
set the establishment on fire to *perhaps a séance?* Technocore needed a
framework for survival, not an interpretive poem. An unexpected warm,
fuzzy feeling about her mother was not a good reason to abandon her
common sense, and she had roughly thirty years of anecdotal evidence
to prove it.

Stepping out into the cold air, Dylan pulled her collar a little closer
as the sting settled into her cheeks. Watching her breath rise in short
puffs, she inhaled the smell of pines. There was something comforting
about the cold, clean smell of the city. When she was little, Dylan had
thought of the rain as a bath for the world. Every day, nature washed off
the day before and gave itself a clean slate. It was reassuring.

Rounding the corner, she met the heavy wood-and-glass-plate double doors of Cruise's Coffee House and yanked on one brass handle.
Stepping inside, she was flooded by the warm, familiar scent of coffee.
The shop had been there since she was in high school, and although
they had several locations throughout the city, it still felt like the small,

local homework joint she knew. Covered in dented wooden tables and old dark leather chairs, the house had its own roaster, and if you woke up early enough, you could smell the beans roasting across town.

Wandering up to the packed pastry display case, Dylan bit her lip for a moment before deciding to splurge on a chai latte and a piece of pie. Dessert was usually a special-occasion treat for her. But since she'd come back to Seattle, it seemed more like a close friend she had resisted calling until things became dire.

"Hi, what can I get for you?" the woman behind the counter asked, the usual friendly-coffeehouse-employee look stuck to her face.

"If you had to choose, which pie would you get? Apple or berry?"

"Oh." The woman's magenta lips puckered as she thought about it. "They're both good. What are you drinking?"

"Chai latte."

"Definitely get the apple with that one." A voice from behind startled her. The barista looked up and nodded in agreement as Dylan turned to look at the speaker. Mike Robinson stood smirking down at her, as if catching her off guard in a great pie debate were an inside joke.

"Hi, Dylan," Mike said, his voice mellow against the whirring of the espresso machine.

Dylan blinked a few times, staring at the gray cashmere covering his broad shoulders, racking her brain for the right response. Her sister was right: even Bernice, sworn enemy of the Robinsons, would think he was good looking. Honestly, who looked good in sweater-vests after the age of ten?

"Dylan?" Mike was still smiling, but one eyebrow was raised in a question.

"Um . . . sorry, I was spacing out. Long day." Dylan shook her head, pulling herself up to her full height and tearing her gaze away from the well-fitted vest. She wished she were wearing her heels or at least not such dorky tennis shoes. She also wished she hadn't left her vocabulary at home. Since when did she greet people with *um*?

"Are you together?" the woman behind the counter asked.

"I'm not that lucky, but a guy can dream," Mike said. His smile was innocent enough, but his eyes betrayed him as they ran a hot look over her, giving her a fleeting up and down. Dylan's heart rate tripled almost as fast as the goofy grin appeared on her face. He thought someone would be lucky to get coffee with her in her gym clothes. Mike tilted his head toward her bag, the fleeting look of mischief still playing around his eyes. "Are you staying?"

The sound of his voice jogged her brain. Gym clothes were irrelevant, because Nicolas had the regular honor of seeing her in them. It was still a flattering thought, though. He was Sexy Robinson, after all.

Fixing her face, she tried to say sure, but whatever came out was more babble than a word. Dylan nodded and wished her ponytail would stop bobbing around. If she couldn't use her words, she wanted to at least salvage what was left of her adult image.

"Then yes, we are together. May I also have a chai, please?" Mike said, adjusting the strap of his computer bag and drawing Dylan's attention back to his shoulders.

"Two chais and one apple slice," the woman said, cheerfully ringing them up as Dylan slid her credit card across the counter and into the woman's hand.

Mike opened his mouth to say something, but Dylan cut him off. "I insist. As a thank-you for solving the light situation."

"I don't think asking my mother to redirect a spotlight deserves particular thanks. But I'll accept it nonetheless," he said, scooping up the pie and a mug of chai. Dylan replaced her credit card in its proper spot in her wallet, then picked up her mug and followed him to the table. She wanted to think she was smiling over the neat leaf design in her foam, but she acknowledged it was nice to have an unexpected chai with someone who was at least charming enough to flatter her and pretend she was a catch.

Mike set the slice of pie down on a low coffee table and collapsed into an oversize leather chair, leaving the adjacent love seat for Dylan. She set her drink on the table and lowered herself onto the cushion, tucking her legs under her. Across from her, Mike pulled out a tablet and started poking around. His denim-clad legs were so long they nearly hit the edge of the table.

"So what are you doing here? Dinner with the parents again?"

"Sort of. I was dropping something off, then decided to force myself to go over my lecture notes before I get home, because"—he looked up from his tablet and smiled at her—"the last thing I want to think about when I get home is teaching a bunch of sleepy undergrads. What are you doing here?"

"I don't even want to talk about it."

"That bad?"

"Yes." She groaned into her palms and closed her eyes, as if by shutting them, she could shut out the mountain of information she needed to sift through.

"Tell me about it."

Dylan moved a hand, cracking one eye open and fixing it on Mike, who was situated in the chair exactly as one would imagine their professor to be. Straightening herself up, she took a big breath, considering how best to gloss over everything.

"I'm listening," Mike said, still looking like he wanted to know why her term paper was going to be late.

"Fine," she said with a massive exhale. "I might be in over my head at work, and when I got tired of the paint on my office walls, I thought, *Go home, get some food, a little peace and quiet, then try solving this whole Technocore mess.* Only, it's my parents' house, so that is like going to a preschool and expecting order. Thus, I'm here." Dylan felt the tension leave her shoulders as she watched Mike process everything.

"Preschools are a great place to conduct business." He deliberately took another sip of chai, managing this with a straight face before busting up. Dylan's smile gave way to laughter. The image of her in a suit conducting business at a plastic table with three-year-olds made its way through her mind.

"How are you in over your head? On Friday night you seemed to have the world figured out. It's been four days. What changed?" Mike asked, smiling over the edge of his cup.

Dylan debated for a moment how much to tell him. Sure, her parents didn't trust the Robinsons, but Mike seemed all right. Besides, who was a PhD student going to sell corporate secrets to? Really, half of the details surrounding her job were already in the press. Taking a deep breath, Dylan leaned in. "Okay, but you can't tell anyone this, because I am legally obligated to keep my mouth shut."

Mike's grin was lopsided as he tried to force a straight face. "Secrecy. Got it."

"When I assess a company, one of the first things I do is talk to the staff to find out what's going on," Dylan said, tucking her hands in her lap to keep from flailing them in the air. "This is only my first day of staff interviews, and it's already a mess. Worse, it is a mess my boss wants turned around in just over two months."

"That seems a little quick to try to fix a company recently rated an 'egomaniac haven' by *Time*." Mike frowned and took a breath before adding, "What are the problems? Maybe there are a few quick fixes you can start with?"

"My plan exactly, Professor." She grinned into her mug. "However, it's clear the quick fixes are going to involve some concessions from everyone's favorite hoodie-wearing CEO."

"First, I'm going to put it out there. I like hoodies. They're comfortable—"

"And yet you didn't wear one to work. Because you know deep down hoodies are a curse upon the human race and the tech industry. Mark Zuckerberg effectively took the pocket protector and replaced it with a hoodie, dooming all nerds to look like they're coming from the gym at all hours of the day."

"You give the hoodie too much credit. Nothing can dethrone the pocket protector." Mike leaned forward and picked at the pie with a fork. After taking a bite, he added, "The rest is yours. I only wanted a little." Dylan cocked an eyebrow at him, and he waved the fork at her to continue. "Back to the issues at hand. Tell me what's wrong with the hoodie wearers."

"It comes down to three things. First, the employees feel underappreciated and overworked, like most people. Then there's the whole disappearing-management act. Technocore used to be so small that three years ago everyone knew everyone by name. Employees had direct access to Tim. Now, he has an entire floor to himself, where he is holed up with the coffee cart." Dylan paused to catch her breath as Mike hissed in disapproval. Hogging the coffee cart was the equivalent of commandeering the watercooler in another office. It was corporate-culture massacre. No one wanted to be caught outside the CEO's office chatting about the Seahawks when the guy decided to get a cup of coffee.

"Okay, what's the third?"

"You know what the third is."

Mike inclined his head. "Yeah, but I want to hear your professional diagnosis. This is interesting to me."

Dylan wanted to hug him. No one found her job interesting—not her family and certainly not Nicolas. Hell, half her coworkers thought it was boring. "Fine. No one wants to work at douchebag central. That video of the fight with the old ladies was the final straw."

A few months ago, Gunderson and several of his friends had gotten into a shouting match with some elderly women from the community softball booster club over who had the right to sit closest to home plate. Someone had actually recorded Tim shouting, "Move it, Nana! Technocore bought these damn seats." One of the poor octogenarians had started crying and begged to wait until the next inning because her grandbaby was playing third. Eventually, the women had picked up their walkers and shuffled slowly out of frame, mumbling about how rude young people were. The internet had had a field day.

Mike pursed his lips, his eyes sparkling.

"Say it," Dylan mumbled, picking up the fork and taking a big bite of pie.

"I think your professional assessment of 'douchebag central' is funny. I mean, maybe I wouldn't phrase it like that to Tim, but it's funny."

"I was thinking it would go over better as *Technocore isn't well received by the community*."

"Hmmm . . ." Mike wrinkled his nose.

"What?"

"I mean, that's true. But the bigger issue is, people are embarrassed to work there, right?" Dylan nodded through a mouthful of pie. "Maybe you should tell him that. I mean, phrase it better. But make sure he knows his behavior impacts all the employees."

"You're right," Dylan said, setting the fork down. Mike's gaze flickered over to the pie for a moment. "Please. No one ever has just one bite. Go on."

"Two bites, then," he said, picking up the fork.

"So tell me. What are you teaching?"

"Same class as last year. A course on student motivational frameworks," Mike said, sighing heavily and exchanging the fork for his tablet. Dylan's thoughts drifted as he started in on an overview of the course content. She decided there were probably fifty undergrads running around the University of Washington with a crush on him on any given day. She couldn't blame them. Sitting in a worn leather chair, talking about education, Mike Robinson was quite possibly the most adorable person in the city, if not the state.

"But what about your work at the museum? How does that fit in?"

"I teach one class each semester as part of my doctoral fellow-ship. Someday in the very distant future, I will defend my dissertation, receive my PhD, and earn the right to have only one job. Until that time, I will continue shaping the minds of youth. Scary as that is." He laughed, tapping on his tablet.

Dylan watched the muscles in his shoulders move as he flipped through slides and wondered where he bought his button-ups and if he was single. *People who look good in sweater-vests are not single,* Dylan reasoned, then stopped.

What was she doing? Whether or not he was single and looked good in a sweater-vest was not a concern of hers. Neither were the muscles under the vest. A twinge of guilt crept toward her conscious-ness, and she bit down on it, jaw tightening. Maybe she could convince Nicolas to give sweaters a try. Not that he would take her advice. But a girl could dream that her boyfriend would try something new every once in a while without—

Dylan cut her relationship musing off midthought. She wasn't sit-ting with Mike in this coffeehouse to daydream about his sweater—or anything else, for that matter. Grabbing her notes, she spread them out and started looking for the best easy fixes for Technocore. Dylan felt herself slip into fix-it mode as the chai worked its caffeinated magic on her exhausted mind. She began listing like a woman possessed. Every so often, either she or Mike would reach out and grab another bite of pie. But otherwise they worked in comfortable silence.

She was in the middle of a brainstorm on community image reha-bilitation when Mike stood up and stretched his long frame. Pulling her attention away from the page, she looked around to find the café emptying out.

"Looks like they're shutting down. Are you ready to head out?"

"I guess so," Dylan said, untucking her feet and setting them on the ground. Holding her mug, she began looking at her piles of papers and wondered how she'd managed to spread out so much.

"Here." Mike reached out to take her empty mug, gently brushing her hand and sending tingles down her arm. Her eyes shot up and met the flecks of gold in his, her chest squeezing for a fraction of a second. The pause was almost unnoticeable, just long enough for Dylan to wonder if he felt the static, too, when Mike grinned. "Did you want to hang on to it?" he chuckled, lightly pulling the cup from her hands.

"No." Dylan forced the air back into her lungs, her answer sounding more like a cough than a laugh. He hadn't felt it. Neale was getting to her. There was no sexy static. She laughed at her imagination as Mike walked to the counter to drop off their mugs.

Dylan carefully replaced her files in her bag to avoid imagining any more electricity between them. "Did you walk here?" she asked over her shoulder, wedging the last file in place.

"Yup. You?"

"Guess we're walking back together. Don't let our parents see us." Dylan watched Mike's easy expression creep toward a smile and felt relieved. No sparks. She could walk home knowing a moment ago had been a fluke. "How's the fundraising going?" she asked as she ducked under his arm and out the door, feeling the cold push against her skin.

Mike hesitated, sucking air between his teeth. "Honestly, not well. My museum is in a low-income neighborhood; most big donors don't know we exist. It's hard to convince people to invest in something they've never heard of before, in a part of town they'll never go to, for people they've never met." Mike's scowl deepened as they passed through the golden shimmer of a streetlight, the glow catching the edges of his jaw, reminding her of Bruce Wayne in old Batman cartoons.

"I could help." Dylan felt herself speaking before she had fully thought about what she was offering.

"Really? Are you an expert in museums too?" Mike laughed, his face relaxing in the pale-gray light left by the cloud-covered moon.

"Well, no. But I'm good with public perception and business-plan assessment," Dylan answered. She reminded herself that no matter how swamped she felt at Technocore, she should help. Every child, regardless of their financial means, deserved a top-notch learning space.

And then there was Mike. He looked so stuck in the mire. How could she not offer to do something? Surely if she could help Technocore, she could find a way to help him. And it had the added benefit of making amends for all the souls Bernice said she was claiming.

"You mean it?" Mike stopped, and she realized they were in front of her house.

"Of course. I need good karma since I'm working with Technocore. Who knows—maybe your project will balance out all the bad and keep me off hell's doorstep." She laughed, butterflies beating erratically in her chest as the weight of Mike's eyes rested on her.

"Okay." Mike sounded genuinely surprised. "Feel free to stop by anytime to see the museum in action. No pressure, if you're too busy."

"I can stop by Friday afternoon. I heard Tim usually leaves the office by noon, so I should be free." Dylan waved a dismissive hand and forced herself to sound casual. After all, helping a friend was not a big deal.

"I'd like that."

For a second Dylan thought he might hug her, and she panicked. It was one thing to get chai with Mike. It was another to go around cuddling him when Nicolas was at home, probably missing her and their email ritual. Taking a deep breath, she tried to capture a few of the more aggressive butterflies in her stomach and reminded herself that hugging an old friend was not cheating, even by Nicolas's paranoid standards. Mike rocked forward and back on his heels for a second, his hands firmly in his pockets as if he were waiting for something.

That something turned out to be his mother's floodlight, which snapped on and bathed the street with white light. Dylan jumped back guiltily, as if one of the Robinson women were watching them from behind a curtain. Mike let out a breathy chuckle.

"See you Friday," he said, lifting his chin toward her disaster of a front lawn.

"See you." Dylan took another step backward as Mike turned, fishing his car keys out of his bag. Shaking her head, she turned to face the statue-covered yard.

"Hey, Dylan," Mike called, forcing her to rotate around again. "For the record, I don't think you're going to hell." He began slowly walking backward in the street.

"For what?"

"Fixing Technocore." He shrugged, still ambling backward. "I mean, how many people would be out of a job if you didn't? Really, some could argue your work is saintlike."

"Oh, please." Dylan rolled her eyes.

"I mean it. Night."

"Night," Dylan called, her cheeks getting hot despite the chill.

Mike turned with a wave to face his car, and she went inside. Dylan was halfway up the stairs to her room when she realized she was still smiling.

CHAPTER SEVEN

Dylan sat quietly reading the pirate romance outside Tim's office. She figured he already knew about the book, so she might as well finish it and give it back to Layla. It was only polite. She had planned to present the issues to Tim on Thursday, but in a usual bout of Tim-itis she had received not one but three can-we-push-our-meeting-back emails. He had only agreed to see her Friday morning—now afternoon—after she'd pointed out that even if he didn't use her expertise, Technocore was still paying Kaplan for her time. She hoped the email sounded businesslike and not like the desperate plea it was. She could only dodge Jared's check-in calls and emails for so long before he pulled the plug on her.

Dylan flipped the page and wondered how a book could go from steamy to improbable so quickly. The pirate and the heroine had broken up over stolen gems exactly two paragraphs after sex on top of a moving carriage. *Who comes up with—*

KTHUNK.

Tim's office door burst open, interrupting her thoughts. "Dylan, I'll be right with you. Layla, can you make me another mocha?" Tim called as he sprinted toward the bathroom door.

"Sure thing," Layla shouted at the door. Glancing at the book in Dylan's hand, she smiled. "Good, isn't it?"

Dylan nodded. Loath as she was to admit it, the book was riveting. After carefully replacing her bookmark, she put the book back in her purse. Layla might dog-ear pages, but Dylan wasn't about to start folding up a borrowed book.

"Ready?" Tim came sprinting out of the restroom and snatched his mocha off the little shelf Layla had set it on.

"Yes, sir. Lead the way."

Not that Tim had waited for her. By the time Dylan closed the office door, he was already behind his desk, wearing a hands-free headset. She decided to ignore this. There were weirder things about Tim Gunderson than his propensity for wearing headsets for in-person meetings.

"What do you got?" Tim said, clicking the end of a pen.

"Well, I have narrowed Technocore's challenges into three opportunity groups."

"What does that even mean?"

"You have three big problems," Dylan said, translating her own business jargon. Usually, executives preferred she say *opportunities* in place of *problems*. It was easier to claim plausible deniability if someone sued.

"Oh." Tim's pale eyebrows shot toward his hairline. "That many?"

"Yes. The good news is there are several small, immediate steps you can take to start fixing them." As Dylan began making her case for staff morale and leadership accessibility, Tim remained still save for a few pen clicks, his gaze focused on the ceiling.

"The last one is more difficult to change, but I think we can manage it with some creativity." Dylan tried to soften the blow. "Some employees have the perception that Technocore is not a community player. Consequently they feel . . ." She hesitated, searching for the phrase she had practiced over the last few days. "Well, they feel uncomfortable telling people where they work. It makes recruiting and retaining good employees a challenge."

"Are you sure this is a real problem?" Tim's skepticism rolled off him as he clicked his pen again.

Dylan almost snatched the pen and his stupid headset from him. Smoothing a small wrinkle in her skirt, she took a calming breath before continuing. "Look, Tim. I can lie to you. But you hired me because I help take companies that are dying and bring them back to life. If you want Technocore to flounder until the board puts it out of its misery, fine."

"So you are a necromancer." Tim snort-laughed. When she didn't laugh, he added, "Because you raise zombie companies," then started snort-laughing again.

Dylan's stare was incredulous. "You do recognize these problems are severe. You do not want to make it to zombie-company level, right?"

Tim stopped laughing. "Sorry." He did not look sorry.

She needed to try a new tactic if this was going to work. "Yes. I get the analogy. But, Tim, this is serious. For you and for me. You're right; I'm a necromancer of sorts. But even I can't bring you back if you keep going the direction you are headed."

Tim smiled as if he had missed the point, and Dylan braced herself for another round of *Dylan of the Dead* jokes. "I know this is mission critical. We hired Kaplan, after all, but I don't think you need to be that intense. Really. I built this company. Now that I know there are problems, I can fix them."

"Great. The document in front of you outlines the research in more detail if you have any questions." Relief began to trickle over her. Once the primary issues were agreed upon, it was just a matter of getting his signature on the next steps. From there she could work with her own team to get things done. No more waiting around for him. "I have outlined a number of actions we can take to get things going. I want to run a couple ideas for a staff-appreciation group by you, and—"

"Not necessary," Tim said, clicking his pen once more.

"I'm sorry?" The pen was giving her a nervous twitch.

"Your big-picture analysis is great. But I know this company inside and out. I can fix it."

"You want to contribute to the development of a strategy, then?" Dylan paused.

"No, I mean I have a solution."

"Well, great. Very proactive," Dylan said, praying she sounded diplomatic. "What would you like to do?"

"I mean, I haven't nailed down the specifics. But I'll let you know when I know."

Dylan balked. The entire process was devolving from slightly ridiculous to completely absurd in record time. Tim grinned and leaned back in his chair, this time putting his feet up on his desk. Taking another deep breath, she imagined what her report to Jared would look like:

> *Jared: I have discussed the issues with Tim. His solution is to put his feet up on his desk, click his pen, and bark orders at no one into his headset. I'll let you know when I have details.*
>
> *Dylan*

That was not going to work. Readjusting her tactics again, she said, "I'll put time on your calendar early next week to go over ways I can help implement your vision?"

Or redirect the strategy entirely, she thought.

"Just be on the lookout for an email from me with the details."

"Of course." She might be sick. So far, emails with good news from Tim Gunderson were entirely foreign to her.

"All right, I gotta make a call. Talk to you soon, you necromancer, you." Tim giggled through his nose as he took his feet off his desk.

"Can I expect an email from you by Tuesday afternoon?" she asked, placing a stranglehold on her composure as she put the papers back into her satchel.

"Yes, or close to . . ." Tim waved as if to signal that they were done, then screeched into his headset, "Petey man! How are ya?"

With a curt nod, she walked to the door. Offering a small smile to Layla, she made it inside the elevator before her seething burst from her.

"Gee, Dylan. I know you have done this a hundred times. But I'm such a genius I don't need your opinion. Oh, I know I'm paying for it. I roll around in money for fun, so wasting it doesn't matter to me." She gestured wildly around the elevator, imitating Tim's voice.

Feeling the elevator slowing to a halt, she smoothed the front of her blouse and took a deep breath, forcing composure on herself before she stepped back into the complex cubicle layout that marked the way to her office. Dylan pushed down on her door handle and did her best not to slam the door behind her.

Setting her bag on the desk, she looked at her flashing voice mail light. She knew it was Jared before she even looked at the caller ID. Typing in her voice mail pass code, Dylan leaned against the edge of the desk, waiting for the robo-inbox to finish reading the time and date of the call while tension built in her neck.

"Dylan. Jared here. Calling because I'm reading your last few daily reports now, and it says here that you have meetings with Tim and other Technocore leaders scheduled for this week. Got to say, that really disappointed me. After our conversation, I thought we were on the same page about being a team player." Jared sighed heavily into the phone, as if the act of Dylan doing her job was painful to him, before he continued. "I'm reminding you that you need to get approval from me before you schedule these sorts of meetings. I'm still the lead manager on this project, even if I am not on site at the moment. Let me know that you understand what I am saying and how the meetings went."

For a moment, Dylan's rage tuned out the sound of her voice mail robot asking her if she would like to save the message or delete it. How could he possibly be upset with her for doing the most basic parts of her job? If he wanted to approve meetings, they would never get anywhere. Especially if he wasn't reading her progress reports until three days after she sent them.

Sinking into her chair, she pressed her fingers over her closed eyes for a second. If it was so important that he know about her every move before it happened, he should be in Seattle. It wasn't like she had time to waste, and Jared hadn't exactly been responsive to his email lately. Unless he considered his pointless midnight check-in missives responsive, which she certainly didn't.

Deciding to handle Jared's impossible request later, Dylan focused on her actual problem: Tim. There was a chance, albeit a small one, that Tim would change his mind and review the documents she'd left behind. Or maybe he would come to the same conclusion about next steps on his own. Taking one more deep breath, Dylan opened her eyes to the sound of the phone ringing.

"Dylan speaking," she said through a forced smile, grabbing a pen. Consulting 101: customers could hear smiles on the other end. Consulting 102: always be ready to take notes.

"Um, hi, Dylan. It's Charlie from security." Charlie's voice wobbled.

"Hey, Charlie. What can I do for you?"

"I was checking on you. Seeing if everything was, you know . . . okay?" There was a pause before the rest tumbled from him: "'Cause there are cameras in the elevator. I watch them."

Dylan wanted to kick herself. It was her luck that Charlie would be monitoring the cameras in the elevator when she acted like a toddler in it.

"That's sweet of you. I was letting off steam," Dylan said, trying to make talking and gesturing to oneself sound as normal as possible. "Tough meeting."

"Deep mentioned you had a plan. Tim didn't go for it?"

Of course Deep had. "Not yet, but he will. And he did start this great company; his ideas might be even better." The corporate can-I-help-you smile was back in full force.

"Not likely."

Before Dylan could stop herself, she laughed. It wasn't the most professional thing to do, but she did feel better.

"Keep your fingers crossed for me, yeah?"

"Sure thing. Walking people out of the building is depressing."

"Thanks, Charlie."

Smiling in spite of herself, Dylan smoothed another invisible wrinkle on her blouse and decided that Charlie's call was a sign to get lunch before "hanger" took control of her entirely.

～

The familiar smell of home cooking washed over Dylan as she entered the Skillet. Its decor greeted her with a perfect lumberjack-chic balance, complete with wood-paneled walls and waiters bedecked in plaid. The massive windows let in what little gray sunlight the city had to offer as she slid into a plush moss-colored booth. The diner was one part hipster pretension and one part perfect burger, neither of which she objected to, if she was honest.

Today was a guilt-free-hamburger kind of day. In fact, eyeing the specialty drinks, she thought pretty much the entire Technocore project deserved a treat. Vowing to come back for a boozy milkshake when she didn't have to go back to work, Dylan had finished ordering "the Burger," complete with whatever bacon jam was, when her phone rang.

Nicolas almost never called during the workday unless it was an emergency. While she wasn't sure what she could do from Seattle about a leaky pipe, she felt like she should pick up. After all, she had missed yesterday's call because she was with Mi—*busy*, Dylan course corrected midthought.

"Hello," she answered, unpacking the pirate romance.

"Hey, babe. How are you?" Nicolas asked, concern in his voice.

Dylan exhaled, happy to have a sounding board. Nicolas wasn't the kind of guy who listened to every small detail of your day. But if you told him about a problem and the solutions you were mulling over, he could be helpful. And she needed help. "Nicolas, I'm worried about this assignment. I basically pulled an all-nighter developing solutions, only to have Tim tell me that he is a genius who can solve his own problems."

"These guys always think that. Would you really be there if he was that smart?" Nicolas scoffed.

"He seems to think so." Dylan smiled up at the owner of a tattooed arm dropping off her iced tea.

"So what are you going to do about it?" Nicolas asked, just like she'd expected. There was a comforting order that came with being able to predict her partner's actions.

"Honestly, I think I have to let him try. I figure if it works, great. If it blows up, I'll either be out of a job, or Tim will give me an opportunity to do what he hired me for."

"I guess that'll work," Nicolas said, sounding distracted. "Listen, I was calling for a reason. When you texted last night saying you couldn't talk, I thought maybe there was a serious problem. But now I know it was work—"

"Wait, you didn't call when you thought there was a problem? That doesn't make sense," Dylan joked, waiting for Nicolas to join in. After a beat of silence, though, Dylan took a sip of iced tea. "Sorry, go on."

"It's just unusual for you to change our schedule. Must be the Seattle air." On the surface it sounded like a joke, but Nicolas emphasized the word *schedule* to let her know that he was irritated with her deviation from it. Dylan chafed at his rebuke but let it go in favor of excitement as her food began making its way to her. The sooner her burger arrived, the sooner she could eat instead of talk.

"Anyway, I was calling because I wanted to update you on the case," Nicolas continued, "and to tell you our shower is doing something odd."

"Oh." *Better than the toilet.*

"So I can't make it this weekend. But since the case wrapped, I can probably make it in a couple of weeks, before I head into mediation on the next one."

"Great!" Dylan said, more to the food that was set in front of her than to Nicolas. "I'll give my parents a heads-up."

"I don't think I can take off any extra time, though, so your office will have to find flights from Friday to Sunday."

"It's short, but it'll be fun. I can't wait for you to see where I grew up," she said, munching on a bite of burger. Whatever bacon jam was, it was amazing.

"It should be a good time," Nicolas said in a businesslike tone. "So about the shower. The super—"

"Nicolas, I'm so excited you are coming to visit! But I have to finish up and get to a meeting. Talk to you soon. Love you." Dylan hung up before he could add anything. If she got off the phone, he would figure it out or bathe in the sink or something.

Sighing, she set the phone down and turned back to her burger. Sure, his visit wouldn't be for as long as she'd hoped, but relationships were based on compromise, and this was a place to start. They could always come back for the holidays. Glancing at her incoming emails, Dylan rolled her eyes at another check-in message from Jared. Typing out a quick response with her progress (yes, she had met with Tim; yes, they were taking steps), she felt the pressure return like a ton of bricks on her shoulders. Stuffing the phone back in her bag, she thought of a few different ways to relax before heading back to the office, none of which seemed particularly appealing.

Mulling it over after another bite, Dylan instinctively asked herself the question she most dreaded: *What would my family do?* Picking up a french fry, she turned the idea over in her head. They'd skip work and go play around until a solution to their problem came to them. Dysfunctional as they could be, the idea wasn't all bad, Dylan reasoned, especially if she could skip school responsibly and come up with the ideas she needed for Technocore.

~

She wondered if this was wise. At the diner, visiting Crescent Children's Museum had seemed like a great idea, and Mike sounded genuinely excited she was coming to see the place. Now, standing in front of a formidable-looking structure, she was less sure. The building was old enough that the Washington climate was taking its toll, and bits of moss and lichen had started growing in the cracks between the roof and on the stone steps leading up to the heavy wood doors. Crescent must have been beautiful when it had been built in the 1940s, but now its graying cement facade looked tired. Dylan reached for a heavy brass handle and gave the door a hefty pull, pushing her doubts about the visit aside.

While the outside might have been imposing, the inside was warm and inviting. The floors were old, serious-looking marble with black, red, and white geometric designs covering every inch, but the dim sconces had been replaced with a variety of brightly colored light bulbs. Glancing up at the map in front of her, Dylan realized that the colors corresponded with the different sections of the museum. What would have been boring wood-paneled walls had been covered with inviting banners, advertising exhibits like the waterworks, the sounds-and-signs room, and still others focusing on various forms of art. Dylan walked up to the massive oak counter built into the floor. School was not out yet, so the museum was slow. Only one woman wearing a brightly colored cat T-shirt was behind the desk, attempting to solve a Sudoku puzzle.

"Hello," Dylan said, trying not to feel guilty as the woman jumped in surprise.

"Hi. Can I help you?" she asked, pushing her Sudoku to the side.

"Yes. I'm here to see Mike Robinson."

"Is he expecting you?" the woman asked, already dialing what Dylan guessed was his extension.

"He should be. I spoke to him a few minutes ago." Dylan threw in an extra smile for good measure.

The cat-shirt woman nodded before speaking into the receiver. "Hi, Mike, there is a Ms. . . . ." She glanced up, waiting for her to fill in the blank.

"Dylan Delacroix."

"A Ms. Delacroix here to see you." Dylan listened to mumbles on the other end as the woman smiled affably. "Sounds good," she said before shifting her focus back to Dylan. "He says he'll be right over."

Dylan nodded and went to study the big calendar of events by the door. She was vaguely aware of the happy shouts of children's questions floating through the stone corridors every so often. *Actual whispering is a skill you acquire over time,* she thought, then amended that. Whispering was a skill you acquired if you were lucky. As far as she knew, Deep had never learned to whisper, and it didn't seem likely that she would learn anytime soon.

The sharp click of dress shoes on marble pulled her attention away from whisper skill development. Dylan whirled on her heel as Mike strode down the long corridor, looking like what magazines thought people at museums looked like. He was dressed in dark-gray slacks and a smoke-infused light-blue dress shirt, and his walk was intentional, not hurried. As if walking in colorfully lit corridors were the same as being in his living room. He had his sleeves rolled up and his collar unbuttoned. She wanted to hand him a tumbler full of scotch and an old book. Unless there was a polo pony and an Aston Martin waiting outside, he could not have looked more like a character in an Annie Leibovitz photo for *Vogue*.

"Thanks for coming," Mike said as he drew closer to the large calendar, an easy smile tugging at the corners of his eyes. Mike leaned in to give her a quick hug, made slightly awkward by her bulky bag. Dylan realized that, outside of her first night home, she had not touched Mike. Or even come close enough to smell the aftershave he used. Earthy and fresh. Not floral.

Mike left his hand on her elbow as he turned to face the woman at the desk, reminding her more forcefully of the first night on his front steps. Dylan felt her stomach tighten, remembering the reassuring muscles that had steadied her. Fighting an instinctual urge to lean into the security of his arm, she readjusted her necklace and her thoughts.

"Gloria, I'm going to take Dylan on a short tour. If anything comes up, feel free to call my cell." Turning back to face Dylan, Mike added, "I was surprised you showed up."

"Did you think I wouldn't come? I always come." Dylan smiled, adjusting her handbag to rest under one arm.

Mike paused on an inhale, dropping his arm from her elbow and biting down on his lower lip. Tilting his head to the side, he blinked at her. Dylan's mind replayed her last words as Mike shut his eyes and took three deep breaths. Did she have ketchup on her top? She looked down and was relieved to find no food attached to her attire. Looking back up, she met Mike's gaze as he shook his head slowly. Exhaling, Dylan asked, "What?"

"You always come, huh?" Mike said, trying to press his grin into a straight face, his eyebrows raised mischievously.

"I . . . that . . . that . . ." Dylan opened her mouth and then closed it, the heat of a furnace burning in her cheeks as she realized how her words could be construed. She had been thinking that he looked good when she'd first seen him. But, she reasoned, that was in a strictly scientific-observation sort of way. It certainly wasn't the cause of her perfectly innocent words. Mike was just twisting them. "That is not what I meant."

"Sure it wasn't," Mike said. "Are you trying to tell me something, Dylan?"

"No. No. I'm not trying to tell you anything." If Dylan had thought she was overheating before, it was only because she hadn't known the humiliation she felt could get any worse. "No. Really, that is not what I meant."

"It's fine. You don't need to be embarrassed. I'm happy for you." Mike stared at her for a long moment before clearing his throat. "Shall we start in the theater?"

"Yes. Let's do that," Dylan said, making her words crisp. Running a hand over her hair, she tried to flatten her flustered mind, carefully storing her urges in the irrational corner of her brain, where she could blame them on her upbringing. "The theater, huh?"

"It is the best place to get a sense for what we do at the museum."

"It sounds like I'm about to get the donor spiel."

"You are. The top-donor speech, as it is. Only the special donors get a guided tour."

"From a director, no less."

Mike gave a lopsided smile at his own title, tugging half of Dylan's heart along with the curve of his lips. She took a deep breath, practically begging her misbehaving thoughts to go back to their corner. She was here to see if she could help, not to ogle. "Don't get too excited," he said. "A donation of two hundred fifty dollars or more constitutes a 'special donor.'"

"That will change. Soon as you get this room up and running, Crescent is going on the map as a cutting-edge children's facility."

"Facility? That sounds clinical."

"It's not clinical. It's professional," Dylan corrected, watching the other half of his smile catch up to the first.

"If it gets me a paneled sensory room, you may use all the business jargon you want."

"You may as well start calling it a children's facility now. I don't lose often, buddy."

"I wouldn't have asked you here if I thought you did."

"I was kidding." Dylan laughed as they rounded a corner and passed through another set of heavy doors, complete with a brass lion handle from the movies.

"I wasn't."

Dylan almost tripped over his confidence. If she hadn't been a professional high-heeled sprinter, she might have. Mike did not break eye contact with her, self-assurance vibrating off him. She wasn't sure what to do with the compliment, so she redirected the conversation toward the massive stage at the back of the room. "So this is the theater?"

"Yes. This is the point in the tour where I dazzle you with childhood-development theory and my vast knowledge of experiential learning."

"By all means. Dazzle away." *Dazzle away?* Dylan hoped he developed sudden amnesia and forgot the entire trip to the theater, or at least the part where she stopped forming cohesive thoughts.

"Right." Mike nodded solemnly. "At Crescent our mission is to provide children with experiences. Not unlike adults, most children learn by doing. By providing kids with more than a nameplate and facts, we give them a chance to act on the knowledge they have gained. Our theater offers children the opportunity to dress up and act out different concepts and professions. Chances to be doctors, astronauts, and scuba divers all in one location." Mike paused and looked at Dylan a little sheepishly. "This is the part of the tour where I admit to rigging the space so there are guaranteed to be children playing in here for donors to see. Your visit caught me off guard."

Dylan laughed, feeling less self-conscious now that she had some company in the self-deprecation department. "Impressive. Please explain the mechanics of staging playtime. I may need this trick later."

"Homeschool groups. They usually require a couple of days' notice, though." Mike shrugged the sheepish look off, replacing it with the confidence he had worn moments ago. "Continuing on, unlike adult museums, which are largely observational, Crescent subscribes to the experiential-learning model. Take, for example, our waterworks space." Mike began walking in reverse up the sloped auditorium. "This is where I impress everyone with my ability to walk backward while answering questions."

"It is impressive. You are out here giving away tour trade secrets. I might steal your job." Dylan felt her smile surface as her Gunderson-induced panic subsided. Crescent and Mike, the self-narrating tour guide, were just what she needed.

"Honestly, this one comes with years of practice as an undergraduate campus tour guide. I'm not worried about people in the consulting world mastering this skill overnight."

"Someone's getting cocky. If you trip, I want you to know I'll laugh."

"I wouldn't count on it. Never fell once in over ten years." After throwing a quick glance over his shoulder, Mike twisted around to face the installations as they walked into the next room. Dotting the room were dozens of freestanding structures, all brightly colored and built at elementary-schooler height. Looking to her left, next to a glass case Dylan could make out a massive cartoon drawing of a raindrop explaining how clouds worked. In the case was a tiny ecosystem, miniature clouds dropping even smaller buckets of rain on a little cityscape of Seattle. As Dylan watched, the clouds slowly stopped raining and cleared up. Despite the twenty-five-year age gap, both Dylan and the sticky-handed child watching the display were astonished.

"The clouds will reform in fifteen minutes," Mike said, noticing her squinting in the direction of the display. Dylan arched an eyebrow in lieu of asking for an explanation. "There is a heating coil under the city that—" Mike broke off midsentence, moving from Dylan's side and making a beeline for one of the installations.

"Oh, buddy, you really don't want to drink that," Mike said, scooping a child away from a dripping stalactite in an impressive arch. The rumpled little boy, surprised by his impromptu flight path, clung to Mike's forearm until his feet were on the ground. He looked up at Mike and gave a small forlorn glance at the stalactite display before toddler-running back to an aggressively bored-looking teenager furiously tapping on his phone.

"What no one tells you in school is that being here is one part museum advocate, one part childcare provider," Mike said, walking back toward Dylan and readjusting his sleeve, which had been pushed farther up his toned forearm.

"What happens if the kids drink the water? Does an alarm go off?" Dylan asked, remembering the feel of his arm under her hand. Taking her gaze off him, she watched the teen as he took the rumpled boy by the hand, still oblivious to his previous antics.

"No, no alarms. We don't want to traumatize any of them. And we chlorinate the water to kill germs." Mike shook his head and smiled before adding, "But last week I caught a kid trying to pee in it, so really, I wouldn't vouch for its potability."

"I can kind of see where it looks like a big toilet," Dylan reasoned. Mike guffawed, throwing her a sideways look. "What? I know I shouldn't say that given my parents' profession, but if we are being honest here," she added with a sharp gesture of her free hand, "you can't tell me that doesn't look a little like a toilet."

The idea of peeing in public was something Dylan usually found mortifying, but here she was giggling like bodily functions were adorable. She blamed Mike for this.

"I feel like his mother would have made the same excuse if she wasn't busy being horrified."

Hanging a hard right at a set of heavy doors marked EMPLOYEES ONLY, Mike started down an empty hall. Without the brightly colored lights, the marble floors gave off a distinctly less welcoming, more financial-institution vibe.

"This closed section leads to the sensory space," Mike said as they continued down the corridor, the sound of Dylan's heels bouncing off the bare walls. She stopped abruptly as Mike plunged into the massive black hole that appeared at the end of another right turn.

"Um . . . ," Dylan called into the darkness. Her pulse quickened as the formerly friendly children's museum turned into the beginning stages of a horror movie. The sound of Mike shuffling around in the dark didn't do much for Dylan's courage level.

"I'm looking for the light. I thought I left it . . . on . . ."

Taking three cautious steps into the blackness, she found herself groping around her purse for her pepper spray. Maybe Neale was right. Maybe the Robinsons were charming ax murderers after all.

"Got it!" Mike yelled, filling the room with the Rapturesque white fluorescent lighting often used for nighttime construction projects. Blinking, Dylan quickly stashed her pepper spray—and her humiliation—back in her purse, vowing to stop listening to Neale.

Unfortunately, the lighting did little to help the horror story appeal of the space. The walls might have once been cream but had slowly faded to a depressing shade of grimy beige. Large pieces of murky clear plastic hung over what Dylan assumed were windows, the massive, earthy, ornate wooden frames barely visible under the dust and bits of plaster.

"What was this place?"

"It's labeled 'grand room' on the floor plans. Although I'm not sure what a grand room is, honestly."

"Huh." Dylan felt gravel and loose chunks of whatever covered the floor beneath her heels and tried not to wrinkle her nose. Perhaps Mike saw the potential for a sensory room, but all she saw was a lawsuit waiting to happen. Nicolas would have a field day suing this place.

Dylan grimaced at the missing ceiling tiles, then looked back toward Mike. He was studying the hunks of absent wall plaster with the sort of intensity usually reserved for avoiding looking at other things. *Or people*, Dylan thought.

Using the stained walls around his head as a cover, she watched Mike for a moment. His usually relaxed posture was noticeably absent, replaced by a spine that was too straight to be comfortable. Her inner business consultant kicked in as she ran down her CEO diagnostic checklist. Normally relaxed hands jammed in pockets—check. Shoulders a fraction of an inch too high—double check. Avoiding eye contact at all costs—also a check. Zero indication that he was still breathing . . . Dylan paused to observe his rib cage for a second. Although his torso filled out his shirt quite nicely, there was no way he was moving a lot of air through it. Check.

All nervous, protective gestures present and accounted for. Taking a deep breath, she exhaled. "Wow."

"Wow good? Wow bad?" Mike asked, narrowing his eyes.

Every fiber of her knew that Mike was showing her a very dear but exceptionally impossible dream. It was a miracle the city still considered the structure sound enough to let children—or even dogs—in with this section still standing. When she'd said she wanted to help, she had thought she'd write a personal check, maybe beg her dad to pony up. But this project was so much bigger than what her puny charity budget could manage. Still, a deal was a deal, and she was nothing if not good for her word. She had to try, or risk being as flaky as the rest of her family.

"I can see it . . . ," Dylan said, careful to meet Mike's gaze. Dream lawsuit or no, she couldn't tell Mike the truth about his plan.

"Really? I know it's rough," Mike answered. His shoulders dropped the appropriate distance, but his face read as skeptical.

"Yeah. I . . ." Dylan's eyes cast wildly about for some redeeming quality in this troll cave. "I love the chandeliers. Are those brass?"

"I was a little worried about them structurally, what with the water damage." Faux genuine as her response was, Mike was willing to grab the life raft. Taking a massive step over piled-up scaffolding, he walked toward the center of the room. "I want it to be paneled to the edges, like the Sky Church."

"Sky what?" Dylan watched the ground and tried to gracefully circumnavigate the pile of junk so she could stand next to him. Mike stopped pointing at the wall long enough to aim an incredulous stare at her.

"Sky Church. The venue inside MoPOP." When recognition didn't immediately dawn on her face, he tried to rephrase it. "You know, the venue in the Experience Music Project, now MoPOP? The wacky-looking museum—"

"I know what the EMP is. I live in an artist hive, not a bunker. I just haven't actually been inside of it."

"You're kidding. You've never been inside the Hendrix museum?"

"Does riding the monorail through it count?"

"You can't keep telling people you were raised here. You gotta see it. Add it to the list." It was Dylan's turn to look incredulous. "Don't act like there isn't a checklist running through your head right now." Mike's good-natured smile returned as he poked fun at her.

"Gee, you remember my absolute best traits. Thanks for that." There was no point in denying "the list" existed, and they both knew it. "Now, tell me what you want to do."

Smirking, Mike began rambling around the room, pointing to various aspects of the space and noting planned changes. Sure, the alterations would cost more money than either of them had access to, but Dylan imagined defeat on someone like Mike would be more heartbreaking than she was prepared to handle. She didn't regret her small albeit deeply impractical lie.

"—like the Bezos Center at the Museum of History and Industry." Mike's words pulled Dylan back into the room. She'd missed whatever had prompted him to wave wildly at the back wall, but she was pretty sure that if it was named after the founder of Amazon.com, it was expensive.

"Haven't seen that one either?" Mike tried to mask a look that fell somewhere between offense and pity. "How can you be the child of artists?"

"Don't ask me questions based on the assumption of normal parentage. My parents think dogs are appropriate messengers."

"They're whimsical, is all."

Dylan threw her free hand over her heart. "Aw, thank you. 'Whimsical' might be the nicest way anyone has ever called my family weird."

Mike shrugged a lazy shoulder, turning back toward the open doors. "What can I say? Whimsy suits them."

Dylan smirked. "I'm sure you want their whimsy in your life as much as you want a triple bypass."

"I don't think your family is nearly as odd as you think they are," Mike said, navigating back toward the construction light. "The whole feud thing aside."

"That's because you don't have to live with them." Either she was missing something, or Mike had managed to locate a level of reasonable she had yet to see her parents display. Both thoughts were equally unnerving, albeit for opposite reasons, so she pushed them aside as she stepped carefully to the door, grateful to be away from the uneven flooring.

As they walked back through the hall, she weighed her options. She didn't have time for a pro bono project. Especially with Jared breathing down her digital neck every fourteen minutes. Still. There had to be a way she could sell using some of her time on this. It was obvious Mike needed help, and she could use a distraction. She'd poke around for a while and write a check to the museum when she left. Nothing massive, but certainly something bigger than "special donor" money. She had basically run Nicolas's workplace-giving drive for the last two years. How much more time consuming could this project be?

"Maybe you could come up with a list of some spaces I should see? Y'know, so I can get a better sense of what you want to do here."

"Dylan Delacroix, is this your way of trying to trick me into taking you out?"

"That is not what I am asking." Dylan rolled her eyes, refusing to let Mike embarrass her again.

"Just checking." Mike shrugged, putting one hand in his pocket. "You actually want to help? You aren't just making a pity offer? I value honesty, and I promise I can take it if you really don't want to do this."

"I'm being honest. I want to do this." Dylan's pro bono scheme was only half-baked, but she added extra emphasis on "want" anyway.

"I know you said you would help. But I figured you'd tell me to open the windows in there and learn how to plug in a light." Dylan narrowed her eyes, reinforcing the idea that he should choose his next words wisely. "Not, you know, actually invest your time. You have an important job and all." He exhaled, his other hand dropping to his side.

She let loose a laugh that sounded more like a groan. "Trust me, it is not as big a deal as it sounds. Besides, I might be able to swing this as a pro bono project for Kaplan." Dylan regretted adding that detail the second it escaped her mouth. Mike's smile was giving off a glow that rivaled the fluorescents in the hallway. "Don't get too excited. That isn't a promise or anything. And you'll probably have to do most of the legwork—"

"No. No. I'm happy with whatever you can do." Mike cut her off mid-expectation-management speech. "I'm glad someone else even thinks it is a viable idea."

Dylan's mind spasmed. This was hardly a viable idea.

Mike's excitement saved her from having to develop a response to the room's usability. "But yes, I can put together a list of places to check out. I'll drop it by your house next time I stop by my moms' place."

"Great," Dylan said, as much to reassure herself as to encourage him.

Crossing back through the colorful entrance, she dodged a few eager third graders. School had let out, and the space was starting to fill up. Mike looked perfectly at home surrounded by roughly a hundred screaming children. Normally, Dylan would have found the entire thing overwhelming, but between Mike grinning and occasionally waving at kids who recognized him, the museum was suddenly the single most charming place she had ever set foot in.

Hesitating at the visibly sticky door handle, Dylan decided the museum's charm had its limits. Mike must have taken her reluctance to touch the door as a sign he should open it. Leaning in, he reached around her shoulder to push the handle of the door. The familiar and unusual heat of another body so close sent shivers through her. She stood in front of the open door a fraction of a second longer than she meant to, enjoying the sensation of being near another person. Particularly one who waved at kids and had a jaw sculpted out of marble.

"So I'll come by later?"

"Yup. Absolutely." Dylan wasn't sure if he was asking a question or gently encouraging her to move out of the doorway and stop trying to snuggle with him. She hurried through the door, pretending to furiously dig around in her purse for her keys, as if they were not always in the second-innermost pocket. After shuffling around a lipstick and a few pens for good measure, she pulled out her keys, feigning a look of triumph.

"Thanks for coming by," Mike said, relaxing against the doorjamb. Dylan decided he probably tossed that same casual, seductive grin at anyone from fellow PhD students to benefactors. Whatever. It worked for him, and she needed to leave right now, before it worked on her too.

"Yup. See ya!" Dylan waved and executed one of her better speed walks to the car, willing herself not to look back. She hopped into the driver's seat, buckled up, and started the car with the kind of efficiency a NASCAR driver would envy. Exhaling, she looked at herself in the rearview mirror.

"Okay, Dylan. For everyone's sake, please never use the word 'yup' again."

CHAPTER EIGHT

Dylan let herself sit idle in the driveway for a second, wondering if helping Mike with Crescent really made sense. Didn't she have something good with Nicolas? Should she really be palling around with some other guy for a community service project?

Pushing herself out of the car, she decided that there was nothing going on between herself and Mike that constituted a threat to her relationship with Nicolas. This was her mind making some impressive mental leaps. Her imagination really had nothing to do with the guy next door and more to do with her and Nicolas's dry spell. It was just kind of hard to feel sexy when he was shouting into his phone all the time.

"That you, Dyl?" Neale's voice singsonged from the kitchen as Dylan crossed the front door threshold and shrugged off her coat. She looked down at her heels and then the rug and decided to keep her shoes on.

"Coming." Dylan pressed her cold fingers to her cheeks to mask the flush, then pulled her shoulders back and strutted into the kitchen.

Giving Dylan a once-over, Bernice scratched a fleck of dried glaze on her neck. "You're home early. How was your day?"

"Busy. I decided it'd be good for Kaplan and Technocore to pick a pro bono project." Dylan felt the white lie slip off her tongue and hid it by turning toward the sink for a glass of water. Her mother could smell lies; she was sure of it.

"Really? What is it?" Neale asked.

"I think everyone at Technocore recognizes they haven't been a community player, and Crescent Children's Museum is looking to do some pretty cool cutting-edge tech stuff."

Dylan turned away from the sink as her mother's eyebrow stretched toward her in-need-of-a-touch-up roots. "Oh? The good-looking boy across the street's place?"

"Mom. You know his name." Dylan exhaled.

"I know his last name. But I can't blame you, sweetheart. The good-looking ones are always a bad idea. Don't worry—we've all made that mistake. Trust me." Bernice winked at Neale.

If Dylan hadn't already swallowed her water, she would have choked on it. "Mom. No winking. It's gross, and I know for a fact neither Neale nor I want to hear the story behind it."

"Actually—"

"No, we don't." Dylan cut Neale off and shot her a look that wielded more than daggers.

"Fine. Another time. Let's just say your mom really lived her wild oats."

Dylan gagged, torn between repulsion and her urge to correct Bernice's expression.

"How did all this come about?" Neale asked, an unusually present look crossing her space-queen visage.

"Today was tough. Trying to set up procedures with Tim." Dylan ignored Bernice's scoff at the consultant jargon. "So I went out and ate a hamburger, and I still didn't feel any better, and then I decided on a pro bono project. A feel-good thing to wash the taste of Technocore out of my mouth."

"Who doesn't love a 'feel-good' project in the middle of the day?" Bernice used air quotes around the words *feel-good*, as if her meaning might not have been conveyed by her shit-eating grin.

"Mike Robinson is a pro-BONE-o project," Neale snorted.

"He probably tastes better than a hamburger too," Bernice said, her deadpan playing to the extreme of Neale's laughter.

"Okay, ew. Sex jokes with my mom and sister. Yuck." She felt herself giggle and swallowed the laugh, irked that a little piece of her mother's humor had found a way to amuse her. Mike must have been rubbing off on her if she was starting to find Bernice's jokes funny.

"Dyl, that wasn't even the best I could do. Mom and I haven't devolved into jokes about washing your mouth out yet."

"Give us credit. We didn't say *that's what she said* or anything," her mother cackled.

"I'm not sure you deserve credit for only stooping to the second-lowest rung of raunchy humor."

Dylan was spared further indignities by the doorbell ringing, followed by Milo's bellowing from somewhere on the second floor. Stacy didn't actually wait for anyone to answer the door; instead, she walked in just in time to catch Henry shouting, "Don't ring the doorbell. It makes the dog bark."

"Hi, Henry."

"Hello." Her father's voice carried remarkably well over Milo, whose fervor had died down to a half-hearted yowl.

"Hey, Stacy. Don't pay attention to Henry. He is in a conceptualizing phase. 'Any small distraction.'" Bernice mimicked her husband, walking into the hallway to give Stacy a frigid hug. "Of course, you don't need to ring the doorbell."

Stacy wrinkled her nose at Dylan from over her mother's shoulder but otherwise said nothing about the Delacroix's notoriously fickle relationship with their front door. She knew Stacy found her family to be a blend of endearing and strange, an attitude pretty much anyone who set foot in the Delacroix's home more than once had to adopt.

When they were younger, her friend had asked why her parents didn't move to somewhere like Fremont, where all the other well-off artist types lived. With a motto like *The Freedom to Be Peculiar* and a giant troll statue under a bridge, Fremont was more the Delacroix's speed. In the end, Dylan had explained that in Fremont, her parents were two of many peculiar artists. In Green Lake, the Delacroix had the distinct honor of defining *peculiar*. A long-standing feud with their neighbors was just poutine on whatever cuisine Bernice had managed to char that evening.

"Ready?" Dylan reached for her coat around Bernice, who looked like she was about to invite Stacy in for another round of racy jokes.

"My toes so need a pedi. Like, I-won't-even-wear-my-flip-flops-into-the-salon-level bad," Stacy said, shaking her head in disgust.

"Want me to drive?" Dylan asked, snatching up her keys and hoping it wasn't obvious she was trying to get them out of the door fast.

"Sure," Stacy said, waving to Neale, who was drinking the rest of Dylan's water in the kitchen.

"Are you girls coming back for dinner?" Bernice asked, her tone too innocent for Dylan to be comfortable with the question.

"I don't think so. Dyl, I was thinking we could try the new Ethiopian place by my house?"

"Sounds great. It does look—"

"Not as good as who you had for lunch," Bernice interrupted Dylan with another cackle, which Neale echoed from the kitchen.

"Okay, Mom. I love you," Dylan said, wrenching the door open.

"I don't get it," Stacy said, looking bewildered.

"Long story. I'll explain in the car."

"Okay. Bye, Delacroix," Stacy called over her shoulder as Dylan nudged her out the door.

Pressing unlock on her keys, Dylan sighed in exasperation as the car lights flashed. "As soon as she asked about dinner, I knew she wasn't done with the jokes."

"What was she talking about?" Stacy asked, jumping into the high seat of the SUV.

Dylan started the car and carefully backed out of the driveway, aiming her gaze and her words over her shoulder and away from Stacy's prying eyes. "It's just my family making fun of me for agreeing to help Mike Robinson with a project. This happened over lunch, so now she is making snack jokes."

"She really can't help herself. The dirty jokes are part of her charm."

"You might be the only person who finds her jokes charming."

"Come on, she's funny. She isn't *that* bad."

"Remember the salad dressing incident at the volleyball game?"

"Okay, that was bad," Stacy said. "But it was like fifteen years ago. Plus, I like when a woman in her sixties can laugh at sex. Everybody likes to pretend women stop even knowing about sex after menopause. I like that Bernice isn't playing the no-sex-for-women game."

"Bernice has never played a societal-expectation game in her life," Dylan said, shrugging as she turned left. Stacy might have been right about her family making slight improvements in their behavior, but Dylan would rather be present for the freezing over of hell than admit it to her friend.

"Well, that's true," Stacy capitulated as a sly smile crept across her face. "So you are working with Mike, huh?"

"Yes. Don't make that face."

"I'm not making a face."

Stacy was absolutely making a face. She lacked any form of subtlety, and behind her hot-pink lipstick she was trying her hardest to suppress a smile that said more than enough.

"If you start making Bernice jokes, I swear I'll turn around and drop you back off at my parents' house."

"Fine. No jokes," Stacy said, throwing her hands up, then letting them fall to her lap with a smack. "But isn't he cuter than Ghost Boyfriend?"

"Why are you calling Nicolas 'Ghost Boyfriend'?"

"Because no one but you can see him." Stacy laughed. "He's tethered to your Texas apartment, Casper-style."

"You spend too much time with Neale." Dylan's chuckle came out in an unladylike snort-laugh. "Nicolas isn't a ghost. He just isn't big on the cold and eating unfamiliar foods. It makes travel tricky."

"And you are okay with that?" Stacy asked, her lip curled slightly.

Dylan paused. She'd stopped asking herself that question after Nicolas had freaked out over Thai green curry on a date. She just chalked it up to his quirks about deviating from known quantities and ate whatever she wanted when he wasn't around. It wasn't that he didn't want her to eat Thai food. It was just that he was a creature of habit, which she liked most of the time. Hell, his dedication to structure was what had drawn her to him in the first place. Their life was the exact opposite of her childhood, which Dylan found comforting. Or at least she'd thought she did, until Stacy had brought it up.

She glanced over at her friend, trying to prepare an answer, when Stacy's expression relaxed. "Whatever. If it's what you like, then I guess it works for you." She shrugged before adding, "For the record, I agree with your family. Mike looks delicious."

"Please. I have to see this person regularly. I don't want a bawdy laugh track running through my head every time I talk to him about fundraising or our parents' latest fight or whatever."

"Bawdy, huh? Impressive use of SAT words."

Dylan flipped on her blinker and turned into the parking lot of Richie Nails. "Tell me what's new with you."

"I want you to know I'm giving you a free pass. Don't think I didn't notice the subject change. We are so coming back to Mike." Stacy unbuckled her seat belt and jumped down from the car with a dainty hop. "Actually, things have been great at work. I got a tiny pay bump." She held the door of the salon open with one hand and her thumb and forefinger together in front of her face with the other, emphasizing how little her pay raise was.

"That's fantastic. Congratulations!" Dylan squealed as she walked through the nail salon's door.

"Yeah, but that's not all. Hi, Tammi," Stacy said to the older woman moving toward them. Dylan and Stacy had gone to this salon since high school, back when Stacy had thought that sparkly acrylic claws were the height of nail fashion. The trend had never caught on.

"I almost didn't recognize you. You look so adult in your work clothes," Tammi said, giving Dylan's shoulders a squeeze. Despite being about half Dylan's height, Tammi ran the staff at Richie Nails with an iron grip. Not even her husband disobeyed a Tammi order. If she told Dylan to sit in a chair, she did it without question. Even Neale listened to her. "We haven't seen you in a while."

"It's been forever. I have been swamped with work in Texas." Not a lie, but Dylan felt guilty all the same. Giving Stacy a hug, Tammi tossed a glance at one of her manicurists, who began filling a basin without batting an eyelash.

"I said the same thing," Stacy said, throwing Dylan a reassuring smile. At least Stacy understood that life with Nicolas was demanding and having Jared for a boss was nearly the same as having a second boyfriend. Albeit one she liked a lot less.

"You girls take your shoes off and go over there. I'll grab your colors." Dylan almost protested but stopped herself. Tammi had begun selecting their colors after Stacy made a particularly questionable nail-art choice. At the time, she'd been irate and convinced that the two of them were out to destroy her business reputation. Dylan helped broker a color-selection compromise, which saved Tammi's reputation and Stacy's fashion sense. She remained proud of her solution to this day. In many ways, Tammi choosing colors was Dylan's first corporate-productivity project.

Setting their shoes aside, they settled into their pedicure chairs with a couple of gossip magazines each, Dylan turned back to Stacy. "You were saying about work?"

"Oh yeah. So I got a raise. But you know Dr. Marshall teaches dentistry at UW, right?" Dylan hadn't known that Stacy's boss taught in the dentistry program, but she nodded anyway. "He suggested I apply for a master's in dental hygiene. And I think I'm gonna do it."

"Look at you. First a raise. Now graduate school." Dylan bounced in her chair, causing her manicurist to tsk. She put her foot back in the basin with a mumbled apology.

"I know most people think it's silly that I even got a bachelor's degree. But there are some real upsides—"

"Stace, stop. It isn't silly at all. It's awesome." Dylan sighed. By *most people*, Stacy meant her family. In high school, she had entered a city college program to complete her associate's degree at the same time as her high school diploma, then started working right away. There was good money in the Castello family business, and her family didn't see why she wanted to go to a university if she "only wanted to clean teeth," as Mrs. Castello put it. Instead, Stacy had put herself through night school, working at Dr. Marshall's clinic during the day.

"I'm not getting above myself or anything. It isn't curing cancer. Although we can help identify it. But you know what I mean." It was Stacy's turn to fidget and earn a nasty look from her manicurist, who was steadily trying to remove the stubborn remnants of her bubble-gum-pink polish. "A lot of times, we are people's first line of care. And Dr. Marshall said that with a master's, I could teach other hygienists someday."

Stacy stopped to catch a breath, and Dylan seized the opportunity to halt her self-sabotage. It felt like physical pain to watch her friend buy into someone else's vision of her. "Don't say what you do isn't important. It is. Think about how many little ones sit down in your chair, afraid, and leave happy and healthy."

"You should've seen the one I had today. I get a sick joy out of calming those kids down."

"Exactly. Which tells me you are on the right path, and I'm exceptionally proud of you. You put yourself through college with this. I didn't even have a real job in college, unless you count beer consumption. In which case, I was paid very well." Dylan smiled.

"Well . . ." Stacy paused, chewing on her words for a moment. "I'm glad you are proud of me, because I wanted to ask you a favor. I need a character reference. It's a short letter. You can say—"

"Done. I'd write a novel if it meant you getting into graduate school."

"Really? At first I thought I should ask Sandra at work, but then I found out you were in town. And you have known me way longer. It seemed like a sign. Does that sound bananas?"

"Yes, but I like your brand of bananas," Dylan said, watching the smile on her friend's face spread.

"Okay, girls," Tammi interrupted and handed a color directly to Stacy's manicurist without flourish. "Stacy—for you, a new shade of pink. Something softer than your usual, but I think you'll like it."

Pushing up one sleeve, she shook out her semiblonde extensions and fixed a hard look on Dylan before producing an electric-yellow bottle. "You work too much. Learn to have a little fun."

"Oh no, Tammi. I haven't changed that much." Dylan twisted the corners of her mouth southward but tried to keep her tone light. Technocore was in the business of running over business owners, not her.

"You need to be bolder too." Tammi turned to the technician and added, "Give her a smile," then walked away without another word.

Dylan grimaced. In Tammi's kingdom, there was no dissent. *And this is why God invented nail polish remover,* she thought.

~

Dylan was in the habit of checking her email before she got out of bed. This was a ritual for her and Nicolas, and half the time it left one or both of them in a foul mood. Listening to the sound of Milo running in his sleep, she briefly entertained the notion of giving up the phone ritual. It wasn't like Nicolas was here to see her brush her teeth before touching base with the company. A small sense of dread filled her stomach as she rolled toward the edge of the bed to grab her phone from the side table, where its alarm was cracking out a generic, upbeat "wake-up" tune.

A flurry of emails from Jared requesting time to "dialogue" greeted her. But still no email from Tim announcing next steps to the staff. It had been a week, and given Jared's I'm-in-charge-so-get-back-to-me-ASAP voice mail, Dylan wasn't sure she could wait much longer for Tim to act if she wanted to stay employed. By the time she finished putting on her eyeliner, her nerves were so on edge she skipped breakfast to get to the office quickly, hoping to put an end to the tension building in her neck and shoulders.

The drive over was torture. If she hadn't spotted Tim's Tesla parked in the very first stall, Dylan thought she would have been relieved to see her temporary office. Sliding into her desk chair, she noticed the blinking red light on her phone, indicating that Jared had left at least two voice mails. She picked up the phone, sucking in a deep breath and her stomach at the same time, as if the act alone would keep the sinking feeling from kicking in.

"Hey, Dylan?" Brandt's voice accompanied a timid knock on the door.

"Hi, Brandt. What can I do for you?" she chirped, overjoyed to have her ill-fated phone call interrupted.

"It's just . . . um . . . I think Tim tried to make some of your changes . . ."

"That's great."

"Well . . . maybe. Do you want to see?" Brandt started fidgeting in a way that made Dylan think he was one uncomfortable question away from biting his nails.

"All right. Lead the way."

Brandt's face twitched into what was supposed to be a smile but looked painfully like a grimace. She saw why as soon as she entered the break room. A Costco flat of off-brand diet pop sat on one of the countertops with a tabloid-size sheet of paper taped to it. Inching closer, Dylan reread the words she was actively trying to pray away.

It has come to my attention that you all would be happier if you had quick access to caffeine. Have a pop on me!

Benevolent Leader (Tim)

In bright-red pen, someone had scratched out the *ben* in *benevolent* and turned it into *malevolent*. Another person had scribbled, *Where's the coffee cart?* And *These aren't even cold!* Right next to several other people who'd shared similar, less politely phrased sentiments.

"*Malevolent* is a little dramatic." Throwing a sidelong glance at Brandt hovering in the kitchen doorway, Dylan snatched the paper from the top of the flat and tucked it under her arm.

"I don't get it. We said bring the coffee cart back to a central space." Brandt whispered his concern, even though anyone within hearing distance was likely to agree.

"I'm going to guess he thought this was an acceptable substitute until he could figure out how to get a cart for every floor," Dylan lied, rotating her hand in a big circular motion, as if the action would somehow make the lie more probable. The look behind Brandt's glasses suggested he was not buying it any more than she was. "Are these on every floor?"

Dylan knew the answer before Brandt nodded.

"Hell," she said, doing her best to keep her curse words to a moderate volume. "Brandt, I need a favor. Can you take these signs out of the kitchens?"

"No problem."

"Don't throw them out. Shred them, or someone will fish it out of the recycling and keep being snarky."

"Got it." Brandt stuffed his hands into the pockets of his fleece and took off.

"And, Brandt," Dylan called into the hallway, forcing him to draw up short, "if there is space, would you please put these in the fridge?"

Brandt nodded and sped toward the cubicle jungle. There were two staff kitchens per floor. Dylan was lucky most people got in late. A half hour more, and this would have been a bad-office meme in twenty seconds flat.

Shaking her hair over her shoulder, she trotted back to her office. As she reached for a sticky note to remind herself to show Tim how people felt about his handiwork, the red light on her phone caught her eye.

"Seriously, man. Hold your horses." Dylan slouched. Sighing heavily, she accepted that her morning was quickly moving from unpleasant to downright bad. Skipping all three of Jared's voice mails, Dylan picked up the phone and allowed herself one more eye roll before dialing the number she wished she didn't have memorized.

"Dylan. I left you a series of messages. Did you get them?"

Dylan rested her elbow on her desk, drawing in a deep breath. "I did. Seattle has a hands-free law, so I couldn't call you back in the car."

"That is awful."

"Well, there is some truth to—"

"Anyway, I'm following up on my voice mail from last week. You do understand that you are not to move into the next phase of the project without clearance from me. Especially when the work product from that phase will be seen by Technocore's board or Kaplan's leadership. Am I clear?"

Dylan managed to smother the urge to point out that she'd said as much in each of her emails to him this week and that nearly every phase of her job was intended to produce something someone important would see. If Technocore improved its performance, then people would know about it with or without her saying a word. That was literally the whole point of her being here. But she'd been to this particular Jared rodeo before. It was useless to point out the logic holes in his statement. Better for her to do whatever the phone equivalent of smile and nod was. In this case, she said, "Crystal clear."

"Good. Then I have something else I want to cover with you. I have a phone meeting with the upper-level guys today, and they are going to want an update on Technocore. Have you made any progress at all? Should I be concerned?"

Dylan gritted her teeth and sat up. "As I mentioned in my daily report, time on Tim's calendar is difficult to come by; however—"

"You need to manage up with him. You can't expect him to be onboard with the changes because he hired Kaplan."

Dylan had a hard time hearing Jared's words over the sound of her molars grinding. *Managing up* had to be one of the worst phrases in the world. Any consultant worth their salt should have banished it from their vocabulary years ago. It was patronizing to the person receiving the advice and made the manager who supposedly needed guidance sound clueless. Which wasn't totally off in Tim's case, but still.

Tuning back in, she caught the last bit of Jared's rant. "Tim doesn't know what is going on."

"It is interesting you say that; before we got on the subject of managing up, I was going to mention some of the steps he has taken at my suggestion."

"Really?"

"Yes. It was difficult to get time on his calendar but well worth the wait. He . . ." Dylan's eyes ran roughshod around her office, looking for a lifeline to throw herself. Landing on the tabloid-size note on her desk, she shrugged. "He is delivering thoughtful handwritten notes to key employees, along with beverages." Using her shoulder to hug the phone to her ear, Dylan reached up to massage her temples. She prayed the "thoughtful handwritten notes" hadn't made their way to the internet yet. Otherwise, Charlie would be in her office with a cardboard box for her things in the next five minutes.

"Good step in the right direction. What's your timeline for the other changes?"

"We are still working on that. I'm trying to take it in manageable chunks with Tim."

"I hate to break it to you, but you need a concrete timeline. Empower yourself."

"I feel pretty empowered working with Tim to get things done on Technocore's timeline." The silence on the other end felt like a long-distance stare-down with Jared. She imagined his face turning the same shade as his favorite salmon-colored sweater.

"Good." Jared's tone suggested her response was anything but good. Dylan decided to go for the *W*, as Nicolas would call it.

"I think a good source of information for your meeting would be my daily progress reports. Feel free to ask me any questions as you read through them."

Dylan used this long pause to begin mentally identifying her savings accounts and their balances in case she needed them at five o'clock.

"Could you forward them to me so I don't have to search my inbox?"

"Of course." Dylan hoped he could hear the *screw you* in her client-is-always-right smile. "Since I have you here, I wanted to check and see when you might arrive in Seattle. We are almost three weeks into the project, and since I need your approval to move forward, I just thought some sense of your timeline might be helpful."

Jared coughed into the phone. "We'll have to connect on that another time. Right now, I need to head to the conference room for the partners meeting."

"No problem." Dylan didn't bother to point out that earlier he'd said that he needed the information for a call. No need to push the issue with him. "Good luck with your meeting."

She waited for the call to be disconnected before slumping back into her chair and throwing her elbow over her eyes to think through her options. She didn't want to get fired from Kaplan. Usually, she liked her job, and consulting was a small world. She would have a hard time getting hired somewhere else.

She could quit. The thought made Dylan queasy. She had worked hard to stay on the junior-partner track. The idea that someone who thought *empower yourself* was an acceptable phrase could destroy her career was too much. She didn't want to start over somewhere new.

A rumble in her stomach made Dylan aware that the nausea-and-headache combo she felt might not be entirely Jared induced. Slowly standing up, she decided to grab a store-brand diet pop for caffeine's sake and pulled an emergency granola bar from her desk drawer. The cubicle jungle was starting to come alive as she reached the staff kitchen and plucked an only slightly cold pop from the shelf. Dylan waited until she was on the damp patio before allowing herself the satisfying hiss-click of a freshly opened can of not-Coke. Crunching into her granola bar, she attempted to button her coat with the free fingers of her granola bar hand.

Finally accepting that her buttons were not a priority, she polished off the rest of the granola bar in four big bites and began planning Nicolas's visit. Stacy might have been wrong about his picky eating, but she was right about his absence. It was a little weird. His visit would be a good chance for him to get to know her less obvious past. Dylan secretly suspected that most people thought she made up stories about her childhood. But she wasn't that lucky. Or creative.

After taking a final sip, Dylan dropped her empty can into the recycling bin and decided she was ready to think about Technocore again. She reached for the cold metal door handle in time to startle Deep, who was pushing on the other side.

"God, girl. Do you enjoy scaring me?" Deep said, clutching her collarbone and walking backward into the office.

"Maybe a little. What's up?"

"Just thought I'd get some air." Catching the look on Dylan's face, Deep added, "Fine. After I saw the picture, I thought you'd need moral support."

"What picture?"

"You haven't seen it yet?" Deep said, her eyes shifting around the office, as if willing someone else to come by and show Dylan "the picture." "You were out there so long I thought—"

"Deep, show me the picture."

"I hate doing this. I thought I was going to bring comfort, not be the grim reaper of consulting photos," she said, her neon-orange nails tapping lightly on her phone screen. As she waited, Dylan wondered how Deep could pull off that color when she herself could barely wear sparkly yellow on her toes. Then Deep handed her the phone.

"Oh."

It was all Dylan could manage while staring at a photo of the knockoff pops with Tim's gracious note. The caption read: *A love note to my office from our CEO. Presented without comment.* Which would have been true, except for the delightful hashtags *#TechnoTool* and *#GunderpantsStrikesAgain.* The person had been thoughtful enough to tag the location of the photo, in case any of the 173 people who had already liked it were unclear on where this individual worked.

"Guess Brandt wasn't fast enough to get all of the notes," Dylan said, blowing air past her bottom lip. Looking back down at the photo, she paused, incredulous. "You liked this?"

"You have to admit Gunderpants is kinda a funny nickname," Deep said, wrinkling her nose.

"No, I don't have to admit it."

"Come on—" She elbowed Dylan's side.

"It wasn't his finest hour. Don't repeat that."

"Besides, I figure once Tim finds out about it, Marissa is doomed anyway, so I may as well give her a like before Charlie has to march her out the door."

"Tim wouldn't really sic Charlie on her, would he?" Dylan asked, hoping for something better than she expected. Deep raised a perfectly manicured eyebrow but didn't answer.

CHAPTER NINE

Dylan woke up with a start and glanced around her room, that familiar disoriented sensation creeping over her. Trying to get a grip on her surroundings, she stopped to listen to the sound of absolutely nothing. It felt wrong.

Rolling over, she squinted at the clock, its little red numbers blinking 8:14 a.m. That was about the time she usually woke up when an alarm wasn't involved. Rubbing her face, she sat up, still marveling at the silence. Her heart rate slowed to a normal pace. It was the Saturday after the world's longest Friday.

Gingerly setting one foot on the floor, Dylan noticed her door was cracked open. Someone had taken Milo with them. She swung her other leg onto the floor, heaved herself out of bed, and shuffled down the first flight of stairs before stopping to peek into Neale's bedroom. It wasn't like Neale made her bed, but as far as Dylan could tell, the sheets were in the same rumpled state as they had been in the day before, implying that Neale had crashed at a friend's home.

When she'd padded down the second set of stairs, Dylan found the kitchen as empty as Neale's room. She could tell her mom had been there, because she'd left half a pot of coffee in the coffee maker. This was a Bernice hallmark. Make one massive pot of coffee and drink it throughout the day. Dylan found stale coffee gross, so she gently pressed her hand to the glass. The carafe was still warm. Safe to assume this was not yesterday's coffee. Her mother had left the house.

"Am I alone?" Dylan asked the coffee maker. It was too good to be true. The odds that anyone was ever alone in the Delacroix household were like the odds of winning the Powerball. Just shy of impossible, and just regular enough to make you believe it could happen.

Daring to hope, Dylan crept toward her father's study. If she wasn't alone, she certainly didn't want anyone knowing she was up, or they would take away the blessed silence. Poking her head around the door, she found a very empty and oddly tidy room. The giddy sensation of being alone kicked in almost instantaneously. Part of her wanted to run upstairs, put on a towel, get some ice cream, and watch TV, because there was absolutely no one to see her do it. Another part of her wanted to make a new pot of coffee and read a very large book. As she stood in the hallway, Dylan realized that either of these activities required her to sit on the furniture. The dust and dog hair alone were enough to put her dreams of towels and tomes on hold. Far from discouraged, she found her joy turning to unmitigated glee. This was her shot to engage in her favorite de-stressor. Cleaning and dance hits of the late 1990s and early 2000s.

Dylan hustled back to the kitchen, dumped out Bernice's coffee, and set on a fresh pot before catching sight of herself in the kitchen window.

"Ew." She cringed at the sight of her pores. Blaming Jared, she ran up to the bathroom to find a pore strip to suction to her nose. Then she skipped back down to the living room, where she flipped through the family's dated catalog of CDs until she found what she was looking for. Janet Jackson's self-titled masterpiece, *janet.* Shaking the tension out of her shoulders, Dylan dance-walked to the kitchen, poured herself a cup of coffee, then grabbed a dust rag and some Endust with the other hand. After bumping the cupboard closed with her hip, she got started in the living room, crowing along with Ms. Jackson.

~

After seventy-five minutes and twenty-three seconds, Dylan had managed to successfully scrub the living room and work up a good sweat. Stopping only to tear the pore strip off and confirm that her skin was suffering under the stress of Technocore, she hit rewind on her favorite song, "If." Dylan was about to start on the floorboards in the hallway when the doorbell rang.

"Neale!" Dylan shouted over the music, silently cursing her sister for forgetting the door code. When she'd pushed herself off all fours, she ambled toward the door, admiring the dust and grime that had situated itself on her college sweatshirt. Yanking open the heavy door, Dylan threw a hand on her hip and glared . . . at the opposite of her sister.

"Hi. Am I interrupting?" Mike asked, looking up from their ancient door mat. Rounding his shoulders forward, he slid his hands into the pockets of his dark jeans, adding, "Sorry. I can come back."

"Oh no. I thought you were Neale. You're not interrupting." Dylan casually repositioned herself behind the door, on the off chance that he hadn't noticed the layer of dirt crusted onto her pink running shorts.

In a moment of horror, she realized that the dirt wasn't her most pressing problem. Her father had left the outside speakers on again, so the entire neighborhood had been listening to Ms. Jackson's sexy alto for nearly two hours. She felt heat creep up her neck and flood her face, which she was pretty sure matched the Pepto-Bismol color of her shorts despite the melanin in her skin. "I'm so sorry. I didn't realize that the outside speakers were on. I'll turn it off right now. Please tell Linda and Patricia it was not intentional."

"I think they actually prefer Janet Jackson to choral reproductions of indigenous chants." Mike's face split into an easy smile. "Oddly enough, that is not why I'm here. I wanted to see if you were around to go look at a couple of museums. If you aren't busy," he added, gracefully nodding at the dust rag she was clutching.

116

In the background, Janet filled Dylan's panicked silence by describing exactly what she would do if she was someone's girlfriend. Somehow, she had imagined a lot less spontaneity and messy topknots when she had offered to do this with Mike. And a lot less sex music.

"Yes. Sure. Let me get changed," Dylan croaked, doing her best to casually speed walk toward the stereo as Janet let everyone on the block know whose name would be called out in bed.

Dylan smashed her index finger against the power button with so much force that it hurt. Her yellow ankle socks slid on the newly Pine-Soled floor as she dashed back to the hallway. Mike stood motionless by the wide-open door, wearing a bemused expression.

"Sorry. You can come in," Dylan said, motioning him into the house with one hand and trying to wipe off the dust with the other. "Wait." Dylan threw out the hand she had been using as an emergency lint brush. Mike stopped midmovement, his hand on the door handle, like they were playing Red Light, Green Light. "Did you mean we should leave now? Or sometime later?"

"You're in charge. Whenever works best for you. If you need some time, I can go." He used his thumb to gesture over his shoulder at the door.

"Oh no. Now is fine. I just didn't want you to be sitting here waiting when really you meant later but were too polite to say. Then I'd be holding you hostage when you had somewhere else to be." Dylan started with her favorite circular hand gesture as if it would make her rambling more eloquent. Mike began shaking his head, the polite smile shifting to outright amusement.

"Nope. I'm all yours."

He turned to shut the front door, and she noticed the criminal fit of his jeans. Not obviously tight but fitted enough to give a girl some idea of what she was working with. Not that she was looking. This was Janet's fault.

"Okay, then." Dylan pulled her mind off his backside as he rotated around. Gesturing to the only truly clean room in the house, she added, "I'm gonna get changed. Make yourself at home."

She dashed up the stairs as fast as her brightly colored socks would carry her and ripped the dingy sweatshirt off her body. Shedding the rest of her clothes into a pile on the floor, she wondered how she'd managed to find a wearable rainbow to clean in. Hadn't Neale recently pointed out that she owned no color? Obviously she hadn't looked at her workout gear.

Silently thanking the sisters of Alpha Zeta Delta for their patented five-minute-ready routine, she grabbed a pair of jeans, a gray cashmere sweater, and the blue scarf that matched her ballet flats. Hustling into her favorite all-purpose casual outfit in two minutes, she thought, *Still got it.*

Next, she made her way to the bathroom, preparing for the phase involving tinted moisturizer, mascara, and blush and mentally committing any extra time to a quick swipe of lipstick, when she got a good look at her face and stopped cold. A ring of lovely white pore-strip gunk encircled her nose, which was a stunning shade of red from where she had removed a layer of skin and blackheads before Mike had arrived.

"Sexy, Dylan. Very sexy."

Throwing some water on her face, she hoped Mike thought the slime was part of the general dirt she was wearing and not her pores giving up on life. To be safe, she gave herself an extra thirty seconds to add some lipstick—better to draw attention to some other part of her face—before moving down the stairs, conscious of how anxious her steps sounded.

Dylan hit the bottom stair and rounded the corner to find Mike settled in a chair, scowling at Kierkegaard.

"Ready?"

Mike jolted, the lines on his face vanishing. "That was fast."

"One of the many lessons I learned from my soros. The art of getting ready quickly and the finer points of Malthusian economics. Although that turned out to be less helpful." Dylan shrugged and readjusted her scarf.

Mike chuckled, walking into the hallway and standing behind Dylan as she opened the door. Her body and mind resumed their old war over his sudden closeness, with her body attempting to lean in and her mind asking it to stay still and act like she had some semblance of self-control.

"I have something for you," Mike said, reaching into his pocket and extracting a folded-up square of paper.

"What's this?" Dylan's brain stuttered to change gears as she accepted the paper, forcing her to acknowledge that lust and coherence were at opposite ends of the communication spectrum. The laugh lines on Mike's face deepened as he watched her unfold the page, the top of which read,

A Highly Organized List of Places Dylan Asked Mike to Take Her To

"I didn't ask you to take me anywhere. You showed up at my house," Dylan said, over Mike's laugh.

"I recall you specifically asking for a list."

"I did. But this title is inaccurate. It should read, 'A List of Places Mike Recommends Dylan Research.' The list is basically void with this title." Dylan laughed in spite of herself.

"I have a pen. You can change it in the car." Mike smiled, leaning in toward her and nudging her with his shoulder so she was forced to look up at him. "Will that work? Or do you need me to retype it?"

"You're obviously new to listing, so I'll accept it . . . this time." Dylan felt herself smiling up at him, despite her most platonic intentions. Folding the paper and placing it in her back pocket, she asked, "Just confirming that the rest of this list is accurate. We are going to the Burke first, correct?"

"Correct. I thought I'd drive, since asking for a favor, then forcing you to sit in traffic feels like bad form."

"Fine by me," Dylan said as they crossed the street.

Mike pressed the clicker on the new-model navy-blue Subaru SUV so Dylan could hop into the passenger seat. Of course he would drive this car. She smiled at her seat belt and suppressed a laugh as he ducked into the car. Glancing at her over his own seat belt, he stopped. "What?"

"Nothing."

Mike arched an eyebrow and began easing the car down the road at a careful four miles over the speed limit.

"It's just, you would drive this car." Dylan laughed the sentence out before she could stop herself. "It is the most consistently Mike thing in the world. If someone had asked me in high school what car you would drive as an adult, I could have guessed this car down to the color."

"This car is amazing. What I'm hearing is that I've had consistently good taste." Mike's smile lingered on her for a second before he turned to face the road.

"I was thinking less amazing and more along the lines of a super safe dad car."

"Well, it does have an excellent safety rating. Which I'm pretty sure makes me sound like I'm one birthday away from bringing snacks to soccer games."

"Worse than that. It sounds like *I'm five years into juice boxes and fruit leathers.*" Dylan snickered.

"I'd have way better snacks than that." Mike looked incredulous. "Fruit leathers? Give me some credit. I wouldn't humiliate my kids. I'd do a good job on snack day."

"That is reassuring. Just because you drive a dad car doesn't mean you are gonna be the cheap juice guy." Dylan very much doubted that anyone would think of him as the Capri Sun dad. Sexy dad? Maybe. Crappy-snack dad? Probably not.

"No way. That guy drives a minivan." Mike laughed, turning into the parking lot near the museum and throwing the car into park. Reaching for the door handle, he threw a sly grin over his shoulder. "For the record, this is the most predictable thing about me. I take risks in other places," he said, holding Dylan's gaze for a second before smirking and sliding out of the car without another word.

Dylan froze, hand on the door handle. She was pretty sure they weren't talking about cars anymore, and now her mind was involuntarily going in all the directions her body had attempted to go earlier.

"Pull it together," she mumbled before pushing the door open and making a mental note to leave this part of the conversation out when she talked to Stacy.

Without so much as acknowledging his ambiguous statement, Mike moved forward. "I wanted to show you this one first, because it is a great example of a traditional museum, but also because they have an exceptional education program."

Dylan forced her mind to shift gears as they walked toward the front of the building. She had driven past the Burke a million times and been to the museum with her father almost as many. However, she had never really stopped to look at the building until now. The Burke, technically titled the Burke Museum of Natural History and Culture, was a city icon. While the boxy building itself was not that exciting, the museum made every inch of the landscape interesting. Indigenous art and statues were everywhere, blending into the grounds, some covered in the bright-green moss that, if left unchecked, would reclaim every surface of the city. But at the Burke, the moss was intentional, as if to signal that the museum was a part of nature itself.

"I always liked this place," Dylan sighed, nostalgia tugging at her as they climbed to the front entrance.

"I know. Every time I visit, I feel like I should've taken a school bus," Mike said, pulling the door open and fishing his wallet out of his back pocket. Dylan hustled to the counter to pay before Mike got through the door. Whether or not he would admit it, she was pretty sure her job was more lucrative than being a PhD student working at a struggling nonprofit. Holding out her credit card, she opened her mouth to ask for two tickets. Mike cut her off, gently placing his hand on top of her outstretched hand and smiling at the teenager behind the counter. "Hi. I work at the Crescent and the UW. I have my ID."

Dylan deliberately didn't notice his hand. The way it warmed her own, cold from the gray outside. She didn't notice the size of it or the way his hand felt, not heavy but present.

Instead, she chose to focus on the teen, who shook his hair out of his face and smiled the distinctly northwestern smile of someone who is friendly but in no way wants to be friends. "Welcome to the Burke." He paused to look at the ID. "Let me get you a couple of passes." The teen stopped to hit three quick keystrokes before holding out two stickers. Mike lifted his hand from hers to accept the tickets.

"Thank you," he said, handing one sticker to Dylan, who suddenly felt the emptiness of the hand that still held her credit card. Half smiling, Mike added, "Most museums in the area have an agreement. We waive entrance for each other."

"I should have guessed." Dylan's laugh was breathy as she returned her credit card to its assigned spot and peeled the sticker from its back. "You were saying this is a good example of how museums can include children." She cleared her throat and looked up at Mike, his own sticker firmly affixed to the front of his black jacket.

"Right," Mike said, looking up and collecting his bearings. "We want to go this way." He began navigating through the museum's lobby, past the mounted skulls belonging to the long-dead reptiles that had once called the area home. Mike moved through the space casually, allowing her time to take in the dinosaur skeletons and recreations of prehistoric landscapes as they made their way deeper into the room. "So as background, what you'll notice is most museums dedicate a space for children and then a much larger space to house the actual collection," he said, angling them toward a corner of the museum that was, in fact, specifically dedicated to children. "The educators basically create a program around the collections' setup."

"Is that bad?" Dylan asked, tearing her attention away from a massive creature etched in stone and anchoring it to Mike's cheekbones. She had to give his genetic combination credit. Most people wouldn't be interesting enough to physically compete with a fossilized stegosaurus.

Mike hummed low in his throat for a moment. "It isn't so much good or bad as different."

"How so?" Dylan avoided pointing out how diplomatic his answer was.

"The programs are well designed, but space limitations often force museums to use a lot of 'find and observe' techniques. Less of the touch, feel, smell, and do that most children learn with."

"Is that why children put everything in their mouths? To learn? Here I thought it was a death wish."

Mike laughed, the sound rolling across the room. "Exactly. Although with toddlers you never know." He began pointing out features of the museum, dodging the occasional overexcited tiny human as they made their way around the brightly colored room. Dylan couldn't help but be drawn in by his passion as he described the theories behind the books and worksheets dotting the child-size tables. It struck her that Nicolas didn't talk about his work like this. *Precision*, *drive*, and *competition* were all words she would use for the way he approached work. But *passion*? Dylan wasn't sure about that one. Wandering around the room with Mike, she hoped she talked about her job the way he did. It was easy to make fun of consultants, but she loved fixing companies and helping people enjoy where they spent the majority of their waking hours. If she sounded like Nicolas, that was something she wanted to change.

Slowly, Mike made his way around the room, letting the minutes tick by, before coming to a stop in front of a crate of rubber creatures.

"That is about all there is to see. Unless you want to check out the rest of the museum."

"Do we have time?"

"The schedule is entirely up to you. My time is yours."

Dylan froze for a second, torn between her need for expediency and her desire to look at the giant fossil in the corner. The battle between her inner list maker and her six-year-old self had the potential to be a long one. Mike must have seen it on her face, because he shifted his posture toward the door and smiled before adding, "I can always come back with you. We can literally come anytime you want. Does that help?"

"I'm going to hold you to that promise." Dylan's mouth quirked up. "I have one request. I want to look at that one over there. Then we can go." Dylan pointed at the fossil, not bothering to hide her enthusiasm.

"I knew it." Mike chuckled and started walking over to the piece. "Everyone loves that one."

"You mean everyone under the age of ten? Because that seems to be the crowd."

Mike shrugged. "I'm not here to judge. But we're lucky we are tall. We won't be able to get any closer. At least not without pushing a few first graders."

Dylan was nearly finished squinting at the plaque that read DASPLETOSAURUS when she took a shoulder to the thigh, sending her off balance and straight into Mike's side. He wrapped a steadying arm around her, driving a warm shiver right through her. Dylan blinked up at him, enjoying the feeling of his touch lingering for just a fraction of a second longer than she expected. Mike gazed down at her for a moment, licking his lips, before dropping his arm and breaking the spell.

"Ouch," Dylan mumbled, feeling the absence of his closeness more than the pain of taking a shoulder to the leg. A light-headedness set in so swiftly that it caught her off guard. It wasn't that she desired Mike, per se, she reassured herself; it was more the missing feeling of physical closeness that made her head spin.

"Doing okay?" he asked, his voice low over the hum of activity.

"I'm all right," she said, in response to her mind as much as her body. Dylan reached down to rub her leg, hoping she didn't bruise. "I think it is time to give my spot to the future linebacker over there." The healthy-looking nine-year-old who'd pushed past her didn't seem to notice she had knocked into anyone.

Mike laughed gently. "The Seahawks could learn maneuvering tactics in a children's museum. Don't worry—you take enough shoulders to the knees, and you toughen up," he said, cutting through the crowd toward the car.

"Where to next?" Dylan asked as they ambled across the parking lot.

Mike squinted, unlocking the car as his eyes adjusted to the new light. The Seattle gloom had a living quality to it. It had shifted while they were inside, and the gray now made the world look like it was bathed in a bright smoke. It wasn't anything close to sunny, but it was as close as the city was likely to get. The familiarity of it made Dylan feel at home.

"I'm thinking MoPOP next."

Dylan smirked, thinking about the neon Gehry at the heart of downtown. "My mother called it 'ghastly' the other day. I can't wait to tell her I visited."

"She is still holding a grudge, then?"

"I think she wants to be. In reality, she wishes she thought to put that much shiny metal over the train." Dylan was only half telling the truth. MoPOP was a target of constant derision for longtime Seattleites. Designed to look like the sections of a heart, it was kindly described as bold or bizarre. If the person describing the museum was less charitable, they would call it ugly.

"Mom still thinks it looks like someone had too much time and money on their hands and not enough common sense," said Mike. "Don't tell them they agree on something."

"Oh, certainly not. Linda and Bernice will never know we were together. That can only make the grudge match worse."

"I gotta say, risking parental wrath is worth it. I like hanging out with you."

"Your secret is safe with me," Dylan said, catching his eyes for a second. With the change in light, they looked closer to a smoky green than the honey brown they had been in the museum. Not that she noticed his eyes. Or remembered their shifts or anything. That would be inappropriate. And driving around laughing at their mothers was not inappropriate.

～

A shiny baby-blue artery loomed overhead, signaling their arrival. Dylan had to admit that as absurd as an acid-trip-inspired heart-shaped museum was, the space was impressive. Someone had put tremendous thought into the museum's playground, which soared in a whirl of colors and sounds as they walked past it. A massive sculpture with cranks stood on one end, surrounded by people of all ages pulling different levers, which caused bells to chime. Dylan looked up, expecting Mike to start explaining the academic concepts behind the park. As if reading her mind, he stated, "I love this park."

"It's clever. A musical park in front of a music museum."

"It encompasses more than one of the senses and links action to reaction. It's so well done." Mike took an extra second to smile at the kids who were careening wildly down a metal slide, their backsides soaked through with rainwater, as a gust of frigid air rushed off the sound toward them.

Dylan shivered and rubbed her hands together, wishing she had thought to bring gloves. Slowly, Mike took his hands from his pockets and turned to face her, wrapping his around hers for a moment. Looking down at their hands, Dylan could have sworn her heart and every other part of her body had frozen. Except for her hands, which were growing warmer with Mike's touch. Looking up at Mike, Dylan realized that the heat coming from his hands was nothing compared to the four-alarm-fire look in his eyes.

She swallowed hard as her thoughts began to collide with one another. Dylan knew she should move. It was one thing to help Mike with a project; it was another thing entirely to let him hold her hand when she had Nicolas waiting for her. It was just that she enjoyed the feeling of being wanted, even if it was in the smallest gesture or casual glance. But it was unfair to Mike for her to pretend her loyalties didn't lie elsewhere. She had Nicolas, and that was, mostly, enough for her. Dylan looked up at Mike. Before, she could chalk the flirting up to harmless banter, but this was something altogether different. That look was asking her for permission to take something she couldn't give.

Reluctantly, she pulled her hands from Mike's as another gust of wind ran off the water. "Should we go inside?"

"I think that's a good idea. Otherwise, we'll freeze out here." For an instant, Mike's face flickered with disappointment, but he managed to force a little brightness into his tone before walking toward the door. He rubbed the warmth back into his own hands as they stepped through the front entrance. "How about you hang here for a second and I'll grab our tickets?"

"Sure." Dylan was only half listening as her guilt was pushed to the side. The rest of her attention was dedicated to the chaos around her.

Every nook and cranny of the space invited staring. While the outside of the building was covered in shiny sheets of brightly colored metal, the interior's vaulted ventricles were mostly the hue of wet concrete, with strategically placed bursts of orange and pink drawing crowds to the museum's basics. Sound poured from an absence of color to her right. Curious, she wandered toward the blackness, grateful her height let her see over most of the people waiting to enter. She recognized the slow weight of Eddie Vedder's voice, singing something off the album *Ten*—Dylan couldn't quite remember the title. Something about fleeting thoughts . . .

"Ready?"

Dylan looked up to see Mike holding more stickers and looking like a kid on the playground outside.

"Do you remember what this song is called?" she asked, reaching up to take the sticker from him. Mike stopped, looking at her quizzically.

"What? I know it's Pearl Jam, so spare me the pained native-Seattle-grunge-child look." Dylan rolled her eyes.

"'Even Flow.' You have been gone a long time," Mike said, leaning his sculpted shoulder into the word *have* for extra emphasis.

"Are you sure you and my mother aren't best friends? Bernice says the same thing all of the time."

"Did you forget who Chihuly is too?" Mike laughed at his own art joke, and despite her best efforts not to, Dylan found herself giggling. It was impossible to forget the man behind every piece of large-scale glass art ever. That would be like forgetting who'd painted the *Mona Lisa*. Mike nodded as they passed the man working the entrance to the dark room.

"I'm not that—wow."

Dylan stopped flat, suddenly understanding what the dark room was. And why the space was called the Sky Church. The cavernous room was mostly empty, save for a few small white couches in the center. What looked like enormous billowing clouds lit with a black light floated from the ceiling, lazily dipping in and out as she tipped her head back. Dylan felt herself trying to breathe in time with their movement as the walls around her shifted. Children sprawled on the floor in front of colossal screens, which wrapped a two-story-tall crooning musician around the building.

"Cool, huh?" Mike whispered at her side. Gently nudging her elbow, he inclined his head toward a spot on the couches vacated by two petite men. Mike and Dylan glided across the floor and squeezed onto the couch to watch the rest of the video. The room was so vast and so personal that it felt like Dylan was melting into the music and darkness, becoming part of the building itself. She ignored how tightly she and Mike had packed themselves into the couch. And how the lights played with his features, highlighting his nose and the muscles in his neck. Instead, she directed her focus toward the room, shimmying down the couch so she could watch the ceiling and the screen at the same time.

The next video hit the walls with a blunt force that made both of them jump. Dylan's hand flew to her scarf with a compulsive urge to put her heart back where it belonged. Laughing next to her, Mike leaned in. "Ready to go upstairs?"

She felt her cheeks heat up as his words brushed the soft spot on her neck below her jaw. Was she going to spend the rest of the afternoon looking like she had just gone for a run, or was her body going to give the hyperactive-spatial-awareness thing a rest? Giving her head a shake she hoped passed for a nod, she stood up and tried to duck out of the view of the people watching behind her, slinking toward the elevators.

"The children's area is on the third floor. This space is the closest to what I hope to do at Crescent." Mike sounded giddy as he spoke over the heads of several people who had managed to pack into the elevator with them.

"This is bound to be exciting," Dylan said, giving Mike a bit of side-eye as he rocked on the balls of his feet.

"Be as sarcastic as you like. Your mind is going to be blown."

Mike strode out of the elevator like a dog being let loose from his crate. Noticing she was about ten feet behind him, he stopped short, joy radiating from him. The floor was covered with kids, the most excited of them being the grown man in front of her.

"Tell me about this place." Dylan gestured around before carefully tucking her hands in her pockets, away from fourth-grader germs.

"I don't have to tell you; you're going to *experience* it," he said, leaning heavily into the word.

"Did you just make a pun out of the Experience Music Project?"

Smirking like a cat who'd caught a canary, Mike wiggled his eyebrows.

"Punny! Your soccer dad is showing." Dylan laughed despite herself.

"Before I show you around a truly wonderful interactive children's exhibit, I'd like the record to reflect that puns are really more grandpa-joke territory." Mike flashed a hundred-watt smile.

"Fine, old man, lead the way." Dylan extended her arm in an after-you gesture as he reached for a set of double doors.

The reason for his enthusiasm slammed into her like a brick wall. The space was soundproofed well enough that she hadn't been able to hear what was going on behind the doors. Once inside, she could see that every corner was covered in instruments. At the center of the room, a giant screen was surrounded by children tapping at digital versions of drums, while small sound studios held guitars, keyboards, and other instruments hooked up to monitors. Mike made a beeline for one of these rooms, grabbing Dylan's hand and weaving around the children yelling to one another.

Inside the small room, things quieted down again. In front of her was a keyboard and a computer screen listing exactly three songs: by Journey, the Beatles, and the Jackson 5.

"Isn't it great!" Mike's smile was bordering on Christmas-level big as he gestured to the panel in front of him. "This software is so cool. Pick a song."

"And do what with it?" Dylan looked down at the keyboard and over at Mike. "I don't have a musical bone in my body. I know you know this; you can hear my dad hollering clear across the street."

"That's the best part. You don't need skill. The program is here to teach you, in a soundproof, almost judgment-free setting." The corners of his mouth quirked as he said this, giving away what little sincerity he managed to muster. "Besides, you aren't required to sing. Just play."

"Oh, is that a challenge? 'Cause I'll sing if it's a challenge. Then we will see who's laughing." Dylan poked at a button marked *I'll Be There* and shook off her inhibitions. Outside of one drunken karaoke mistake roughly five years ago, she had yet to sing in front of another soul. For one thing, she was terrible, and for another, Nicolas didn't like her to drown out the car stereo. He claimed the sound from his speakers was too nice to spoil with her screeching. *Luckily, Nicolas isn't big on road trips*, she thought, stretching out her arms and half watching as the computer walked her through a series of quick keyboard exercises.

"Let's try again," the robot voice said as she mashed at the keys with one finger, trying to remember the pattern the software had taught her. She was vaguely aware of Mike laughing as she squeaked in frustration.

"Hey, buddy, you think this is easy?"

"No. Not at all. I think the kids around us are tiny musical prodigies, and that's why they picked it up so fast."

"I'm sorry not all of us played the tuba in middle school." Dylan sneaked a look away from the screen to catch him wrinkling his nose.

"I'd pay money for you to forget about that."

"Never. I'm going to ask your mom for pictures, then mail a copy to you on your birthday every year so you don't forget where you came from," Dylan said, managing to properly execute the pattern despite the distraction.

"That is low. I've grown as a person. My musical taste has improved dramatically and—"

"Congratulations! Let's put it all together," the computer cheered, cutting Mike short.

"Wait, there's more?" Her triumphant smile faded as the screen split. On one end was the piano part, and on the other a young Michael Jackson clutched his mic, ready to croon his twelve-year-old heart out. "Shoot."

"Hope you are ready to sing," Mike crowed as Dylan hacked away at the pattern she had already forgotten. Fortunately, she knew the words. She packed away whatever inhibitions she had. This was the two of them in a soundproof box, so what did she have to lose?

Taking a deep breath, she let loose the opening line of the song.

Mike grimaced as Dylan continued to poke at random notes with one hand, gesturing wildly with the other. "You better start singing!" she threatened in between verses over the sad protestations of the keyboard.

"I was wrong. No need for me to sing too."

"Do it," Dylan demanded.

Mike's mischievous grin lasted a beat before he joined in with his own interpretive gestures, his appalling falsetto testing the padded walls. Risking a glance at the booth window, Dylan could see several kids giggling at him. He either didn't know or didn't care. Dylan had to admit that if she was going to howl with someone, she was glad it was someone who also knew the words to a Jackson 5 song and made up his own dance moves.

By the time the Jacksons wailed their last "la la las," Dylan had given up on hitting a single key and resorted to voguing over Michael's wails. She descended into cackles as she struck a final pose, and Mike bowed to the not-inconsiderable crowd of children who had gathered to watch two adults lose their marbles. Tapping her elbow, he waved to the door. "We should let them use the room for its intended learning purpose."

"Being an adult means sacrificing for the next generation," Dylan sighed, taking the scarf from around her neck and reaching for the door.

Within three seconds several kids had rushed into the room, excited to try.

"As much as I want to relive every tragic-sounding episode of *Carpool Karaoke* with you, I feel like we should try to hit one more place. I don't want to take up your entire day." Mike moved back toward the elevator, smiling at her over his shoulder as he wove around the other guests. She felt her heart squeeze, even as she mentally listed all the other things she should be doing with her time. As much as Dylan didn't want to admit it, her family might be on to something with the whole spur-of-the-moment-plan thing. Being spontaneous could be fun. Or at least it could be fun depending on who she was with.

Perhaps it was the magic of the museum getting to her, but Dylan felt like she would happily surrender her day to Mike. Yes, the living room needed dusting, but listening to a grown man bay at the moon for her benefit was far more enjoyable.

~

"If we create spaces for children, they should be allowed to be children in them," Mike said, a forgotten bite of salad stuck to the fork he was holding. "School gives them the rote stuff. I want to provide an avenue for children to explore those ideas through play. But I also want an experience that shifts as kids grow."

"It's the difference between children completing a worksheet and the space being a worksheet." Dylan leaned over her sandwich, wondering how he managed to make his enthusiasm this infectious. She wasn't sure she had a passion for experiential learning, but by the time her stomach had started growling in the Seattle Art Museum, she was convinced he was on to something big with Crescent. The question was how to get donors to buy into his vision. It wasn't as if she could convince every one of her parents' collectors to spend a day at the museum. She could ask Tim . . .

Dylan dismissed the thought almost as soon as it crossed her mind. She couldn't even get the guy to send an email, and when he did "follow directions," the end result stayed in the news for days, so why would she inflict him on Mike? That would be like giving someone a parakeet for the holidays. Cute, but way more work than they signed up for when they agreed to the office white elephant. Tim was not the answer to this problem. There had to be a better solution. She just needed a little time to think on it.

"Right!" Mike waved his fork around and seemed to notice it for the first time. "Anyway, I don't know if you could tell—I get worked up about this stuff." He laughed. "But no more. Tell me, what's new with you?" he asked, finally eating the bite of salad.

"It's been busy. But good!" For a small second, Dylan thought maybe she sounded less obtuse than she felt.

At least, until Mike quirked his eyebrow over the rim of his iced tea. He took his time finishing a sip, then answered, "Go on." He leaned back with the good-natured smile of someone who could wait all day for her to speak.

"Well, work has been challenging, but I expected that," she conceded, finishing off the last bite of her sandwich and picking up her napkin. She took a moment to watch the smoky clouds roil by and decided they had about an hour before it started to rain with intention. "My attempt at convincing Tim to be decent is still trending on social media. So there is that."

"Yeah, I was trying not to ask about it," Mike admitted, taking another sip of his drink and leaning forward conspiratorially. "What happened?"

"You are a gossip, Mike Robinson. You should've just come out and asked."

"Me? Never. Being a gossip requires me to turn around and tell someone. I plan on telling no one. So what's the deal?"

"It was bad. But what made it worse was, he was genuinely trying to make it better," Dylan said, dropping her napkin on the table and throwing her hands up. "We had a whole chat about moving the coffee stand back to the lobby. Then, BAM! Diet off-brand pop. I mean, what the hell?"

Mike shook his head, his now-dark eyes fixed on her. "That's not ideal. Do you know how you are going to fix it?"

"Beyond demanding he run his next cockamamie idea by me? No. Besides, by Kaplan standards this is a relatively cataclysmic failure. I'll be lucky to be employed come Monday."

"Cockamamie, huh? If I'm a Capri Sun–wielding soccer dad, you are someone's grandmother." Mike's smile was gentle. "But really, I don't think you're out on your ass over this."

"Well, that's kind of you, if not unrealistically optimistic," Dylan said, taking a big gulp of her latte. "The share prices did dip on Friday, after all."

"No, really, if they were going to dismiss you, I feel like they would have done it by now, if for no other reason than to find a scapegoat to stem the blood flow and restore investor confidence or whatever. But everyone knows Tim is difficult, so I suspect the powers that be don't think sacrificing you is the answer." Mike looked at her like this was the most obvious conclusion, then started to crunch the ice in his glass like his parents hadn't paid for braces.

"I think you might be giving the wheels of bureaucracy too much credit. But since it's reassuring, I'll take it."

Mike laughed. "Fine. So outside of work, what else?"

"What else?" Dylan repeated, drumming her fingers on the table, dredging up the visit she had almost forgotten. "My boyfriend is coming to Seattle."

Dylan watched Mike's eyes narrow briefly when she mentioned Nicolas. A small part of her mind cracked with disappointment, even if being honest was for the best.

Mike's expression recovered quickly, and he said, "That's exciting. When?"

"In a week. His ticket is part of my benefits. Don't want to waste free airfare." Dylan wondered if the amount of perky she was pouring on was too much.

"It's nice they give you a visitor ticket while you are working away from home. Any big plans while he is up here?" Mike took the opportunity to crunch another piece of ice.

"He hasn't met my parents or sisters before. I'm hoping he'll change his mind about being outdoors and we can hike with my family. I'm sure you remember my dad flyering your house over the Olympic National Forest."

"Ma had a cow." Mike smirked. "How long have you all been together?"

"We met in college." His head quirked up fast, the skepticism rolling off him. "But we didn't start dating seriously until four years ago. Lived together for three," she rushed on, watching his head move slowly back to center, his eyebrows still near his hairline. "What I like about him is that he understands how important structure and routine are for me. Like, once I mentioned how having to run across town to pick up this dress I'd had altered for his firm's holiday party was going to throw off my entire schedule for the day. He just went and picked it up for me. Didn't even mention it—just texted me a picture of him holding the dress at the tailor's shop."

Mike leaned back against the seat cushion and nodded affably. "That's nice. But I'm hung up on the fact that you've lived together for three years and he hasn't met your parents. That seems . . ." Mike paused, searching for a word as he studied the remaining ice in his cup. "Unusual."

"Well, yes. But if you think I work a lot, you should see his schedule. He's a divorce attorney."

"That would keep you busy. Do you usually spend holidays in Texas?" Mike's forehead relaxed, but he managed to hold on to the quizzical expression.

"Mostly. His family is there, so it's easier to skip the whole airport thing. They are big fans of cruises to the Caribbean." Dylan shivered. She could probably live the rest of her life without setting foot in the Galveston port again.

"And you want to go on the same cruise every year?" Mike asked, the twinkle returning to his eyes.

Dylan waited a beat to answer, squirming in her chair. "Okay, no. I hate cruises. They are like giant, roving, highly orchestrated germs." Mike's chuckle seemed to fill up the entire restaurant. "Don't laugh. They're weird."

"Have you ever considered telling him you hate cruises?" Mike said, his lips maintaining a hint of a smile as he crunched more ice.

"God, no," Dylan said, but she regretted her honesty as Mike tilted his chin at her. She began to circle her hands as she worked through the crashing explanations in her brain. Years of being lost in foreign countries while her parents drove on the wrong side of the road should have made Dylan appreciate a cruise. However, it had had the opposite effect. Worse, Nicolas had no framework for understanding her boredom. He'd probably take it personally, so instead, she spent one week a year trying to convince herself to like cruises. It mostly worked. Looking up from her relationship analysis, Dylan found Mike still waiting. "Meh, it's not worth the fight."

"If it works for you, I can't judge. I'm not seeing anyone, let alone living with them. But I didn't live with my last girlfriend, and I still met her parents." Mike sighed, shaking his head and smiling. "In fact, they took the breakup harder than she did. They still send me Christmas cards."

"If my parents could get it together to send Christmas cards, which they can't, I suspect none of our exes would make the list."

Mike fixed his gaze on her. "Before we take apart your parents' holiday traditions, I want to go back. What do your parents think of him finally visiting? Have you informed Henry he won't be hiking?"

"Let's not talk about Bernice's feelings on the capitalist-industrial divorce complex or the fact that my father may be planning to throw mud at him." Dylan was pleased to see Mike chuckling at her blatant attempt to change the subject. She laughed, but the thought of trying to get her parents to behave with Nicolas was more terrifying than trying to get Nicolas to book his ticket to Seattle.

"Back to our mission," Dylan said, rubbing her hands together for extra emphasis. "I have some ideas for getting this sensory room funded. I have a former client who was big into facilitating stock gifts. I can connect you to him. Also, have you thought about a live text-to-donate drive at the fundraising gala?"

CHAPTER TEN

Dylan pulled into the office at 7:15 a.m., determined to answer a few of Jared's emails before she dealt with Tim's panicked messages. She was impressed the meme hadn't reached Tim's consciousness until early Sunday, limiting the number of *URGENT* emails he could send. Dylan had considered writing to him that applying the little red exclamation point to his email and adding *READ ME* to the subject line was overkill and part of his perception problem. Instead, she'd simply answered that she was aware of the meme and that they would take mitigating steps on Monday. What those were, she had no idea.

"Morning, Charlie," Dylan called, breezing through the heavy doors. "Can you do me a favor and give me a call when Tim comes in?"

He arched his eyebrow like she was asking a trick question. "I don't think it's against any of our policies. Is it?"

"If it is, I won't tell."

Charlie's manner eased. "In that case, I'll do it. Although do you really want to be the first person he sees after, you know . . ." He shrugged in place of saying *the meme*.

"He's gonna have to see someone first—may as well be me. Talk to you soon."

"Bye." Charlie's voice floated into the elevator bank as she pressed the floor button with the corner of her laptop case. Sure, she had spent her weekend covering herself in little-kid germs, but that didn't mean she needed to get everyone else's germs too.

Exiting the elevator, she ran through her plan for the day. Step one: head off any high-pitched emails from Jared. Step two: cut Tim off before he could try another diet-soda stunt. Step three: stay employed long enough for steps one and two. Kaplan was notorious for removing consultants over the weekend and replacing them on Mondays, so she'd decided Mike was probably right when by Sunday evening no one had called her about getting a ticket home.

"Still, there is a first time for everything," she said under her breath, waiting for her computer to boot up. As expected, she had no fewer than seven emails from Jared, the previews for which all read something like:

Dylan: Things are out of hand . . .

Tipping the last of her coffee back, she scrolled through her unopened emails, trying to decide which of Jared's missives to answer first, until an email from Barb Maisewell caught her eye. She wouldn't email gossip. Barb was way too savvy for that. But really, what other interaction did she and Dylan have beyond the occasional tabloid article about their favorite guilty pleasure cooking reality show?

Hi Dylan,

I hope you are enjoying your time at home! Quick question for you. Has Jared been up to Seattle since you got there?

Thanks,
Barb

Dylan was disappointed that Barb didn't include an article from *EW* or something but decided answering a work email from Barb was better than dealing with Jared's. She hit send on a quick "nope" email, complete with an *In Touch* link on the reality chef's latest dating exploits, as her desk line rang.

"Hi, Charlie, is the eagle on the move?"

Without missing a beat, Charlie answered, "Ten-four. Be prepared. He looks rough."

"Thanks for the heads-up."

"Good luck."

The click on the line gave Dylan a jolt. She didn't have a plan or even the semblance of a plan. Despite having spent an impromptu Saturday with Mike, she wasn't ready to call herself a fan of improvisation just yet. She walked to the elevator doors, silently thanking her maker that Tim was in early enough that other people weren't around to see her trepidation.

Whatever comfort the silence of an empty office provided dissipated the moment the elevator doors opened. To say Tim looked destroyed would be an understatement. If that hoodie had less than a week's worth of dirt on it, she would be shocked. After a moment's hesitation, Dylan stepped into the elevator.

"Hi, Tim," she ventured. The weight of the elevator bearing them upward was almost as heavy as the silence, and Dylan stifled the impulse to check on her chignon, look at her phone, or do anything other than count the seconds until she could get out of the metal box of misery she was riding in.

Finally, Tim grunted something that could not be construed as a word in any language. She decided to take it as an opening. "Let's talk about Friday."

Tim took a deep breath, shaking his head and jamming his hands into his filthy pockets. "I don't get it. What do people want from me? Based on everyone's reaction, you would think I shot someone. I swear people were nicer to that soccer dude who ran over someone with his Porsche."

Dylan bit her lip instead of pointing out that it was actually a baseball player who'd tried to crush fans at the supermarket with his Lotus. Tim was looking to vent about someone who drove a more obnoxious car than him, and she could understand that. Sort of.

"Tim, why the diet pop?" It was all she could manage as the elevator doors chugged open.

"Your document said people missed the coffee cart. Coffee equals caffeine. Give the people caffeine." Tim's voice had gone up about six octaves as he unlocked his office and stopped short. "Fuck."

Dylan peeked over Tim's shoulder into his office and cringed. In a decade of studying terrible corporate leaders, she had never seen anything like this.

Dixie Cups everywhere. Full of diet soda. The cups were lined end to end on the carpet, bookshelves, and all the chairs. They'd even managed to balance them on his computer monitor. Whoever had pulled this off must have spent all weekend carefully filling tiny cups and placing them on every possible surface. They'd avoided the space where the door opened, but that was it. She almost laughed until she caught sight of Tim, who was misting up.

"I'll go get a garbage can."

"Can't we call maintenance?" Tim sniffled at his sneakers.

Dylan paused. She wanted to be delicate, but he'd earned this one.

"No, Tim. We need to clean this up ourselves. The cups and the reason for them." Tim's shoulders sagged as he rubbed his eyes, while Dylan retrieved a small wastebasket. "Before we start, take a picture. This is a practical joke, and we need to make sure you laugh at it."

Tim stopped rubbing his eyes long enough to look at her like she might be possessed. "This is not funny."

"Well, it's going to be when we get you on track. Think of this as future laughing."

"That doesn't even make sense."

"Take the picture, damn it." Dylan was pretty sure she had never cursed at anyone she worked with, let alone a client. She took it one step further and shook the trash can at him. "Now, get to gettin'."

To her surprise, Tim pulled out his phone and took the photo. Glancing at the screen, he changed angles a few times and snapped more pictures.

"Okay, it's not a photoshoot."

"If I'm gonna laugh, I want it to look good," Tim said, taking the can from her and walking as far into his office as he could before crouching down and looking up at her expectantly.

Dylan looked down at her dress and realized that the pencil cut was going to be problematic as long as she was wearing her heels.

Slowly, she stepped out of one shoe and then the other and stooped to hide them as close to his office wall as possible in the hope that no one else would see her crawling around on the floor without shoes. Jared could never say she didn't go the extra mile for the client. Sitting next to Tim, she picked up a sticky cup of flat pop and dumped it into the trash can before stacking it into another empty cup.

"This sort of feels like a waste," Tim sighed. "Do you think we could put the cups in the staff kitchen for water or something?"

Dylan stopped dumping flat pop out to look at Tim, waiting for the punch line.

"What?"

"Tim, that is the kind of thing that gets your office filled with cups in the first place. Ask yourself, *Would I want to use a stale, soaked-through, diet-soda-covered cup?* If the answer is no, then don't do it to your staff. Even if it saves money."

"It was just a question."

"No, it wasn't. Be honest: if I hadn't called you out, would you have done it?"

"No." Dylan arched an eyebrow, and Tim amended, "Probably not." When the second eyebrow went up, he shrugged. "Maybe."

"Gross." Dylan wrinkled her nose, picking up the next cup and tossing the liquid before fixing Tim with a stare. "Explain this logic to me. I'm trying to understand how I could give you a document outlining that people here feel underappreciated—taken advantage of, even—and you're wondering how to reuse paper cups."

"Does it matter?" Tim shrugged and adjusted his stance slightly to take advantage of the additional few inches he'd cleared. Noticing she had halted dumping cups again, he stopped trying to make himself comfortable. "I built this place. Money was tight for so long. They don't know that."

"Don't they?" Dylan let the skepticism hang in the air before selecting another cup to toss. "People without loyalty don't feel betrayal, Tim. They feel like they helped you build this place. And you are over here acting like you did this alone. It's rude and self-centered." Tim's posture hadn't been reading proud, but in that moment, whatever was left holding up his hoodie deflated entirely.

"Steve also said that," he conceded. "Do you think he did this?"

"If he did, you earned it." Dylan laughed at the idea of the haggard COO helping everyone exact an exceptionally petty revenge. Catching the lines deepening on Tim's forehead, she added, "For the record, no. I don't think Steve did this."

"Steve's always been a cheerleader." Tim moved farther into the room, allowing Dylan to tuck into a new corner of the large office. She hated to admit it, but the prank had given her a chance to have the meeting with Tim that she had hoped for when she'd started.

"Let's move away from the who and move to the repair," she said. "We know people are frustrated because they feel their contributions are being diminished. The truth is, when you were a smaller company, a coffee cart was a perk, but now free pop—or honestly, moving the cart back into a central place—isn't gonna cut it." She stopped to take a breath and stack more gooey cups, then added, "You have to take concrete steps to improve the culture. I've outlined some of them in the document you have. Do you want to reread it, or shall I go over them?"

"No. I'll give it a critical read."

"That's what I expected. Look at you, already making strides, Mr. Founder and CEO."

The joke seemed to have a positive impact on Tim. "Anything else?"

"Yes. First, I'm going to give Deep and Brandt the okay to form the staff-appreciation group." Tim flinched and opened his mouth, but Dylan was faster. "It won't conflict with your plans. They'll work on small strategic efforts, like potlucks and happy hours. You'll still oversee big moves."

"Fine." Tim's shoulders sank again as he asked, "Next?"

"Second, promise me you won't go buying office beverages again."

"I'll leave that to facilities from now on. Scout's honor. What else?"

"Third, we are going to draft a good-natured social media post about how one stupid stunt deserves another," Dylan said, duckwalking a few inches to reach more cups. "It'll help people's perception of you, both inside and outside of this place."

"About that. There was nothing in the document about public perception. What are we doing there?"

"Right now? Nothing. We need to clean up the house before we move to the front yard."

"Does that make sense?" Tim asked, and Dylan instantly regretted giving him a compliment. That ego was way too quick to rebound.

"Please trust me."

"We can revisit that at our next meeting."

Dylan rolled her eyes so hard she was glad Tim was focused on dumping out pop. Of course he would approach this like a negotiation. "Fourth, you will ditch that repugnant hoodie. What did you do, fish it out of a lake?"

Tim looked perplexed, as if he hadn't really thought about what he was wearing. Sniffing the sweatshirt, he gingerly peeled it from his body and answered, "This was in the back of my car."

"That is worse than a lake."

"Is it?" Tim asked, like finding stale clothing in his fantastically tacky car might not be a bad thing.

"It really is," Dylan said, shaking her head hard enough that her hair wobbled. "One more thing." Stopping to make eye contact one last time, she added, "If you insist on driving that flashy car, promise me you won't wear anything you find in it ever again."

~

Dylan flipped her blinker on and turned into a generic apartment complex off Queen Anne, looking for an open visitor spot. Since coming back to the drizzly city, she had finally managed to get somewhere at Technocore. So when Stacy had suggested she come over for dinner at her place, it had seemed like the perfect way to cut loose and not obsessively check her email for the first time in weeks.

Dylan put her shoulder into the turn and did her best impression of a race car driver pulling into a pit stop, then threw the car into park. Using her purse as a hair shield, she dashed to the door marked 55 and knocked with more force than she needed.

"All right. Lordy, Dyl, I'm coming!"

"It's cold," Dylan shouted at the door, smiling as the petite bleached blonde yanked it open.

"You're cold because what you're wearing is ridiculous. Can you get a coat that isn't for show?" Stacy stepped aside, allowing her friend into her home.

"Lady, this coat is Burberry," Dylan said, reaching in for a hug.

"Then you paid way too much money just to be cold," Stacy laughed.

"I'm sorry if I'm not ready to go full Bernice to avoid freezing. Besides, it was a gift from Nicolas. He loathes synthetic fabric without a brand name," Dylan said, playfully removing her coat. Taking note of her friend's eye roll, she changed the subject. "Your place is darling. I love it."

The space was small but cozy. An oversize and overstuffed brown couch stood in the corner, covered in throw pillows. Dylan noticed one of her mom's pieces on the wall and realized Stacy's place felt so much like home because it looked a lot like a clean, reasonable version of her own.

"Anything look familiar?"

"Did my parents pawn off those end tables on you?"

"Yes, and the rugs. Shake off the dog hair, and they are good as new." Stacy smiled, bouncing into the galley kitchen and turning on a string of decorative lights. "Your mom pointed out that the overhead lighting is dreadful, so I use these now. More peaceful, don't you think?"

"Wait, my mom's been here?" Dylan tried not to sound stunned as she removed her shoes and set them in the shoe rack. Bernice was barely capable of caring for her own home. How she'd helped Stacy set up her apartment was a pure mystery.

For the second time in a handful of days, it occurred to Dylan that there might be more to her family than chaos. Maybe she was just too close to the source to see around it. The thought exhausted her. Dylan had enough problems at work. She didn't need to spend her precious free time examining hard truths that had been self-evident until this trip home.

"Both your parents, actually. When they found out I had my own place, they got super into decorating it. I guess it makes sense; Billie and Neale don't have their own spots, and it's not like you're dying for help." Stacy laughed as she opened the fridge.

Dylan's ego smarted. Her parents had never even offered to help. Then again, she'd probably made it clear their help wouldn't be all that helpful to her. Nicolas loved stark lighting and sharp edges, which would have stopped her father dead in his tracks. As much as it ached to hear, she was glad her friend had let them decorate.

"Whatever you got from them, it looks far better in your home than it ever did in ours," Dylan said, coming to stand in the kitchen.

"You're sweet. Mimosa?" Stacy's bob popped up over the fridge; she was holding a bottle of prosecco that cost about seven dollars and a big thing of Tropicana.

"The predinner cocktail of champions?" Dylan laughed. "Sure."

"Good. I was dying for one on the way home, so I'd be having a mimosa with or without you. I know you drink fancy predinner drinks these days," Stacy joked, handing her a glass that was a lot more prosecco than orange juice.

"Laugh all you want. Once you have had a real martini, you never go back. Cheers," Dylan said, raising her glass and following her friend back out to the giant brown couch.

Taking a big sip of her drink so it wouldn't spill, Stacy flopped onto the couch. "So how's it goin'?"

"I think I'm getting somewhere with Technocore." Dylan paused to take another sip. "This whole pop thing was actually good."

"I saw he posted a joke about it on social media."

"I kind of thank God for the prank. It made Tim way easier to work with today." A warm, floaty feeling started to creep over her brain, and Dylan cautioned herself to slow down on the drink. "Also, remind me to tell you about Mike and the museums after this."

"What?" Stacy drained her glass and eyed Dylan, waving at her to finish up.

"He was easier to work with. It took an hour for us to clean up—"

"Boring!" Stacy shouted, dragging the *o* out for longer than was decent. Dylan wanted to blame the champagne, but Stacy would have responded that way if she had been drinking water. "Screw Tim—tell me about Mike," she said, moving her eyebrows around conspiratorially.

"Actually, cleaning up the cups was pretty cool too." Dylan dodged her friend.

"Girl, don't try it. Spill."

"I feel like this is going to be a lot less exciting than you think it is."

"I'll be the judge of that," Stacy said, producing a bag of prepopped popcorn that Dylan suspected was stored near the couch for nights like this.

Taking another swig of her mimosa, she started from the top, complete with a recap of Bioré's lowest moment and their unexpected concert for the under-eighteen crowd. At some point Stacy topped off their glasses, noting that the visitor parking was twenty-four hours, so Dylan could always leave her car overnight.

"So basically, you went on a sexy-time museum date," Stacy said when Dylan stopped to catch her breath.

"What? No. How did you get that out of this story?"

"How could you not?" she said, giving Dylan a wink. Stacy tried to roll an *r* to go with her shimmy, but it sounded more like a gargle than a come-hither.

"I don't even know what that sound was."

"But you know what it meant." Stacy devolved into giggles, taking Dylan with her. "This guy is an experienced fundraiser. He doesn't need your advice; he wants your time."

"I see your point, but I also feel like"—Dylan began turning her wrists, looking for the word she wanted—"you're wrong." She laughed. "He knows I'm seeing someone, anyway."

"What? Ghost Boyfriend? Does anyone really know you're dating him?" Stacy asked.

"Please stop calling him that."

"He's too healthy and all-American looking to be real."

Dylan snorted. Nicolas could look a bit buttoned up in pictures. She tucked the joke away so she could tease him about it the next time he told her she was smiling too big. Now she had proof he needed to loosen up a little. And really, who thought smiling big was weird, anyway?

"I want to point out that I know Mike is a capable fundraiser, but I'm an excellent securer of corporate relationships." Dylan navigated away from Nicolas and hoped that the sudden onset of champagne hiccups didn't detract from the message.

"I'm sure you add value. But you must admit Mike is very striking."

"If I admit that, can we move on?"

"No. But I'll give you a break and circle back to the whole good-looking thing later," Stacy said, cramming a handful of popcorn into her mouth.

"Fine. He is very striking," Dylan said, taking a smug sip of her drink and enjoying the shock on Stacy's face. "See, I'm not too uptight to admit when someone's good looking. Spread the word. Definitely tell my mom."

"Whatever. You did that under extreme duress and the influence of my dear friend prosecco."

"Deal's a deal, heffa. Now, tell me about your life," Dylan cackled.

"You are diabolical," Stacy said, draining her glass for the second time. "I do have something for you. I printed out all the recommendation stuff for my master's program at work, in case you didn't see the email."

Dylan's brain cringed. She had seen Stacy's email and hadn't gotten around to clicking on the link, let alone writing the letter. She'd make time for it as soon as Nicolas left.

"I'm sorry. I saw the email and got so caught up with everything I didn't have a chance to answer."

"No worries, you still have like three weeks, but I know you are busy. That's why I printed it out," Stacy said, tucking the papers into Dylan's bag before returning with more snacks and a second bottle of prosecco. "We won't finish this one, but I have an awful date to tell you about, and that should not be discussed with an empty glass."

~

"Cheap prosecco is the devil," Dylan mumbled as she tried to push her half-curled hair into something that resembled a bun. At some point she and Stacy had decided that Dylan would stay over instead of bothering with a cab. The following morning looked more like a comedy of errors than her standard routine. She was running so late that Stacy ended up lending her a bright-pink sweater to throw over yesterday's dress, implying that the bottom of her dress was so neutral that absolutely no one would recognize the outfit from the day before. On the upside, there was no shortage of toothbrushes at her friend's house, so at least Dylan didn't have to wait to use her emergency office toiletries.

She couldn't remember the last time she'd gotten into the office after nine o'clock, but she also couldn't remember ever taking a walk of shame from her best friend's house, so really this was shaping up to be a week of firsts. Fishing Advil out of her handbag, Dylan palmed a few tablets and took a big gulp of coffee. She could already feel the first dose wearing off and made a mental note to stop by the kitchen to fill up her water bottle in an effort to stave off the dreaded twenty-four-hour hangover.

When she unlocked her office, the red message light blinked at her. Hitting the power button on her computer, she picked up the phone and punched in her voice mail code, then instantly regretted the choice.

"Dylan, Jared here. I want to touch base with you about the Technocore project details. Better to cover them over the phone. Ideally, before you check in with anyone else. Call me back."

If there was a countercure to Advil, Jared's voice was it. "Delete," Dylan grumbled, channeling Stacy. Seeing a mass message from Tim, she caught her breath.

All:

I have heard you loud and clear. The pop was a bad idea, and the accompanying message an ill-conceived attempt at a joke.

"At least he kept that part of my draft," Dylan mumbled, resting her head in her palm and reading on.

It has come to my attention that you all feel under-appreciated. I want to fix that, starting next week, with a trip to the exclusive Silver Pines Retreat in the Olympic National Forest. We will take a luxury bus up on Thursday and be back Sunday afternoon. I hope this will give us all a chance to reflect and heal as a group.

Thank you for your dedication to Technocore,
Tim

"Oooh, pink sweater. That looks good on you." Deep's voice floated through the doorway, her pixie cut swept into a style that made her look like she should be working at a fashion magazine.

"Good morning," Dylan said, surprised by her own chipper tone. For a brief moment, she had forgotten her sorry state long enough to appreciate that someone noticed her trying out a new color. Even if the new fashion choice was more luck than decision-making.

"Is it a good morning? I mean, maybe the good news is Tim isn't a benevolent leader anymore. The bad news is he's making us work through the weekend. How is this better than diet pop?"

Dylan grimaced. "He is trying."

"I can tell," Deep said, flopping into a chair across from Dylan's desk. "I'm here with an FYI because I like you way more than the last fifty consultants. The bullpen is freaking out about finding childcare and canceling weekend plans."

"Thanks, I'll have Steve send a follow-up email clarifying a few things." And by *a few things* she meant *everything*.

"Also, the interns want to know if they are going to get paid for this, or are they being forced to work for free?"

"Ugh." Dylan tossed her head back and closed her eyes before the room started spinning. "Do me a favor and spread the word that all of this will go strictly by the HR code. People aren't getting screwed over," she said, reaching for her water bottle and righting her head slowly.

"Will do. Rough night?" Deep asked, giving the Advil on her desk a once-over.

"Never drink cheap prosecco on a school night."

Deep laughed. "Or if you are going to do it, you should probably keep extra in your desk."

"I'm not even gonna think about drinking cheap champs again," Dylan said, hoping her face didn't look like her stomach felt.

"Honey, never let the next morning stand in the way of a great evening. I've got crackers in my desk. I'll bring them over."

"Deep, when I feel less terrible, I wanna know what you're doing with your evenings that you have this kind of wisdom and crackers at your disposal."

"I'm not sure you're ready for those details," she said, leaving with a smile that held way too many secrets. Returning with the crackers, Deep said, "I thought knocking would be unnecessary, all things considered."

"You are my hero." Dylan pulled open the box and yanked at the plastic sleeve. When she'd finally liberated a cracker, she attempted a nibble before noticing that Deep had plopped back down in the seat across from her.

"Not to kick you when you are down, but I'm going to guess you didn't catch last night's TeraBlog?"

"No," Dylan said, trying to keep the crumbs from flying out of her mouth. She'd signed up for the tech gossip blog when she'd come to Technocore but didn't spend a lot of time on it. First, she had no idea who most of the people featured were. Second, she didn't need to read about Tim's latest mishaps because she was present for most of them.

Deep pulled out her phone and started reluctantly tapping at the screen. "Let me say that it can and has been way worse. This is just mildly cringey."

Dylan brushed the crumbs from her fingers into her wastebasket before taking the phone. The photo, provided courtesy of Tim Gunderson, showed him making some sort of prayer gesture to a confused-looking older man, his candy apple–red car posed carefully in the background so the reader could see his *NO HANZ* license plate. Dylan bunched her lips into a tight O.

"Keep reading," Deep said, leaning back and fighting to keep the distaste from her perfectly highlighted cheekbones.

Seattle's Tesla-Wielding Millionaire Repents

Tim Gunderson, the beleaguered founder of Technocore, donated his notorious red Roadster to a local shelter on Monday night. Gunderson said of the car, "I'm hoping it can be used to transport families during what is arguably one of the most difficult times in their lives. Shelia [editor's note: Gunderson named his car] got me from place to place, and now she can help other families do the same."

Since Gunderson tweeted the news, many can't help but wonder if a standard tax-deductible gift might have been more helpful. Still others noted that there is no guarantee that Gunderson's company will be afloat in six months, so it is probably best he hold on to those pennies.

"Well," Dylan said, picking up another cracker. "At least he buried the meme."

"Brandt said the same thing. Frankly, the picture looks stupid, but the idea wasn't all bad. The shelter will probably sell the car, but at least we don't have to see it in the parking lot anymore," Deep said, exhaling slowly. "I can't figure out what brought it on or why he felt the need to hire a photographer to document it."

"That's my fault. I gave him everyone's feedback, and I think he may have overcorrected."

"I heard people have been putting bus passes in the office mail for him," Deep giggled.

"Is 'people' you?" Dylan half laughed, using air quotes, before remembering her headache.

"I wish. I'm too lazy to pick up passes just to give them to Tim. Maybe next time, though."

"If I do my job right, there won't be a next time," Dylan said, feeling better as the crackers worked their way through her system.

Deep stood up and smiled. "In that case, I'll pick some up this afternoon."

CHAPTER ELEVEN

Dylan drummed her fingers on the steering wheel, releasing some of her nervous energy as she crept toward the airline sign Nicolas was waiting under. To her family's credit, they were keeping the jokes to a minimum, and her dad had even made an attempt at dusting. Dylan was so grateful for his effort that she hadn't even told her father that she'd gone back over his dusting job after he'd left the house. If she didn't know any better, she would say the Delacroix were excited to meet her "ghost" boyfriend. She just couldn't decide if their excitement was a good thing or a whole kettle of mess waiting to boil over.

Inching closer, Dylan spotted Nicolas yammering into his phone. She flailed at him through the windshield until Nicolas gave her a brief smile and a wave. After pulling up to the curb, Dylan hopped out of the car, risking the drizzle to open the trunk and greet him.

"Well, Mark, you and I both know how this ends. Hi, babe," Nicolas said, giving her a quick kiss on the cheek and handing her his luggage.

"Hi," Dylan said to his shoulder as he jumped into the passenger side, covering his head with the in-flight magazine. She wished she'd borrowed the magazine to cover her own hair as she dragged his luggage to the back of the car, shutting the hatch, and then darting around to the driver's side.

"All right, Mark. Gotta go; my girl picked me up . . . yup. Talk Monday," Nicolas said, then hit the end-call button and reached over to turn up the heat in the car.

"I also have seat warmers, right here in the center," Dylan said, looking over her shoulder and feeling a fresh blast of hot air hit her. The airport was not made for so many people, and the Seattle drivers were so busy out-nicing each other that it was nearly impossible for her to figure out when people were letting her go and when they were doing the required no-you-go dance.

"How was your flight?"

"Turns out Kaplan's companion ticket only covers business class."

"I'm surprised they gave you business class. Half the time consultants don't even get that," she said, waving as another car stopped to let her over, essentially halting traffic for no reason other than being polite.

"I'd revolt," Nicolas said, clucking his tongue.

"Luckily it's not a long flight. And the magazines in business class weren't so bad," Dylan said, grinning at the road and waiting for him to laugh at the joke. The car stayed silent, and she cleared her throat, trying again. "I'm so excited you're here. My parents can't wait to meet you. Dad even made an attempt at using cleaning supplies."

"It should be good. And even if it isn't, it's a short trip."

The blue glow of his cell phone highlighted the harder edges of his face as Dylan attempted one of her father's calming yoga breathing techniques. Gripping the steering wheel, she faced forward and addressed the elephant in the SUV.

"Nicolas, I know their lifestyle can be unorthodox, but this is important to me."

"I know, babe," Nicolas sighed, pocketing the phone and leaning across the console to kiss her cheek again. "It'll be fine. I'm sure your family is less unusual than you say. Besides, parents always love me. I even googled your mom's and dad's work. I'm ready for this."

"Thank you. That is all I needed to hear," Dylan said, relaxing her grip on the steering wheel.

"Where are we staying?"

Dylan had decided it was best to introduce Nicolas to the family in doses, until she could be sure the transition was smooth. Besides, there was no way both of them would fit in her childhood bed, especially with Milo constantly trying to crawl in.

"Just down the road from my parents' house. Near the university. The place is supposed to be cute, and I figured you might be hungry. There is a Seattle staple nearby that you have to try. It's a burger place everyone—"

Dylan's breath caught, and she sighed, interrupting her own thought. The drive into the city from the airport was one of the most gorgeous views from any airport ever. Even on the wettest days, the picture-postcard skyline, complete with cranes and the Space Needle, seemed to reach out of the water, its lights twinkling like rare gems. It was always stunning. No matter what, she always felt like she was home the moment she saw it. "I love this view."

"It's nice," Nicolas said, flicking a glance out the window, the blue glow of his phone back in full force.

Dylan decided to enjoy the low hum of the radio until they reached the hotel; that way Nicolas wouldn't have to split his attention. After a few minutes and several more no-you-go turns, she parked at the hotel and bounced around to the trunk. As she finished heaving the suitcases out of the back, Nicolas appeared around the bumper, giving his phone one final tap and pocketing it again.

"Well, this looks decent," he said, grabbing the handle of his roller bag and moving toward the front door. "I looked up the burger place you said was good, and everyone on the internet agrees. I think we should try it."

~

Dylan sat on her hands so she couldn't fidget. In a totally uncharacteristic move, she had forgotten her wrap, flat iron, and round brush at her parents' house, meaning that she was sporting her curls for the first time in roughly ten years. She didn't mind the curls, but she wasn't crazy about the level of unexpectedness that came with them. Today was not the kind of day for surprises, even harmless strange-hair-day ones.

Dylan tugged at a lock of her hair, catching Nicolas's eye before she looked down at her watch. Of course, her family was late.

"I see why you straighten your hair," Nicolas said, stirring three raw sugars into his coffee.

Dylan wondered what the hell that was supposed to mean, but before she could formulate a full response, the diner bell jingled, and her mother's voice filled every available crack in the room. "I don't know why they hate firecrackers. And if the Robinsons are going to paint the house—Dylan!"

Henry began frantically waving as Bernice marched toward the table. Gently nudging her dad forward, Neale appeared wearing something that had only recently belonged to Dylan but was now covered in strategically placed holes and haphazard lace. The whole ensemble was very "Miss Havisham meets the Olsen twins."

"You must be Nick!" Bernice said, stopping in front of Nicolas's chair and gazing down at him with her arms wide, waiting for him to stand and hug her.

Nicolas blinked at her for a moment. Slowly getting up, he stretched out a robotic hand. "I go by Nicolas."

"Oh. I'm sorry," Bernice said, still holding out her arms.

"You are Nicolas," Henry shouted, opening his arms wide and filling up whatever space Bernice's alto did not manage to reach. Dylan squirmed in her chair, waiting for Nicolas to hug her family. Never mind that Bernice rarely gave hugs, and when she did, they felt like stone-person hugs.

"Hello," Nicolas said, rotating the hand that Bernice either ignored or didn't notice toward Henry.

Neale floated around behind them, waving in short jerks, which felt a lot less strange as Dylan watched her parents imitate Christ the Redeemer. Her mother and father spent a lot of time staying in one pose as part of their jobs; their arms weren't even close to tired. Nicolas glanced at her, and she mouthed, "Hug." Out of the corner of her eye, Dylan could see the waiter coming over with menus.

As if out of some horrific family nightmare, Henry caught sight of the server and shouted, "Calvin! Good to see you."

Calvin clearly mistook Henry's pose as a hug for him and, without missing a beat, embraced Henry, then Bernice and Neale in turn. "Where have you been? Haven't seen the Delacroix in a while."

To Dylan's horror, Calvin's hug didn't prompt Henry to give up on Nicolas, who was still standing there staring at the whole family like a deer facing down loud, oddly dressed headlights while they chatted with Calvin. Dylan's anxiety alarm began screeching in her head as she hopped out of her chair and wrapped her arms around her mother for a granite hug.

"Mom, come sit next to me," she said when Bernice finally released her from her death grip. Hanging on to her mom's arm, she pulled Bernice into the nearest chair before calling to Henry, "Dad, let Calvin do his job. Come sit down."

"Right. Are those for us?" Henry asked, pointing to Calvin's menus.

"They are. I'll be back with your coffees."

Plucking the menus from Calvin's hand, Henry took to passing them out before having a seat. Once he selected a chair, Neale meandered over to the last chair, next to Nicolas, and sat down.

"We were saying our neighbors are ghastly," Henry said without preamble or prompting. He looked slightly wonky with his purple glasses perched on the tip of his nose to read the menu.

"Is this the thing with the neighbors?" Nicolas asked Dylan as Calvin reappeared. She nodded briefly and smiled as he rolled his eyes.

"But their son is lovely. Isn't he, Dylan? Noble profession, teaching is." Bernice narrowed her squint in a way that suggested she wasn't just trying to read the menu. Dylan's heart pounded at the mention of Mike. The last thing this visit needed was Nicolas asking questions about their neighbors. A few small hiccups aside, she liked her life in Texas. She had a good thing going for her. Or mostly good, anyway.

"Mom, he works in a museum."

"A children's museum. So he's an art lover too." Never one to let a detail get in the way of her point, Bernice added, "And he is getting a PhD."

"Anyway, his parents are fascists," Henry added.

As Calvin took orders, Dylan tried to get a pulse on everyone at the table. So far, it seemed like Henry was oblivious to the hug snafu. Neale had probably picked up on it but had already decided not to care. Bernice, on the other hand, would likely take the slight to her grave. Fortunately, she had a fair number of wrongs to keep track of, so Nicolas could bounce back from this with either a few well-placed laughs at her mom's jokes or a couple of good jokes of his own.

"Nicolas, tell us about yourself. Dylan says you're an attorney?" Bernice asked as soon as Calvin left the table.

"I practice family law at Grey, Campbell, and Keller. We cater primarily to high–net worth individuals to protect their assets." Nicolas applied his most winning smile as he said this, pulling his shoulders back and taking a seated power stance.

"What does that mean?" Neale asked, tearing open a sugar packet and dumping half of it onto the table before noticing and shifting to let her coffee cup catch the rest.

"I work primarily on divorces, with the occasional annulment thrown in."

"That sounds"—Bernice paused, and Dylan could see her mother trying to pick out a convincing lie—"like a very challenging job."

"Especially if alimony and children are involved. I've one client who is working through his third divorce; I swear every wife tries to take him to the cleaners. But that's why he retains us." Nicolas smiled around the table, relaxing a little.

"It sounds like this guy is bad at being married. He'd save himself a lot of money if he gave up on the idea altogether," Henry said, laughing.

"Yes, but then the firm wouldn't get paid. His bad choices are good for business," Nicolas chuckled in response.

"Capitalism at its finest." Neale shook her head, her curls moving with her disgust. Dylan forced a nervous laugh from her throat as Bernice and Henry grimaced at each other.

"You know, Bernice, I was thinking about it on the flight up here—I remember a client had one of your pieces as a point of contention. Both she and her husband loved it. In the end he was willing to take less in the settlement to keep it." Nicolas smiled again, clearly thinking this was flattery.

"My work was a bargaining chip?" Bernice waved her coffee spoon at Nicolas.

"People use sentimental possessions as leverage all the time. That is basically what keeps me in business. Otherwise, they could get an eight-hundred-dollar divorce through some half lawyer online."

Bernice looked like someone had just told her that she'd received a lifetime ban from REI. Dylan's spine stiffened as her mother's lip curled, prepping for a rant that could only end in something terrifically insulting to God, country, and at least one man sitting at the table, when Calvin appeared with their food.

"All right, who had the marionberry french toast?"

If her father hadn't already hugged him, Dylan might have done it. Waving as her scramble came up, she was relieved to see Bernice relinquish the rant in favor of munching on a bite of pancakes. Working to change the subject, Dylan said, "Mom actually has a show coming up soon. What's the series called, again?"

"*Three Souls*." Bernice smiled, and her entire body softened. "It's an exploration of aging, parenting, and what it means to rear souls as your role in society shifts."

Neale, who had appeared to tune in when she sensed a Bernice diatribe, gave Dylan a helpful nod and asked, "Is it mostly canvas work, or have you decided?"

"I'm still working with the gallery, but I think mostly canvas. Maybe a few of my earlier bronzes. I'm not sure that I want to put them on the market. But your father thinks seeing the progression of my work is important for this show."

"And you don't have to sell them," Henry pointed out.

"Yes, but you know how it is. Once collectors know a piece exists . . ." Bernice shook her head, taking another bite of her food.

Breaking off a piece of his muffin, Nicolas said, "It's funny—I had no idea art like yours was so expensive." He chuckled, then added, "I mean, the divorce piece wasn't even a big painting."

"Well, not everyone likes to hang *Animal House* posters on their walls," Bernice quipped.

Just like that, the calm Dylan had restored vanished. All she could do was hope Nicolas would cram the rest of his muffin into his mouth so he couldn't fit any more of his foot in there.

"Art comes in price ranges like anything else," Neale said diplomatically. "There is a market for art, and people purchase what is meaningful to them at a price that makes sense for the market; thus the market supports itself."

Nicolas was flustered, surprised Neale had explained a basic economic principle to him and that the principle applied to the fine art world the same as any other market. "I mean . . . it's good Bernice can support herself with art. It's a tough business."

"Well, we can't all be employed sucking the algae off of foolish men with too many wives," Henry said, scooping the last bite of breakfast onto his fork. "But we do okay."

Dylan racked her brain, trying to remember the last time her father had slung an insult. That was usually her mother's domain. She opened her mouth to jump in but wasn't fast enough.

"It is unfathomable that a little lady like me can support myself. Sometimes, I even support my family," Bernice said, mawkishness dripping from her words.

If Nicolas had missed Neale's tone, he certainly picked up Bernice's and Henry's. Unfortunately, he was not the kind of man who backed down in a fight. "I took a class on entertainment law in school. Artists are so involved in the creative process that pricing and selling their work can be difficult, because labor doesn't always match the buyer's price expectations. Not to mention the constant shift in consumer tastes. It's why making enough money to support yourself is difficult."

"You took a class in law school?" Neale snickered.

"Good thing you are familiar with our struggle." Bernice folded her napkin.

Dylan's head swiveled like a woman possessed as she searched for Calvin. They needed the check before someone threw food. Probably Henry, but Bernice was still holding her fork in a menacing way, so she couldn't be sure. Catching Calvin's eye, she waved with only the faintest hint at discretion. This was an SOS situation. She couldn't risk a subtle gesture being missed.

"Can I get you all anything else?" Calvin said, holding the bill.

"I think we are all set." Dylan forced a cheery grin onto her face as she sweat through her cardigan.

"I can take the check." Nicolas held out his hand in a way that was both apathetic and demanding.

"I know we are paupers, but really, I think we can treat this one time," Bernice said, bristling. Calvin looked confused for a moment before handing the check over to Bernice. At least Calvin knew where his bread was buttered.

"Thanks, Mom!" Dylan said. "Y'all have any plans for the rest of the day?" She half listened as Bernice made an empty attempt at salvaging the conversation. When she'd envisioned this meeting, she thought she'd worked through every possible scenario. Somehow, she'd never imagined Nicolas would bring up the business model of the art world or question her parents' ability to provide for their family. Yes, she'd grown up without a bedtime, but did Nicolas actually think she'd been raised naked and starving in the streets?

As they trundled to the cars, Henry and Neale took over her mother's attempt at conversation, until they reached her dad's battered hatchback. At some point, Henry had scraped the side of a parking garage wall and never bothered to take the car in, so the exposed metal was rusting. Like most things, Dylan had long ago accepted that this was normal for her parents and stopped caring. But at this moment, she felt piercing regret over not trying to get it fixed before Nicolas arrived. If she was lucky, he'd only make fun of the car for the next few weeks. But with the way things were going, his mocking time frame was quickly expanding past a few months.

"Guess we will see you both later," Bernice said, pulling on the still-locked door handle.

"All right, Mom, I'll give you a call about tomorrow." Dylan hugged Neale.

"Nice to meet you all." Nicolas waved, getting into their car. Watching the pack of Delacroix make a left out of the parking lot, Dylan exhaled, debating where to start.

"Well, that was unique." Apparently, Nicolas had already digested the experience.

"Initial meetings are difficult," Dylan said, trying out her most gentle consultant coaching voice. "I mean, you know what they say: never discuss politics, money, or religion over dinner."

"In the case of your parents, they probably need to talk about all three. Last Thanksgiving, you were wondering how your family plans to retire."

Dylan gritted her teeth. "I did say that . . . about my sisters. But really, their retirement or my parents' retirement is none of our business. Everyone in the family has made it this far in life, so maybe we can just let it go."

"You say that until they're living on our couch."

"You know, I'm not worried about it, so maybe you shouldn't be either." Dylan prayed to God there was some Skrillex knockoff on the radio she could use to drown out Nicolas. She didn't care that it sounded like an android grudge match, as long as she didn't have to hear his analysis of her family.

"Well, I don't know what changed, because you were worried about it six months ago," Nicolas said, shaking his head.

"I guess I've just made peace with the uncertainty." Dylan shrugged, irritation causing her hands to shift from ten and two on the steering wheel.

Nicolas gave her hands a less-than-friendly look, inhaling before he said, "I wasn't going to say this to your parents, but artists fall out of popularity all the time. And their stuff isn't exactly mainstream. What your dad does is weird."

"Okay, let's not talk about them," Dylan said, jamming her finger on the stereo's power button.

"You're nothing like them. Don't worry."

"I'm not worried," she said, turning the radio up and scanning for whatever could pass as dubstep. Her family was quirky. That wasn't bothering her. The man next to her was a different story.

~

Dylan's family thought Nicolas was a "toad," according to Billie, who'd texted her exactly twenty-five seconds after her parents left the restaurant. A text from her notoriously absent second sister felt like a bad omen. Deciding against bringing Nicolas over to her parents' house, the next day she picked up her hair products while he waited in line at the original Starbucks. She'd tried to explain that it was like every Starbucks he had ever been to, but it was on his itinerary, and he'd insisted on visiting, so they'd agreed to meet for a second attempt at a family meal and a wander through Pike Place later.

As she wound her way toward the market, Dylan thought it wasn't an altogether bad thing that Nicolas was doing something on his own. Since yesterday's breakfast, she'd been trying to come up with a way to address the debacle with her parents, but the three attempts she'd made had been met with some combination of confusion and sarcasm. Dylan was so frustrated that she had nearly thrown her wine at him over dinner last night. She had been excited for his visit, and now that he was here, he felt like a pair of old shoes she had worn one too many times to be comfortable. Then again, they had been together for so long; maybe she just needed to visit a cobbler. After all, she had never been bothered by things like his googling every one of her restaurant suggestions. Both of them liked to know what they were getting into. So why was this chafing at her now?

Dylan wasn't sure what was happening, but she did know that the space apart gave her time to come up with a strategy to control the conversation. Hell or high water, she was not letting him bring up her parents' finances or letting Neale call him *the Asshole Formerly Known as Nick*.

After locking the car, Dylan made her way over to the market's entrance, where Nicolas was standing. Smiling over at her, he said, "You were right, babe. It was like every Starbucks. I thought it would be different."

"At least you checked it off your bucket list."

"True. And I got a mug, so I'll have something to show everyone," Nicolas said, waving the coffee cup at Dylan. "Where are your parents?" He glanced over her shoulder.

"Probably parking. They said they'd follow me out the door."

Nicolas looked down at his watch with a frown. "It's already 10:07."

"They probably went farther down the block. My dad can't stand circling for a parking spot."

"They are seven minutes late. In the law world I could bill for this amount of time." Nicolas laughed at his own billable-hour joke.

"You can use that line at your next company party." Dylan smiled and reminded herself that people's parents hated their partners all the time, and those relationships still worked out.

"There they are," Nicolas said, still chortling. He nodded at her as if she were in on something hilarious and waved at her parents.

Dylan looked up to see her mother striding toward them like she was going into battle, complete with heavy-duty hiking boots. Henry was wearing the exact same outfit as yesterday, a fact Nicolas would normally comment on if he weren't openly giggling at Neale's sartorial choices. For Neale, it was not nearly as odd as it could be. True, fascinators and crocheted coats weren't common, but once you got past the Moon Boots, she was just wearing jeans and a T-shirt with a few too many zippers.

"Ready for a bite?" Henry called as the three Delacroix darted across the street, overestimating a gap in the traffic and causing drivers to hit their brakes. Her father smiled all around but did not attempt a hug.

"Sure are," Nicolas said, mirroring Henry's jaunty tone. Her mother rolled her eyes and shot Dylan a dirty look. For her part, she would rather her boyfriend and father out-jaunty each other than take the tone they'd shared over breakfast yesterday.

Her plan was to keep things as brief as possible. Grab conchas at the bakery and wander the market. An hour in and out. Dylan hoped the act of walking would loosen everyone up. Nicolas could be funny, and if she could catch the right situation, her family would see that. By the same token, the market was packed with artists and artisans making a living with their crafts. If she was lucky, Nicolas might even observe how people like her parents paid their bills. Then they could finally put the whole tired financial conversation to bed.

"There are a lot of people here." Nicolas jostled into her, pulling her attention back to the present.

"The market is always crowded on weekends," Bernice said, slowly herding the group toward the bakery stand.

From the outside, Pike Place seemed entirely composed of tourists waiting for the fish throwers, but a number of locals were always mixed in. For all the standard fare, the sellers at Pike's always managed to have that one ingredient you couldn't find anywhere else. A rare spice or a funny cut of meat was easily had here, making it worth a local's time to brave the selfie sticks. And there were a lot of selfie sticks out today.

Neale perked up. "This is one of the oldest public markets in the country."

"I didn't know that," Henry said, intrigued by Neale's random factoid.

"Yup! Before the market was built, farmers used to take their goods to wholesalers on Sixth, who would then sell them to consumers at a ridiculous price. Eventually, some corruption was exposed, and it led the farmers to found the market."

"Interesting," Bernice said over her shoulder.

"Before World War Two something like two-thirds of the sellers were Japanese Americans. They were forced out, because people are trash," Neale added, fully leaning into her role as tour guide. "Many of them didn't recover their stalls."

"Shameful." Henry frowned at the nearest stand as they waited in the bakery line.

"Now there are two primary beefs at the market. One is between the crafters and the farmers over space. The other is with the city. The market provides social services and low-income housing that city ordi-nances frequently threaten," Neale finished, sucking in a deep breath. "Hi. May I have two orejas? Please."

"How do you know all this?" Nicolas asked, half smiling as Henry and Bernice placed their orders.

"Neale loves random facts. She learns everything about a subject. Then surprises everyone with this font of information like seven years later," Dylan said, smiling up at her sister before turning her attention to the woman taking orders. "Hi. How are you?"

"Good. What can I get for you?"

"Concha and a coffee, please," Dylan said, her attention pulled between the woman behind the counter and her sister's explanation of which books she'd read on the history of the market.

"Same as her," Nicolas said, gesturing to Dylan, then turning back to Neale. "You sure read a lot. Of course, you have the time."

Neale's forehead wrinkled, as if searching for a way to see reading as a bad thing. When she found no logical explanation internally, she asked, "What do you mean?"

Despite the roughly five thousand people surrounding them, Dylan was convinced the entire market could hear a pin drop, her family was so still.

"You have a lot of time on your hands given your career." Nicolas chuckled and walked away from the counter to let Henry pay.

"What is wrong with you?"

For a heartbeat, Dylan believed she had only thought the words. At least until Neale smiled at her, and Nicolas stopped smiling.

"What do you mean?" He phrased the question exactly how Neale had a few moments prior, but the words were menacing. Neale's smile was replaced with one of abject disgust as Nicolas's neck began to turn the color of a rare steak.

"All the information Neale shares, and you decide to pick apart her career?" Dylan could not make herself back down. Out of the corner of her eye, she could see Henry paying, his eyebrows dancing up his forehead.

"I was joking, babe."

"No, you weren't. You thought you were slick. Couching cheap shots in a joke," Dylan said, shaking her head and starting a brisk walk back toward the parking lot.

Nicolas blinked at her for a second before pulling even with her shoulder to answer. "What has gotten into you? You always say your family is not normal."

Dylan tried not to shove people out of the way as she made for the exit. Checking over her shoulder, she could see her parents and Neale exactly five feet back, doing the worst acting jobs of their lives. If this was how they pretended not to eavesdrop, she would hate to see them onstage.

"I can say that because I say it with love. They are my family."

"Babe, I like them too."

Dylan snorted.

"I'm thinking about you. Do you want them siphoning off your 401(k) when they get old?"

"Siphoning?" She bit back a response about her parents' money and focused on the real problem. "What I wanted was for you to try, just a little," Dylan said, reaching the entrance to the market. "I wasn't even asking for charm, just kindness and a modicum of respect." Her voice rose more than she had anticipated. Nicolas hated for her to speak too loudly in public, and she was sure she'd never hear the end of it later.

"I didn't mean it like that. I meant that they aren't really stable. Neale doesn't even have a job," Nicolas said, pulling on her arm.

"Nicolas, they are artists. Not war criminals." Yanking her arm free, she started to fish around in her purse for her keys. "Do you know how much business savvy it takes to be working artists? I'm sorry we can't all have CPAs for parents. Actually, no, I'm not."

"What's that supposed to mean?" Nicolas asked, narrowing his eyes.

"For the love of God, your parents go on the same cruise every year. How do they not die of boredom? I know my family is odd. But that is just as odd as half the stuff my parents do. Odder, even!"

"That's absolutely not true."

"The thing is, years of cruising with your parents, and I never tell them it's odd, because I respect them and I love you. That is what you do for your partner: love their familial quirks."

"Mine aren't odd, and they certainly aren't the mess you have. I see no reason to pretend."

Dylan's head jerked sharply from the parking lot to where her family was standing, now openly listening and completely offended. Her head felt light. Was this what their relationship was? Her talking and him ignoring? Constantly correcting and restructuring her? Was the order he brought to her life worth shrinking every last piece of herself? She couldn't get any smaller. There was nothing left to shrink unless she disappeared altogether.

Dylan's upper lip curled. "It's like you didn't hear a damn thing I said. So maybe you'll hear this. Find a different ride to the airport. Then find a different girlfriend."

"Oh!" Bernice shouted, forgetting to be an observer. Dylan turned on her heel and began a dash to her car that would have made an Olympic sprinter jealous. Her only goal was to get in the car before Nicolas had a chance to say so much as a single *but, babe* . . .

"See you at home," Henry called from across the parking lot. "Proud of you."

"Thanks, Dad," Dylan shouted, trying not to feel completely uncool as she leaped into the driver's side and slammed the lock button. She could hear Nicolas shout something shrill but couldn't make out the words. Forcing the car to start, she took a deep breath and tried to steady her hands.

"This is okay. You are a smart girl, and you are going to be okay." She repeated a silly mantra she had read in *Your AAA* magazine. She took one deep breath and glanced in the rearview.

"Oh shit."

Nicolas was making his way toward the car and standing in her way so she couldn't back out. "I am not doing this," she shouted at the rearview mirror before realizing that he couldn't hear her. Without thinking, she threw the car in drive. The SUV groaned as she drove over the cement parking block into the flower bed.

"Sorry. Sorry. Sorry," she apologized to the plants, her shoulders bunching toward her ears. She had just enough time to be grateful there weren't any pedestrians on the sidewalk when she cruised over the curb and onto the road.

Glancing back to the parking lot, she could see Nicolas standing there flummoxed, hands outstretched like she might still try to back out. Across the street Neale was sitting on the sidewalk shaking with laughter, while Bernice raised the Black Power fist, wiping tears of glee from her eyes. Henry was in the middle of a one-man slow clap.

Dylan blew through a yellow light, rounded the corner, and felt herself relax. Sure, she had destroyed her relationship, but at least she'd never have to listen to Skrillex again.

CHAPTER TWELVE

"What did I even do?" Dylan asked Milo, a cup of coffee tucked into her lap. The massive dog wasn't adding a lot to the conversation, but he was taking up most of her twin bed, so there was that. Reaching out her foot to give the dog a tummy rub, she looked out the window. The skies were getting rough, and a big rain was headed her way, echoing the maelstrom in her head.

"The thing is, dog, I'm not upset about this. Maybe I'm numb right now?"

Milo moved a little to the left, seeking a better scratch.

When she'd gotten home, Dylan had immediately gone to her room, and for the first time in her life, her family had given her the blessed gift of privacy. Probably because they were still talking about the morning's incident and didn't feel they needed her opinion on the proceedings. Bernice had brought her a cup of coffee and a granite hug, but other than that she was on her own to work through the end of her relationship.

She had expected waterworks and the big pitiful moments that had characterized her college breakups. When Dylan was younger and she and a boyfriend had gotten in a fight, she would find her baggiest, saggiest pair of sweatpants and wallow in her sense of loss until a friend forced her to get glammed up and go out or the threat of poor grades had dragged her to class. Instead, she'd spent the better part of the last few hours staring into space, alternating between rage at having spent so much time with someone who couldn't find it in himself to even feign decency and the desire to try to work it out. Dylan looked over at her phone. Nicolas was probably just going through airport security. She could catch him before he got on the plane, and they could try to find a way forward.

A way forward that didn't include her family. Dylan cringed. Her family wasn't perfect, but if today proved anything, it was that they were there for her, in their own weird way. Any other family in the country would have been ashamed of a child defacing a flower bed to get away from an angry ex. Her parents were delighted by it. They were proud of anything she did that went against the social grain. And while Dylan couldn't say that she understood the pride that came with watching your child deface public beautification efforts, she was grateful for it just the same.

But Nicolas had good traits. He was circumstantially funny, and he always organized their bathroom without her ever having to mention it. He made dinner reservations so they didn't waste time waiting in unnecessary lines. It wasn't like she had spent the last few years with a monster. At least she didn't think she had.

"He's on the board of the local youth center, for goodness' sake! It isn't like he's evil," Dylan said to the dog, who again shifted a little more to the left, causing her to pause midrant.

Nicolas might not be evil, but he wasn't forgiving. The same guy who happily wrote checks to get new basketball nets every year was still holding a grudge against the neighbor who'd scratched his car, even after she'd left a note and paid for a new paint job. Dylan took a sip of her coffee, feeling her heart deflate. The market incident was the kind of thing he would never let go of. He might forgive her or only bring it up once in a blue moon. But forgive her family? Not a chance.

A few months ago, she'd have understood—probably even walked away from her family without much hesitation. She might have missed the occasional Sunday phone call from her dad or the weird memes Neale sent her, but she would adjust to it eventually. Now, it seemed like a lot to give up. Maybe it was just being back in Seattle, but she couldn't reconcile Nicolas's growing list of dislikes and his snide comments. The order he brought to her life wasn't worth the catalog of petty grudges she needed to hold to be with him. Dylan had developed enough of her own stability. She could be left alone, and she wouldn't implode.

Strange as it seemed, after years of running from her family, she was less afraid of turning into them than of becoming so rigid that she was careless or, worse, cruel. Her family was okay. And it wasn't like Dylan had any intention of moving in with them or starting to dress like her father, but when push came to shove, they did love her unconditionally. Even if that love was quirky and loud and got on her last good nerve. She couldn't say that about Nicolas. His love was based on a prescription, a narrow list of behaviors and traits he could tolerate, and she just didn't have it in her to be those things anymore.

Milo snorted in agreement, bringing her back to the room and the rapidly cooling cup of coffee in her hands.

"You're right; I'm a smart girl. I'll be okay," Dylan said. The large dog groaned and stretched himself off the bed in an oddly feline way, then flopped down on the floor to signal his disinterest in the continued assessment of her downward spiral.

"I just need to make a few phone calls, research storage units, then moving companies," Dylan mumbled, looking for a pen and notepad to start her list.

Catching sight of her work computer, she remembered another less-than-happy surprise. Turning to her canine therapist, she added, "I forgot about that stupid retreat. I need to make a packing list too."

~

The overwhelming smell of pine trees hit Dylan as she swung herself out of the driver's side door. Feeling the cold settle into her cheeks, she was glad she'd raided Bernice's extensive collection of Nano Puff jackets. Her mother might be the only person every shade of pea green, sky blue, and fuchsia looked good on. But the jacket did pack into tiny spaces, so at least Dylan was traveling light while looking like a paint sample from the eighties.

Squinting across the parking lot, she could see Deep lugging an enormous orange suitcase toward a rustic-looking great hall, whose heyday had probably been sometime before Nixon was president.

"Need help?"

"No. I need civilization," Deep said, twisting the suitcase over the gravel and looking up. "What are you wearing?"

"I'm warm, and that is what counts," Dylan said, dodging a particularly large puddle. "Are you running away from home or something?"

"Ha. Ha. I'm allergic to nature. My mother is the Queen of the Outdoors. I spent every summer until I was eighteen backpacking and memorizing plants and shit," Deep said, shaking the hair out of her eyes. "I've made a full recovery. Thanks for asking."

"Are you serious? We should form some sort of support group. Children of REI Addicts. This jacket is from my mother's exceptional collection of quilted, waterproof paraphernalia."

Deep stopped to heave the suitcase up the first step to the hall entrance. "Well, that explains a lot."

"You understand how the jacket happened to me?"

"God, no. I understand you. The jacket is unforgivable. I'd rather freeze to death than be seen in a Gene Simmons reject."

"Geometric is making a comeback," Dylan chuckled, grabbing the handle of the suitcase to help her heft the thing.

"Even if it does, that sad shade of mauve will never—" Deep paused as they reached the glass door. "Oh my God."

"No."

"It's so—" Deep said, choking on her words, a massive grin creeping across her face.

"How did no one vet this?"

"I don't think anyone needed to—wait for it—"

"You better not make that pun." Dylan recoiled from the door.

"Wait for it."

"You are the worst."

"Vet anything. Get it? 'Cause they are all dead!" Deep cackled, her breath fogging up the glass in front of them. "Don't worry. I'm sure someone prayed for their souls." She doubled over, forcing Dylan to take a second look at the hall. She could almost feel her email exploding with complaints as she faced the window.

As expected, there were animal heads mounted on the walls. What was not expected was that those heads would still be attached to stuffed bodies, taxidermized and mounted on shelves, teeth gnashing and claws bared.

What Dylan never could have dreamed of was that they would be carefully arranged around the most massive crucifix she had ever seen.

"I don't understand the theme of the decor. How are these two things even related?" Dylan asked, once Deep had straightened up.

"Are you setting me up for jokes?"

"You're right. Don't answer me," Dylan said. She sucked in a big gulp of air before reaching for the handle. "After you."

"Jesus walks ahead of—"

"Don't make it worse," Dylan hissed, grabbing the suitcase and pushing it through the door after her friend.

In contrast to the smell of pines outside, the hall smelled like fluorescent chlorine and the kind of powdered eggs that came in a box.

"So luxurious," Deep said as they stopped to take stock of the room.

To Dylan's relief, Tim had not situated himself under the giant cross. Rather, he was posted uncomfortably at a makeshift check-in table, arguing with what looked like the campground director. Whatever they were discussing, Tim was not winning the argument.

"I should go check in with the boss."

"I'll pray for you," Deep said, wheeling her massive suitcase over the lumpy linoleum toward what looked like a school lunchroom counter.

Weaving her way through the crowded room, Dylan watched Tim yank at his hair with one hand before dropping it to his side with force. The camp director took a step back to put space between himself and an agitated Tim. This was a bit of an overreaction on the camp director's part, since Tim couldn't have been more than 155 pounds soaking wet, but Dylan picked up the pace anyway. The last thing she needed was a headline about Tim Gunderson beating up a Christian-camp director.

"Good morning. Dylan Delacroix. Nice to meet you," she said, extending her hand to the camp director.

The man paused a moment, taking in her jacket, before reaching out. "Joe Woychowski."

"Pleasure to meet you. How's it going?" Dylan tried to sound casual as she strategically positioned herself between Tim and Joe. Joe was a stout individual, but Dylan had nearly a foot on him and a good four inches on Tim. She decided her size might be a mitigating factor if either one of them got out of hand.

"This ignoramus will not let us switch campsites." Tim wasted no time restoring the frost Dylan had worked to thaw.

"And as I explained in my email this morning, we understand he made a mistake, but we are unable to correct his error because another company has already booked the luxury site."

"So . . . what? I'm stuck with a pack of wild animals on the walls, bunk beds, and no Wi-Fi?" Tim threw his hands in the air at "no Wi-Fi."

"Let me understand. Tim, you meant to book a different campsite?"

"Yes. Dylan. Explain to this man that we are a *tech* company. No Wi-Fi equals no work. Plus, all the stuffed animals are creeping me out. Their eyes follow you; did you notice?"

Dylan suppressed a shudder and avoided eye contact with the bobcat above Joe's head. "Can we make this site work? You mentioned bunk beds?"

"Yes. This site is primarily a children's church campsite."

"Must have been why it was a good deal," Tim said under his breath, eyeing an elk across the room.

"We have enough beds for everyone. Each bunkhouse sleeps twenty-two people," Joe said.

"Right. So we can make this space work. Thank you, Joe. Would you mind getting us a few site maps so we can start getting people settled in?"

"Not a problem," Joe said, glaring at Tim as he turned to go.

"We can't stay here. What the hell are we gonna do? Tell campfire stories? Then this guy is telling me they have one, just one, desktop computer we can access in the reading lounge, which, by the way, only has Baby-Sitters Club books."

"Good book series."

"Really? I was more of a Baby-Sitters Little Sister fan." Tim stopped his rant to give her a sideways look, then shook his head. "Doesn't matter. We're screwed."

"Hardly. I don't know what else you have planned for the next couple days, but we can make this work." Dylan forced herself to believe what she was saying. Pulling her eyes off the walls, she looked around the room. The novelty of posting the decor on social media was already wearing off, and people were getting antsy.

"Were you going to expound on how we are not screwed? Or just say something hopeful and wait for someone else to strike gold?" Tim said, waving his hand in front of her face.

"No need to be mean. I'm not the one who booked a kids' campsite without consulting the consultant," Dylan said, looking down at him and serving up the extra sass that had been hanging around since she and Nicolas had broken up.

"I'm sorry." Tim put his hands up in submission. "Can you help?"

"Well, I'm trying. But don't think we won't dissect this once we get back to a place with Wi-Fi," Dylan said. "I think we act like this mix-up is a team-building exercise." She paused to let him finish rolling his eyes before she continued. "Take an activity out of Team Building 101 to assign cabins. Make everyone get in groups of eleven by favorite ice cream or animal or something."

"Then what?"

"Let them get settled in. After that, you run a modified version of your plan with pens and paper. I'll make a run to the store for poster board, and I'm sure they have markers lying around here somewhere."

Tim looked around the room, apprehensive. "I guess I don't have much of a choice. We can't send people home after they got all the way up here."

Dylan thought more than a few people would probably like to go home, especially after catching sight of the walls, but she nodded anyway.

"No time like the present," he added.

"Actually, we should wait until Joe gets back with—" Dylan said, but Tim was already on the move, pulling his shoulders back and striding toward the giant hearth under the cross. Dylan's eyes roved around the expansive room, eventually finding Joe holding a megaphone and cradling a stack of paper. She waved him over as Tim hopped onto the hearthstone, shouting to little effect. The people nearest him turned around and took three steps back to get out of spit range, but the hall was so big that the sizable crowd stationed by the coffee stand hadn't even noticed he was talking. Shrugging, Tim lifted his hand to his mouth and pulled off a wolf whistle that would be the envy of gym teachers across the continental United States.

"Welcome!" Tim stretched up, cupping his hands around his mouth in an attempt to amplify the sound. "I hope you all had a pleasant ride up to this majestic site. Mounted animals notwithstanding."

A few people in the front snickered before a woman yelled, "We can't hear you."

Taking an exaggerated deep breath, Tim shouted, "This better?" Without waiting for the answer, he plowed on. "Like I was saying, welcome! We are going to start by getting sorted into our cabins."

"Got your maps," Joe whispered, finally appearing at Dylan's side.

"Still can't hear!" the woman called again.

"I said, we are going to get into cabins," Tim screeched, causing the people near the front to jump back another foot.

"Great. And if I could just borrow this," Dylan said, reaching for the bullhorn in Joe's other hand.

"Oh no. I need that to help people find their cabins." Joe moved the bullhorn away from her as if she were a toddler reaching for something with a Mr. Yuk sticker on it. Tim's voice cracked as he continued to scream at the room.

"Joe, you're gonna have to do me a solid," Dylan said, taking her best big-sister tone and grabbing onto the bullhorn. Giving the horn a hard yank, she managed to wrench it free from Joe's death grip, eliciting a gasp from the man. Stumbling backward at the sudden release of the hotly contested item, she smoothed her jacket and her tone—"You'll get it back, promise"—then marched over to Tim and thrust the thing at him as another round of "whats" went around the room.

"Is this better!" Tim shouted into the shrieking bullhorn. A volley of squeals sent hands over ears as the people in the front gave up and walked back toward the coffee stand, leaving Tim a good ten feet of room.

Dylan made a mental note to have Brandt pick up a PA system at some point and silently thanked her lucky stars that Tim hadn't decided to have this professionally filmed "for posterity."

"You may have noticed we are at a children's campground and not a luxury retreat. There was a mix-up in scheduling, but it is in keeping with the theme of the weekend, which is"—Tim paused for dramatic effect—"invention!" Clearly, he had expected applause here and stopped talking to wait for it. The awkward moment stretched into a half minute of silence. Finally he explained, "It's invention because we want you to explore new ideas . . . like a curious child." Tim spoke more slowly and moved his free hand in a come-along-with-me-here-people gesture. When the clapping still didn't start, Tim shrugged. "Whatever. Anyway, we have a few hours before dinner, so what we want to do is divide everyone into cabins."

Tim instructed everyone to get in groups of eleven people based on their birth month. He continued through the room like a motivational speaker, asking what month each group was and pairing them with another group from the same month, then yelling, "Fantastic! Head over there to that gentleman with the stack of papers, and he will get you situated," before moving on to the next group.

"We'll gather for dinner and a keynote session at five thirty," Dylan said to the first group when they approached for cabin assignments. Observing the blank stare most of the group members gave her, she made another mental note to get copies of the schedule to hand out at dinner. Just one of about fifty mental notes to take care of before everyone reconvened in the dwelling of the dead animals.

"Hey, Dylan?" Brandt's voice came from behind her.

"What's up?"

Brandt curled his lanky frame inward before speaking. "The bunk beds don't have sheets."

"Shit," she said, not caring if the giant cross and every dead animal in the room heard. It was going to be a very long two hours.

～

"I can't believe I maxed out my credit card at REI," Dylan mumbled, passing more sleeping bags to Deep.

"Better or worse than maxing it out at the hunting-goods store?" Deep asked, grabbing a bag full of neatly arranged pillows from the back of Dylan's packed car before closing the hatch.

The two had spent the better part of the last two hours cleaning out every sleeping bag provider in the region, while Brandt had stayed in the great hall cramming pillows into cases that Tim had managed to track down from a home-goods store. Judging from the pink princess pillowcases, Dylan suspected he'd had to clean out the place too.

"I think the woman behind the counter was wearing a newer model of my jacket," Dylan said as the pair began inching toward another cabin about a hundred yards down a muddy gravel road.

"I'm just saying I've never seen so many crossbows in one location. I spent so much money I'm pretty sure I landed myself on a government watch list," Deep said as they jumped out of the car again.

"At least it will make for a funny story when you have to explain it to the NSA."

"Too bad Tim didn't get a Model X. The thing would have been useful right now."

"Don't say that. He is probably looking for a reason to buy a new Tesla," Dylan quipped, rearranging a few more of the puffy monstrosities that blocked her rearview mirror. "Thank you for doing this. I know Tim isn't easy to work with, and I'm a relative stranger, so you have zero obligation to help. But I appreciate it."

Deep looked at her with a joke in her eyes. "Don't mention it. It seems weird, but I'm not ready to give up on Technocore yet. Tim and I knew each other a bit in college. I majored in fashion and happened to be good with design. He took a chance on me as a front-end developer. Who else would have given me a shot in tech with my résumé?" She sighed, looking out the window, then back at Dylan again. "I was about to call it quits when you rolled in. You seemed tougher than the other consultants, so I thought I'd give you a chance."

"I don't know that I'm tougher, but I'm glad you stayed. This would suck without you." Dylan laughed, switching off the car. "Let's grab a bite and see what program Tim has in store for us."

"I'm excited about the food part. Tim's program, not so much."

Giggling, they made their way back toward the taxidermized palace. As Dylan reached for the door handle, the smell of bleach and something altogether unpleasant hit her. Looking around the room, she could see adults stuffed into lunchroom tables that reminded her of the second grade, while the line for food wrapped around the room.

"I have an energy bar in my purse. Maybe I'll eat that," Deep whispered, eyeing a yellowish substance on someone's plate. "Do you think that is mac and cheese or pureed squash?"

"Does squash come in that color?" Brandt asked as he passed them, heading toward a table under a dusty black bear.

Wrinkling her nose at her friends, Dylan followed Brandt toward the table. Settling in, she relaxed as Brandt and the other interns began to grill Deep about some TV show all of them were following. Apparently, Deep had taken the unpopular stance that this season's villain was the best character in the show's history, upsetting nearly every other fan at the table. Dylan hadn't seen the show, but she did her best to needle her friend while taking in the feel of the room. Sure, the food looked marginally inedible, but people seemed to be having a good time. She was about to jump up and grab cookies for the table when Tim started making his way to the newly acquired PA system.

"Good evening. I hope everyone has settled in nicely." Tim's voice carried over the hall, instantly quieting everyone down. "I know today has been a busy one, so I won't let this run too late. I thought that for tonight's prime-time session we could all use some inspiration, so I wanted to talk about why I started Technocore. Like many companies before it, Technocore started with an idea."

"Oh God." An intern with short curly hair sitting next to Brandt slumped. She waited a beat, then got up and wandered toward the cookies, her face lit by the aggressive glow of a cell phone that had appeared faster than anyone could blink.

Tim started into his childhood, which sounded more mundane than he seemed to think it was. He clearly envisioned this as his own inspirational TED Talk. Unfortunately, Dylan didn't find him nearly as interesting as the talk done by the biochemist turned radical nun or that kid who'd figured out how to print new computers using a paper clip and some recycled shoes. Looking around the room, she saw that René from sales had put his head on the table and fallen asleep, and the guy next to him was about fifteen seconds from unintentionally joining him.

"No one is watching," Dylan said under her breath.

"That's not true," Brandt whispered back, nodding at the giant cross above Tim's head. "God is always watching. And in case he gets bored, the animals are watching too." Brandt snickered into his Styrofoam cup.

"Stop it," Dylan said, trying unsuccessfully to suppress a grin as the curly-haired intern returned with a plate full of cookies. As Tim droned, she lost track of how many stay-awake cookies she ate, as well as the number of times René woke himself up snoring.

"So that is the true meaning of what we've done here. And what Technocore really means to the world. Thank you for being a part of that. Have a great night, and let's do some inventive thinking tomorrow!" Tim said, then paused for thunderous applause. Instead, he received a polite smattering of claps mingled with the grunts and scratches of people trying to free themselves from the cafeteria benches.

Dylan cataloged as many employee responses as possible. She always felt that specific feedback was particularly helpful in instances of clueless failure. And this was nothing if not a spectacular failure to read the room. She took a full-body breath, trying to imagine the way she felt in yoga class. It almost worked, except for the part where her inhale smelled like burnt popcorn. Extracting herself from the table, she looked around the room to find Tim missing. She had to hand it to him; the guy knew how to exit the scene of a catastrophe.

"You won't get out of feedback so easily," Dylan whispered to herself, making her way toward Joe, who was still holding his precious bullhorn and a stack of maps.

"Hi, Joe. Any chance you know which cabin Tim is in?"

Joe eyed her with an impressive display of nausea and suspicion. "Why do you want to know?"

"Because I'm an ax murderer, Joe," Dylan said, before she could stop herself. Gritting her teeth as Joe took a small step back, she added, "I want to give him feedback on tonight's session, and as you can see, he is gone."

Joe's frame relaxed. "He does need feedback," he said, nodding his head aggressively. "Cabin twenty-three. Medic's hut. Need a map?"

"I know where it is. Have a good one," Dylan said over her shoulder before making the short walk to the hut across the way. Of course this schmuck was staying in the medic's cabin. It was a single with a private bathroom.

Dylan let her fist hit the door with more force than was strictly necessary, hoping the act would warm up her fingers.

"Who is it?" Tim's voice called from the other side.

"Dylan. Thought we should go over some feedback from today," she said, beginning to do the it's-cold stomp on his doorstep. The latch popped, and Tim cracked the door open and stood aside to let her in. "Thank you," she said, gliding into the warm cabin and rubbing her hands together.

Dylan's eyes darted around the room, looking for the animal heads that had come to be the hallmark of her time at the campground, and was pleasantly surprised to find there were none. Instead, the cabin sported the rustic shellacked wood one expected to see in a medical hut. Glancing at the miniature waiting room, she spotted the faux-leather pea-green chairs and ancient *Highlights* magazines that had lived on the coffee table of every medical office since New Edition had topped the charts. Looking at a medicine cabinet with a carved red cross hanging over it, Dylan spotted packaging. Squinting at the lettering, she made out the most insulting words she'd seen all day: *1,800 thread count Egyptian cotton.*

"Seriously, dude?"

"What?" Tim asked, nervously glancing around the room.

"You got yourself fancy, high–thread count sheets when everyone else is trying to squeeze into *Doc McStuffins* sleeping bags. Even your CFO is sharing a cabin," she said, gesturing to the sheets before crossing her arms. "And where is the actual doctor?"

Tim toed the carpet with his sneaker, working up to an acceptable explanation. "It's technically a nurse's cabin. And since we didn't bring medical staff, I figured—"

"There's no medical staff here for an emergency?" Dylan didn't care if she sounded shrill. They were forty-five minutes up a mountain. Someone was bound to twist an ankle. Shaking her head, she said, "Actually, don't answer that. We have bigger problems, believe it or not."

"Look. I know I botched today."

"Not sure that is a strong enough word."

Tim glowered at her for a moment, then exhaled, his shoulders sagging. "I sort of ran out of time to execute my vision. And I couldn't have my slides or the sound effects without Wi-Fi. I was off my game."

"Sound effects would not have helped. Trust me." Dylan shifted from one foot to the other, letting her irritation loose. "Level with me, because we are both one more bad idea away from losing our jobs. Do you actually have a plan, or was this whole thing put together all higgledy-piggledy?"

"Higgledy-piggledy?" Tim said, eyeing her with humor.

"You know exactly what higgledy-piggledy means."

"Did you notice I gave everyone credit in my speech like you suggested?" Tim said, his voice rising an octave. When the diversion didn't work, he caved. "No, I obviously don't have a plan."

Dylan arched an eyebrow at him and took a deep breath. "I know you brought some fancy gadget to write with. Go get it."

Tim turned his back on her to find something to take notes with. As he rifled through his bag, he said, "I know everyone thinks I'm a joke. But I made a great company with an excellent product. If people would recognize how good Technocore is at cybersecurity, they'd leave me alone and let me do what I do. I just want a chance to do this my way. I don't want to be like all the other founders who sell out or get fired 'cause they can't hack it at their own company."

Dylan understood this on a gut level. In an industry where so few founders became leaders, it was natural for Tim to want to do things his way. It was the curse of tech success, and in a weird way, it had begun haunting Tim the moment he'd started hacking.

"If only we lived in that world, but your reputation matters as much as the product." Dylan sighed, settling herself into a waiting chair and switching back into problem-solving mode. "Next time you have an idea, ask yourself, A: Is this moving the company forward technologically? B: Will this crush anyone's soul? And C: Am I acting like that CEO from the ride-sharing company who got fired for being an asshole?"

"I met him, and he wasn't great in real life," Tim said, coming back with a shockingly plain yellow notepad.

"For now, let's use him as your behavioral baseline. If you can see him doing something, please don't do it."

"That is a low bar."

"Well, do better and we can raise it. Assuming we still have jobs," Dylan said, shrugging. "Now, list what sucks."

"Like, in the world?" Tim asked, looking oddly scandalized for a grown man.

"No. At this campground. And put food at the top."

Tim nodded. "Also, the coffee . . . and no Wi-Fi."

"Activities. Oh, don't look at me like that." Dylan shrugged off Tim's hurt glance.

"People management. Too many people going one place, so we shuffle everywhere."

"Let's call that congestion. What else?"

"The decor," Tim said, leaning forward and getting into the exercise. "The animals are always watching."

"Write it down!" After Tim had finished scrawling *animal heads* on the paper, she asked, "Anything else you can think of?"

"Outside of there not being a bar? No."

"Well, write down a bar. Then we can get going."

Tim stared at the notepad, hesitating. "It's a long list."

"More importantly, it is a list that we can pay to fix."

"I don't think we can get someone out here to take the heads off the walls that fast," Tim said gently, as if he might hurt her feelings with the truth.

"Oh no, the heads are staying, but where we spend our time can change. For example, we can add more campfires and hikes to the program."

"You are good at making lists," Tim said, looking at her with something that bordered on respect.

"You ain't seen nothin' yet," Dylan answered, rolling her neck from side to side.

Passing her the yellow notepad, Tim asked, "So what happens next?"

Standing up to stretch her arms out wide, Dylan felt like she was getting ready for a race and not a long night of fixing things. Massaging her left shoulder, she said, "I'm gonna need your credit cards."

CHAPTER THIRTEEN

Dylan stared down at the tube of Icy Hot, then smiled back at herself in the mirror. Her hair had managed to curl over the course of the corporate retreat from almost H-E double hockey sticks. Instinctively, she tried to reach up to arrange it. Wincing, she lowered her arm and squeezed a large amount of the not-so-pleasant-smelling gunk on her hand, then slowly tried to apply it to the dead center of her back. The ropes course was finally catching up with her body, and it was clear that while she might have the technical skills to climb, the muscles required were in serious need of some attention.

She was proud of the way the retreat had turned out. After a night of pounding on doors, begging caterers, and bribing several store clerks to open early, she had arguably one of the better saves in her career. By the time the second day had started, she had a continental breakfast catered. Brandt spent the night polling people's special skills and found an employee who was a yoga instructor in his free time to lead a few sessions. Someone else had worked as a children's camp counselor and managed to make up arts and crafts for those grown-ups who wanted a break from the outdoors. Deep even agreed to revisit her childhood trauma and lead a sort of botanical hike for groups. At the end of the rib eye dinner, everyone had been working on their friendship bracelets and smiling through *Moana* movie night, complete with spiked hot chocolate and cookies.

Changing how she approached the sore spot on her back, Dylan thought about how to report on the more substantive parts of the retreat. Jared had left a number of panicky messages for her and would be less than impressed with her revived interest in the high-ropes course. Tim and a few of the senior leaders had done some brainstorming around departmental issues, including how best to use the newly created staff-appreciation committee. She just hoped that was enough.

"Dyl, you gonna be ready soon?" Neale's voice floated up the stairs.

"Probably gonna need another fifteen minutes," she said, shaking her head and pulling on her shirt before lowering herself onto the bathtub ledge to put on flat shoes. Somehow, she'd let Stacy talk her into going to another townie bar down the street.

Gritting her teeth, she used the top of the toilet tank to push herself up, marveling at the indignity of her situation. Glancing in the mirror, she looked at her hair more closely. She hadn't intentionally worn her hair natural since she'd realized there was a way to control it. But in this light, the curls didn't seem like a bad thing. Sure, they were all over her head, but wasn't that what hair did? It worked for Neale. Not that she was a great barometer of social norms. Still. Dylan paused.

She'd started pressing her hair in middle school, a pit of hell that killed off any girl's need to stand out real quick. After a while, pressing her hair was a part of her morning routine. Something she did on autopilot. And, of course, Nicolas liked her hair straight, which had mattered at the time. But she wasn't sure she liked maintaining it every day anymore.

She'd let go of glitter dusters after middle school. Why couldn't she let go of this too? Taking a deep breath, she unplugged the straightener with unexpected speed, preempting her internal tug-of-war before it could get started.

"Finally," Neale hollered from the living room, clearly listening for Dylan's slow shuffle down the stairs.

"I can't believe Stacy talked me into this," Dylan said, muscles hissing as she leaned heavily on the banister to support her jerky hop from one foot to the next. "And what is the rush? The place is two feet away."

"Martini Sunday," Neale said breezily before looking up. "Oh, is that your natural texture I see?"

"That place has a martini special every night of the week. And I don't have time for the straightener *and* your beloved martinis in my current state."

"And to think Billie said you were too uptight to stop pressing your hair."

"Billie should know better than to bet against me."

"I guess she owes me money." Neale smirked, fishing around in the stack of coats by the door. Finding one of Dylan's, she put it on with a dissatisfied sniff.

"That's mine."

"No wonder it's so dull."

"Gee, thanks."

Neale didn't move to take off the coat, so Dylan began rummaging around for another one. "Climbing is a serious workout. I've never been so sore."

"Who even are you? Curly hair. Climbing things . . ."

"Shut up. Do you have your wallet? Or were you gonna use mine too?"

Neale shrugged and reached for the door. "I'm just saying, for a retreat that almost went up in preserved-animal flames, it sure seems to have made you a new woman. Or turned you back into the old one. I'm not sure which yet."

Letting out an exasperated sigh, Dylan walked through the door. "My grand transformation will never be at the hands of Tim Gunderson. Let's go."

"Definitely back into the old one," Neale said, grinning.

~

Smells like mistakes, Dylan thought as the heavy door closed behind her with a whoosh of cold air. The Brick Heart was around the corner from Lenny's, but it might as well have been the same place, down to a woman who looked suspiciously like Mrs. Claus working the door. The bar was primarily lit by neon signs advertising different beers, some of which had stopped being available to the public sometime in the early nineties. The cracked vinyl of black booths duct-taped together seemed to be a major feature of the decor. The sticky floors, however, were unintentional. Or at least Dylan thought they were. Glancing up, she noticed Stacy waving at them from a booth close to one of the windows, the red light from the neon above her head giving her hair a pink tinge.

"Come on, Neale," Dylan said, looping her arm through her sister's and pulling her toward the table.

"Hey, Delacroix. I was starting to wonder where you all were," Stacy called, scooting farther into the booth to make room for Neale and eyeing Dylan as she carefully lowered herself across from them, trying not to howl in pain on the way down. "What happened to you?"

"Long story. It involved taxidermy and a ropes course. I need a drink before I tell it," Dylan chuckled.

"Well, the good news is, we can fix that. And drinks are half-off. Although, Dylan, these are not the gold-laced martinis you tried to order at Lenny's," Stacy said, waiting for Neale to exit the booth before pushing herself off the sticky seat and landing on the floor with a bounce.

Dylan listened to the pair laugh as they made their way toward the bar, giving her a chance to lift herself out of the booth without anyone hearing her groan. By the time she managed to reach them, Neale was ordering while Stacy chatted animatedly with a guy who was obviously mistaking friendly for interested.

"Do you want a Rollercoaster or a Galactic martini?" Neale asked, eyeing her with that strange combination of expectation and judgment only a sister could level. The choice between amusement parks and space was an important one. Dylan needed to select carefully.

"Coaster."

"Told you she had excellent taste," Neale said, all smug smiles aimed at the bartender.

"You were right. With the sweater, I pegged her for a space drinker," the bartender said to Neale before halting, one hand on the tap of whatever dispensed her drink. Looking at Dylan, he said, "You look familiar."

Dylan tilted her head to the side, looking hard at the guy behind the bar. His baseball cap wasn't helping her facial recognition much.

"Did we go to high school together?" Dylan asked, hoping the question would stall him long enough to give her mind time to retrieve his name. "Roosevelt?"

The guy nodded and stared at her. Dylan realized that he was tilting his head to mirror the way she held her own head. Glancing at Neale, who seemed bemused by the situation, she took a deep breath and prepared for the most charming apology she could manage in this den of regrets. He was Neale's . . . associate or friend or something, after all. "Honestly, I remember your—"

"Dylan? Neale, I didn't know your sister went to high school with us!"

"Well, you and I technically didn't go to school together. I'm younger than you," Neale said, as if that explained everyone's lapse in memory.

"It's CJ. CJ Rodriguez." He gestured to his barrel chest with both hands.

"Oh!" Dylan said. She vaguely remembered the name and had the sense that she hadn't enjoyed his company in high school.

CJ, on the other hand, seemed genuinely excited to see her. "Neale talks about you all the time. You look different. When did you get to be so awesome?"

"She was always awesome. You just didn't notice."

Dylan recognized Mike's voice before she turned around to face him. He smiled casually at CJ, his weight shifting slightly onto his right foot. The first thing Dylan noticed was his gray button-down, which fit a little snugly around the chest and was made of some soft material that looked both unfussy and warm. She wanted to touch that chest, then amended the thought. This was a science-project sort of urge. Dylan could never pull off intentionally wrinkled flannel bedsheets in shirt form, but Mike sure made it work. She just wanted to know how.

"Thank you." Dylan took her Rollercoaster from CJ, grateful for the neon glow, which masked the heat in her cheeks. Hell, she was probably blushing all over.

"Hey, man, how's it going?" CJ said, reaching a jovial hand out from behind the bar to shake Mike's. "Haven't seen you in a while."

Mike's gaze swept over Dylan, causing another flush that she was positive not even the neon glow could hide, before turning his smile toward CJ. The pair engaged in the complex man handshake Dylan never fully understood. Her handshake analysis wasn't doing much for the flush, but it did take her mind off the fact that whatever was in a Rollercoaster tasted a lot like Pine-Sol smelled.

"I'm good. How you been?" Mike asked.

"You made it," Stacy said, turning her attention away from the guy she was talking to and clapping her hands like a kid at a birthday party. The disappointed guy wandered away after taking one long look at Mike. Dylan couldn't say she blamed him. The guy was not about to compete with someone that appealing, and if he had thought he could, Stacy's reaction cleared that up real quick.

"Yeah, I was able to wrap up dinner with my brother early, so this worked out perfectly." Mike's deep voice rolled over whatever music was passing as a reference to the bar's glory days. "Do any of you need a drink?" he asked, eyeing Dylan's precariously full Rollercoaster and Neale's surprisingly empty one.

"You can get those in a pitcher," CJ offered, grabbing a bar towel.

"I'll get that. And a beer, please," Mike said, glancing at Stacy's drink, which was less full than one would have expected given the electric taste. Turning back to Dylan, Mike added, "If you all want to sit, I can bring 'em over."

"Sounds good," Neale called from her perch near the bar. She began her saunter to the table, ignoring that the question had not been addressed to her.

"Thank you," Stacy said, grabbing Dylan's forearm and weaving her way back to the duct-taped booth, leaving enough time for Dylan to smile and mouth, "Thanks" over her shoulder before focusing her attention on keeping her drink from sloshing on the floor. Not that it would have mattered to anyone, but Dylan was rather keen on not adding additional safety hazards to the space.

Releasing Dylan's arm, Stacy sidled into the booth, where Neale was already at home, and leaned in conspiratorially. "Oh my God. Dylan, he's into it!"

"Please. Based on what? The fact he's buying *all* of us another round?" Dylan made a small circular motion with her glass to indicate they were receiving the exact same benefit. Noticing the potential for spillage, she took another sip.

"Or the fact that he was checking you out. Get it!" Neale said, bouncing up and down and shimmying her shoulders.

"Okay, stop. I saw no such thing, and I was there."

"Of course you didn't. You dated that tool for how long?" Neale took a break from her shimmy to sip her drink, then yelled, "But not anymore."

Dylan used Neale's return to dancing as a moment to think. Mike was always flirty. She figured he did that with everyone. The stay-at-bat theory or whatever. But maybe Stacy and Neale were right? She might not have been completely honest with herself when it came to Mike's intentions. Now that she thought about it, she wasn't sure that she could say the same about honesty and her intentions either.

"I'll bet he does a lot of squats," Stacy said, leaning outside the booth to get a better look at his backside. The obviousness of Stacy's act pushed Dylan's self-reflection to the side of her mind.

"Probably the kind with that bar thing over his shoulder." Neale nodded, trying to lean over Stacy for visual confirmation of their theory.

"You two, stop. Don't be creepy," Dylan hissed, taking a bigger sip of her drink, hoping it might wash away whatever humiliation she felt stuck to the back of her throat.

"We're not creepy. You're a prude," Stacy answered, leaning back into the booth, forcing Neale to sit upright. "It is really unfair, you know." She stopped and adjusted her T-shirt before continuing. "I don't think you should be allowed to be that good looking and have a PhD. You can either have brains or beauty, like everyone else."

Neale nodded in vigorous agreement and took a sip of Dylan's drink, as if she didn't have the dregs of her own sitting right in front of her. Taking her drink back, Dylan conceded, "People like him exist to remind us that we did not win the genetic lottery."

"To think, in some backwoods part of the world, someone hates him for being a successful minority with two moms," Stacy said, leaning into her palm and staring at the back of his head. Dylan wondered if he could hear them.

"Nope," Neale shouted, confirming Dylan's fears. "Nope, if they ever saw the guy and read his résumé, they would love him."

"True. But you are assuming someone that backward can read." Stacy giggled into her glass.

Dylan opened her mouth to say something about the folly of making assumptions around literacy and social values, when Stacy straightened and hissed, "He's coming back."

A surefire way to let someone know you are talking about them is to go dead silent as everyone turns to look at the person. Dylan chastised herself for being too addled to face forward, make up a conversation, dig in her purse, or touch the sticky stuff on the walls. Anything would have been less awkward than watching the guy walk over, beer in one hand, Rollercoaster pitcher in the other.

"Hey, Dylan, can you scoot over?" Mike asked. If he had noticed the awkward staring, he was too polite to react to it.

"Of course," she said, beginning a hop-slide to the end of the booth, her muscles stinging with each pop up.

"Perfect timing. We were just about to hit the celebration phase," Neale said with a shake of her shoulders before draining what was left in her glass. Next to her, Stacy mimicked her actions, but with considerably more bounce.

"What are we celebrating?" Mike asked, setting the pitcher in the center of the table, then lowering himself into the space Dylan had made for him.

"Dylan's breakup! It was fantastic. I wish you could've seen her in action," Neale said, smiling at her big sister like she had won the Fields Medal in applied mathematics.

For a brief moment, Dylan fully understood what the phrase *sororicidal tendencies* meant. Stacy readjusted her posture with such force that Dylan was surprised she didn't hurt her neck trying to look at her. To Mike's credit, he was considerably more smooth about adjusting his torso, his broad shoulders angling toward her. Mike's well-shaped eyebrows had managed to quirk up, accompanying the tell-me-more expression on his face.

"I'm not sure we were actually celebrating," Dylan said, finishing her drink with less panache than either Neale or Stacy. She willed her pointed look to convey the *shut the hell up* she was thinking to Neale, who ignored it.

"I'm just saying you told him about himself in public and drove over a median to get away from the guy when he blocked your car."

"It was technically a sidewalk with a flower bed," Dylan said, as if the specifics of what she'd driven over made the story more reasonable. For a small second, she considered melting into the floor, preferably before Neale started quoting the exact language she'd used. At least until she remembered the state of the floor. Dylan really liked the sweater she was wearing. It was cashmere.

"He sounded like the worst," Stacy said, reaching for the pitcher and pouring some for the three women.

"How was he the worst?" Mike asked, turning the full weight of his gaze on Dylan before swallowing his beer.

"He wasn't the worst. He just wasn't . . ." She shrugged under the intensity of his look. How could she explain Nicolas? For years, his behavior had seemed logical, in a way. Nicolas's rules for their life together provided a kind of structure at a time when it seemed like she never had any. "He was kind of . . ."

"He steamrolled people. And he wasn't nice to me," Neale said, winking at her sister.

"How could anyone be mean to our Neale?" Stacy asked, sounding like someone's tipsy aunt.

"Good riddance. You are too good for someone who is unkind," Mike said, an easy smile running across his face.

"He is worse than unkind—" Stacy started, and Dylan began to wonder how quickly demons found new hosts to possess, when Mike cut her off.

"Right, maybe let's call him a transcendental asshole?"

Stacy began cackling, while Mike snorted at his own joke and eyed Dylan as she unclenched her jaw. A snort-laugh was something she deemed goofy. Yet it was having a catastrophic effect on her heart rate, which had spiked since Mike had strolled in wearing that sexy bedsheet shirt. Dylan forced her heartbeat to steady and took another sip of her drink. It tasted less like industrial cleaner now.

"Mind if I have some?" Mike pointed to the pitcher.

"Of course! You bought the thing," Neale said, picking up the pitcher and pouring some directly into Mike's beer glass. Noticing Mike blanch at the combination of Roller-Whatever and beer foam, Neale added, "You won't be able to taste beer anymore. Trust me."

The clean freak in Dylan gagged as Mike shrugged and picked up the glass, eyeing it dubiously before taking a sip and wincing. "Oof. I won't be able to taste anything after that."

"It grows on you," Neale said.

"Does it? Because I'm not convinced," Mike said, sucking air in through his teeth. He set the glass down. "So, Stacy, what's new? I hear you may be going back to school?"

"Yes," Stacy said, straightening up in the booth, her posture implying seriousness. "I want to be the kind of person dentists look at and go, *What do you think?* You know what I mean?"

"Makes perfect sense," Mike said, taking another tentative sip of his drink, this time without choking. "So what goes into this program? More clinical work, I assume."

If it was possible, Stacy perked up even more. "Yes. It is a lot of clinical work; basically you become a dental therapist. I want to continue working with children." Stacy drained her glass, looking over the rim of it as she smiled. "Dylan is actually writing my character reference."

"Sure am," Dylan said, feeling her gut drop a fraction of an inch. She still hadn't looked at the paperwork Stacy had given her, but it would go on the top of tomorrow's to-do list.

"Glasses are empty," Neale announced, as if it were new information to everyone at the table. "Dylan, there is a little left in the pitcher; why don't you finish that? Stacy and I can get more." She began pushing at Stacy's thigh for her to let her out of the booth, like Stacy was also a Delacroix sister. Which, in a way, she was.

"Oh. Right. Okay," Stacy said, grabbing her purse and jumping off the bench.

"Be right back," Neale said, bouncing down the vinyl seating after Stacy.

"Do they need another pitcher?" Dylan frowned as the pair giggled their way to the bar, each of them occasionally looking back at the two they had left behind.

"Do either of them have to drive anywhere?" Mike asked, looking over his shoulder.

"No. They don't. Let them have all the disgusting liquor they want, I guess."

"God, it's gross, right? I was worried I was the only person who thought so."

"So gross. But it's on sale, which makes it seem like a lot better deal than it is." Dylan shrugged one shoulder. Her skin prickled where Mike's glance landed, and she forced herself to stop noticing the sensation.

"Sometimes cheap is just cheap. When a drink tastes like this, I'm not sure free would be considered a good deal."

"Ugh, and they are bringing more. We need a plant or something to dump it into," Dylan said, then added, "The floor is pretty sticky; maybe we put it there."

"This doesn't seem like the kind of place where you need to be concerned about safety," Mike laughed, poking at a hole in the duct tape patching the booth.

"Tell me, how's building the experiential-learning room going?" Dylan said, feeling herself relax at last.

Mike sighed heavily, leaning his full weight against the booth. "My vision has stalled."

"Stalled how?" Dylan asked. Placing her elbow on what looked like a clean patch of table, she rested her head on her hand and leaned toward him. Mike had a gravitational pull that was difficult to resist. Worse, she wondered if she even cared to fight gravity when Mike pulled himself out of his slump and turned to face her. She stopped short. Mike was a bad idea. Gravity or no, he was still a Robinson.

"I'm having trouble finding funding. Even with that stock-gift guy you connected me to. The problem is, our donor base is too small to take advantage of something like that. You may have noticed that Crescent's pockets aren't exactly deep." Mike's smile barely masked the sting of his honesty. "We've gotten a couple big meetings. No bites yet. Lots of 'Let me know if you secure some funding; then I'll pitch in.' Which is another way of saying no."

Dylan laughed, leaning in a fraction of an inch closer. "How are you pitching this to people?"

"Mostly with a lot of enthusiasm and crappy drawings that an intern put together. Another issue is that I'm asking people to imagine a thing that doesn't exist. I just—" Mike stopped short and cocked his head to the side, his eyebrows drawing together as he looked out the window.

Glancing over her shoulder, Dylan sat up quickly. Stacy and Neale were on the other side of the glass, looking like two dogs caught chewing on a shoe. The pair had been huddled together, trying to sneak back to the Delacroix house, when Mike had noticed them. For a moment the four of them blinked at each other. Then Stacy waved, causing the duo to devolve into a fit of laughter as Neale pulled out her phone and texted someone.

"What the hell?" Turning to face them fully, Dylan threw up her hands as Mike began to laugh behind her. Neale held up her phone and untangled her arm from Stacy's just as Dylan's phone buzzed.

You too were good without us, so we leave. Can you bring me coat home?

Suppressing the urge to laugh at her sister's drunk typos, Dylan looked up to find Neale gesturing to the coat on the other side of the bench. She had just enough time to give the pair a dirty look before Mike stood up and snatched the coat up, putting his considerable wingspan to good use, then gave Neale a thumbs-up. Looking down, Dylan typed out a message and pointed to her phone.

Real smooth. Assholes

Neale smirked and showed the message to Stacy, who doubled over with a fresh fit of laughter. Waving her thanks, Neale pulled Stacy upright and began to strut away, her head held too high to be considered sober or respectable.

"Guess they aren't bringing those drinks, then," Mike said, a wide smile on his face. "Really, it's for the best. We were just gonna dump them on the floor."

"I should've known they'd skip. Since when does Neale buy pitchers?" Dylan laughed, shaking her head.

"Well, unless you want something else, do you want to get outa here?"

Dylan knew exactly the kind of "outa here" he meant, but her blood still stopped running for a long second. She imagined his sheets felt a lot like that shirt looked, and she wouldn't mind being in them, as long as he was there too. Without that shirt. She shook her head, putting a halt to her racing thoughts. "Two of these are more than enough for me."

"In that case," Mike said, scooting out of the bench, "let's go."

Dylan smirked at her own misguided physical response and began the slow, painful slink out of the bench with what little grace she could muster. Feeling her muscles howl as she stood, she turned back to Mike. "Before my sister and very best friend decided to skip out on us, you were saying that no one wants to invest until someone else invests."

"After you," Mike said, pushing the door open. "Basically. I need to find someone who'll take a quarter-million-dollar risk, just to get a bunch of other people to take that same risk. On the upside, the other fundraisers like your live text-to-give idea, so that's something."

Passing through the door ahead of him, Dylan noticed that he was still carrying Neale's jacket. "Want me to take that?" she asked, before adding, "Never let it be said you have inexpensive taste, Mike."

He made a small noise that was somewhere between assent and a laugh. Handing her the jacket, he said, "Unfortunately, there is a difference between having expensive taste and having expensive things. The higher-ups aren't saying it yet, but I think I may have to retire this dream and put in some blocks or some other tired experience."

The night air felt good against the Rollercoaster-induced flush. At least, she thought it was the drink that was causing the flush. Risking a glance upward, Dylan decided that Mike had a nice neck. The kind where someone's head would fit comfortably between his shoulders and his face. It was a neck made for being close to, for cuddling, as well as other, less . . . neighborly things.

Dylan paused, thinking of her current living situation and the possible city-ordinance violation her parents were planning to file against the Robinsons. She shuddered, deciding to focus on the less distressing aspects of her off-limits neighbor. Like his work situation.

"Maybe I could help some more? I still have a month left on my placement out here, and I don't do much, except try not to get fired, so I may as well do something good with myself." She was mostly babbling now, filling their walk with more acceptable thoughts. "I do know a fair number of well-connected people through my parents' work and Kaplan. Maybe I could introduce you? Help you get some better meetings?"

"Are you being serious?" Mike had stopped walking, focusing all his attention on her. "I mean, you already connected us to the text-to-give company and the stock-gift-facilitator guy."

"Of course I am." Dylan tried to act affronted, as if the idea hadn't just walked half-clothed into her head. A small voice in the back of her mind suggested that connecting Mike to actual money would be a lot harder than giving him the email address of a few civically minded former clients, but she pushed it aside. If by some miracle Kaplan didn't fire her, it would look good on her résumé, and the partners took pro bono work very seriously. It would be a win-win for her career and for Mike. Spending more time with him was just an added bonus.

"Well, if you are serious, I'd love to go over donor names with you." Mike looked genuinely surprised, even a little touched.

"*Pffff.* Serious as a heart attack." Somewhere in the back of her mind, an alarm sounded that her promises might be bigger than her actual skills. But surely she could learn this. Jared basically played charity golf every other weekend, so how hard could this be?

"In that case, I think everyone at Crescent would murder me if I didn't at least try."

"That's the spirit."

Mike began walking again and bouncing on his toes with the kind of enthusiasm that would make Stacy proud. "I mean, I know it's a long shot, but we have an event in three weeks. This is a super late addition to the program, but for that much money, I'm sure my big bosses would be willing to rearrange the evening to make a big announcement about the room."

She heard the words *three weeks* and cringed internally. She didn't know a lot about fundraising, but even in the business world, finding millions of dollars in three weeks was a stretch. Unless you had a connection. Which she had just billed herself as having. "Exactly."

Dylan was vaguely aware she was leaning toward him as he spoke and cursed his magnetism. He was all easy charm and comfortable shirts. Or smiles. She was pretty sure she meant smiles. She frowned at herself and attempted to redirect her focus to Mike's words.

"—maybe we can go over a list of names to try to get meetings with tomorrow? Do you need more time? Maybe the day after?"

"Let's say Tuesday so I have time to think," Dylan said in her best no-big-deal voice. She reasoned Mike was over the moon about the prospect of reviving the sensory room, and she could use some positivity heading into the homestretch with Technocore. Three weeks of concentrated time together doing something good for the world would be enjoyable, especially with Jared breathing down her neck.

"Dylan, this is just fantastic. I'm not gonna lie—I decided to come out for a sorry-about-your-dream drink, and then there you were. It's like fate." Mike began moving down the sidewalk again, streetlamps highlighting the excitement on his features. They were nearing their parents' respective homes, and suddenly Dylan felt like walking much more slowly. If they reached their driveways, the magic of the moment would die in the floodlight of the Robinsons' motion sensor.

Mike must have noticed the hesitation in her pace, because he looked down at her, concern scrawled across his forehead. "Dylan, are you all right? I don't mean to pry, but breakups are hard. You don't have to answer the question beyond yes or no, but I'd be remiss if I didn't ask you candidly." He took a deep breath, pulling the shirt tight across his chest, a hint of a joke crossing his face. "I mean, he did understand what a *routine* meant to you."

She laughed, rolling her eyes at her own reasoning. "Routines are overrated." Nicolas was the last thing on her mind. However, there was no polite way to tell Mike that she was more interested in what was happening under his button-up, so she settled for, "You know, I think I am. Who knows, maybe it is just shock, but believe it or not, I'm kind of okay with the whole thing."

The skepticism slowly abated from Mike's brow. "I believe you, but I also believe that just because everyone else thinks he was a jerk doesn't mean he lacked any redemptive qualities. You lived with him for years, so I'd understand if you are hurt by it ending and want to be able to express—"

"You are a very good, sweet person. You know that?" Dylan interrupted, suddenly torn between breaking the spell and falling into his orbit. "Really, I drove over a flower bed to break away. I'm fine."

"I'll take your word for it. All I'm saying is that it's okay to not be okay. If you ever want to talk, I'm here."

"I'll keep that in mind."

"I'm at my parents' place all the time. You are always welcome to come over to the house . . . as long as you don't drive through our front lawn afterward." Mike smirked and turned toward his driveway.

"I'll leave that to my parents."

"That's all I ask," Mike said before stopping midmotion and tilting his head to one side. "Actually, hold on."

Mike stepped deliberately into her space, his expression focused and steady. His eyes were dark, and the intensity made Dylan feel hot all over. Her lungs stopped working, her heart fluttering in her chest. She looked up at him. Mike bit down on his bottom lip as he reached up, running a hand along the side of her face. Was he actually going to kiss her in the middle of the road, between their parents' houses?

Dylan's lips parted unconsciously as he leaned closer, still holding her gaze. If she was going to put a stop to this, the time was now. She forced air into her lungs but felt the sentence she should say make its way back down her throat as Mike's hand gently cupped the side of her face. Who was she kidding? She would not be putting a stop to this, parental wrath or no.

He moved an inch to the side, sending a tingle of anticipation through her. Seconds seemed to tick by as Mike's gaze jumped down to her lips, then flicked back up to her eyes. His breathing slowed to a whisper of a movement, and Dylan felt her thoughts haze over with desire. If he delayed this kiss any longer, she was sure she would lose her mind. He ran a thumb over her left cheekbone, then drew his hand away and stepped back.

"Eyelash," he said, holding his hand out to her.

"What?" The word came out sharper than Dylan intended.

"Eyelash. What did you think was going to happen?" Mike's expression was somewhere between naughty delight and mock innocence.

"Not . . ." Dylan opened her mouth, searching for words. She felt like she had run headfirst into a brick wall, her senses completely disoriented. He was supposed to be kissing her right now, not waving stray body hair in her face.

She could almost strangle him. Of course he wasn't going to kiss her in the middle of the road. The guy was a general flirt and sworn enemy of the family. Dylan gave herself a shake and tried again. "The way you were moving all slow. I thought it was a bug or something."

"A bug? You didn't think anything else?" Mike said, looking down at the eyelash he held. Gazing back at her, he raised his hand and blew gently on his thumb. The gesture shouldn't have been sexy, but it was making Dylan wild.

"Yes. I mean, no. What else could it be?" Her head was officially a mess. She needed to get out of the middle of the road before she humiliated herself any further.

"I was asking you," Mike said, a playful lift at the corners of his mouth as he looked her up and down.

"Apparently, an eyelash." Dylan eyed her parents' front yard. Unfortunately, her father had recently added lights to the Tiger, so there was no way she could hide behind it until Mike left and she could retrieve her dignity from where she had dropped it at his feet.

"Well, if that's it. I'll let you go inside." Mike exhaled slowly.

She wasn't sure if she had truly never been a hugger or if so much time with Nicolas had turned her into someone who "didn't do hugs," but either way, now seemed like a bad time to sort that out. Instead, she reached out and patted Mike's bicep. In the moment, it seemed like the best in-between action. In the split second afterward, she was sure it was the most awkward of all possible options. She had just enough time to notice his bicep flexing under her touch when Mike looked down at her hand and then back at her as if he was suppressing a laugh.

"I'll see you soon," he said, shaking his head and walking backward out of her reach.

"Night," she said, putting her arm down faster than she'd ever thought possible.

Still walking backward, Mike crossed into his moms' driveway, bringing on the white floodlight of doom. "Night, Dylan."

The Robinsons' light reminded her of alien-abduction movies, and she thought it might not be all bad if they descended and took her out of this humiliating moment. Recognizing only Neale would actually wait for the aliens to save her, Dylan made a breakneck limp to her front door. Growling at whoever had locked it, she furiously typed in the code and prayed that her mother hadn't reset it. Mercifully, the door clicked open, allowing her to fall into the hallway without risking a glance backward.

It sounded like Neale and Stacy had either gone elsewhere or found somewhere in the house to crash that wasn't the living room, which was just fine by her. Dylan wanted space. Shuffling toward the first staircase, she decided it was probably good she had not tried to make a move on Mike for at least two reasons. First, because there was no clear indication he wanted anything from her. It was an eyelash, for Christ's sake. In fact, after that arm pat, his expression had shown the most pitying look anyone had given her since her sorority sisters had insisted she throw out her toe socks during sophomore year.

The second, she thought as she winced up a step, was that she was too sore to do much of anything right now anyway.

CHAPTER FOURTEEN

Dylan tried not to readjust her hem as she walked toward Masu Bistro. She didn't need to be nervous. In fact, she'd managed to scrounge up a list of names for Mike, just like she'd promised. Admittedly half of the names were from Deep, who might have googled local philanthropists, and Charlie, who'd absolutely read them in the *Seattle Times*.

Walking past one of the roughly three dozen trendy sandwich spots in Capitol Hill, Dylan tried to focus on anything other than her nerves or adjusting her skirt, so naturally, her thoughts landed on her mother. More specifically, Bernice and Neale doing the Free Vagina dance in the hallway the morning after the Brick Heart. It was meant to inspire her to date again after so many years tied to "that wet sack of cow excrement," as her mother had put it. Really, it was mostly lewd gyrations and the pair of them shouting "Free the vagina!" every so often. The entire event was somewhat amusing but also left Dylan with a deep urge to demand more anatomical accuracy. They really wanted her to free the clitoris, after all.

Rolling her eyes, Dylan gave in to temptation and adjusted her skirt ever so slightly before pulling on the door handle of the sushi spot. Stepping through the doorway, she was struck by the intimacy of the place. Unlike half the restaurants in the neighborhood, Masu was small, with a massive black counter at the center of the space. She and Mike had decided to grab a late dinner, so only a few patrons were scattered at the tables clinging to the edges of the restaurant. Once her eyes adjusted to the dark, she spotted him installed in a corner of the bar near an exposed-brick wall, chatting affably with the chef behind the counter.

Dylan smiled and waved, the gesture reaching dorky levels of enthusiasm. So much for playing it cool. Taking a deep, calming breath, she smelled hints of oil and pickled ginger. Dylan focused on the familiarity of those smells over the backflips her stomach was attempting. Mike said something to the chef, whose shoulders shrugged as laughter crept into his face, before he turned away to work on an order from a customer across the bar.

"Hey there," Dylan said, shrugging off her khaki trench coat and placing it on the back of her bar chair.

"Hey. Glad you could make it." Mike stood up, giving Dylan a brief moment to assess him. Gone was the soft shirt, replaced by a well-fitted navy-blue sweater that could only be described as some kind of sexy Mr. Rogers situation, over a white cotton T-shirt and gray slacks that probably came from a place more reasonably priced than they looked.

Dylan smiled at his outstretched arms, determined to do a better job hugging him than she had a few nights back. Leaning into him, she felt her skin humming, as if all the static electricity in the air had suddenly decided her body was the place to be. As she inhaled his spicy smell, the buzz picked up, and she wondered how someone managed to smell like a kitchen and so good all at the same time. Probably the same way his arms managed to feel fit but not intimidating. He gave her a tight squeeze before relaxing his hold on her. Dylan let go, unexpectedly missing his warmth, and took a step back. Clearing her throat, she settled into her chair.

"Did you find the place okay?"

"More or less. This area has changed so much since the last time I was home," Dylan answered, risking a glance away from her menu to look him over once more.

"I swear something new opens every other week. When I first moved in, I planned to try every spot in the neighborhood. Then I found this place, and now I'm that guy who eats at the same restaurant three nights a week." He laughed at himself, sitting sideways on his barstool and relaxing his solid shoulders into the wall behind him, pulling the Mr. Rogers sweater taut across his chest.

"You like what you like. No shame in that." Dylan feigned a casual cool. She expected the tingling sensation to decrescendo after she sat down, but it had no intention of doing anything like that. Recrossing her legs, she perched the platform of one heel on the strip of wood that functioned as a footrest before testing it with the full weight of her limbs as she relaxed. The shoe suddenly hitched down the thin wood, causing her to jerk forward as the heel hit the strip. Dylan squeaked and caught herself with her forearms before she managed to go face-first into the bar.

Mike's forehead creased as Dylan tried to right herself with all the grace of a baby hippo exploring its first mud bath. "We can move to a table, if that is easier for you. I didn't think about your shoe of choice when I picked this spot," he said, inclining his head toward the heel she was trying to untangle from the clutches of the stool.

"No, no. This spot is good," she said, attempting a lower-abdomen crunch to extract her shoe, silently thanking Pilates for whatever core strength she possessed.

Mike looked at her with more than mild concern. "Are you sure? Because it's not like the place is—"

"What can I get started for you?" the chef asked.

Dylan had never been more grateful for a conversation to be interrupted as she finished righting herself with a shimmy so her backside was once again centered on the stool.

"Mike, you are the expert. Any recommendations?"

He lifted an eyebrow at her chair but let it drop when Dylan glanced back down at the menu without additional comment. "Maybe we order in rounds? I usually let Chef pick. He never lets me down. Except for that one urchin thing. I did not like that."

The chef cackled, as if it was one of the better jokes he had played on a patron. "You said you were in the mood for something wild!"

"I believe my words were 'something new and unexpected.'"

"Shoulda been more specific." The chef's expression looked like a cat who'd caught a mouse. "But I won't do that to your lovely date. What are your opinions on sashimi?"

The man asked this question in such a mundane tone that Dylan was halfway through, "Love it!" before her mind tripped on the word *date*.

"Good, good," he said, retreating to the other side of the counter to grab something.

"Thanks, Chef," Mike said, ignoring the man's assumption. Apparently, he was not bothered by the idea that someone believed he was on a date with his familial archrival. Or he hadn't been listening carefully.

Would it be bad if we were on a date? Dylan thought as the buzzing kicked back into high gear. Wouldn't Mike think it was a little soon for her to be dating again? She didn't miss Nicolas or anything, but should she at least pretend for the sake of propriety? Or had propriety gone out the window when she'd driven over the flower bed? Because it seemed that way.

Feeling her thoughts spiral, Dylan reached for the security of the list in her handbag. "Right, so. Down to business," she announced, extracting the list and placing it on the counter between them.

Mike laughed and moved off the wall. "Ah, yes. If we yell it to the whole restaurant, Chef will revise his assessment, and this will definitely not be a date."

"That is not what I was doing." Dylan put on her best innocent smile.

"You are about as sneaky as a Mack Truck." Mike chuckled, pointing to the list of names. "I know we aren't on a date because your list isn't titled *Dylan and Mike's Date List*."

"I just want to be efficient. Don't want to waste our time," Dylan said, leaning into the joke—she needed to practice flirting now that she was single anyway. Why not start here? "We can be on a date later tonight."

"Somehow, I don't believe you. I know how seriously you take list titles. Now you are just toying with me."

"Me? Never." Dylan tossed her hair over her shoulder, doing her best to lean into the idea of practice flirting. She smiled, catching the eye of the chef as he made his way over to them with a board of sashimi, looking like a tiny arc of two-by-two matching bites of goodness.

"It's cool. Skip the chitchat. I don't need to know how your day was." Mike sighed before leaning in to take the board from the chef. "Thank you. This looks great."

"Fine, we can eat first. Then list," Dylan said, mixing a bit of wasabi in with her soy. Picking up something that looked like unagi, she added, "So how was your day?"

"It was great—thanks for asking!" Mike said, a sarcastic grin written on his face as he popped a bite of food into his mouth.

"You wound me." Dylan placed her hand over her heart. "Really, how was your day? I promise I'm not asking so we can cut to the chase. I genuinely want to know." She also wanted to know how his lips managed to maintain a whisper of a smile while he was chewing, but asking that felt intrusive.

"It actually was an enjoyable day," Mike said, carefully affixing a bit of ginger to another bite. "I spoke with my boss, and they said they can add the sensory room to the program. I'm so excited I already started looking at construction crews."

"Really?" Dylan asked, shifting uncomfortably on her stool. It was one thing to babble mindlessly about helping him; it was another watching him stake his career on her dubious claims. Still, she had a list. It wasn't as if his coworkers had promised him a spot onstage or anything. All he would have to do was say no one would take his calls and move on with his day. At least, she hoped it worked that way. "So what does that mean for you?"

"It means they will plan both table space and program space for the sensory room, assuming your list works out. I can't say thank you enough for—" Mike paused, turning his ear toward the speaker nestled into a dark corner of the restaurant, pulling Dylan's attention with it. "Sorry. It's just . . . is this D'Angelo?" His expression was bemused.

Listening, Dylan wrinkled her nose. "It totally is—2000s slow jams and sushi. Unexpected."

"'How Does It Feel' is not exactly what I think of when I eat sushi." Mike shook his head and picked up another bite as Chef wandered over with a new plate, this time with seaweed-wrapped rolls topped with scallops and a spicy sauce.

"Raw fish and sex music. Oh, baby, oh, baby."

"Pretty romantic date," Mike giggled into his water glass, causing Dylan to snort at her scallops. After taking a drink, Mike shielded his smile and mumbled, "Look at Chef."

The mischievous grin had disappeared and been replaced by a dignified-looking chef, carefully wiping down counters as he sang every seductive word under his breath. Dylan turned her head to face Mike and hoped the chef couldn't catch a clean look at her laughing.

"He is clearly a fan," Dylan managed to choke out as Mike's gaze jumped back and forth between her and Chef, his shoulders shaking from the effort of not laughing out loud. Dylan tried to glance at the chef again but couldn't without losing it.

"Don't look. It makes it worse if you look," Mike said, angling his body away from the counter so he was facing her again. Tilting his head farther away from the chef, he added, "Distract me. How was your day?"

Still chuckling, Dylan tried angling her body farther away from the counter, making her parallel to Mike. "Honestly? The best part of my day may have been putting this list together."

"I don't believe that. Surely someone told a good joke or something."

Dylan picked at another scallop. "The amount of time I spend actually doing my job versus putting out fires is like a one-to-seven ratio. I'm basically a month away from the dreaded quarterly-earnings report, and things still aren't on solid ground."

"What does your boss say about all of this?" Mike asked, leaning in on his forearm and snagging a bite for himself.

"Besides *what the hell is going on?* Not much." Dylan shook her head. "And that is the weird part. Realistically, if quarterly earnings are posted in a month, that means we have about three weeks left to get stuff to the higher-ups for approval, and he still hasn't darkened the doors."

"Does he usually show up on your projects?"

Dylan's laugh sounded more like a sigh of resignation. Picking up another bite, she said, "For little projects, no. But for something this high profile, Jared has made it abundantly clear that I am just the muscle. He is supposed to have final approval on any- and everything."

"But someone has to have noticed he isn't here. I mean, they can't see him at his desk every day and think, *Yeah, he is definitely doing a good job up in Seattle.*"

Dylan scoffed, shaking her head. Mike asked her another question, and she started to relax, letting the natural flow of friends at dinner take over. At some point the chef brought over more food, and she found herself mellowing into the kind of food coma only an intimate corner, sushi, and the sultry sounds of slow jams could provide.

"Billie is doing well?"

"By all accounts. I rarely hear from her. She is more of a call-when-she-needs-something kind of person," Dylan said, around the straw in her water glass.

"So you know she is doing well since she hasn't called." Mike smiled, leaning toward her on his elbow. He had never really leaned away after the chef had started singing. The thought of the chef brought Dylan back to the room. He was no longer behind the spotless bar. Glancing around, she caught sight of the staff quietly sweeping under empty tables and chairs, trying as best they could to discreetly pack up for the night. Her eyes darted to her phone; it was well past ten, and they hadn't even touched her donor list. As if her eyeing the room were a signal, Mike straightened his posture and looked around, alert for the first time in hours.

"I don't know where the time went. We didn't even look over the list," Dylan said, stretching up, aware of Mike's gaze following the lines of her arms toward the ceiling. She wasn't the least bit disappointed they hadn't talked business, but for the sake of propriety she added a pout to her tone.

"Not my most productive meeting but certainly the most fun. We should probably go before these poor people are trapped here all night," he said, passing the server some cash. They stood, and he held Dylan's coat for her. "If you don't mind staying out, we could find a coffee spot that is open late and finish up."

"You mean get started?" Dylan asked, slinking into her coat and placing the list in her handbag.

"I mean, ten thirty is my bedtime, but for you, I can make an exception. Maybe stay up till eleven fifteen."

"Ten thirty? And here I thought that sweater was just for show. Turns out you are an old man." Dylan smiled and began weaving her way toward the door, conscious of the movement of her hips as she swayed around tables and chairs. "I like the sound of coffee."

"Good. I think the Tabby Cat is open late. My place is around the corner. We can grab my car and drive over. It isn't super far, but I don't think we want to walk this late."

Feeling Mike reach past her elbow to open the door, Dylan turned. "If your place is around the corner, why don't we just go there? Unless you are secretly a tea drinker or something?" She tried to make the suggestion sound like a logical conclusion as opposed to what it actually was—a casing of the joint. Dylan was dying to know what Mike Robinson's man cave looked like.

"Of course I have coffee. I'm not a monster."

"Fine. Your place it is," she said, smiling at the server who was hanging back to lock the door behind them. The woman winked, and it took all of Dylan's inconsiderable stealth not to wink back. She hadn't started the evening on a date, but whether or not Mike knew it, they were on one now.

CHAPTER FIFTEEN

Dylan spent the entire walk over praying Mike's house wasn't covered in black IKEA furniture and college posters. That would have spoiled the magic of the entire evening. Now, standing in front of an old brick building, she reasoned that nothing this classic could house the sad remnants of a man clinging to his glory days. Once she thought about it, if the sweater was any indication, he might have skipped over the postcollege man-child phase altogether. After twisting the key in the lock, Mike held the door open.

"After you. I'm on the fourth floor."

The building was old enough that Dylan didn't bother looking for the elevator. Instead, she crossed the black-and-white-checkered tile floor toward the worn mahogany staircase and started the climb toward his apartment. Dylan liked to think that spin class kept her in decent cardiovascular shape, but by the second floor she was starting to sweat under her trench coat. Looking for something to take her mind off the endurance event that was getting to Mike's apartment, she caught sight of a gaudy red-and-gold door wreath with something that looked suspiciously like a papier-mâché unicorn one floor above them.

"What is that?" Dylan asked as they rounded the stairs to the top landing.

"Hmmm?" Mike asked, turning his focus from the key in his hand to the door she was pointing at. "Oh, that is Mrs. Warnly's good luck ornament. She makes them. Even gave one to me for the holidays last year. I have yet to display it." Mike smiled wryly as he turned the handle.

"At least you have one neighbor who likes you and wants good things for you." Dylan shrugged up at him with a hint of mischief.

"Even if those good things are pretty dreadful looking," Mike whispered as they walked in. Dylan shivered. His presence felt like the movement of the earth around the sun. An unavoidable truth, drawing her in. Intentionally shifting her thoughts, she moved into the entryway, giving Mike room to hit the lights and toss his keys on a hook by the door.

"Welcome," he said, stepping out of his shoes and placing them on a rack hanging on the back of the hallway closet door. As if he had been reading her mind, Mike began to carefully unfasten the buttons of his sweater, furthering Dylan's sexy Mr. Rogers fantasy. Slowly, he peeled off his sweater to reveal a white undershirt stretched across his chest, hugging the curves of his shoulders, leaving his biceps exposed as he hung up the sweater.

Subconsciously, Dylan knew she was staring. She knew this was rude, and she was certain she didn't care. His back was to her, and it wasn't like her mouth was open. At least, she hoped it wasn't, since he chose that moment to turn around. He held her gaze for a beat before tilting his head like he was studying a curious artifact.

"You doing okay?"

"Totally fine." Dylan felt the heat in his stare radiating in her cheeks and looked around the narrow hallway for something to feign interest in. How was she this awkward? Sure, she hadn't been on a date for the better part of a decade, but this was someone she knew well. She didn't need to be nervous. Giving herself a shake to refocus, she pulled the soy sauce–spotted list from her bag and shrugged off her coat. Slipping out of her heels, she sighed with the relief that came with taking off dress shoes at the end of the day. "Feels good to take those off after all those stairs. Must be how you stay in shape."

Mike laughed. "I suspect that has more to do with the jogging. I usually take the elevator, but you seemed pretty gung ho on the stairs, so I just went with it."

"There's an elevator?"

"The door is built into the staircase." Mike chuckled as he padded down the hall into the living room. "I'll start the coffee. Make yourself at home."

"I thought this was the sort of fancy old place that only had a dumbwaiter. I may have been in heels, but I wasn't about to try to squeeze all of me into a two-foot box," Dylan called, her eyes following him to the kitchen.

"Wouldn't have judged if you had tried it. Four flights of stairs is a lot of stairs," Mike chuckled over the rattle of dishes and the closing of cupboard doors.

Dylan allowed the apartment to draw her attention away from the kitchen. There was not a shred of obvious collegiate furniture or paraphernalia in sight. In fact, the place had a distinctly grown-man vibe. He had painted the walls a warm shade of Bermuda gray that made the room feel relaxed. A sensation only enhanced by the oversize chocolate-brown sofa and armchairs. In place of a coffee table, he had a battered wooden trunk covered in a stack of about three weeks' worth of *Sunday Times* back issues and a few junk mail catalogs doubling as coasters.

"So this is where you live," she said, wandering deeper into the space as the smell of coffee crept from the kitchen. "It feels so grown up."

"Thanks," Mike called as the coffee maker sputtered.

Dylan walked toward a delicate glass dining set to look at his art. On one end of the dining table was a large vintage opera poster; on the other was an abstract piece composed of broad, romantic brushstrokes with grayish undertones and a warm streak of berry red running through it.

"I got lucky. I found this antiquing with my mom."

Mike's voice grew less muffled, and she turned to find him holding a mug out toward her.

"Thank you," Dylan said as Mike passed her the steaming mug. "I didn't know Linda was into antiquing."

Mike laughed, the sound as warm as the coffee in her hand. "It was a short-lived phase. Mom was an amateur collector, but Ma is a professional declutterer."

"Sounds like Patricia. I bet there was never a week where my dad didn't try to raid your trash when y'all weren't home."

"Oh, he did it while we were home too." Mike smiled at this, as if he was letting her peek inside the Robinson family dynamic. "My parents act annoyed, but a small part of them likes to see what he can do with junk. Did you want cream or sugar?"

"Cream, please."

"Your parents are quite talented. I hope you know how much I admire their work," Mike said, turning to walk back to the kitchen.

"You have no idea how nice that is to hear."

Careful to follow at a distance, Dylan did her best not to stare at his walk, then deposited herself on the couch. Leaning forward to peruse the newspaper stack, she caught sight of her electric-yellow toenails and froze. She had forgotten all about them until now. Their eerie smiles grinning at her as if they knew the game. After checking to see if the coast was clear, Dylan stood up and tucked her knees under her. Sitting on her feet was tricky in a pencil skirt, and she listed to one side, pulse fluttering at the sound of Mike closing the refrigerator. Using the trunk, she pushed herself upright with enough force to leave her slumped against the back of the couch, her knees hanging off the edge but her feet safely under her, as Mike returned, clutching creamer and a package of cookies.

"I love your place. It feels like a not-creepy gentlemen's smoking club," Dylan said, gesturing widely with the arm that wasn't pinned to the side of the couch, as if sprawling on his furniture were perfectly natural.

"Glad to know my house feels like the good kind of boys' club," he laughed, placing the creamer and pack of cookies on the middle of the trunk, next to the old newspapers and the list she had left there.

"If it were even close to the creepy kind, I'd have hiked back down that Mount Everest of stairs. Somehow I can't picture you being a creepy-club kind of guy."

"I'll take the compliment." Mike's smile was lopsided. "Cookie before we dive in?"

For a brief moment, Dylan considered forgoing both the cookies and the creamer, but then she noticed the name on the package—Tim Tam. Leaning forward, she bunny hopped to the center of the couch, careful to keep her feet stowed beneath her. Mike's smile spread into a full-blown grin as she came to a halt facing him and reached out for a cookie.

"I love these," Dylan said, ignoring the question written on his face as she took a bite.

Mike raised an eyebrow and nodded at her knees. Dylan chose to ignore this, too, adding creamer to her coffee instead. Turning back to Mike, she leveled what she hoped was a charming, who-me smile. Shaking his head, Mike said, "Fine, you don't have to explain," and picked up a cookie. "I became obsessed with these while studying abroad in Australia during undergrad."

"Does studying abroad in Australia really count?" Dylan asked, reaching for another cookie.

"More than a semester at sea does," Mike laughed, then added, "which is to say, barely. But I did have a good time wasting a semester and not learning another language."

"Fair enough. I didn't go anywhere in undergrad, so what do I know?" Dylan giggled.

"You learned to live in Texas; that feels pretty foreign to me."

"Well, more foreign than a semester at sea, anyway."

"So we can both agree that a semester at sea is a party boat?"

"Absolutely."

Mike grabbed another cookie and dunked it in his coffee. He crammed the whole soggy mess in his mouth in one massive bite, chuckling at his own lack of grace. "That was a display of basically everything I learned in Aus." Grabbing the list, he added, "Shall we get started?"

"By all means," Dylan said, hop-scooting closer to see the list. Mike did not move the paper between the two of them, so she leaned into him to see the names. Even at her ridiculous angle, she was aware of how close they were, her knees gently nudging the muscle in his thigh as she crossed him. Her copy was safely stored in her bag, and she silently thanked the gods of surprise dates that she hadn't mentioned it earlier in the night.

"You know these people?"

"Or know people who know them," Dylan hedged, cautious of committing too much to a few of Deep's more ambitious Google additions. Brandt had begged her to add Tim, but after his last escapade with philanthropy, Dylan had decided that her instincts were right. He could humiliate himself on the charity scene without her help.

"This is fantastic," Mike said, leaning back ever so slightly so he could look Dylan in the eye. "Steve Hammond. I see him at events all the time. It would be great if we could get him to do something."

"I think we should be able to meet with Steve." Dylan smirked. Mike had picked the one name she could actually get a meeting with. Assuming he wasn't busy firing a fresh wave of Technocore employees.

"Seriously, this is so great." Mike bounced forward, grabbed two cookies, then leaned all the way into the couch's soft leather back. Taking a bite of one, he extended the second cookie to Dylan. Tingles shot through her arm as their fingers brushed. Dylan paused, cookie still in hand, to look at him. Mike's posture straightened, pulling at an invisible string somewhere deep in her stomach. She held her breath and Mike's gaze, willing herself not to shrink from whatever was between them.

"So . . ." Mike cleared his throat, still looking at her.

"Yeah, I'm just gonna do this."

Taking a deep breath, Dylan leaned in. The kiss was sweet, almost shy. But there was something delicious in the reserve of it. Her lips just brushing his, as if testing their realness, ensuring he wouldn't disappear from under her. His arm wrapped around her, softly at first, then pulling her closer to him as the kiss deepened. Sliding her free hand around the back of his neck, she let the clean, soft edges of his haircut tickle her fingers. She slipped her tongue across the bottom of his lip, testing the boundaries between them. Mike responded, moving boldly and pulling her in closer, so she could feel the hard muscles in his torso. He tasted like the sugary treats she had just eaten. Vaguely aware her own cookie was melting in her hand, Dylan couldn't help it: she giggled.

"What are you laughing at?" Mike's voice was on her lips as he leaned his forehead against hers, his breathing uneven.

"My cookie is melting."

Mike laughed, and Dylan could almost feel his smile touch her own as he tilted his head to look at the hand that wasn't wrapped around him. Chocolate had managed to drip all over her arm. Dylan sensed his reluctance as he released the hand at the small of her back, allowing her the space to roll back onto her calves. Carefully, she disentangled her arm from around his neck and slowly brought the softening mess of a cookie to her mouth.

"Want some?" Dylan mumbled through a mouthful of cookie, holding up her chocolate-covered hand.

"Maybe later." Mike bit down on his bottom lip as she began to lick the chocolate off her thumb.

"Suit yourself. It'll just take me longer to clean up before we can get back to business." She shrugged.

Mike leaned over, close to her ear, and whispered, "Take your time," then flicked his tongue across the corner of her mouth, adding, "You have melted chocolate all over your face," before leaning back again.

Dylan instinctively followed him forward, still working on the chocolate attached to her ring finger. As she did, her knees dug farther into his thigh. Mike winced and shifted away from the pressure.

"That can't be comfortable," he said, tapping a hand on her knee.

Dylan worked at the chocolate on her finger a little longer than she needed to, trying to come up with a good reason to keep her feet hidden. Pursing her lips, she watched as Mike tilted his head expectantly.

Exhaling, she pulled her feet out from under her, stretching her legs across Mike's lap. "I got a really bad pedicure. Like, embarrassingly bad."

Dylan watched in horror as Mike looked down at her metallic-yellow toes. The terrifying smiley faces on her big toes grinned up at him.

"Wow. That is just . . ." His body shook as he pressed his lips together. "It's just so . . . weird."

"I know. Don't laugh," Dylan said, trying to retract her legs from his lap. "I'd have removed them if I'd known I was coming here."

"I feel like your feet are watching me," Mike said, placing a hand across her legs and looking away from her toes, laughing into his own shoulder. "How do you go to the bathroom?"

"Honestly, I try not to look. I can't find the nail polish remover, and once my shoes are on I keep forgetting to buy more. You know my parents' house." Dylan chuckled. "My toes are too terrible; I have to put them away," she said, trying to bring her legs back from across his lap.

"No, no, no. It's fine," Mike said, still laughing as he slowly moved his hand up her calf, past her knee, finally letting it come to rest featherlight on her thigh. "We'll just have you sit in a different position or something."

"Or we could do things that don't involve sitting."

Dylan said the words fast so she couldn't talk herself out of her desire. Mike stopped laughing and grew quiet, squinting at her, the crow's-feet at the corners of his eyes taking shape.

"Like, maybe we find the room in your house that has options for other . . . activities." She trailed off, not quite meeting his gaze. Mike continued to take her measure as she moved her hands in a circular motion, looking for a polite way to suggest sex.

"This escalated quickly," Mike said, biting down on his lower lip. Dylan's face snapped to attention, catching the questioning look on his face.

"We can de-escalate. I don't want you to feel rushed or anything," Dylan sputtered. Suddenly unsure of herself, she looked down at her hands and kicked herself for being spontaneous. She usually considered all the angles. Spontaneity just wasn't her thing. She had made a whole life out of eliminating uncertainty, and it was a good life. Surprises were for people with less Delacroix in their name.

Risking a glance, she caught Mike's pause, his lower lip working overtime, and felt her heart stutter. Who was she kidding? The boy next door wasn't going to drop years of animosity for an uneasy truce with someone whose parents' had toilet papered his house two years ago.

"Let's forget about it. Best not to trust a Delacroix," she half joked, fighting the deflated feeling that came from misplaced hope.

Mike's eyes narrowed. "I trust you. Why wouldn't I?"

Dylan's chest expanded. "Because my parents lied about clogging the storm drain in front of your house?"

"Yes, but you didn't lie about it. Besides, we spray weed killer on your lawn whenever you all go on vacation. Dylan, you've always been honest with me. It's one of the things I like about you." Mike reached out and ran a hand down her arm. "I'm okay with escalation. Assuming you are."

Dylan leaned into him, surprised by the rush she felt. The pure bliss that came with taking a risk. Enjoying the slow gathering of electricity between them, she kissed him once again, slower and deeper this time. She waited, feeling Mike open to her, before backing away. "As long as you don't make fun of my pedicure."

"Done." Mike kissed her again, then tapped her thigh and looked over at her feet, his lips pressed into a thin line of impish delight.

"Don't say it."

"Wasn't gonna."

"Sure," Dylan said, nudging him with her shoulder before swinging her offending pedicure off the couch and onto the floor, unpinning Mike so he could stand. Extending his hand toward her, he lightly pulled her to her feet. Then, still holding her hand loosely in his own, he began to walk past the kitchen, toward what Dylan assumed was his bedroom.

He flipped on a lamp, a sheepish look on his face. "I always make my bed, but if I had known I was going to have company, I probably would have put away the dry cleaning. Maybe thrown out the empty Amazon boxes."

"People with emoji toes should not throw stones," Dylan said, the corners of her mouth quirking upward as he relaxed. There was something comforting about him making his bed every morning. A surprising shared appreciation for the rightness that came with ordering one's space.

Dylan turned in a slow circle to get the full effect of his taste. It had the same adultness to it that the rest of the apartment had. The room was all dark woods and steampunk accents. At the center was a king-size bed, crowned with a large chocolate leather headboard and covered in a peacock-blue duvet. Making it 360 degrees, she faced Mike again, who appeared to have significantly more interest in her than in the decor.

"I like this room." Dylan nodded with surety. "And I'm assuming you have condoms. I like you, but I really don't want to be pregnant right now."

"Bedside table. I'm not interested in being a dad just yet either."

"In that case . . ." Dylan shrugged, feeling coy as she unzipped her skirt and stepped out of it, resisting the urge to pick it up off the floor and fold it nicely. Instead, she reached for his belt buckle, while he tugged the staggeringly well-fitted white shirt over his head. Dylan paused mid–pants unbuttoning to admire what jogging had done for him. He didn't have the kind of body that intimidated a partner; rather, it was just the right amount of muscle and fat. Like Mike could still have a beer or a second slice of cake with her. She reached up to his bare shoulders and ran her hands down the planes of his chest, stopping only when she hit his pants. Giving them a hard pull over his well-developed backside, she let them fall to the floor with a muffled thud before looking up at him.

He traced a hand down her spine, his touch barely above a whisper. Mike paused. "You sure about this?"

"Yes. And if I change my mind, I promise you will know."

"Fine," Mike said, gesturing to the divot between his pectoral muscles. "For my peace of mind—last call on any other smiley-faced toes or other hang-ups I should be aware of."

Dylan smiled, shaking her head as she began toying with the top of her blouse. Midway through unbuttoning, she looked down and squirmed. Men did not need to match anything. If their underwear was clean and lacked holes, it was considered nice underwear. Glancing back at Mike, she wrinkled her nose.

"I sense a hang-up," Mike said, gently touching her arm. "What is it?"

What on earth had possessed her to keep the stupid bra when the panties were missing?

"My underwear doesn't match," Dylan said, feeling her shoulders sag.

Mike shook his head and waited, watching her with concern. "Seriously, what's bothering you?"

"I'm being serious," Dylan said, feeling foolish as the silence between them spread.

Mike's brow furrowed for a moment as he studied her. When she didn't flinch, his shoulders began to shake as he wrapped his other arm around her, drawing her in close. Placing a kiss on the top of her head, he laughed, "Do you think I care about your underwear matching?" His voice was muffled by her hair as he continued, "I can barely even see what color it is."

"Yes, but it's not a very good first impression," Dylan said into his chest, feeling the tension drip from her shoulders.

He stepped back to take a long look at her. "If I can get past your feet smiling at me, I think I can get past your underwear." He reached out and carefully unbuttoned the rest of her blouse. Pushing the left strap of her bra to the side, he leaned over and kissed the spot where the offending item had been. Pausing an inch away from her sensitive skin, he added, "In fact, I couldn't care less if your underwear ever matched."

Dylan felt herself smile as he kissed her collarbone, one hand snaking around her back to undo the clasp on her bra. Gentle kisses ran along her neck as her bra came undone. Placing another series of kisses on her right shoulder, he removed the last strap and let it fall to the floor. Her skin prickled with the sensation of his touch as he reached around her mismatched panties. As she drew her hand across his collarbone, his body tensed with her nearness, anticipating what the rest of the night had in store for them.

"Can we take these off too? Or is there more you need to share about the state of your underwear?" Mike asked, pulling at her waistband.

"No. These can come off without further explanation."

"Finally." Mike exhaled, his chin resting against the top of her head. Taking a step back, he pulled at the last of the mismatched set, let it fall next to its counterpart, and guided her toward the bed.

CHAPTER SIXTEEN

Where has Milo gotten to? For the last few weeks, the dog had made it a point to wake her up every night with some combination of farting, sleep running, and trying to fit his massive body into her tiny bed. But it was 4:53 a.m., and she couldn't find the dog anywhere.

As she rolled over, her pulse spiked, the fog lifting off her mind. The dog wasn't in the bed because she wasn't in her bed. In fact, she was in a much larger bed with admittedly cleaner sheets. And in that larger bed was Mike. Dylan willed herself to relax, pulling the duvet cover up to fill the cold space where rolling away from him had left her skin exposed. In the dark, she felt herself take on a Cheshire cat grin, although she hit pause on doing a happy dance, which would probably wake him up. She'd managed to have "a little fun," as her mother would have put it. Actually, more than a little fun.

Remembering her family, Dylan wrinkled her nose and tried not to think about how to explain where she'd been the night before. Would they even notice she hadn't been home? Not that she needed to be home; she was a full-grown woman. That said, she'd get asked questions she didn't have answers to. She moved over to take a closer look at the clock, and her heart rate began to dance as she thought through her situation. If she managed to set the feud aside, which she couldn't, her whole life was in Texas, or at least the bits of it that were still intact. Her job, for however long she had it, was there. Her friends—also in

Texas. Her possessions, although still at Nicolas's place, were in Texas. Mike knew she was only here temporarily. He couldn't expect this to continue for any length of time, could he?

Dylan rolled onto her back and saw Mike peacefully dozing with one arm tucked under his cheek, the other stretched across the space where she had been a few minutes before. Her eyes widened as she looked over at him, thoughts hiccuping. It was now 4:57 a.m.; she was in someone else's comfy bed, after some damn good sex and a nice evening.

A nice evening with a guy who was kind and had asked her to stay. Dylan had started the night with every intention of doing the best she could to get out of dinner without damaging him or anybody else. She was supposed to be helping. Instead she had done the exact opposite.

"Oh my God," Dylan mouthed at the ceiling, her agitation growing. She could not possibly stay. Here Mike was, all smiles and thoughtful gestures, and she was basically holding herself together with double-sided tape. She silently threw back the covers, then began the painstaking task of searching an unfamiliar room for her things, talking herself through her next move all the while. As far as she could tell, the best thing to do was to get out of there. Tomorrow she could buy him dinner or something and tell him the truth. After a glass of wine or three, she could be honest about the googled list and what was left of her mess of a life in Texas. She could even tell the truth about the likelihood of her being successful at Technocore. She just couldn't do it right now. Or first thing in the morning. Mike would probably try to make her breakfast.

The guilt would eat her alive.

Fumbling as she slunk into her underwear in the darkness, she cursed herself for not bothering to gather and fold her clothes the night before. After locating her skirt and blouse, she tiptoed into the hallway, grateful that they hadn't stopped to turn the lights out the night before. She pulled open the closet and gathered up her coat and handbag. Glancing at her shoes, she decided to put them on in the hallway, avoiding the obvious click of heels against wood that would signal her departure. Reaching for the door handle, she flipped off the hall light. If she couldn't be honest, the least she could do was save him some money on his utility bill.

Backing into the hallway, Dylan pulled the door shut, then slowly released the handle until she was sure it wouldn't make a sound in the lock. Exhaling, she turned and glanced across the hall.

A woman who could only be Mrs. Warnly looked at her with disapproval, eyeing the heels in Dylan's hand. She smiled at the grim-looking woman, who was wearing a roller set and clutching a newspaper. She did not return her smile. Mrs. Warnly knew she'd just left a nice boy sound asleep without so much as a note, and the woman did not approve. Dylan wasn't sure she could blame her as she crept toward the staircase, shoes still in hand.

~

Dylan turned into the Technocore parking lot and began the hopeless circle for a parking space, cursing Tim. When the company had moved into its new building, he'd severely miscalculated the number of parking spaces required for the staff. After all, he and the executive team had reserved parking. He didn't really care if there were only forty spaces for roughly 2,500 employees. Making a mental note to bump the proposed parking-shortage solution up the high-priority list, she swore and started driving toward the surrounding streets to try her luck.

She found a spot, and her tired body groaned as she got out of the car. Earlier in the morning, she'd managed to get back into her parents' home undetected and sneaked in a power nap before forcing herself out of bed and into the shower. Unfortunately, she still needed about four more hours of sleep before she would feel rested. Clutching the biggest coffee travel mug she could find, Dylan heard her phone ding as she stomped across the damp sidewalk. She felt around the bottom of her purse, anxiety coursing through her body. Would Mike text so soon? She hoped not, because she hadn't the slightest idea what she would even say.

When she finally located the source of the ding, *Nicolas* scrolled across the screen. Secretly she was grateful he'd refused to be listed in her phone as *Boyfriend* or with any sort of heart-based emoji. He said that was demeaning and exclusively appropriate for teenage girls. She disagreed, but it did save her the trouble of having to fix his name in her phone.

Forcing herself not to tap her pointy-toed houndstooth heel as she waited for the elevator, Dylan practiced breathing in and out while consistently checking the number above the elevator door. She'd started to wonder who on the second floor was taking so long to get out of the stupid thing when the door finally opened. She rushed in and jammed the little "close" arrows before turning back to her phone.

Hey babe. You haven't been answering my calls.

Watching the "..." that followed his text, indicating he was typing another message, a pang of nostalgia leaned on Dylan's solar plexus. Not long ago, a checking-in message from Nicolas would have meant something to her. A rare moment of him demonstrating that he was thinking about her.

I really want you to hear me out. I think you'll feel better once you've heard my reasoning.

Dylan snorted as the nostalgia bolted from her memory, replaced with a reminder of the roughly fifty-seven text messages she'd received every time she hadn't answered his calls and he'd wanted something from her. The thing with Mike might be complicated, but he wouldn't demand she talk to the super about their toilet anytime soon. Comparing Nicolas to Mike was like comparing a Fig Newton to a Tim Tam. One might be better for her according to the nutritional label, but the other was clearly a superior choice by every other reasonable measure.

> I don't like how we left things. We were fine before your family was involved.

Nor would Mike trash-talk her family. And he had good reason to dislike them.

> Please. Let's talk.

Dylan bit down on her bottom lip, tired of Nicolas's emotional manipulation. His version of begging might have seemed cute to him, but she thought she would feel even better if he just left her alone. For the sake of her stuff not being in the street like in a nineties R&B music video, she answered:

> I'm OK with where we left things. We can arrange for me to pick up my stuff when I return in three weeks.

As soon as she hit send, his typing bubble appeared, and Dylan secretly wished the Wi-Fi in the building wasn't so good. She didn't need to see the response right away.

> Babe. Do we really need to throw away all these years over your family?

Her fingers flexed in frustration as she tapped back:

> Again, I'm comfortable with the way we ended. I'll contact you when I'm back in town.

Doing her best to smile as she passed employees in the cubes on the way to her office, Dylan caught his reply:

Fine. Don't forget the apartment is in my name. The locks may not be the same until we have a chance to talk.

Dylan rolled her eyes so hard it was a miracle they didn't get stuck in the back of her head.

This feels like you are manipulating me. But, if a call is required in order for us to amicably end this relationship, I'll give you a call tomorrow night.

Fitting her key into her office door, Dylan sighed. Was holding her things hostage even legal? If anyone would know how to make her life hell, it was the shark of a divorce attorney she lived with. She should have predicted him doing this. Had she been honest about the odds of their relationship ending, she might have.

As if the world could sense her apprehension, her desk phone began to ring. Glancing at the caller ID, she groaned as *Jared* scrolled across the screen. She let it ring twice more before straightening her spine and picking up the receiver.

"This is Dylan."

"Dylan, Jared here. I left you a couple messages this morning."

"Yes, I saw. I was just making my way through my voice mail." Dylan fought to keep the irritation out of her tone. His clipped delivery made it sound like she had not returned his call since 3:00 p.m. last Friday, not 9:32 a.m. the same day.

"I don't know if you have seen the trending #TechnoDisasters and #TechnoFails reports on our clients, but Technocore has scored high again. And not in a good way."

"You know, that doesn't surprise me. We had a rough start at the retreat, but if you dig deeper into the hashtags, you'll see a surprise turnaround in—"

"I don't care about the turnaround," Jared shouted, taking her by surprise. "What I care about is results. I'm not seeing them in all of this junk."

Dylan cleared her throat, trying to decide how best to proceed as her boss breathed heavily into the phone. There probably wasn't a right way to talk him through this, but the alternative of crawling under her desk to wait it out seemed just as unlikely to yield positive outcomes.

"I can see why it seems that way. But share prices are holding steady, which implies investor confidence, and again, within the trending posts there is actually a change in tone—"

"I don't need excuses. I need—no—*expect* results."

"And I think you are seeing them. It's a real vote of confidence the board hasn't scheduled a meeting, released a statement to shareholders, or—"

"I don't give a shit about what the board hasn't done. Those assholes created this mess. I want a report on the immediate outcomes of the retreat, action items okayed by Technocore management, and workforce-retention projections tomorrow. Understand?"

It took Dylan a moment to process being cursed at by a man who was almost assuredly wearing a sherbet-colored cardigan and boat shoes.

"My understanding was that you would like to be part of the review process before we start putting together some of the documents that both Kaplan and Technocore directors will need to approve."

"For God's sake, did I stutter?"

"No, you were quite forceful in your language. It's just Technocore is also *your* assignment, and I think if you were present, you would see the tenor of the workplace is rapidly improving, even with the stumbling blocks."

"At the rate you're going, there won't even be a client for me to visit. Get your shit together, or get your bags, because I will fire you. Clear enough?"

Dylan's mouth went dry. Jared had been nasty for weeks, but this was a new rock bottom. Trying to keep her voice steady, she answered, "That is a tall document order. Typically, four of us would analyze this kind of data and make a recommendation a week or so later. You do realize you're asking for a grand total of one hundred sixty hours' worth of work in two days? Even if I pulled an all-nighter, I wouldn't have enough time to produce a quality product."

"Get it together or get out," Jared spat. "I'll look for the documents."

The line went dead. Dylan sat motionless until the please-hang-up-or-try-this-call-again voice spoke into her ear. Gently, she set the phone back into its cradle and looked at her closed office door to ensure no one was watching, then let several unseemly descriptors fly.

By the time she had reached *profound dickhead*, she had rage shakes. Whatever had crawled into his undies and bitten him was no excuse for cursing at a colleague. That wasn't just bad managerial tactics; it was bad manners. For a moment she considered sending him a picture of her middle finger and storming off, but then she caught sight of Deep walking toward her desk, chatting with the socially awkward guy from Accounts Payable, and stopped short. Jared was a certifiable asshat, but he wasn't chasing her out without a fight. Not when things were just starting to turn around.

Taking a deep breath, she opened a document to start an outline of the items he'd requested when there was a knock on her door. Tension seeping into her jaw, Dylan glanced up at Brandt's perpetually pale face in her window. He was smiling and waving at her.

"Good morning," Brandt said as he stepped through a miniscule crack he'd opened in the doorway, as if a thin opening made his presence less of an interruption.

"Good morning. How's it going?" Dylan leaned back in her chair, aiming for a relaxed posture she did not feel. The specter of the world's worst manager hung over her head like a curse, and she would be damned if even a hint of Jared's attitude made its way into her office.

"Your hair is curly!"

Dylan laughed at the look of genuine surprise on his face as he came to stand directly in front of her desk. "Don't tell anyone. It's my best-kept secret."

"Not anymore, it's not." Deep strolled past Brandt with an excess of confidence and plopped down in the chair across from her. "If I had hair like that, I'd never be bothered with a flat iron again." Studying her appearance, Deep cocked an eyebrow at her. "Any particular reason you've got curls and came in after nine a.m.?"

"None whatsoever." In another life, Dylan was almost positive Deep had been a child of Bernice's. It was like she could smell a good story waiting to be told.

"It is very unlike you," Brandt added, without any of the implied suspicion Deep's question had carried.

"Just feeling lazy. I figured with this rain it wouldn't matter what I did."

"But that's never stopped you before," Brandt pointed out.

Deep's smile was devious. "Does it have anything to do with List Guy, because we googled him, and wowza!"

Dylan's bark of laughter cut her friend short. "Enough about Mike. Did y'all come in here to ask why my hair is curly?"

"Don't think I didn't notice you changing the subject," Deep said, giving her a suggestive wink. "No, we didn't come to chat about your hair or List Guy. Brandt and I were thinking we could go to lunch and talk about staff-appreciation-committee stuff? We had an idea for a game night."

The word *no* was halfway out of her mouth before Dylan caught herself. There was no way she could deliver what Jared was asking for, so why couldn't she take twenty-five minutes to walk over to the corner store with them?

"Sure. But can we make it a late lunch? Like one thirty?" Holding up a hand, she added, "Kaplan's breathing down my neck on some stuff."

"Of course," Brandt said. "Told you she'd come."

"Guess I'm getting lunch." Deep inspected her perfect manicure, smiling. "We had a bet. You never come out of this office. I thought for sures Brandt would be picking up the tab."

"You bet on me being antisocial? Brandt, thank you for your loyalty," Dylan said, in mock pain. "Deep, you just had an off day. I'm a hermit." A bit of the tension rolled off her shoulders as the three of them giggled. "Anything else I can do for you before lunch? Any other bets I need to settle?"

Brandt's gaze twitched over his shoulder. Dropping his voice to just above a whisper, he said, "Do you think you can help get our reimbursements for the retreat pushed through? I hit the limit on my card, and I don't want to pay the interest on that thing."

Deep nodded along. "Bailing Tim out of dead-animal jail left me broke."

The corners of Dylan's mouth twitched up. "No problem. I'll get it taken care of today." Her phone began to ring again as she said, "It's the least I can do." Glancing at the caller ID, she smiled apologetically. "Speak of the devil—it's Tim."

"We can finish discussing everything at lunch," Deep said.

Dylan nodded her assent as the pair walked out the door. Side-eyeing the phone, she felt the dull throb of deadline panic pick up a notch. Sitting up straight, she cleared her throat. "Hi, Tim."

"Dylan. How's it going?"

Dylan took a moment to appreciate that Tim did not launch directly into business with her. This was an improvement. Jared's beloved hashtag watch wouldn't measure it, but Tim was getting better at being a boss. "I'm doing well. I think our minds must be linked, because I wanted to talk to you about next steps from the retreat."

"Yeah, I have a plan for that, and I'm going to need your help."

Dylan felt her eye twitch. "Fantastic. I know the staff-appreciation group is eager to get going."

"We'll do that too. But this is top secret. I need you to meet me for an off-site tomorrow morning in the Industrial District."

"Industrial District?"

"I don't want to spoil the surprise. I'm sending you the address. Be there or be a hexagon!" Tim laughed with too much enthusiasm for a man who'd just invited her to a warehouse district with no explanation.

"I have a pretty packed day tomorrow dealing with Kaplan. Can you give me a time estimate?"

"Uhhh . . . couple hours." Tim said this like he was a fifth grader trying to pick an answer that sounded correct on a math quiz.

Stress settled into Dylan's chest, eking its way down her spine. She didn't have an hour, let alone several, but this might be her only shot at a longer block of time with Tim to get Jared's requested documents approved. Forcing herself to stop grinding her teeth, she said, "Okay, but while we are there, we have got to work on the long-term plan for employee retention and next steps postretreat. Deal?"

"Sure. We'll get everything hammered out tomorrow."

"All right." Dylan thought she could hear Tim squeak with delight and stifled a laugh. It was not a very adult sound. "But if there is a plane hangar or a stabby-looking warehouse involved, I will be long gone in under a minute."

"Once you see what I have planned, the warehouse won't freak you out." Tim said this in such a dry tone that she couldn't tell if he was being sarcastic or if a warehouse was actually involved. Before she could ask a clarifying question, Tim added, "All right, my Rolfer is here. Gotta go!"

"Hey, Tim. One thing," Dylan said to the dead air on the other end, then shook her head. Of course Tim was into Rolfing. In fact, she was only surprised it had taken her this long to get confirmation. Pushing her frustration about wasted time aside, she opened a window to email him about Deep's and Brandt's reimbursements. Typing out a quick *please do this*, she blew out a long, strained breath and scheduled the message so that it would go out in roughly an hour and fifteen minutes, hoping to catch Tim post-Rolfing.

Attempting to swallow her mounting anxiety, she reasoned Jared had said close of business, but he hadn't said in which time zone. She could send him the documents by 5:00 p.m. Hawaiian Standard Time tomorrow, and he couldn't say she hadn't followed directions.

"This'll totally work. Not." Dylan groaned, slumping over in her chair. "Don't give up. You're a smart girl. You can figure this out." Inhaling through her nose, she picked her head up and tried to work.

She achieved laser focus on her work for all of thirty-five seconds, when her phone chimed again, causing her heart to leap into her throat. Massaging her left shoulder, she reached absently for her purse and pulled out her cell phone. "Shit."

Dylan dropped the phone on her desk almost immediately as Mike's name scrolled across the screen. The hairs on the back of her neck stood up as the phone continued to ring. She'd barely had a moment to think about anything since getting to work, including Mike. She certainly wasn't ready to deal with her choices yet. Holding her breath, she waited for the phone to stop ringing and prayed he wouldn't leave a message.

Not that she didn't want to talk to him. She just didn't know what she wanted to say. *Sorry I lied. I don't know half the people on that list, and my life is garbage. How do you feel about trying again from a place of honesty?* seemed like not the right place to start.

The phone stopped ringing, and she exhaled audibly. Whatever she planned to say needed finessing, and she would say it . . . after she got through Jared's demands. And Tim's absurd meeting. And everyone else's requests.

The phone buzzed, and Dylan glared at the device, which was seemingly hell bent on her listening to her voice mail. Picking up her cell, she held it as though she might be physically ill.

Mike's familiar voice crept through the line, comforting despite the dread his words induced. "Hey, Dylan. Turns out Chef knew something about sushi and slow jams that we didn't." He paused here, and the image of him nervous as he chuckled at his own joke came to her uninvited.

"So you were not here this morning, and I thought I'd check in with you. Make sure everything is, uh . . . copacetic." She imagined him rubbing the back of his head as he tried to find the words he needed to reach her. Despite herself, she smiled, thinking of him in his sweater, pacing around, wearing a hole in the floor of his apartment.

"Anyway, could you call me back or text me so I know you weren't abducted by aliens last night? Okay, talk soon. Bye."

Shaking her head, Dylan willed the smile off her face, allowing the tension in her shoulders to return. She didn't need to be endeared to Mike right now, no matter how adorable his voice mails were. The only thing she needed was to get through today; then they could talk. Until then, she would keep afloat by any means necessary.

Typing fast, she pulled up Steve Hammond's calendar and looked for a vacancy tomorrow. After throwing a hold on a chunk of time, she picked up her phone, stomach muscles clenching, and typed out a text to Mike.

Hey! Sorry, you were passed out and things at work went off the rails. We've got a meeting with Steve Hammond for 3:30 tomorrow. Maybe we can grab a bite after? Sushi and slow jams not required, but much appreciated.

Tossing the phone in her purse like it was made of lava, she closed her eyes to stop the room from spinning. If she stayed in the office for another minute, she'd be sick. If she could just find a quiet place, literally any quiet place, to hunker down, she might actually survive the next twenty-four hours. As it was, panic had her sweating so hard she was pretty sure even her shoes were full of water. Dylan reminded herself that she had pulled off some pretty impossible-sounding tasks before. She didn't have to panic. She just needed to get out of the office.

She closed her laptop, threw the computer into its case, and grabbed her coat. She wasn't sure where she was going; all she knew was she was in over her head, and she didn't want to hyperventilate or barf on Technocore's third floor.

~

Dylan sat in the car, breathing in through her nose for five seconds and out through her mouth for eight, like her middle school choir teacher had taught her. She had been using this trick to fight a state of near-debilitating dread since she'd bolted from the office a half hour earlier.

As she forced herself out of the car, the fresh air hit Dylan like a blast of cold, pine-scented reality, and she yanked on Cruise's door. This time of day, the place was mostly empty, save for a few college students who looked as stressed as she felt. Trotting toward the counter, she attempted to maintain whatever calm she'd regained on the drive over as the barista finished wiping down the espresso machine. Sure, she was in a hurry, but she wasn't pressed enough to want old milk from the steamer hanging around her beverage.

"Good morning. How are you?" the guy behind the counter asked, his red stapler tattoo smiling up at her from his forearm.

"Hi, I'm fine, thanks. Can I have a small double latte, please?" Dylan said, forgoing the usual polite exchanges. Best not to get sucked into a conversation when she was exactly three heartbeats away from an anxiety-induced blackout.

"Oh, a double. Someone has a busy morning," Stapler Tattoo said, smiling despite the fact that Dylan looked like she was ready to tear her hair out.

"Sure is," she said, her best please-leave-me-alone smile stuck to her face.

"Anything else I can get you?" the guy said, tapping at the screen in front of him.

Dylan eyed the pastry case but decided against getting anything. If she got started with sweets now, she would be eating them all day. "Just the latte, thank you."

"No problem." The barista smiled, accepting her credit card. After a moment, he flipped the screen around for her signature. "All right. I'll bring your latte over to you in a moment."

"Thank you," Dylan said, hustling over to a large corner table. In a flash, she began laying out her papers, the pressure behind her eyes mounting with each file she pulled out of her bag. As she took in the sheer volume of paper, her mind began to haze over at the edges, the insurmountable volume of work pushing her past the point of overload.

"Here you go," the barista chirped, causing Dylan to look up in a frenzy. He rocked back on his heels as her overwhelm washed over him. "You seemed like you needed a little something to pick you up, so I made you a foam leaf."

"Oh." Dylan blinked at him for a moment, wondering if she was experiencing some sort of pressure hallucination. It was the only explanation for why this man was talking to her about leaves when her entire world was rapidly crashing around her ears. When the barista didn't disappear, she looked down at her latte. There in lovely foam art was indeed a leaf. She racked her brain for what the appropriate pity-leaf-design etiquette was and settled on, "That was kind of you. Thank you."

Her phone began to buzz, *Stacy* scrolling across the screen. *No time for that right now,* Dylan thought, gritting her teeth at her phone as well as at the barista, who was still beaming at her. Switching the phone into airplane mode, she turned her attention back to her computer, giving the guy a silent hint that he could leave her in peace. Much to Dylan's dismay, he coughed loudly, offering her a hint of his own. When she did not look up, he said, "Rough morning?"

Did she have some sort of sign taped to her that said **Interrupt Me!**? Instinctively, Dylan reached around to feel the back of her blouse before recognizing that this was highly unlikely. Reminding herself that this person was trying to be helpful, she sighed, eyeing the leaf design. "You have no idea. It's not worth discussing."

"What happened?" Of course she'd managed to find the one nosy barista in all of Seattle. "I still have like three hours left on my shift." The guy shrugged, settling into the chair across from her. Dylan nearly kicked herself for having said anything. Now she was trapped in a polite exchange with no way out but friendly chitchat or yelling. Shouting was a bad idea. She didn't want to get kicked out of the coffeehouse. Repacking and unpacking somewhere else would take another hour. Not to mention the stress. Fine. If he really wanted to know. She would make him sorry he'd ever asked.

Taking another deep breath, Dylan laid the last twelve hours out for the complete stranger in front of her, leaving out nothing except names. She might only be employed at Kaplan for another few days, but that was not a good enough reason to relax her spotless client-confidentiality standards. By the time she'd confessed everything, the barista was staring like she had just admitted to highway robbery. "So yeah, I'm roughly twenty-four hours from finally losing my job. I'm being held hostage by my ex, while alienating the boy next door—"

"Technically, the man across the street," the guy said, holding up an unusually delicate hand. Examining Dylan's incredulous brows, he demurred, "But I see what you mean."

"The thing is, I don't want to give up. I've worked hard and done well at my consultancy. I hate that I'm in this pressure cooker where I'm bound to throw it all away." He opened his mouth to add something, but Dylan pressed on, her voice rising. "And I like a lot of the people at the company I'm working for. I don't want to let them down. Even the CEO, who I like . . . sometimes."

"But do you have to give it up?" he asked, watching as a customer strolled in and stopped short of the counter to consider the menu mounted on the wall. "Your job, I mean."

"Well, not technically. But I'm between a rock and a hard spot."

Glancing at the customer again, the barista stood up, looking put out over having to do his job. "Okay, if a brand-new consultant came to you with this problem, what would you tell them?"

"Calm down. You are perfectly capable. All you need to do is sketch an outline for each document, then fill in what you can. That way the bosses can see your thinking and provide feedback, as opposed to wondering why one piece is perfect and nothing else is even started. It looks like better time-management skills." Dylan shrugged.

"One, that was way more detailed than I expected. Two, just do that." The guy shrugged as if it were that easy. "You're smart. You'll figure it out."

"That's kind of you," Dylan laughed, mentally preparing a rebuttal until the customer stepped up to the counter and threw the barista a hurry-it-up-dude look.

"I'll check on you later. Good luck," he said, wandering back to the counter with less hurry than the waiting customer expected.

Watching him wander away, Dylan smiled at the unexpected pep talk. Yes, the barista was prying, but he wasn't wrong. She just needed to get through the next few hours. Then she could head back to the office, and everything would be okay.

The caffeine from her half-drunk latte began to work its way through her overtaxed system, and her mind shifted gears, pushing aside the stress, making just enough room for her to focus. Dylan glanced behind her to see if anyone was listening, then realized that at this rate, she didn't care if the whole coffee shop thought she had lost it. Pulling her shoulders back, she whispered, "He's right. I'm smart. Focus, Dylan. You got this." Then she started working.

CHAPTER SEVENTEEN

Dylan yawned as she tipped her blinker toward the parking lot belonging to the kind of warehouse she'd told Tim she wanted nothing to do with. She'd managed to get into a flow state at Cruise with Tyrell, the overly friendly barista, making sure that each shift change kept her in a steady supply of snacks and caffeine as she'd organized the good, the bad, and the ugly from the retreat. It wasn't until well after dinnertime that she'd even remembered she'd put her phone in airplane mode. When she'd turned the phone back on, the deluge of messages had been so overwhelming that she'd switched it right back off, vowing to return every single call and text after she made her deadline. When Cruise had finally closed at midnight, she'd carried on her work at home until her mother had started to make phone calls to France at three thirty in the morning. Even in French, her voice had carried through the house, eventually forcing Dylan to put in ear plugs and give up working.

Scanning the parking lot, she didn't see a car that looked like something Tim would drive. As she considered the risk of being murdered in the parking lot if she leaned her seat back to catch a power nap, a pounding on her window sent her heart into her throat. Attempting to strangle the rest of her scream, Dylan took in a semideranged-looking Tim in a neon-orange bicycle helmet, his ludicrous grin fading at the sound of her screeching. Clutching the place where her heart was making an effort to escape her chest, she rolled down her window.

"What is wrong with you?"

"Why are you screaming?" Tim asked, looking around the parking lot in terror.

"You can't just come out of nowhere pounding on car windows in abandoned parking lots."

"I'm wearing neon," Tim countered, as if that rendered terrifying her impossible. Unluckily for him, all it did was serve as a reminder that she hadn't gotten nearly enough sleep to notice a millionaire in a tragic spandex color combination.

"Still not a good excuse." Dylan angled her chin at the warehouse. "What are we doing on the set of CSI?"

Tim's face folded back into a delirious V shape. "Staff appreciation!"

"I don't understand."

"I need to get inside and get changed before Taylor arrives." Tim held up a bicycle saddlebag. "Come on, Dylan. Don't worry; you won't get hurt. I play capoeira."

With that, Tim turned and marched toward the big metal doors of the warehouse. She doubted Tim's capoeira was as good as he claimed, but the odds of anyone attacking a man in a fluorescent catsuit seemed pretty slim.

Dylan continued to cling to her coffee mug as she got out of the car and crossed the aluminum threshold of the warehouse; a strong sense of dread began to creep through her. Just behind the security desk was a large window, presumably for a foreman to survey whatever was happening on the floor. In this case, Dylan had a clear line of sight into what appeared to be a massive garment-production factory on one half of the facility and a packing operation on the other. Tim took that exact moment to strut by the window in his fitted exercise attire, the effect of which was rather like a visual punch to her psyche. Whatever this was, it was real, and Tim was loving it.

She walked past the unmanned security desk and crossed onto the manufacturing floor, where Tim was speaking animatedly with a woman at a sewing machine. Looking up, Tim waved her over. As soon as she was within earshot, he launched into introductions. "Dylan, this is Lois, our head seamstress for the day. We are talking about production timeline. Lois, this is Dylan; she is going to be our floor manager."

"Nice to meet you," Lois said, extending her hand and fixing Tim with a glare.

"Nice to meet you as well," Dylan said reflexively, then paused, processing Tim's words. "I'm sorry, Tim—may I have a word with you? I think I need clarity around your, uh . . ." Dylan halted, searching for the most delicate way to phrase *stupid idea*, and came up with, "Vision."

Tim rolled his eyes and exhaled like a preteen, just to be sure Dylan understood how irked he was, before adding, "Excuse us, Lois."

Stepping over a few power cables, she took a large sip of coffee before beginning. "Tim, yesterday you said this would be a few-hour meeting. Now I'm a floor manager. What is going on?"

"Well, at the time I thought it'd be a few hours, but after talking with Lois, it seems more like a day project."

"What project?"

"Staff appreciation!" Tim gestured around the room as if it were obvious. "Your analysis said staff feel 'unheard and underappreciated.'" Tim put the words in air quotes, his bicycle bag waving along with the motion. "I thought this up on the way back from the retreat."

"Okay. But what is it?"

"This is why it's great. I pulled a staff list myself. All two thousand five hundred plus, including part-timers, and—shoot. Taylor's here," Tim said, looking at the woman who had just crossed into the workspace, the same look of apprehension on her face that Dylan was wearing. Tim continued, "I wanted to change. Oh well."

Catching sight of Tim's neon getup, Taylor sauntered over, clutching the strap on a fringe-covered cross-body bag, which was oddly formal, given her jeans and sneakers.

"Taylor, good to see you. I was just giving Dylan the backstory on our project. Dylan, this is Taylor from the *Seattle Examiner*; she is here to do a story on the staff-appreciation effort."

"I didn't realize you invited anyone from the press," Dylan said, willing her eyebrows to retreat down her forehead. Somewhere in her trapezius muscles, her sense of agitation blossomed into a full springtime of terror.

"Hello," Taylor said, her hand still firmly clamped on her purse.

Dylan nodded briefly before fixing Tim with a stare that would melt Satan. After his last brush with the press, he should have learned his lesson about arranging his own photo ops. Apparently she needed to have a more explicit conversation with him. And find a good PR trainer. But all that would need to wait until tomorrow, assuming she still had a job on Friday, which was in clear and present danger.

Locking eyes with her glare, Tim shuddered and cleared his throat, turning his attention back to Taylor. "As I was telling Dylan, today is all about thanking Technocore's employees. I came up with this whole thing in a dream and have been making calls all week to make it happen. Over here, we have people working on custom employee jackets, complete with their names on the front and monograms on the cuffs. Then we have hand-calligraphed certificates of appreciation, which will all be signed by me and accompanied by a handwritten note. Then there are the personalized thank-you mugs." Tim paused, smiling before asking, "Can you tell I'm big on customization?"

"This sounds expensive," Taylor said, eyeing the people huddling over sewing machines.

"Oh, it is. I hired every seamstress within a hundred miles of the city. Finding a space with enough power was a challenge. And the permitting!" Tim wiggled his eyebrows.

Dylan took the mention of permits as a sign she should intervene. "Tim, let's hold off on sharing exact details until we have a chance to discuss what Lois was telling you."

"Yes. Lois mentioned there was a problem with the employee name files. Nothing is in alphabetical order. They just need to alphabetize every individual piece before we can start stuffing the gift bags."

"Sounds time consuming," Taylor said, now eyeing Dylan, whose expression was hovering somewhere between murder and total annihilation.

"We have the warehouse until midnight, so it shouldn't be an issue," Tim said. Ignoring the apoplectic sounds coming from Dylan, he added, "If you don't mind, I'd love to change out of my bike clothes before we continue. Perhaps you can get some background on our recent efforts from Dylan." Without another word, Tim turned and sprinted toward the back of the warehouse.

"Is he always like this?" Taylor asked, startling Dylan out of her delirious fear state.

She had to get rid of this woman now, before things got any worse. And with a Tim idea, there was no way things wouldn't get worse. Taking a deep breath that did nothing for her racing pulse, she said, "I'm sorry, but there has been a misunderstanding. Tim is not available for interviews. I'm afraid I'll have to ask you to leave."

"That's funny, because Tim was pretty confident he could be interviewed when he offered me exclusive access to this event. I guess I could go back and write about how Tim had some crony kick me out when he began behaving erratically while dressed like an inflatable dancing puppet. It isn't as good a story, but something has to go in my column."

Taylor shrugged like there wasn't a threat lurking in her words, and Dylan's mouth went dry. This was her worst Technocore nightmare come to life—a walking ultimatum carrying a fringe-covered bag. Her mind clawed at its caffeine-soaked edges, desperately searching for an alternative that wouldn't result in bad press. As it was, letting Taylor see "staff appreciation" was more likely to produce a positive outcome than roundly kicking her out of the warehouse would.

"Fine." Dylan sighed. "But I think we had better set a few ground rules." She hoped her tone conveyed a level of authority she neither felt nor possessed. "First, I'm a consultant, and I'd appreciate it if you did not name me in your piece." She took another deep breath, pulling her posture yardstick straight. "Second, please consider the conversations Tim and I have confidential. I'm sure you can understand why having a reporter quoting them verbatim would risk trade secrets."

The reporter rolled her eyes. "I'd never report on anything for the sake of salacious reads, and certainly not—"

Holding up her hand, Dylan interrupted, "I'm sure you wouldn't, and it is not my intention to imply you have low ethical standards. But I'll need your word just the same. With the clear understanding that the full and considerable weight of my company will bear down on you and the *Examiner* should you violate our good faith agreement." She wasn't entirely sure what *good faith* meant in legalese, but Nicolas used it as a threat all the time.

Taylor had the decency to look momentarily crestfallen at the realization that her big break was probably not going to come today. "Of course."

"Thank you. I don't mean to sound abrupt, but we have a lot to do here, and I need to have a chat with Tim, so if you will excuse me. Please, make yourself comfortable," Dylan said, gesturing toward the sole metal chair by the door, which Taylor promptly ignored, turning instead to wander along the gift-bag tables.

Hauling as quickly as she could through the door Tim had slipped behind, she called out, "May I have a moment?"

Tim jumped two inches off the ground, looking left and right, before realizing the voice was coming from directly behind him. Turning, he adopted a hangdog expression. "I know what you are going to say."

"Do you? Let's hear it," Dylan said, fighting the urge to cross her arms and scowl. It was too close to Bernice, and she wasn't ready to turn into her mother this early in the day.

"You are going to tell me we need to work on addressing the deeper employee concerns, let the staff committee handle everything, and that this is not the two-hour warehouse task you were promised."

He's oddly spot on, Dylan thought. Taking a slow sip of coffee to gather her composure, she smoothed the front pleat of her wide-legged slacks before speaking. "If you knew this lecture was coming, why do this?"

"Because I know you are going to make me do those things, and frankly, I don't mind doing them." Tim added the second clause hastily before continuing, "But I wanted to try things my way first."

"I thought we came to an understanding about being a CEO your way and next steps during what is a volatile time for everyone." Tim eyed the floor, giving Dylan room to build up steam. "You recognize that you are putting me in a tight spot here. I mean, the press? Again?"

"Don't worry; she won't submit the story until tomorrow morning," Tim interjected, the guilt still scrawled on his face. "It'll probably go in the Sunday edition."

Tim's eyes stayed fixed on the shiny concrete, his shoulders slumping. His self-reproach pressed on Dylan's anger, thawing her slightly. Sighing, she filled the expanding silence. "I need you to sit here and send a memo to the staff regarding our next steps from the retreat while I sort this out. I sent you a draft to review last night, so it shouldn't take long. Deal?"

"Deal."

"Now, head to the security desk up front and get started." Dylan was surprised by the softness in her tone, given how much she still needed to do for Kaplan. As soon as Tim began walking toward the door, Dylan felt the bile in her stomach make its way toward her throat, forcing her to take another deep breath. It was unlikely Jared would view a warehouse intervention as a good reason for her to be tardy with his outlandish request.

"You are a smart girl. You can fix this." She repeated her new mantra under her breath. Taking out her phone, she clenched her teeth. She hated to do this, but she had to tell Mike that he would be taking the meeting with Steve alone. Ditto for dinner. There was simply no way she would be out of this warehouse anytime before six thirty today. A least she'd managed to set up the meeting before becoming a total flake. And really, helping Mike get a meeting was more important than her being there anyway. When it came down to it, it wasn't like he needed her to hold his hand through the meeting.

She'd just finished proofreading the world's most insufficient apology text when a voice startled her. "Hey, Dylan, got a second?"

Tearing her attention away from the phone, she looked up to see Lois jogging toward her, a gaggle of people walking a few paces behind her. As Lois introduced her to the individuals in charge of certificates, mugs, and bag stuffing, Dylan's eyes began to cross from exhaustion. She listened to the heads of each component, trying to understand where they were in the timeline and what challenges they were facing. While each person explained their needs, she did her best to get a list going. Eventually, she gave up thinking about anything other than the train wreck in front of her and got down to the brass tacks of managing multiple assembly lines.

She was busy orchestrating a cleanup of the boxed dinners the gift-bag-packing crew had demolished when Tim appeared by her side, a cheeky look on his face. In one hand he had a sandwich box and in the other a gift bag. Glancing down at her watch, Dylan winced; it was already past ten thirty at night.

"Tim, I know you said the deadline was twelve midnight, but there is still an astronomical amount of packing to be done, not to mention delivery."

"I have it under control. This is for you," he said, extending the package and the boxed dinner toward her.

As if reminding her she was running exclusively on coffee and optimism, her stomach rumbled. It was so aggressive that Tim looked over his shoulder before recognizing the sound came from her. "You should take this and head home. Thank you for your help today."

"Who is going to make sure this all gets quality checked, packed, and delivered?" Dylan asked, startled by the abrupt end of her tenure as floor manager.

"Me. You have done way more than your fair share." Tim shook the gift bag at her.

"Well, thank you," Dylan said, processing the return of her time. Taking the bag and to-go box, she added, "And thank you for making sure I received something to eat."

Glancing over at her temporary office, she realized that if she hurried, she could theoretically get the outlines to Jared before midnight. "You sure you don't need anything more?"

"Yup. Get a move on."

She wasn't going to look a deadline-saving horse in the mouth. "Thanks, Tim. See you tomorrow."

With that she began cramming things into her purse with a sort of haphazard inattention that made her cringe, then dashed out of the warehouse. After unlocking the car, she threw the gift bag into the passenger seat, only marginally aware of the contents tumbling out as she rushed to ship the documents off to Jared under the wire.

~

"Dylan, you're in the paper!" Her father burst into her room clutching an iPad, the font blown up extra large so he wouldn't need his glasses.

Searching through the fog of sleep deprivation, she tried to discern if this was part of some incoherent dream she was having or if her father was actually making his way toward her. The angles of Henry's clean-shaven face were dramatically lit, like he was telling a story around a campfire with a flashlight, not bursting into her room shouting nonsense with a tablet.

"I mean, it isn't your name—oh! Sorry, Milo." Her father stopped talking as he tripped over the gargantuan dog at the foot of her bed. Milo grunted in protest, the scrape of his paws on the wood floor pulling Dylan into reality.

"Uh-huh. Dad, it's early."

"It's five fifteen. This woman says something about Technocore employee bags and describes you," Henry said, speaking at unreasonable decibels. Reaching out, her father grabbed her foot and shook her leg, forcing Dylan to roll over and open one eye. Henry was real and furiously waving his tablet at her.

"I don't—"

"Here." Henry thrust the device at her with zeal, the glow blinding her temporarily. "I need to find the light," he mumbled to himself, relinquishing her foot. As her eyes adjusted, Dylan could hear her father's socked feet shuffle around the room, searching for the switch. "Damn it, Milo. Move."

She was just about to tell him the switch was over by the door when the story caught her eye:

> On Thursday morning, the *Examiner* received an exclusive invitation to observe the underpinnings of an employee-appreciation extravaganza arranged by none other than Technocore's embattled CEO, Tim Gunderson. Our reporter arrived at an isolated West Seattle warehouse that Gunderson rented for the day in order to surprise his staff with items he termed "personalized, bomb-ass swag." Trailed closely by a consultant doing damage control, Gunderson walked through the massive operation of over 35 freelance seamstresses, engravers, organization professionals,

plaque makers, and swag artists, all of whom had been commissioned to create more than 2,500 employee "thank-you bags" in under 12 hours.

"This wasn't supposed to come out until Sunday," Dylan grumbled, the sleep beginning to lift from her brain. Somewhere in her secondary consciousness, she could hear her father stumbling around the room looking for a light switch and mumbling encouraging things about her not being named explicitly.

Gunderson, who's been in the news multiple times for a series of mishaps, wanted to show everyone he'd turned over a new leaf. However, evidence of the improved foliage was scant on the ground.

As Gunderson ignored warnings from his consultant, the freelancers became increasingly irritated by his whims and the unexpected long hours. "It's certainly something we are concerned about," said Susan Moore, president of the freelancers' union. "It is typical of these tech guys to assume that a freelancer is there to be worked to the bone." When asked if there could be legal repercussions for Gunderson and Technocore, Moore replied, "I don't have all the facts yet. But yes, we are concerned, and we will be investigating the conditions Mr. Gunderson asked his freelancers to work under."

Given the stakes, why Gunderson, often referred to as Gunderpants on employee social media accounts, dismissed the good advice of his consultant remains a mystery to the *Examiner*. At one point, the consultant

could be seen crawling around the warehouse floor arranging sewing machine cables and begging the CEO
to do something more meaningful for employees, like
changes to the break room and parking facilities, as a
way of saying thank you.

"I wasn't crawling on the floor," Dylan said as the lights flicked on. Henry let out a triumphant squawk before returning to the bed and peering over her shoulder. Looking up at her father, Dylan asked, "Does this get any better?"

Henry shrugged in a way that reminded Dylan of her mother and said, "Honestly? Not really."

"I need coffee," Dylan said.

CHAPTER EIGHTEEN

This is not how I envisioned my Friday, Dylan thought as she waited for the light to change. While she waited, she eyed the spilled contents of the staff-appreciation bag still lying on the passenger-side floor. She was cold and tired. The embroidered fleece jacket stared back at her, looking comfortable. It was so early; she could sneak into the office and take it off before anyone saw her in personalized synthetic fabric. As she reached over to grab the jacket, her breath caught in her throat. There, in lovely script italics, was the wrong name.

Or, rather, the right first name but a very wrong last name. Forcing her freak-out aside, she wondered if anyone at Technocore was named Dylan Chavez. Maybe Tim didn't know her last name?

Dread squeezed at her insides, making her skin prickle with sweat. Tim knew her name. There was no Dylan Chavez. There was, however, a Rebecca Chavez in what was left of the front-end development team. The file Tim had sent over wasn't just out of order; it was wrong.

She made it to the office in record time. Slamming her car door with her hip, she took a sip of the hot coffee her father had prepared, grateful for his unexpected thoughtful gesture and relieved to find it wasn't a reheat of Bernice's leftovers from the evening before. Not for the first time, Dylan marveled at her parents' capacity to show up for her on occasion, even though they had literally no idea what she did all day. Her father making fresh coffee was so sweet and startling that

Dylan had almost hugged him. In fact, she would have if she hadn't been in such a hurry. Surprising Henry with a hug could mean a substantial time delay, which was not in the cards. Dylan reasoned that later she would give him a bear hug and listen to whatever random joke he wanted to tell. Right now, she had bigger problems.

Rocketing toward her office, she thought through all the possible scenarios for the day. Jared might not even see the article until later in the afternoon. After all, reading through all her half-finished documents would take him forever. Dylan had almost talked herself out of a panic when a stuffed gift bag, strategically placed on a chair in someone's cubicle, caught her eye. The expensive fleece glared back at her, taunting her with *Steve Chou*. Running back around to the front of the cubicle, Dylan yelped. This was Richard Chou's desk.

Horrified, she two-stepped her way to her office, pinning the phone between her shoulder and ear as she opened her computer.

"Tim, it's Dylan. If you get this, call me back. It's an emergency. There's a problem with the gift bags. I'll try to pick them up before the rest of the staff gets here. Okay. Bye."

Punching the red hang-up button, she tossed her phone on a stack of papers and dropped her head into her hands. There was a slight chance she could catch a few of the bags before the 7:00 a.m. shuttle buses arrived, but there was no way she could cover four floors of office space in twenty minutes. Not even if she took off her heels and ran. Dylan reached for her coffee, wondering if there was any way she could clear the early arrivals' desks, then come back for the other staff who came in later. Just as she started to work out the details, her desk phone rang, causing her to jump.

For a second, she hoped it was Tim calling to say he had magically solved the problem and that Steve Chou was a fluke, but her caller ID said otherwise. Dylan almost laughed. Yesterday morning, Nicolas had been high on her list of concerns. Now he would just have to keep waiting.

By the time the voice mail notification flashed, Dylan was committed to trying to grab as many bags off the desks as she could. Or at least as many bags as she could without running through the halls and raising suspicion. Dylan envisioned herself looking stealthy as she wandered past desks, casually sipping her coffee and snatching bags while waving good morning to her coworkers. That could work. She would have to hide them near Tim's office. No way could she fit all those bags in her little room.

Springing out of her chair, she made a beeline for the door, throwing it open rather recklessly for someone about to try to steal a warehouse full of goodies. Dylan squeaked, jumping two feet out of her skin. Deep was frozen mid–knocking motion, also startled by the sudden opening of the door. Clutching the stitch in her chest, Dylan blurted, "Thank God you two are here. I need your help."

"Of course you do. What is it you need today?" Deep said, crossing her arms and leveling an intimidating stare at her.

Dylan paused, trying to sort out exactly what was happening. One minute she had been planning to commandeer two thousand goody bags, and now one very angry friend was strolling into her office, agitation radiating off her like perfume.

"I'm sorry. That was rude." Dylan prodded in one direction, searching Deep's face for a hint. "I was concerned about the bags on everyone's desk and . . ."

Deep rolled her eyes, then glanced over her shoulder at Brandt, who was lurking in the doorway, looking uncomfortably between the two of them. With a short jerk of her head, Deep motioned for him to enter the room and close the door.

Dylan drew in a sharp breath as he turned back around to look at her, hurt written on his face. It was like watching a puppy get kicked. Worse, he had on his name-mismatched jacket. Guess she wouldn't be stealing that one.

"Well?" Deep asked, drawing her back into the room.

Dylan stared back, hoping her face didn't look as blank as her memory felt. She suddenly remembered the abrupt end to her day with Tim. "Shit. Did Tim not approve your expense check? I sent him an email, but I forgot to follow up with a conversation."

Brandt started. "No. He didn't do that, but it's okay. I'm sure you were—"

"You don't remember?" Deep burst. She hadn't shouted, but the words carried the same level of intensity. "Lunch. Two days ago? You just disappeared."

Dylan blinked in surprise. "Oh my God. I'm so sorry." Gesturing to Brandt's jacket, she added, "I was under so much pressure with Kaplan I went out to get coffee and ended up working until three thirty in the morning. Then yesterday Tim went on the lousy rampage you are wearing, and I just blanked."

"You blanked for two days?" Deep said, the tilt of her head changing with her skepticism.

"I did. I'm sorry." The moment the response tumbled out of her, it felt empty. Glancing over at Brandt, who was busy investigating the carpet, Dylan searched for something more to say that would buy her some forgiveness.

"We thought you were hurt," Brandt said, looking up suddenly.

"We thought you had gone out for coffee and were kidnapped or something," Deep said, uncrossing her arms and pointing at Dylan. "We called you like fifty times. Instead you were out here sipping lattes and letting Tim make a fool of our pointless staff-appreciation group." She exhaled loudly and retreated toward the door. Reaching for the handle, she added, "Look. I get it. You are a consultant on a sinking ship. If you don't want to get to know us, fine. Just be a big girl and say so."

Dylan felt her mouth go numb. She wanted to say something, but whatever it was didn't come out, and Deep didn't wait for it. She strolled out the door without glancing over her shoulder.

"Deep acts tough, but she isn't. Her feelings are just hurt. She was really excited about her game-night idea. Don't worry. She'll get past it." Brandt shrugged, moving toward the door. "I know you didn't mean to forget. I'm glad you're okay."

He slid through the door and quietly shut it behind him, as if he had known that Dylan wouldn't have a response for him either.

It felt like someone had placed an overweight suitcase on her chest, forcing Dylan to lean against the edge of her desk and take deep breaths. For a moment, she stood there looking at her closed door, trying to process everything. Of course she hadn't skipped lunch intentionally. She would never choose to treat a friend that way. The whole thing seemed like an overreaction. A small voice in the back of her head said something about how waiting two days to apologize was rude, but Dylan ignored the voice when her phone chimed, indicating that she had received yet another email. She would have to find a way to make it up to the pair of them later. Possibly much later, given the dumpster fire outside her door.

Coming around her desk, Dylan was surprised to see the promised staff email from Tim in her inbox. Willing herself to unclench her fist, she perused the *Big Updates* subject line. A small corner of her heart hoped his big-updates email would include an apology for the jackets. *Or if not an apology*, she thought, *maybe a promise to fix them, along with everything else in the company*.

> Dear Technocorers,
>
> It's been a rough couple of months. Hopefully, the goody bags on your desk go a little way to smooth things over. I want to address some of your concerns from the retreat.

Leadership Doesn't Listen: That is simply not true. In fact, I'm listening all the time. Sometimes leadership makes decisions you don't understand, because your suggestions just aren't plausible given what I know about the company.

You Feel Expendable: I value everyone here. However, if we can transition the president of the United States in three months, we can survive without any one team member. That includes upper management, like me.

Dylan retched. This was a list of ten, and there was no way the points that followed could possibly get worse than what she was reading. She'd practically drafted the email for him. All he had to do was read it over and send out things like *We have formed a committee on employee satisfaction* and *upper-management listening sessions*. Glancing out of the skinny window by her office door, Dylan made eye contact with Helen, a data specialist from the second floor with a countenance like Uncle Sam's. She had interviewed her during the fact-finding process and remembered her as generally kind. But not today. From what she saw on the other side of that glass, Dylan truly understood the expression *death stare*.

Turning back to the email, she began scanning for the cause of the killer gaze. Somewhere toward point eight, she found it:

By now, many of you have met our office consultant, Dylan Delacroix, who has encouraged me to share my vision and expand my leadership style . . .

"What the hell!" Dylan yelped at the screen. Jumping up, she darted over to the tiny roll-down shade, gesturing vaguely to her dress and mouthing, "Change clothes" at Helen before pulling on the balled metal cable.

The shade banged against the window ledge, and she pushed her hands into her hair, pulling hard enough that it looked like she was playing the face-lift game with herself. As the skin on her forehead stretched, she reminded herself to breathe. When that failed, she doubled over, hands on her knees, to count the little circles on the carpet. Anything to take her mind off the sound of blood pounding in her ears and the clutching spasm at her midsection. Suppressing the urge to vomit, Dylan slowly righted herself. Leaning on the door, she closed her eyes.

"You are okay. This doesn't have to end your career. You just have to get through—" Her eyes snapped open as the phone rang, cutting off her personal pep talk. Compressing a horror-film-worthy scream into a minor squeak, Dylan peered at the caller ID.

Still not Tim. She sank into her chair, her hand hesitating over the receiver, watching the red light flash its danger warning. If she didn't answer soon, Jared would go nuclear and start alternating between calling her cell and desk line until he reached her.

It was the third ring. She was either going to answer it or let the emotional blitzkrieg begin. Steeling herself, she picked up the phone. "This is Dylan."

"Dylan. What the hell is going on over there?"

"Beg your pardon?"

"Don't play with me, damn it."

"Jared, I'm not playing with you. It was one piece of bad press."

A copycat of Darth Vader breathed into the line. "One piece? Fuck the press. What do you call the documents you sent me?"

"A perfectly good starting place. There was no way—"

"I knew you couldn't handle this job. You don't have what it takes to make it to the next level at Kaplan," Jared cut in, his tone forcing visions of him foaming at the mouth into her head. Dylan felt the oxygen being sucked out of her lungs, replaced by something much more painful. "Do you have anything to say for yourself?"

"I think you're wrong. My work hasn't hurt share prices at all. Moreover, if you were here, you'd see that people are feeling—"

"Share prices? Is that your measure of success? God, you are an idiot."

"Given our focus on quarterly earnings, I believe that yes, in fact, share prices are the primary metric for determining success, with good press a distant second. The paperwork you asked for is almost a non sequitur," Dylan said, her voice shaky. She knew correcting Jared wouldn't help, but after the morning she'd had, she wasn't about to be berated for the only thing she had done correctly in the last forty-eight hours.

Jared sputtered, "You know what? Get packed. Someone as stupid as you are has no business at Kaplan. Or anywhere, really."

Dylan felt the pit of her insides drop to the floor. She had been dreading this since she'd walked through Technocore's doors. A small voice in the back of her head nudged her to say something. To stand up for herself. The worst had finally come. It wasn't like he could fire her twice. Taking a deep breath, she said, "There is no need for name-calling."

"When someone makes as many bad decisions as you do, yes, there is."

"Fine, fire me. It isn't like you have done any of the work."

Jared let out a strangled squawk. "Do yourself a favor. Go find a cardboard box and put your stuff in it before security escorts you out."

With that, Jared hung up, leaving her in blessed, office-lighting-bathed silence. Her mind began to cloud over with the weight of the last few hours. She'd figured Jared might finally fire her once the staff-appreciation fallout started in earnest. But Deep and Brandt? They were so out of nowhere that they'd left a hollow feeling running through her chest. And that hole was starting to hurt. Like, really hurt.

Come to think of it, her head hurt too. Could she breathe? She was pretty sure she could breathe. As she stood up, the pain in her chest shot up the place in her back where she had hoped steel would be, forcing her to double over, hands splayed across the desk.

"Am I having a heart attack?" she asked the window shade, belatedly realizing that since it was drawn, no one would see her collapse, so no one would find her. Then it would be days before Tim wondered why he hadn't seen her, and eventually her body would be discovered by the socially inept sweat-suit-material-loving geek who'd gotten her fired and caused the heart attack in the first place.

She checked again. Yes, she was still breathing, albeit in a labored, extremely sweaty way. In between clipped inhalations, she took stock of her symptoms. She'd seen a special on heart attacks. It was for women over sixty, but some of that had to apply to younger women, didn't it? Okay, she was sweaty, but not flu sweaty; this was nervous sweaty. Difficulty breathing, check. Chest pain? She stopped, trying to sort through all the signals she was receiving from her body. No chest pain. No pain in her jaw or back either.

"Probably not a heart attack," she whispered, still doubled over. Slowly, she processed the information, counting to ten as she tried to regulate her hiccuped breaths.

"Panic attack," she said to no one, finally sorting her own diagnosis. "I need air, now."

Dylan snatched her keys and coat up into her arms. HR could box up her stuff. Throwing her office door open, she bolted toward the elevator. Jamming the button with her thumb, she jumped in as soon as the silver doors opened. Taking another truncated breath, she repeatedly pressed the close-door button, praying the doors sensed her urgency.

"Come on," she mumbled under her breath.

"Dylan?" Steve's voice startled her from the corner of the elevator. Adjusting his glasses, he added, "I have been meaning to stop by your office. It's not like you to miss a meeting."

"Meeting?" She froze, feeling the sweat on her back grind to a halt. Had Jared already managed to get ahold of Steve? She blinked at Steve and said nothing, marveling at the speed of Jared's retribution.

"With the guy from Crescent. Mike . . . uh . . ." He squinched his eyes shut and snapped his fingers, searching for Mike's last name.

"Robinson," Dylan croaked. Something was off. She had texted Mike, so why hadn't he told Steve she wasn't going to make it? Fumbling for her phone in her purse, Dylan felt her chest start to tighten again.

"That's him. We thought you were coming." Luckily, Steve didn't require an excuse, because the only other words that came to her mind had four letters and were not polite to use with the man who would sign her termination paperwork in a few hours. "Anyway, nice guy. Interesting idea. I have a few questions."

Her fingers brushed the hard coating of her phone case, and Dylan seized it, quickly looking down at the face-ID sensor and scrolling through her list of unread texts. Finding Mike's name, she made a sound that could have doubled for a special effect, prompting Steve to look hard at her. "Are you okay?"

"Yup. Great." Her voice cracked. It was psychologically impossible for her to be further from great at this moment. There, in all its unsent glory, was her text telling Mike she couldn't make it, complete with the typo she'd never fixed before Lois had interrupted her. Just above the unsent text were the three messages Mike had sent her checking in on her whereabouts. Dylan could feel the bile and coffee in her stomach start to claw their way up her throat, visions of being sick all over Steve swimming in front of her eyes. Luckily, the elevator doors began to slide open. A few more inches and she was free.

"You look pale. Are you sure you're well?" Steve asked again, concern wrinkling his nose.

"Totally sure." The doors were finally open wide enough for her to turn sideways and squeeze through. Glancing back at Steve, she added, "Forgot something in the car."

She sprinted through the lobby and pressed the car key's unlock button as soon as she felt the drizzle hit her face. Throwing her bag on the passenger seat, she slammed the door before she let a scream rip through her. Gulping in cool car air, Dylan gripped the sides of the seat as if it were her only hold on reality. The windows began to fog up with her body heat, and the panic started to subside. With its disappearance came the feeling of physical illness.

Mike wasn't meant to be a casualty in all this. She envisioned him showing up for the meeting, jittery with enthusiasm, all good natured with warm smiles. He'd probably sat in the stupid lobby waiting for her, sure she would stroll in any moment, his confidence dripping to the floor with each passing minute. Eventually realizing he'd be taking the meeting alone. She was supposed to be by his side. It was such a small ask, and she had told so many big lies to make him ask it.

Dylan's eyes were burning. Tilting her head back, she pressed the heels of her hands into them. She wasn't going to cry about any of this. Not Technocore or Kaplan or Mike. As she opened her eyes again, her heart squeezed. She had to call him and apologize or at least try to explain herself.

Dylan didn't turn on the car, hoping the chill would keep the nerves at bay. Biting down hard on her lip, she found his number, closing her eyes briefly as she hit the little green call button. After two rings, she began hoping she could leave a voice mail. Maybe he was in a meeting and she wouldn't have to—

"Hello."

"Hi, Mike." She paused, feeling the disappointment that came with an unwanted answered phone call. "It's Dylan."

"Hey." The reticence in his voice stung. "What happened to you yesterday?"

Dylan's heart dropped a few inches toward the snakes twisting in her stomach.

"I'm so sorry. Tim came up with this whole appreciation scheme, and of course it was doomed, and then I tried to text you, but I got interrupted and I forgot to hit send—which I know sounds bad. Then Tim kept me busy all day, and . . . yeah." Dylan let her insufficient, rambling explanation die off.

"So you couldn't call?"

"No." Dylan shook her head, trying to organize her thoughts, remorse threading through her. "I mean, yes."

"It's fine. It was just awkward. He had no idea why I was there." Mike's tone was so different from Jared's. There was no screaming or threats. He was quiet, as if he was leaving space for her to say something that would make it make sense. The softness implied a reset button Dylan couldn't find.

"I was so involved I lost track of"—Dylan squirmed in her chair, looking for an emotional loophole—"literally everything."

"It's just . . ." Mike paused, and Dylan could almost see him rubbing the back of his head, his mouth quirking uncomfortably, as if searching for the right words caused him physical pain. "It just struck me as odd. Then our admin started calling other people on the list, and most of them had no idea who you were; they hadn't even heard of Crescent." The color drained from her face, leaving an empty gray to stare at her from the rearview mirror. Static appeared where her brain function should have been, the last of Mike's sentence coming through as though muffled. "Do you know any of those people? Or did you just make the names up?"

The sound that cracked out of the back of her throat was supposed to be the word *I*, but the vowel never materialized. Mike paused again, allowing more time for her gurgle to turn into a sentence.

Clearing her throat, she said, "I can explain."

"Okay."

"My friends helped me." The fog over her brain seemed to thicken as her lungs tightened. Dylan turned her focus just outside the car windshield, homing in on the little blue badge scanner near the front entrance to the office, and started again. "I thought I'd have time for them to make introductions, before everything went haywire. But I didn't. I messed up. Big-time, and I owe you an apology. I'm sorry."

"Why wouldn't you mention that? I rearranged our biggest fundraiser betting on this." A wave of genuine hurt washed over Mike's words, halting as he tried to process the deception. "The event is two weeks away. There are actual children's developmental opportunities at stake. You could have been honest with me about it. My job. My coworkers' jobs. Why do this?"

Dylan's heart collapsed as he pushed aside her apology. She could almost feel the weight of his lost trust seeping into her, scanning through the scattered bits of reason and trying to create a coherent story line for her.

She struggled to apologize to Mike again, feeling unable to find the phrase she needed. "I don't have a good reason. I wanted to help you, but I got in over my head everywhere else. Honestly. That's it. That's the truth. I'm sorry."

"Help me out here. I'm trying to understand what went wrong. Did I do something?"

Frustration took root in her chest and began creeping its way down her spine, numbing her senses as it went. She didn't know how to explain her life. Couldn't he just accept *I'm sorry* without needing a PhD's worth of understanding around her mistake? *I'm sorry* was literally all she had left to give, and he just couldn't accept it. She snapped, "Were you listening? You didn't do anything. It wasn't even about you."

Mike drew in a sharp breath. Dylan imagined the tension pulling across his shoulders as she listened to him exhale. "You are right. I'm sorry I phrased it that way. What I want to ask is how can I—"

"No." The word slammed against her brain so hard it felt like she hadn't even thought it before it came out of her mouth.

Dylan was done with being manipulated. First, Nicolas with the thinly disguised threats that were supposedly in her own best interest. Next, Tim with the incessant need for cleanup on aisle stupid. Then Jared, shouting outsize demands.

Whatever nice-guy mental jujitsu Mike was capable of, Dylan was not in the mood. She'd messed up, and she'd admitted that. The last thing she needed was another person making her feel bad. There was no possible way that he was sincerely being nicer than she deserved. Not with their family history. This was just another ding in her fantastically shitty trip back to the hellhole that was her hometown.

"I got in over my head, in every possible way," Dylan snapped. "I had to let something drop. Actually, I let everything drop. You were just the by-product of my own personal hurricane."

"I . . . I'm sorry. I don't understand what's happening."

Did he have to apologize? Dylan seethed, her thoughts moving through her unfiltered. Ignoring the roiling in her stomach, she plowed on, her voice rising half an octave.

"I hold it together and follow the rules and be reliable. All those rules and all that order—what did it get me? A cyclone client and a bitch-ass boss." Dylan slapped her hand against the steering wheel. "Worse, I break a few small rules, and I get a one-night stand who is too nice for his own good but can't accept an apology without some long-winded explanation, which I don't have, by the way. Oh yeah! And a floodlight in my decrepit ruin of a childhood bedroom window."

The silence on the other end of the line felt like Mike was working on a mental Rubik's Cube. He exhaled heavily. "Okay, let's deal with those one at a time." His tone was like that of a man talking to a child having a meltdown in the grocery store. Extreme frustration wrapped in a soothing balm. "I'm not asking you to marry me. I'm asking you to be honest with me. Where is this coming from?"

"It isn't coming from anywhere. It is me. I'm a disaster. Just as destructive and dysfunctional as the rest of my family."

"I don't believe that."

"Then you're an optimistic fool." She laughed, the sound hollow. Clenching her jaw, she said, "I can't with you."

"I'm trying here, but I've got a mess on my hands at work." Mike's tone was clipped. Taking a deep breath, she prepared a retort, but this was his breaking point, and he did not leave her the room to continue. "I'm expending massive amounts of energy trying to reason with you right now, and I don't think it's getting anywhere. It sounds like you have some things you need to work out." Mike paused, and Dylan could hear him pacing his office, attempting to regain composure. "Independently."

"Fine." She felt her eyes sting and rubbed them with her free hand. She just needed to get through this conversation; then she could go home and crawl into bed for a year and forget everything.

"At least we are on the same page here," Mike muttered under his breath. "Look, I'm not interested in being a scapegoat or a punching bag or whatever it is you are doing." It sounded as though he had stopped pacing, and his tone softened again. "I care about you. So how about you call me if you work things out or if you want real help working things out. Okay?"

Her heart squeezed, but she had little to say in response. Luckily, her mind was still storming, and she let that carry her through the conversation. "I don't need help."

"All right. Talk to you later," Mike said, his tone heavy. He waited a beat for her response before hanging up the phone, further irritating her. Even his brush-offs were reasonable.

Worse, Mike had sounded sorry too. Glancing at herself in the rearview mirror again, she scowled. She was still an ashy shade of I-just-got-fired green, and any blood left in her face had made its way to her cheeks, reminding her of sinister clowns in movies. The whole look added to her growing sense of horror. What had she done?

In the mirror, Dylan almost didn't recognize herself. What kind of person tore into someone for asking reasonable questions? Her heart plummeted as soon as the words *optimistic* and *fool* circled back to her. Mike didn't deserve to be treated like that. Hadn't Jared just shouted at her for pointing out that he was overreacting? Yet here she was, unreasonably angry at Mike for . . . what? Being kind.

"Holy shit, that was mean," she whispered to herself, nausea washing over her as other parts of the conversation came back. *One-night stand who is too nice?* Those words had come out of her mouth, and she hadn't even meant them. Those words were so hurtful. They were cruel. She was a lot of things, but cruel? Even at her rock bottom, she never wanted to be that kind of person.

Taking a sip of her cold coffee, Dylan choked back the stone lodged in her throat. Dropping the phone into her lap, she looked out the foggy windshield at the fuzzy gray of the Technocore office and shivered, a sheen of her own body heat coating the windows. After blowing on her hands, she jammed her index finger into the start button and waited for the windshield to clear.

"Damn it!" she growled at the hazy walls. She couldn't even get out of her soon-to-be ex-client's parking lot without more failure. Dylan swallowed tears down. Crying was for people who hadn't pulled themselves together after feral childhoods. Women who drove over flower beds to escape ex-boyfriends didn't cry when they threatened them. They didn't cry over disappointing new friends, shitty bosses, bad jobs, or nice-guy neighbors.

Taking another deep breath, she checked her rear windshield and tried to smile at the microscopic patch of visibility opening up. Soon she would be able to safely exit the parking lot and this hellhole of a town. She reached down for her coffee as her phone dinged again. The familiar tone of a text message asking her why she hadn't turned the thing off already. Reminding herself that she couldn't go anywhere, she picked up the phone.

Hey! Did you turn in the recommendation letter?

Dylan froze, the icy temperature outside finally reaching her veins. She stared at the little " . . . " implying there was more message on its way and tried desperately to think her way out of this.

My application page says incomplete and I know everything is in. I'm gonna call. I just wanna make sure my ducks are in a row before I start making demands. LOL!

Stacy had to know she didn't deserve the benefit of the doubt. Dylan hadn't done the letter. Feeling her body start to thaw, she typed out a response.

Holy shit. I had a crisis at work, and I forgot. I am SO SORRY.

Stacy typed back almost immediately.

But you knew the deadline

I reminded you like 50 times

All you had to say was "I'm too busy. No"

Dylan hit send on her half-finished text, eager to get something out there.

I'm so sorry. I'll call them and explain the whole thing

Stacy's response appeared immediately.

I'm going to have to wait until next year and reapply

I'm sure there's something I can do.

Dylan choked on the stale air in the car, willing the vehicle to finish defrosting. She continued typing, afraid to risk another catastrophic phone apology. She needed to ask for forgiveness from Stacy in person.

All my hard work? the stupid standardized tests! my other recommendations? WASTED

I'll drive over now. We can call them together.

Her head began to spin as she read her friend's reply.

Don't

Don't come over. Don't call them.

Your help isn't helpful. Stay out of it.

I'm just so sorry! Tim went off the rails and I basically got fired. Then, I fucked over Mike, too.

Dylan hit send, hoping her list of excuses would buy her the momentary reprieve she needed to reason with Stacy. But as she began typing, Stacy's reply appeared.

Not everything is about you!

Dylan felt her friend's words like a slap in the face. The truth behind them burning as much as her regret. Stacy's typing bubble disappeared as Dylan sat there, her heart breaking. She had to say something.

Feeling her fingers fumble around the keyboard, she hit send on another round of apologies.

I'm sorry.

I completely messed up.

I am so sorry.

Intellectually, Dylan knew her friend had walked away from the conversation, and she couldn't fix it. She couldn't fix anything. Not her job, her old relationship, her new relationship, or her broken friendships. Dylan felt the prickling in her eyes turn into an aggressive sting and cursed the foggy windows. Her nose started to run as a pitiful hiccup escaped her lips. Hunching low in her seat, she could almost see the road through the windshield.

If she could be anywhere else, be *anyone* else—someone with less mess in their past, less disaster in their present, and less nothing in their future—she would be. Blinking at the hulking gray outline of her former building, she gave up caring.

"Fuck it." Dylan put her foot on the brake and her car in reverse. Tucking herself into a crouch, she drove off.

CHAPTER NINETEEN

Dylan didn't bother to fix her nearly perpendicular parking job as she bolted toward the house. She fumbled with the keypad on the door as a frenetic laugh fought to escape her throat. Her mother would change the code on the one day she needed to be home. Jangling the knob in the hope that someone had left the thing unlocked, she fell off kilter as Neale swung the door open.

"Oh God. Did Dad text you too?"

"What?" Dylan blinked at her sister as she pushed herself upright using the doorframe.

"Dad and Linda are at it again over the Tiger. He is so dramatic." Neale rolled her eyes, standing aside to let her sister in.

"I don't . . ." Dylan started into the hallway, then stopped to look at Neale as she closed the door. "What do you want me to do about it?"

"Nothing."

Taking a deep breath, Dylan looked at her sister as tears started to roll down her face. She glanced over at the living room but decided the cleaning job she had done had long since lost out to Milo's fur. Instead she opted for the stairs, gracelessly flopping down as another sob shook her body.

"Dyl, don't cry. I wasn't telling you to fix it. Mom is there smoothing things over now." Neale looked at her sister with a mixture of alarm and horror as Dylan tucked her knees under her chin and wiped at her eyes with her sleeve.

"Thank you," Dylan said into her thighs, a fresh round of tears running down her face. "It's not that. I fucked up. A lot."

Neale settled next to her with more dignity than Dylan had mustered, tucking her ratty tennis shoes close to her sister's chocolate-brown heels. Leaning her head against Dylan's shoulder, Neale asked, "Can you tell me?"

In between ugly sobs, Dylan explained the entire messy affair from end to end. To her sister's credit, Neale did not ask questions. In fact, outside of trying to wipe her sister's nose with her sleeve, Neale didn't interrupt her for the first time since she was old enough to talk. As Dylan rubbed chunks of mascara out of her eyes, Neale lifted her head to face her sister.

"So there is a lot here."

"Your weeklong stint as a guidance counselor is showing," Dylan laughed, looking at the black smudges covering her hands.

"I was really more of an admin at a counselor's office," Neale corrected, a smirk creeping across her face. "I'll put it out there that I'm going to want a different set of details about Mike Robinson later. Knowing you, that requires some wine and a lot less snot, so know that I have notes."

"I might need something stronger than wine for that."

"Weed is legal as long as we aren't near a school."

Dylan giggled at the speed with which her sister replied, then fell silent, the edges of her sweater soaked with tears.

"Dylan, I think we are low enough that I can be frank," Neale said, pulling a piece of Milo's fur off Dylan's sweater. She felt her spine stiffen at the touch, although she knew it was the words that caused the tension. "You have been laid low by that sad, self-important suit wearer," Neale said, hugging her knees, subconsciously mirroring Dylan's posture.

"Which one?"

"Better question: Why do you know so many?"

Dylan looked over at her sister, who met her gaze with benign kindness etched on her face.

"Nicolas."

"I really have." Dylan sighed, sinking back into herself. When Neale didn't fill the space, Dylan felt her thoughts slide out of her mouth. "The problem wasn't really the suit. It was that his personality was his suit. A gray attempt at purchasing class."

"Dylan, that was very biting of you. I'm proud."

"Thanks. I wish I could say it was intentional."

"Okay, but here's point number two, which is out of order and wasn't actually a point I was going to make, but now seems like the time for hard truths." Neale scowled at her own digression, shook her head, and continued. "Anyway. You need to take credit where it's due. The second suit guy. Where the hell is he? You should have a whole team for this job. Instead he sent you and some vague promises about turning up. You deserve credit for all of the good stuff you did at Technocore."

"Easy for you to say."

"Stop it. You being good at your job doesn't make you responsible for Jason being bad at his," Neale said.

"Jared. But yeah."

Neale shrugged at his name as if it were an unimportant detail. "Honestly, just because I don't get your job doesn't mean I can't tell you're good at it. If Kaplan can't see that, do you really want to make partner there?"

"You're right."

"Damn right I'm right." Neale grinned. "Tell me when I've been wrong?" Dylan opened her mouth to start a list, but Neale held up a hand. "Rhetorical question."

Dylan smiled, feeling the dried tears on her cheeks stretch and crack with the unfamiliar movement. "Anything else?"

"What?" Neale asked, staring at a stain on the ceiling.

"You said that was point two. Are there more?"

"You know there is. Don't play."

Dylan felt her neck tighten again. She had been hoping to avoid a discussion where her faults were on greater display.

"Standing up your work friends, even when you are terrifically surprise busy, isn't cool. But the real question is, Why did you make those promises in the first place?"

"I just wanted to keep a lid on everything. Keep people happy. That's my job."

"Bull. Your job was to improve Technocore's image and operations. How does overpromising and underdelivering serve that goal?"

"Okay, enough with the tough questions. Are you going to be a consultant now?" Dylan arched an eyebrow at her sister.

"It looks like Kaplan may be hiring."

"Ouch." Dylan flinched.

"All right, that was mean. I'm sorry, Dylan. Too much tough love?" Neale leaned her forehead on her sister's shoulder, as if the closeness of the gesture would take the sting out of her words.

"I just finished snotting everywhere. Maybe proceed with caution for another fifteen minutes?"

"All I'm trying to say is that you wanted to fix things so badly you made it worse. It's okay to say no. Especially when the request is unrealistic given the other variables."

"God, you sound like me at work."

"No need to sling insults. You know how I feel about nine-to-five." Neale giggled, lifting her head off Dylan's shoulder to look at her sister. "Ready for the superhard stuff?"

"Yes, but be gentle. I still have at least twelve minutes on my snot timer."

Neale laughed, nudging her sister's foot with her old sneaker. "There isn't a gentle way to say this part. You messed up with Mike and Stacy. And I know you don't want to hear it, but you need to fix it."

Dylan's chin trembled, and she focused all her effort on keeping tears off her face as her sister continued.

"All the other stuff you can walk away from. Doing nothing is an option you can respect, but you can't leave them that way and sleep at night. It's just not who you are."

"I know." Her voice was timid, but Dylan worried that if she put any more effort behind it, whatever was holding the next wave of tears back would lose ground.

"Take it from me. Some relationships are too dear to let go of without a fight."

Dylan nodded and felt a few tears dislodge in the process. Neale reached up with the corner of her sweater, prompting Dylan to use the back of her hand to wipe them away and exhale a shaky breath. "You're still right."

"Like I said, tell me when I'm wrong!" She laughed and wrapped her arm around her sister. Neale was taller and her shoulders were narrower, but her arm was long enough to make room for Dylan under her protective cover. Squeezing her sister, she added, "You are good at fixing. You can do this. I wish I could fix this for you now, but I don't know how."

"I don't either." Dylan shuddered as the tears started in full force again. "I never don't know how."

Neale wrapped her other arm around her, pulling Dylan into a strange, crouched bear hug. It wasn't particularly comfortable but was comforting just the same. Brushing Dylan's hair away from her face, Neale planted a kiss on her sister's head, her hair muffling her words. "You'll try. And maybe fail. But you'll sort it."

"Thanks," Dylan mumbled into the little pocket of space between their shoulders.

"It's what I'm here for," Neale said, before releasing her sister and straightening her spine. "We have to get up now," she said, abruptly getting to her feet.

"What?"

"We gotta get up. I can see Mom and Dad coming back across the street, and you know how much Dad loves group hugs and crying together. I'm not in the mood for all of him today." Neale cringed.

Dylan laughed as her sister pulled her to her feet and tried once more to wipe her face with her sweater. She ducked under her sister's arm and smiled. "Any last words of wisdom, oh sage?"

Neale looked out the window, where their parents had stopped to admire the Tiger in the yard, putting on a show for the neighbors, before answering. "You should go get your stuff from Technocore on Saturday, before they march you out of there with a big stupid cardboard box on Monday. That is the worst."

Dylan chuckled before realizing her sister was serious. "When did you ever get packed and escorted out of a place?"

Neale blinked at her sister's question for a moment, then grinned. "Never. I saw it in a Dwayne 'The Rock' Johnson movie, though, and it looked awful." Neale put the actor's wrestling name in air quotes before shaking her head and turning up the stairs. "You coming to hide from Mom and Dad or what?"

~

Dylan steeled herself and scanned her badge to get into the office that occupied her nightmares. She had to admit there was wisdom in Neale's interpretation of the cinematic efforts of The Rock. Getting marched out on Monday would be much worse than shooting them an email saying *Thanks for the headaches. The badge is in the mail.* Her shoulders relaxed as the blue security light clicked. No one would be there to see her shred an astronomical amount of paperwork and leave with a tasteful cloth grocery bag full of possessions.

The emptiness of the place was eerie as she crept off the elevator. It looked like a cubicle wasteland, the appearance of the place growing sadder as the motion-sensor lights shuddered to life. Failed employee-appreciation certificates poked out of every recycling bin lining the hallways. More than one misnamed fleece jacket was crammed into the small wastebaskets or dropped haphazardly on the floor. To her chagrin, Richard Chou's jacket was gently placed on a hanger jammed into his cubicle wall, mocking her with its care. Shaking her head, she made her way over to her office, flipping on the aggressive overhead lighting.

"Okay, girl, you are almost through it." She said this little reassuring number to her corkboard, then straightened her posture before pushing back her desk chair and lifting a stack of papers.

After a half hour or so, her shred bin was looking precariously full, and an uncomfortable stiffness from sitting still had settled into her bones. She stretched up with a yawn, grabbed the bin, and started toward the staff kitchen shredder. A loud thud stopped her in her tracks.

"Ouch!"

A cursory glance at the computer monitors in the cubicle jungle told her that she was supposed to be alone. Shifting the weight of the box from one arm to the other, she grabbed a stapler off a nearby desk. Creeping toward the kitchen with her stapler weapon at the ready, she poked her head around the doorjamb and said, "Hello?"

The figure with his head in the refrigerator yelped and knocked it against a shelf. Yanking his head out of the fridge, Tim turned around to face her, rubbing the spot he had bumped. Next to him stood Steve, holding a cabinet door with one hand and clutching at his collarbone like he was wearing pearls with the other. His mouth was still stuck in a terrified "Oh!"

"Sorry," Dylan said, suppressing a chuckle at the sight of Steve. "I thought I was alone down here. Clearly, y'all did too."

"Good morning," Steve said, regaining his composure and letting the hand at his collarbone drop. "There is no coffee cart on weekends, so we thought we would try our hand at making some."

"I think people have hidden the coffee from me," Tim said, still rubbing his head.

"And the coffee machine, cups, and creamer?" Steve asked, rolling his eyes. "Man, no one is hiding anything. It just isn't here."

"Actually, Tim hid it from himself." She hefted the heavy box of shredding onto the counter. "When you first got the coffee cart, you got rid of all the old machines. Then you moved the cart but never replaced the machines, which was one of my recommendations," Dylan said, shaking her head with a resignation usually reserved for people who lost political races.

"I forgot about that." Tim's eyebrows shot up in surprise, while Steve gave him a sidelong glance.

"Maybe it's time to reinstate our director of operations position?" Steve's tone was so thoughtful that Dylan could almost buy the charade he was putting on for Tim. Rehiring a facilities manager had also been her recommendation. Thinking about her work, Dylan suddenly went still, imploring whatever gods were so effective at bringing rain to the city to cast their magic over her imminent departure. She had arrived specifically to avoid being escorted out by HR, and here was the head of HR looking for a coffee cup.

As if noticing the shift in the room, Steve asked, "What are you doing here on a very early Saturday morning?"

"I . . ." Her brain stalled out for a moment, and she blinked at Steve a few times to jump-start it. Failing to find a better excuse, she called up some of Neale's blasé attitude. "I was told I'd be let go on Monday. I'm here trying to organize things for the next person." Hoping to shift the mood, she added, "Don't want another Marta's-office situation."

Steve and Tim now looked like their brains had stalled and were also in the blink-to-jump-start phase. Dylan's half-hearted chuckle was the only sign a joke had even been made. She reminded herself that HR and CEOs had always been a bit of a tough crowd.

"I don't understand!" Tim sputtered. "No one consulted me on this."

"I certainly didn't authorize your leaving. Who told you this?" Steve scowled.

"My manager at Kaplan. I know things haven't gone as smoothly as we might have hoped, and I understand." Dylan's heart sank, despite her attempts at being gracious.

"That's not possible," Steve said.

"I'm afraid it is. I was told in no uncertain terms to pack my bags. Hence the weekend shredding."

Tim's expression was stoic, while Steve gave the cardboard box of documents an odious look.

"No. What I mean is, Technocore specifically negotiated our contract with Kaplan. Barring some massive act of malfeasance or extreme negligence, it is impossible for them to fire you while you work for us. Did you commit an act of fraud or corporate espionage?"

Steve asked this last question like it was a distinct possibility, forcing Dylan to bite back a laugh. "No. Of course not. I wouldn't even know where to start with fraud."

Tim shifted his weight rapidly from one foot to the next, his eyes darting between the two of them. For his part, Steve fixed her with a piercing stare, as if he were trying to compel a confession out of her with just his eyes.

"Honestly. I've filed my reports ahead of time, and I saved my receipts for everything," Dylan stammered through her dry mouth. Apparently, all the water in her body was making its way to her armpits.

Steve maintained his stone-cold expression for a beat before quirking an eyebrow and guffawing. "Of course you didn't. I see bad behavior all the time. The closest someone like you comes to fraud is reporting the person who committed it."

Dylan forced herself to chuckle, relieved she was not about to be marched out of the building. Tim, on the other hand, looked horrified. Catching sight of Tim's face, Steve doubled over, his cackle only intensified by the CEO's expression. Giving his knee a second hearty slap, he straightened up. "Man, you two have no sense of humor."

"I'm not sure there is a lot of humor in HR," Tim said, turning his nose up.

"There has to be when you're the CEO."

Both broke into a fresh round of howling, reminding Dylan of the cantankerous Muppet movie critics, Statler and Waldorf. When they finally noticed she was still smiling politely, Steve straightened up, rubbed his eyes underneath his glasses, and said, "Yeah. I'll give John a call, but how about we proceed as if you are not fired. Show up on Monday; I'll deal with the rest."

Dylan froze as she tried to make sense of Steve's words. She could see Steve looking at her with a level of nonchalance that made it sound like he unfired people all the time. Next to him, Tim beamed before glancing back at the fridge and grabbing a Coke knockoff product.

"I don't get it."

Steve shrugged. "As you know, we've had a difficult time with consultants. I know John Kaplan from my last company. Good guy. He did us a solid when no one would touch us. I'll give him a call. Honestly, I'm surprised you didn't know about the terms."

"We don't usually see the contract," Dylan stammered, a wave of relief washing over her. "Associates like me just get told where, when, and how long."

"Huh! Who knew?" was all Steve said, as Tim shrugged and took a loud slurp of his pop. "Anyway. You can stop cleaning out your office now."

Dylan's muscles relaxed to a degree she hadn't experienced in months. Her legs turned to jelly, as if she had been holding a wall sit

for hours. Her voice was the only part of her that didn't feel like it had run a marathon. "Thank you."

Unsure of what to do with herself, she started dumping the box of shredding into the bin before something struck her. "Why are you two here?"

Steve grimaced as Tim took a long sip of his pop, looking around as if no one had asked him anything. Dylan watched as the tension stretched between the two of them, until Tim finally broke under the weight of the meaningful gazes Steve was piling on.

"As you know, I made an error. And after consulting with Steve and a few others, but not you, because it turns out you thought you were fired, which explains a lot—you can ignore my emails—" Steve's indignant snort interrupted Tim. Shooting him a dirty look, Tim continued, "As I was saying. After consulting with the team, we told everyone to take the rest of Friday off, our treat. Now, we are here trying to figure out how to rebound."

"Makes sense." Pulling at the sleeves of the ugly sweatshirt she'd borrowed from Neale, Dylan looked between the two men to see if either of them cared to share more. When neither of them said anything, she asked, "What's the plan?"

"I was thinking we do an all-expenses-paid trip to Disney—"

"That's not happening," Steve said, raising a dismissive hand. "I'm thinking a staff picnic or a party cruise. Drink tickets, of course. Don't want people getting out of hand."

Dylan stopped listening. A level of stillness descended over her that would give the gold-painted street performers in Vegas a run for their money. If Steve was willing to book an expensive party cruise, surely she could find a better return on his investment. The gears of her brain began to grind over her chance encounter with Steve on Friday.

"Hang on . . . ," Dylan said, interrupting Steve's concerns about Technocore's lax alcohol policy. She had dismissed Tim's involvement in Crescent thousands of times. But did that mean she needed to dismiss

Technocore's? What if there was a way to do it? Make it bigger, even? Dylan started again, aware that the two men in front of her were waiting. "Steve, you said you met with Mike from Crescent?"

"Wait. What's this meeting?" Tim leaned in, shocked that a conversation had happened without his knowledge.

"A friend of Dylan's who was looking for me to donate to his children's museum. It's not in my personal philanthropy budget this year, but it sounded like a cool project."

"What if . . . ," Dylan said, exploring the idea as it came to her. "Okay, hear me out. The museum needs a big donation, like, more than one person can give. So what if Technocore paid for the sensory room?"

"That is a lot of money." Steve's expression was skeptical, but the words didn't sound like a hard no.

"Obviously. But I think we have a shot at redemption." Rotating her wrist to help her think, Dylan added, "What if we went even further? We could partner with Crescent to develop the program. Give everyone in the office community service hours. For example, staff get ten workweek hours a quarter to spend off site at Crescent, helping them develop the tech, install the panels, run the room. Whatever the museum needs."

"This is exciting!" Tim shouted, bouncing in his organic sneakers. Steve grabbed his collarbone again, and Dylan jumped with surprise.

"Is . . . it?" Steve finally asked, releasing his chest.

"Yes! I used to spend hours at Crescent. I love that place. Now Technocore can be intimately involved in the next phase of its development. We'll have a tremendous impact in shaping the next generation of learners and leaders in Seattle." Tim stopped shifting around and looked between the two startled members of his audience. "Write that down for the press release."

"No." Dylan and Steve spoke at the same time, drawing a look of contrition from Tim.

"I love it," Tim said, his excitement zinging around the small kitchen. Glancing over at Steve, Dylan could see he was starting to catch some of Tim's enthusiasm.

"We could launch it as a pilot. If it works with Crescent, maybe we try it with other charities throughout the region. It gives our employees the chance to get involved in something good, explore new skills, et cetera," Steve said.

"Let's call this guy now. Get Mike on the phone," Tim shouted, his cheeks turning a shade of red that was usually indicative of extreme physical exertion.

A thought jolted her like an appliance with a short circuit. What if Mike had already pulled the plug on the room and said no to the money? Surely, even if he never spoke to her again, he wouldn't do anything to hurt the museum.

"It's Saturday." Dylan hated the deadpan in her own voice, but she needed to slow this train down, lest Mike didn't want her involved anymore and it never left the station.

"So?"

"Who is going to answer?" Steve asked patiently. Clearly he was used to riding out the whiplash effect of Tim's whims.

"I see. Good point. Dylan, isn't he, like, your friend or something? Maybe we just pop by his house?"

Dylan balked, unsure of how to explain just how much she did not want to intrude on Mike at the moment. Luckily, Steve stepped in again. "Tim, that would be weird." Tim opened his mouth to argue the point, but Steve held up a hand and continued, "We can wait forty-eight hours. Let Dylan come up with an implementation plan. I'll work out numbers. You can join me for the call to tell the museum's president. Sound good?"

Dylan found herself inadvertently nodding in sync with Tim and stopped.

"Fantastic. Let's all head up to Tim's office and get cracking. We have a lot to sort out," Steve said, clapping his hands and rubbing them like a dad in a TV show.

"Do you know how to work an espresso machine, by chance?" Tim asked as they strode toward the elevator, the bounce lingering in his step. "Otherwise, maybe we should get a coffee machine or two and test them out today. You know, until we hire a new facilities person."

Dylan smiled despite herself. She had come here in Neale's hideous sweatshirt, prepared to leave as an ex-employee with exactly no friends, no boyfriend, no job, and nothing but a wardrobe covered in dog fur to show for her time in Seattle. Sure, she still had a new fling who wouldn't speak to her and no friends outside of two tech dudes, and her wardrobe was still covered in dog fur. But she had a job again, and that was a place to start.

CHAPTER TWENTY

Dylan tapped two envelopes on the edge of her desk, attempting to funnel her nerves into something less obvious than pacing as she waited for Deep and Brandt. To say Deep had been less than enthused when Dylan had stopped by her desk this morning would be a disservice to the unenthusiastic everywhere. On the upside, she hadn't been entirely hostile, so there was progress.

Her heart dropped along with the envelopes as she saw Brandt sloping toward her office door, Deep sulking behind him. Brandt turned the door handle and stuck his head around the edge. "Is now a good time?"

"Yes. Please come in," Dylan said with more animation than she felt, trying to counteract the apprehension that rolled off her intern.

Brandt's forehead creased as he opened the door an inch wider and squeezed his thin frame into the small crack. Deep gave the door a suspicious glance, then opened it wide to let herself through before closing it without any of the soft touch Brandt had used.

Dylan felt their eyes drilling a hole into her, so she tapped the envelopes on her desk twice to collect her thoughts. This had worked out smoothly when she had rehearsed it with Steve and Tim. In fact, Tim had noted that as he was a master of apologies, her plan had the patented Tim Gunderson seal of approval and an 82 percent chance of success on his "I-really-screwed-up meter." At the time it had been a good joke, but now, as she sat across the desk from the two people she had hurt, it was a lot less funny and a lot more terror inducing.

She stuffed her fear into a small corner of her mind and looked Deep in the eyes, since Brandt was studying the carpet. Setting the envelopes on their side of the desk, she said, "I wanted to give you both these in person. I had a chance to speak with Steve Hammond over the weekend, and we both agreed the pair of you went above and beyond at the retreat. This is your reimbursement, plus the interest Steve calculated. He also wanted to give you both an extra three days of vacation."

Dylan paused, taking in the look of surprise on Brandt's face and the lingering skepticism on Deep's. Bracing herself, she added the bit she had practiced over the weekend. "I can't fix that I didn't get you the money immediately. Or that I let you both down in a big way. But I can say that I value both of you, not just as colleagues but as friends." Unsure exactly how to finish, she exhaled and added, "So I'm sorry."

The fear in the corner of her mind expanded as she waited for a response. Forcing herself to sit back in her chair, she looked from Deep to Brandt and back again. Brandt also seemed to be employing a similar strategy, fidgeting in his chair, eyes darting between the two women as he reached for the check.

"What's the catch?" Deep asked, pursing her lips and leaning farther back in her chair. She left the check where Dylan had set it on the end of her desk. Noticing her posture, Brandt withdrew his hand and leaned away as well.

"I don't know that it is a catch, per se," Dylan started, then stopped as Deep's eyebrows shot toward her hairline, an I-thought-so expression clinging to every inch of her face. Feeling her stomach drop a few centimeters, Dylan sped up her explanation. "It's just, if you're amenable to it, I have a project I think would be perfect for the staff-appreciation committee. It'll be hard work, and it needs to be done in two weeks. So you wouldn't be able to use your vacation for a few weeks, if you want to work on it."

Deep's eyebrows didn't twitch back toward normal. If anything, the purse of her lips became more firm.

"That is the only kind-of, sort-of catch. I swear," Dylan said, raising her hands to display the fact that she wasn't holding any cards.

"What's the project?" Brandt asked, the curiosity in his voice betraying the indifferent look he was wearing.

"It'd be setting up a long-term volunteer program for the Technocore staff at a children's museum—"

"This is pointless." Deep cut her off, leveling a silencing look at Brandt, who'd started to lean forward at the mention of volunteering.

"Sorry?"

"I don't understand why we'd bother planning any community service when it'll just get pushed to the side again. We can't even help our own employees. Hell, our CEO doesn't even know our names."

In all her practicing, Dylan hadn't rehearsed a scenario where reluctance was the response. It wasn't that she'd thought all would be forgiven, but she hadn't expected hostility. She felt the hairs on her arms stand up and rubbed her hands over her skin, trying to calm her nerves. "I know. And I want to reiterate how sorry I am. I understand if you don't want to do it."

"I just don't see how this is any different than all the other half-baked—"

"I'm in."

Both Dylan's and Deep's heads swiveled as Brandt joined the conversation, his tone entirely different from what Dylan was used to hearing.

"But . . . ," Deep said, pausing to collect herself. She raised her hand and nodded her head in Dylan's direction as if she weren't there.

"She messed up. And said sorry. Besides, this sounds cool. You're just being stubborn." Brandt laughed as he said this, then stilled when he caught a murderous glance from Deep. Forcing his expression into something more serious, he continued, "You know you are. It's probably why the two of you are friends."

Now it was Deep's turn to explore the various colors of carpet fiber present in Dylan's office. "It just really sucked," she said, finally drawing her eyes away from the floor. "We told people we were meeting to work on an idea. And that things would be turning around. Then you stood us up. It was embarrassing," she said, crossing her arms.

"Yes, it was humiliating, but things are still looking up. You can't tell me it isn't better around here," Brandt said, his newfound confidence creeping into exasperation.

"I mean. That jacket was kind of funny. And Tim admitted he was wrong way faster. Before he'd have insisted my name was Samantha Khatri."

"And this is a chance to make something even better, Samantha," Brandt chuckled.

Dylan seized on the brief moment of levity. "Look, I can't promise everything is gonna come up roses, but I want to try. And I promise not to stand you up this time."

Deep rolled her eyes, but the tension left her shoulders as she uncrossed her arms. "Fine. What are we doing?"

Relief rushed over Dylan. Fighting the urge to jump up and hug her friends, she pushed her chair away from her desk, a sly smile creeping across her face. "How do you two feel about a field trip?"

∼

Dylan drummed her fingers on the keyboard, waiting for inspiration to strike. A small part of her had hoped she would magically run into Mike when she took Deep and Brandt to visit Crescent. But that hadn't happened, and now she was stuck trying to find words that conveyed why he should answer her call. And she had called.

Once. Then she'd chickened out after the second ring. But today was a new day, and email seemed like a much less scary medium. Or at least it had when she'd promised Tim she would get ahold of him. She reminded herself that at least Tim was excited about an idea that wouldn't make the business section of the *New York Times* for all the wrong reasons.

Rolling her head in a circle, Dylan took a deep breath and started typing.

Dear Mike:

I hope this email finds you well.

I am writing because I had the opportunity to speak with Steve Hammond about Crescent, and after careful

Dylan stopped typing, the cursor blinking at her while she laughed the kind of gut laugh that shook the tension out of her neck and made her wish she hadn't worn a skirt with a restrictive waistband. The only thing that could make this email more boring and less personal was if she attached a spreadsheet with a budget.

Settling back into her chair, she tried again.

Hi Mike,

I tried to call, but I chickened out, so now I'm sending you an email. I talked to Steve and Tim and they are super excited about working with Crescent. They want to discuss specifics and a couple ideas they have this week. Are you around today?

Dylan

She hit send before she lost her nerve. It was still a pretty chicken email, but as far as chicken emails went, at least it was honest. Using the internet to ask for forgiveness seemed gauche. Dylan wanted to apologize to his face without the threat of any of their parents interrupting them. She reasoned that if she could get to his office, she had nowhere to hide even if she lost her nerve.

Leaning back in her chair, she looked up. The office was mostly empty, save for Deep, who was running around with a notebook in a pair of killer stacked heels that said that this particular fashion major had no interest in hearing no. She and Brandt had divided up the monumental task of getting Technocore ready for Crescent's gala. He was in charge of the museum site, and she was in charge of wrangling manpower. Dylan wasn't sure how Brandt was faring, but she was certain Deep wouldn't leave him short of helping hands.

"Next up on the apology tour . . ." Dylan looked over at her phone and wrinkled her nose before picking up the poisoned device. In between Tim's excited flailing, he had managed to ask Dylan roughly 752 personal questions. For a while, she had not considered him a particularly interested party, and her answers had been mostly generic. But by question number 379 he'd started to wear her down, and by number 561 she'd confessed the whole dental school failure to him and Steve, who was surprisingly good at operating a complex espresso machine. In the end, Tim had decided to funnel his substantial let's-make-a-call energy into getting Stacy into dental school.

When asked questions about things like how he would do this and who he would call, all Tim had said was, "Don't worry about it." He'd then disappeared behind his office door for an hour and a half before reemerging with a grin and a goofy thumbs-up gesture, leaving her little choice but to hope for the best from a man whose idea of the best was always suspect.

She'd absolutely considered sitting outside Stacy's house until she came out to talk to her, but Dylan sensed that Stacy was not above calling building security if she was mad enough. Luckily, she had a gala table to fill, and Stacy could never say no to a party that required her most glamour-girl attire.

Opening her text chain with Stacy as a wave of nausea washed over her, she began to tap on the screen.

> I know you are pissed, and you have every right to be. But I think I found a way to fix this and make it up to you. Want to meet for coffee?

Coffee was not gonna sell her friend on a face-to-face meeting, and Dylan knew it. Before the message even finished sending, she started typing again, knowing she needed to send the second text off before Stacy told her to shove it.

> Or, will you be my date to Mike's fancy gala?

> If you hate my proposal, you can throw a drink at me and storm out like a Real Housewife and never speak to me again. And I promise, I will leave you alone forever after that.

Imagining her friend scowling at her phone over a *People* magazine she'd stolen from her office, Dylan held her breath and hit send on the last sentence.

> Whatever you decide, I want you to know that I am sorry. I messed up royally.

Dylan tossed her phone on the desk. It was well past time for her to head home. If she did much more tonight, she'd be the person who sent emails after socially acceptable hours. Everyone hated that person.

Glancing at her inbox, Dylan's heart stopped cold for three full beats. Closing one eye and looking away from the screen, she clicked.

Dylan,

I've cc'd Susan. She's a numbers person and can do a far better job with all of this. Thanks to Technocore for their support.

Mike

She flinched at the workplace email equivalent of *go to hell*, then relaxed the muscles in her face. It wasn't exactly the resoundingly joyful phone call she wanted. But then again, she had called him an optimistic fool, so a barely polite response was probably better than she deserved. If he insisted on being ambushed with an apology, so be it.

Dashing off a quick note to Steve with the woman from Crescent's contact information, Dylan began packing up for the night. Attempting a haphazard shrug into her coat, she fished her phone out from under a pile of papers that needed refiling after her cleaning spree. Scooping up the phone, Dylan noticed a text from Stacy. Feeling exhaustion creep into her bones, she opened the app.

This better be a damn good apology, or I'm flipping tables and throwing wine.

$\sim$

The floodlight didn't blind her as she pulled into the driveway. It should have been a sign something was off. The hairs on the back of her neck should have stood up and paid attention. But Dylan was exhausted, and it was already close to nine thirty as she made her way toward the front door. She pounded in the new code and was greeted by the absence of Milo's howls and Afro-Caribbean drum circles. "Hello?"

Milo came skidding down the hallway, tail wagging so hard it knocked painfully into the walls as he ran. In answer, laughter floated from the kitchen, causing Dylan to freeze. This was polite laughter. Not the raucous mess that usually accompanied her family's joy. She petted the dog as he jammed his nose into her kneecaps and set her coat on a hook, praying that whatever was under it was not covered in some combination of mud, food, or paint. She could hear her father speaking at the most reasonable volume he had used in years.

"What a funny way to solve the problem."

"If only she had solved it intentionally."

Dylan rounded the corner as the room dissolved into laughter, revealing none other than Linda and Patricia Robinson as their guests. Her blood pressure began to rise as she scanned the kitchen for any obvious weapons but found only a half-empty bottle of wine and four people in their midsixties crammed onto barstools. By the time her mother caught sight of her, the mixture of apprehension and curiosity must have solidified on Dylan's face, because Bernice stopped laughing and lifted her glass to her daughter, drawing the room's attention to her.

"Hello, dear. Linda and Patricia just stopped by to ask for the Tiger."

"I'm sorry?" Dylan said, looking around the room.

"Linda was at work complaining about the Tiger in the yard. When her CFO found out who our neighbors were and who made the Tiger, he nearly gave Linda a pay raise to see if he could acquire it." Patricia cackled at this, smiling at Henry all the while. "It's the perfect solution to our current stalemate. Mike's on his way to a conference, so we brought wine and an offer over ourselves."

"The joke is, Linda will still have to see it every day." Henry slapped the kitchen table as he took a sip from his glass.

"Only briefly on my way into the office." Linda laughed, then looked at Dylan's polite smile. "Did you just get home from work?"

"Yes. She has been burning the late-night oil at that job," Bernice said, unaware that she had just botched the colloquialism.

"So late. Do you need dinner? Let me get you some wine," Linda said, looking between Bernice and Dylan with concern before hopping off the barstool and making her way around the kitchen as if she had lived in the Delacroix house for years. Watching her find a glass in the kitchen was almost too much. It was like living in an episode of *Doctor Who*. At any moment the quartet of adults would time travel away from common ground and go back to the long-held tradition of passive-aggressive neighborly bickering.

Unless there was a way to maintain the common ground. The thought twisted around Dylan's tired mind as Linda poured an immaculately precise glass of wine. Not so much as a drop was left to run down the bottle.

"Here you go, hon." She passed Dylan her glass, simultaneously draining her own.

"It's getting late. We should probably get out of your hair," Patricia said, standing up and finishing her glass as well.

"We'll walk you out. You know, this was fun—"

"Actually, I have an idea," Dylan said, shooting her father an apologetic look for cutting him off.

"Oh? What's that?" Patricia said, smiling at Dylan as if she had all the time in the world for her.

"Well, it's just that if Linda's company is interested in Dad's work, I think there may be a way for y'all to collaborate with Technocore and help Crescent at the same time." Dylan paused, suddenly unsure of how to phrase her idea without raising suspicion about her and Mike's not-relationship.

"Yes?" Linda asked, filling the gap in Dylan's thinking time.

"Technocore is partnering with the museum on the sensory room. Maybe Dad would consider a large-scale digital installation, if your company would be interested in sponsoring it and a couple other things at the museum?" Avoiding the temptation to rock back on her heels, she forced herself toward the door with the hope that everyone would follow. If anyone got too curious, she would just open the door and shoo them out. Including her parents.

"I love this idea! Linda, we have got to make it happen," Patricia said, clapping her hands together tightly and bouncing in her ballet flats, the movement reminiscent of her former life as a Grambling State cheerleader. Right now, it seemed she sort of felt like Dylan's personal cheerleader.

"I think it'd be possible. Let me talk to my boss."

"Great. I can connect you to the team at Technocore who are handling the sensory room installation. Shoot me an email if you all decide it's for you. Dad, you can just come to the office with me." Dylan winked, knowing Henry would absolutely clear his schedule for an impromptu Take Your Dad to Work Day.

"I look forward to it," her father said as she reached for the door handle, mentally congratulating herself on a touchy situation well handled.

"You are so thoughtful. Does Mike know you are basically a walking, talking dealmaker for Crescent?"

All internal congratulations abruptly came to a halt as Dylan paused midmotion to process the question she had hoped to avoid. Fixing a smile on the lower half of her face, she held the door open before wading into an answer. "Nope. I'm hoping it'll be a bit of a surprise for the gala. Promise you can keep a secret?"

"This is so fun," Patricia said, overriding the suspicion brewing in Linda's eyes. Giving her wife a short shove through the door, she winked at Dylan. "I take it we'll see you all next Friday?"

"Wouldn't miss it!" Bernice called over Henry's shoulder. Her expression mirrored the suspicion in Linda's, and Dylan thought it was a wonder the two hadn't managed to be friends sooner.

"See you then," Linda called.

"Good night," Dylan said, her tone a hair too chipper for the time of evening. Turning away from the door, she left her father to enthusiastically wave and watch as their neighbors darted across the street.

Dylan waited until she heard the front door click. "Am I in *The Twilight Zone*? The Robinsons were just hanging around the house like old friends."

"Were they?" her father asked, taking his wine into the living room. He stopped to move a pile of books out of a chair before dropping into it. "I guess they were. They came over just after dinner, so they must have stayed awhile."

"Dad, it's like ten," Dylan said, following him into the room. She lowered herself absentmindedly onto a corner of the couch, half-surprised by her willingness to hang out with her parents post–Robinson interaction.

"Well, we haven't talked to them in twenty-five years. It was time for a catch-up." Bernice said this matter-of-factly. "And I dare say we all enjoyed it. Maybe we'll invite them back sometime."

"Ideally, less than twenty-five years from now," Henry said.

"Well, I'm glad you all are growing up." Dylan had forgotten her dad was a lightweight. Half a glass of wine, and he was probably feeling a happy buzz right now. The thought of her parents getting drunk with the Robinsons was too much, so she shoved it aside, sipping her cabernet.

"Besides, I hear Mike might be joining our family."

If the wine had been anything other than delicious, Bernice's words would have triggered her gag reflex. Of course Neale had told. She'd half expected her to. What she hadn't expected was for her mother to completely ignore the boundary. A small piece of Dylan began reconstructing the wall she had neglected to erect when she'd walked in the door. Caught off guard by her parents' normal behavior, she had nearly forgotten who they were. She did not feel like being ridiculed for this one. Was it unreasonable for her to want something other than an emotional disaster zone from her parents tonight?

Shaking her head, she said, "So much for sisterly secrets."

"Oh, come on. You know Neale is a narc," Bernice said, not unkindly.

"Well, if I didn't before, I do now." The smug look on her mother's face faltered as Dylan took a drink of her wine with her feet flat on the floor, ready to bolt before her parents could start on whatever invasive line of questioning they were moving toward.

"For the record, your mom and I like Mike. Always have. Much better than that slick . . ." Henry let his words trail off into his wineglass at Bernice's glare.

"Dylan, don't be mad."

"Mom, you two are privacy-invasion monsters. The anger ship done been sailed." She tried to put jokes behind her words, but Bernice wasn't fooled. She raised an eyebrow at her daughter and looked about ready to say something when her father jumped in.

"Fair point. This is your business. But we claim parental supervisorial port authority." Henry laughed at his half-baked metaphor.

"What your father is trying to say is that while it is hard for us, we can respect your privacy as you work out whatever is going on with the boy across the street." Bernice waved a hand at the front window before shifting the moment away from the levity Henry had managed to infuse. "But we do want to talk about Nicolas."

Dylan snapped, "Mom, honestly. Knowing everything else that is happening right now, do you think he is on my mind?"

"Is he top of your mind? No. But that man is treating you poorly, and he never needs to be top of anyone's mind again."

A feeling of vertigo came over Dylan as her mother's truth settled itself more firmly in her mind.

"You have always been so independent. Even when you were small, you'd get up early, and I mean very early"—Bernice laughed at the memory in this small digression, then continued—"just to iron your clothes and make sure your lunch was appropriately packed. If your sisters left their things out, you'd iron theirs too."

"You were seven going on forty-five," Henry jumped in, warmth radiating from his smile.

"What we are getting at is that, for better or worse, your father and I tend not to worry about you taking care of yourself, because you always have. Until this trip home, we worried about you having fun." Bernice's words were wrapped in a rare kindness, so unexpected Dylan was unsure how to react. A small part of her thought she could relax, while the larger part shouted that little voice down.

"It can be hard when you have a child whose orientation is so different from your own. And parenting adults has its own special set of challenges." Bernice paused, letting her head roll gently to one side, studying Dylan as she searched for the words she wanted. When she found them, she righted her posture before starting again. "Often, we aren't sure what to do with you grown girls. Since our personal ethos is to be left alone, we left you alone for too long."

"You never really needed a parent to begin with. It seemed like the natural thing to do," Henry added, stretching out his legs and wiggling his toes on the rug. "But it doesn't mean we don't care about you and aren't following your life as closely as you will let us. All three of you girls need different things. Neale requires an almost constant audience. Billie dips in and out of our safety net. But you'd rather operate without guardrails, and we want to respect that."

"And that respect will pick up again tomorrow. Tonight, we are parenting," Bernice jumped in, her tone losing its ethereal quality. "We love you. We don't want this hanging over your head. Will you please put a proper end to Nicolas's behavior tonight?"

Henry nodded vigorously at Bernice, as Dylan processed her parents' request. She had always thought of being a Delacroix as a weird brick wall in an obstacle course. A sometimes fun but mostly exhausting element she needed to climb in order to get to where she was going. It had never occurred to her that the brick wall could be there for her to lean against when she needed rest.

Everything in the room felt so vulnerable, as if their careful familial bond were hanging by a spun-gold thread. Half of her wanted to stand up, walk out of the room, and break the bond. But the small part of her that advocated for her to stay was growing louder, demanding she engage. If her parents could admit they were lost, why couldn't she? Was there so much left to lose in telling the truth?

"The thing is," Dylan started, tucking herself back into the couch, "I thought I made myself clear. It's like he isn't taking me seriously." Her shoulders rolled forward, collapsing in, as if her subconscious was trying to make her less of a target.

"I see," Henry said, his expression sobering as he leaned forward to look her squarely in the face. "And how has this been communicated?"

"Henry, what does that have to do with—"

"I'm going somewhere," Henry interrupted Bernice and rolled his eyes. The gesture was so prepubescent it looked absurd on a man in his sixties. Dylan snickered, only pulling it together when her mother caught her eye.

"Mostly texts. A few angry voice mails."

"Oh, honey. Scoot over, yeah?" Dylan pulled her shoulders back and moved closer to the center of the couch so her mother and father could squeeze in on either side of her, the three of them jammed more closely together by their height and matching shoulder width.

Rearranging the puzzle pieces of their bodies, Henry sat back, wrapping his arm around her and clearing his throat. "You tell CEOs off in emails for a living. Why not do the same to Nicolas?"

"It just seemed so childish and impersonal after dating the guy for years. We should be able to part better than that."

"True," Bernice said, throwing her arm over Dylan as well. "But I think we both know the kind of man you drive over foliage to get away from is not someone you treat like a grown man."

"If there is anything I have learned after forty years of gallery contracts, it's get it in writing. Preferably in a language you speak." Henry frowned partially as he added the last part.

Dylan decided she would rather not know the story behind that little piece of advice. "It feels draconian. Like jumping from level two to level ten at light speed." Bernice's right eyebrow joined her left as she pursed her lips. "What, Mom?"

"Well, it's not really my place, but—"

"Spit it out," Dylan said, attempting to adjust under the weight of her parents' arms. The gesture was nice, but she was getting hot under so many layers of skin and sweaters.

"It's just, if you think his behavior is level two, we need to talk about your bullshit scale."

Her father's arm tensed around her, as if shielding her from the directness of her mother's words. The squeeze around her shoulders translated to a squeeze around her heart. Her mother was right. Her bullshit scale needed recalibration, badly.

Somewhere along the way she'd started letting bad behavior control her, first with Nicolas, then with Jared, and even with her clients. As straight talking as she'd thought she was with Tim, how much beating around the bush had she done to cajole him into half decency? It was as if she had gotten so good at repackaging bad behavior that she had stopped seeing it altogether.

"You're right. Civility is just throwing good after bad," Dylan said, slowly nodding in time with her thoughts.

"That's my girl. Cut your losses." Henry announced this like she had won some sort of prize.

"Let's get this email written." Bernice jumped up and ran into the hallway.

"Now?" Dylan asked, a bit startled by her mother's sudden burst of energy.

"No time like the present. Where is your purse?" Bernice called over her shoulder.

"Kitchen," Dylan answered, not bothering to ask why her mother needed her purse.

A moment later the sound of the purse's contents scattering across the kitchen counter crashed into the living room, along with a triumphant "Ha!"

Bernice ran into the room, clutching the half-empty bottle of wine and Dylan's cell phone. She took the phone from her mother, piecing together what she was expected to do. "Do you want me to proofread it?" Bernice asked.

"Mom, no. Remember when I talked about respecting boundaries? This would be one," Dylan said, half joking as she opened her email.

"Okay, but will you at least tell us what you are going to say?" Bernice asked, causing Henry to giggle.

"We are going to work on your understanding of boundaries after I write this email. Dad, stop laughing—I can feel you reading over my shoulder, and that is just as bad."

Henry had the decency to act ashamed. Bernice, on the other hand, took a page out of her husband's book and leaned in closer to try to read as Dylan typed:

Nicolas:

I would like us to communicate through email from now on. I understand the end of our relationship is difficult, but I do not want to be threatened again. Let's keep it civil and behave like adults.

Movers are coming to the house on the 3rd to pack up and take my things away. I will be there to help supervise, and afterward, I will return my key. If there are any final bills to settle, you may email a copy of the statement to me and I will transfer you my share.

Please know that any calls or texts will go unanswered. I expect you to adhere to these ground rules in honor of the time we spent together so we can part on good terms.

Sincerely,
Dylan

"All right. Did I miss anything? Speak now, or forever hold your peace." She held the phone out so both her parents could see her screen. Henry leaned in to see the tiny font, while her mother adjusted her glasses.

"I'm happy with it," her mother pronounced, wrinkling her nose.

"Hit send. Be done with the rascal," Henry said.

Dylan's finger hovered over the screen. Before she could start the downward spiral of second-guessing her second guesses, she shut her eyes and pressed her index finger down, then opened them just in time to see the little blue line finish scanning across the screen. No turning back.

Bernice let out a whoop and jumped up. "I'm so proud of you."

"Me too!" Henry said, reaching over and smothering Dylan in the big hug she suspected he'd been holding off on administering until this moment.

"Thanks, Dad," Dylan said, burying her head into the sweater that was steadily causing her to overheat. When she finally looked up, she saw her mother was still holding the bottle of wine she had retrieved from the kitchen.

"I have to say, Linda and Patricia have good taste in wine. Anyone fancy a celebratory Dylan-just-kicked-him-to-the-curb drink?"

Retrieving her empty glass from where she had set it on a bookcase, Dylan smiled. "Just think, Mom, when Mike and I get married, that could be your Christmas gift for the next thirty years."

Bernice froze midpour to look at her daughter. Henry began to make small, strange sounds that alternated between joy and a cat caught in the dryer. Dylan counted to ten before letting her stoic expression crack. "And you two thought I couldn't make a joke."

Without waiting for her parents to finish processing, Dylan began laughing and grabbed the bottle. With a smile, she finished pouring herself a glass, certain that her parents would catch up on the joke and add a few of their own when they were ready.

CHAPTER TWENTY-ONE

It was common wisdom among Seattleites that it only truly poured on special occasions. As Dylan nudged the car door open with her elbow and grabbed a fistful of slate chiffon, she had to admit there might be more than superstition attached to that belief. Her choice of dress had seemed so reasonable in the cool, dry comfort of an upscale boutique, but as she tried to wedge herself and an umbrella out of the car, she had second thoughts. Deep had convinced her that with her height, something floor length would be showstopping. Now, she wished she'd gone for a cocktail dress.

Dashing to the museum's front entrance, she clicked the lock button on the key and listened for the horn's telltale beep before forcing her way through the museum's front door and letting her skirts fall to the floor. She marveled at the great hall, which had been transformed. The bright daytime fluorescent lighting had been replaced by jewel tones, carefully offset by playful pink, orange, and red uplights. Shimmering drapes hung over the usual posters and advertisements, giving the space a warm, magical hue.

"Thank God you are here!" The sound of Deep's heels clicking against the marble drew Dylan's attention away from the umbrella clasp she was doing battle with.

"You look amazing," Dylan said, giving up on the snap and setting the umbrella in the holder as her friend came skidding to a halt in front of her. The dress Deep had chosen was a black-and-hot-pink color-blocked number that perfectly brought out the rich undertones in her skin. The dress was long sleeve but was cut short, and in true Deep fashion, she had paired it with sky-high bright-pink shoes that showed off her legs and matching pedicure. Even her lipstick matched the shade of pink running through the paneling on her dress.

"Of course I do. You clean up pretty nice yourself. I was right about that dress, wasn't I?"

"It was a bear to get on. Not to mention getting in and out of the car." Dylan shook the glamour wave out of her face as she said this, then smiled at her friend. "But yeah, you were right."

"You look like a 1940s goddess. Very Black Katharine Hepburn. Now we just need Latin Spencer Tracy to show up."

"You can't call him Latin Spencer Tracy," Dylan hissed at her friend.

"Why not?" Deep said, throwing her arms up. "He is Latino. Besides, *brown Spencer Tracy* sounds stupid."

"Because other people will hear you. And then they'll know about him and . . ." Dylan gestured to herself, checking to make sure her voice wasn't carrying.

"You are acting weird enough. Whispering is a dead giveaway."

"I never should've told you about him."

"You're right. But you did," her friend said cheerfully. "Now, I need you in the room. We kicked the museum staff out a few days ago so it'd be a surprise, and I need all the extra hands I can get." Deep hooked her arm through Dylan's and began dragging her toward the sensory room.

"The thing starts in like twenty minutes. You're not ready?" Dylan felt her heartbeat pick up, and she quickened her pace.

"Do I look like an amateur? Of course we're set. Brandt just needs your opinion on the run of show." Deep tugged her down the corridor that led to the sensory room. Dylan stepped onto a blue carpet that had been rolled out and roped off as if she were attending a Hollywood party, complete with dim lighting to add to the mystery of what lay behind the big wooden doors. "Now you get why I insisted on the dress." Deep winked as she pushed on the heavy doors.

Members of the catering staff were hustling left and right, positioning event programs, arranging silverware, and setting out place cards. But the bustle of human activity was nothing compared to the electric hum of technology that touched every corner of the room. The walls and floors had been redone, and massive projectors hung from the ceiling, painting the room in the gray-blue light of a thunderstorm. Clouds and lightning crashed across the walls as the actual sound of pouring rain echoed around her, placing her right in the eye of the storm. The only thing missing was the water itself.

In the center of the room, Brandt stood holding a tablet and shouting instructions over the thunderstorm at Sobbing Frank from the admin team, who scurried over to the tech booth to remotely adjust the projectors a fraction of an inch higher. As Brandt stepped back to survey the progress, he caught sight of Dylan and waved broadly, dashing between chairs to get to her.

"I want a second opinion," Brandt said, skipping the standard greetings, as Deep rolled her eyes. "Deep says start with thunderstorms, but given the weather, I think it has got to be the jungle theme."

"First, this is amazing," Dylan said, rotating 360 degrees. "I can't believe you two pulled this off."

"I didn't sleep," Deep said.

"This is just the prototype. Wait until we get the LCD screens, misters, and heat lamps in here. It's gonna be killer." Brandt's enthusiasm was almost reckless.

"He didn't sleep either." Deep managed a deadpan before cracking up, forcing Brandt back into serious decision-making mode.

"Ignore her. So the room is set to a fifteen-minute timer with a transition over forty-five seconds so that the shift isn't too abrupt for guests. My concern is—"

"Wait. The room changes?" Dylan interrupted him, stunned.

"Well, yes. That's the whole point." Brandt's tone implied Dylan was a bit too slow on the uptake.

"I mean, I know. I just didn't expect we could make all this happen so fast."

"Do you think Technocore is full of newbies?" Deep asked, incredulous. "Of course we can make it happen fast. If the giant screens didn't need to be custom made halfway around the world, we could have executed the whole thing in forty-eight hours." She was using sarcasm to play it cool, but pride was rolling off her.

"My bad." Dylan held up her hands in a mea culpa. Happiness squeezed her chest. She'd helped come up with something that everyone at Technocore could get behind. For a lot of people, tonight would be the first night in a long time that they could be proud of where they worked. She gestured at Brandt, who was squinting up at the projectors again, and said, "Continue."

"Yes. Sorry," Brandt said, shaking his head and pulling his focus away from the projector. "Like I was saying, given the weather, I think a jungle theme is the best place to start the loop."

"Then let's start there."

"I mean, there is the concern that the green may be too jarring—"

"Trust your instincts," Dylan said, using her best calming voice.

Brandt looked as though he might argue when a man in a coat that matched his silver-gray hair appeared, bearing a tray. "Ladies," he said, nodding, and then turned to Brandt. "Sir. We are about to open the doors. A glass of bubbly before guests officially arrive?"

"Yes please!" Deep said, snagging a glass with each hand and passing one to Brandt, who was looking more concerned.

"Thank you," Dylan said, taking a glass.

"Happy to help. My name is Trent. I'm your head server for the evening. Anything you need, just come find me."

With a slight flourish, Trent made a crisp turn and nodded at two members of the waitstaff, who reached for the giant doors. A jazz trio over in the corner began to play as the tech team in the back brought the sound of thunder down to a low rumble.

"But I could be wrong." Brandt jumped back in as soon as Trent was out of earshot. His brow crinkled, the confidence he had gained in the last few weeks beginning to vanish as the clock pelted toward showtime.

"You won't be." Dylan patted him on the arm. "I can feel it. Tonight is going to work out."

Brandt nodded, still looking gray around the edges, but pressed a button on his tablet, changing the walls to a dense, moving jungle scene. A big cat began stalking around the room, right as the heavy wooden doors were propped open, admitting the first guests.

"The jungle is fantastic. You were right," Deep said, nudging Brandt with her elbow and wiggling her eyebrows, drawing a cautious smile out of him. "Now, put that thing away, and let's have some fun."

"Cheers," Dylan said before the three of them took a sip.

Deep twitched her nose at the bubbles, then smiled, looking over Dylan's shoulder. "Go get 'em, tiger," she said and looped her arm through Brandt's, tugging him toward the party without another word. As soon as Dylan turned around, she caught the short, sparkly streak of light headed in her direction and knew what Deep meant.

Stacy was weaving around the big circular tables, working hard to suppress the look of wonder on her face. It almost worked, except for her eyes, which were following a big cat around the room.

Dylan was horror-movie terrified. She'd hoped Stacy would be late so she could find Tim and figure out exactly what he'd meant by "I know a guy" before her friend arrived. Instead, she felt like the miles of fabric in her dress were melting, and soon she would be an emperor wearing some clean underpants and very few explanations.

"You came," she called to her friend in a bald attempt at beating back nerves.

"Well, yeah. I do what I say I'm going to do."

Dylan's smile faltered. "I deserved that."

"Yeah," Stacy said, stopping in front of her friend and looking down. "Don't get me wrong. When I got the call this morning, I was jumping up and down. I'm super happy. But, like, that wasn't cool." Dylan couldn't help feeling like she was missing nearly every edge of a thousand-piece puzzle. Interrupting her friend to admit she didn't understand what she meant seemed like a surefire way to get forgiveness revoked, so she stayed silent. Stacy crossed her arms. "How did you do it?"

"Do what?"

"The UW called and said there was some sort of glitch that made it look like they hadn't received my full application when they had. The thing is, I know you didn't write the letter. I mean, obviously I didn't tell them that."

"Glitch?" Dylan said, dropping all pretense of knowledge. "Honestly, I talked to Tim to see if he knew anyone who could make a call. I had nothing to do with . . . oh." She trailed off, thinking about how long it had taken Tim to make that particular call. The guy wore a headset and kept his feet on his desk; she couldn't imagine a call taking him more than seven minutes.

"What?" Stacy had forgotten to look angry and leaned in, waiting for Dylan's explanation.

"I don't think Tim made a call," Dylan said, looking sideways around the room before leveling her suspicion. "I think he caused the glitch."

"That doesn't make sense."

"I figured a guy that rich had some pull. But the call took him forever to make, and when I asked about the details, he said not to worry about it. At the time, I thought he just didn't want me to feel bad about however much money he had to give them. But I don't think he gave any money."

Reaching out, Stacy began rapidly patting Dylan's arm, her excited dance causing her gold sparkly heels to flash across the floor. "Oh my God. Your boss reprised hacking for me?"

Her whisper-shout carried to a couple placing their purses at a nearby table; they looked up. Raising a silencing hand, Dylan nodded, praying that admitting her boss might have committed a felony wouldn't be the final straw that broke the friendship's proverbial back. Stacy stopped for a second and glared at the couple, who moved on after a few tense blinks. Turning back to Dylan, she started vibrating off the floor, her words a gush of air. "That is so cool!"

"You're not mad?"

"Heck no. It isn't like he got me accepted. He just made sure the red tape didn't stop this woman from getting a fair shake."

"Seriously?" Dylan asked, forcing the hope in her voice under wraps. The last thing she wanted was to rush a friendship recovery, only to have it come back and bite her in the backside like all her other promises.

Leaning in conspiratorially, Stacy smirked. "I'm obviously qualified, and besides, who else can say that a world-renowned hacker and millionaire helped them with their grad school application?"

Dylan laughed. "I promise you I had no idea he was going to fix it like this, but I'm really glad he did." Gathering her courage for the hard part, she added, "Stacy, I'm so sorry for what I did to you. I've been a terrible friend. Not just because of the letter but for missing visits home and not making time to see you. What's wild is that until last week, you were about the only person in Seattle that I wanted to see, and I still didn't give you the time or attention you deserved."

Stacy's kind expression twitched ever so slightly, as if hearing Dylan apologize touched on something deeper. "It's no big deal. Seriously, it all worked out."

"No, it was a big deal. What you said was hard but true. I was selfish. I made everything about me and my work and my relationships, and you paid the price for that."

Looking down for a moment, Stacy let one of her heels wobble back and forth as she took a deep breath. "I'm sorry I said it like that, though. I was just so mad at you. Like, yes, what happened was bad, but I knew you were stressed out."

Dylan smiled as hope filled the cracks in the insecurities of their friendship. The two of them would be okay. Maybe even better, more honest friends now. Watching Stacy's expression carefully, she said, "Can we agree to forgive each other?"

"Yes. Not gonna lie—I missed you, girl." Stacy held her arms out wide for a hug, and the gold sequins on the long sleeves of her dress scratched Dylan's arms. In that moment, she couldn't have cared less about being mauled by a dress. If she never got another hug from her friend, this would be all the hug she ever needed.

Backing away, Dylan fanned her eye makeup, hoping to dry any tears before they did real damage. When she made eye contact with Stacy, who was carefully patting her eyeliner, the pair burst into a wet round of giggles.

"I was so heartbroken over what I did to you." Dylan sniffed twice, still fanning her face with one hand and taking a sip of champagne with the other.

"Oh, I know. I had drinks with Neale yesterday. I was on the fence about rolling through, but then she mentioned Mike and Linda and Patricia. And seriously? We need to catch up."

"Neale is the worst secret keeper ever," Dylan laughed, turning her head and catching sight of the door.

Each muscle in her body hit pause. Mike was standing dead center of the blue carpet, flanked on either side by an elegant older woman. The three of them stopped, wonder written on their faces, as the room began its transition from jungle scene to underwater ocean, the brilliant greens transforming to gentle blues. The aqua light cast shadows over his face, making the angles of his body sharper, from the cut of his high cheekbones to the way his dark suit hugged his waist.

One of the donors elbowed Mike, who was squinting up at the ceiling, directing his attention to a school of fish dancing around the room toward her.

"Oh no." Dylan jumped as their eyes met, jerking her head back toward Stacy with a squeak.

"Ack," Stacy said, following Dylan's eyes to the door.

"Maybe he didn't see me."

"You're six feet tall, and the room is empty. He saw you." To her friend's credit, Stacy angled her body toward the door, as if her miniature stature might shield Dylan from sight and buy her more time to think.

"Holy shit. I'm not ready for all this. Maybe I can hide until it's over?" Dylan whispered, trying to smooth the bodice lines in her dress.

"Wait. You managed to re-up his entire party, and now you are too scared to take credit for it?" Stacy asked, sucking noisy air through her teeth.

"Pretty much. I was so mean. And I flaked. It was way worse than what I did to you, trust me."

"Is he still looking?"

"I don't know," Dylan said, consciously keeping her eyes away from the door.

"Well, I can't turn and look. That's too obvious. Do a casual laugh and glance or something."

"That sounds silly."

"This *is* silly," Stacy said, rolling her eyes. "Just do it."

The sound Dylan forced out of her throat was more like the mangled chuckle of a children's movie villain than a laugh as she pushed the glamour wave out of her face while looking at the door.

Mike was saying his goodbyes to the two elegant women. Straightening up, he looked directly at her and began walking toward them, occasionally waving at a few guests as he crossed the room.

"He is coming." Panic tinged Dylan's attempt at a whisper.

Stacy grinned. "I can get the details later. You're gonna need a little liquid courage for that one. Drink up."

"Don't leave me," Dylan said, reaching for Stacy's arm as she turned to go.

"I have to get me one of those," she said, dodging her friend's grasp and pointing to Dylan's drink. "And look, the family is here. I'm just gonna say hi."

"You are the worst," Dylan hissed as her friend trotted away.

"Don't I know it. Luck," Stacy called over her shoulder, waving at Dylan's parents, Neale, and the Robinsons.

Dylan risked a fleeting glance over at Mike, who had been momentarily sidetracked by another guest. Weighing her options, she decided she would rather face the uncomfortable truth head-on than wait for it to come to her. After all, Stacy was right. She had done all of this for him, and whether or not he forgave her, she could leave here with her head high, knowing she'd made good on her word.

Pulling her shoulders back and her chin up, she grabbed the hem of her dress with one hand and her champagne with the other, making her way toward him. Mike nodded to the guest and turned, his expression inscrutable as he righted himself. Dylan's heart completed a backflip that would have landed her full marks at a gymnastics competition.

"What are you doing here?" an angry voice cawed in her left ear, causing her to choke on a fortifying sip of champagne. Whipping her head away from the hot sound, she staggered back before turning to face the speaker.

Jared stood in front of her, his stocky frame humming with rage. If Dylan hadn't been so shocked by his unexpected appearance, she would have found the sweat running down his faux tan funny. As it was, seeing his Coppertone failure wasn't exactly the good time she had planned for the evening.

"Excuse me?" Dylan said, attempting to regain her composure.

"You were fired. Now you are wandering around Kaplan's party. Leave."

"It's technically Crescent's party."

"Bullshit."

"What's bullshit is you firing me from a contract you couldn't fire me from," Dylan said, surprised by her own directness. Casting a glance over her shoulder, she saw Mike stop walking toward her, his head cocked to one side as he watched Jared rock forward on his heels.

"That," Jared sputtered, "is not true."

"That is not what Steve said when I went in to clean out my office."

"I don't know who this Steve is, but if you aren't out of here in ten seconds, I'll get security."

"What are you doing here?" Dylan said, ignoring the threat.

"I was personally invited by John Kaplan." Jared puffed up at the mention of the company chairman's name. "God forbid he see you. I'm going to do you a favor. Salvage your career and get the hell out of here before he realizes—"

"Dylan!" Tim's tenor carried from across the hall as he hustled around the room. Steve and a couple of polished individuals Dylan didn't recognize trailed behind him, cocktails in hand, jokes written on their body language.

"Hi, Tim." Dylan waved. She turned around to face Jared, who had gone pale at the sight of Tim's joy.

"Isn't this just fantastic? It's even better than what I envisioned." Tim's pure enthusiasm for the project had not waned. He stretched out his arms for a hug.

"It is. I'm blown away by everyone's hard work," Dylan said, dipping in for a quick embrace.

"I wish I were a kid just so I could experience this through their eyes." Tim sounded choked up.

"Dylan, this is fantastic," Steve said as he reached the small group, giving her a side squeeze. Jared squeaked and rocked back on his heels. Steve paused momentarily, but when Jared didn't explain himself, he continued, gesturing to the man next to him. "Have you met John Kaplan?"

A big blue whale reflected back at her from a pair of wire-rimmed glasses that had fallen out of fashion roughly ten years ago. They were set atop a slightly crooked nose attached to a face with a ring of peppered gray hair around an otherwise completely bald head. The entire picture was that of a very rich, very friendly monk. Not exactly the perfectly attired, reclusive partner she had imagined.

Fighting to keep the surprise out of her tone, Dylan extended her hand. "I haven't had the pleasure. So nice to meet you, Mr. Kaplan."

"Pleasure is all mine. And please, call me John," he said, flashing a set of incredibly white and uncomfortably perfect teeth. "Steve tells me you have been doing some fantastic work up here."

"A regular one-woman force of nature." Tim smiled, taking a sip of his drink.

"That just warms my heart. I wouldn't expect anything less from a young lady with such exquisite taste in dresses," said the woman standing next to John. Extending a hand to Dylan, she said, "Estelle Kaplan." If John was the stuff of legend, his mother was the legend itself, and her neck-to-floor black beaded dress looked like it. Dylan smiled and sent a silent thank-you to Deep and her degree in fashion merchandising.

"She is always in that office hammering out idea after idea, getting Tim and me in line, despite our best efforts. Alone, no less." Steve grinned as he said this.

Next to him, Jared made additional sputtering sounds, causing Tim to pause midsip and begin an appraisal of him that read distaste when Jared switched to heavy breathing.

"Jared, is that you?" John smiled at him as if he was just noticing the man.

After wiping his hands on his suit pants, Jared extended a meaty fist to John. "Yes, Mr. Kaplan. So good to see you again after last year's managers' summit. Thank you for the invitation."

"Oh! You work at Kaplan," Tim said, taking in Jared's face, which was slowly transitioning from red to deep mauve. Holding out his hand, he said, "Tim Gunderson, CEO of Technocore."

Jared's eyes looked like a cartoon character's, popping out of his head as Tim mentioned his name. When Jared didn't move, Tim tried again, earnestly asking, "Are you in the Houston office?"

Jared looked like he might begin to foam at the mouth. Undeterred, Tim threw Dylan a meaningful look as if to telegraph his attempt at good social skills before saying, "Dylan's been with us for almost two months now. Do you know her?"

Jared barked and shook his head before answering, "We've met."

"You and Dylan? Of course, you—"

"No. You."

Mother and son exchanged loaded glances; question marks creased across their foreheads.

"I don't think so," Tim said, taking a step back and looking concerned. "Are you all right? Need some water, maybe?"

"No . . . I . . . we . . ." Jared grasped at strangled words before finally spitting out, "I've been at Technocore. Must've missed me."

"I'm pretty sure I'd have seen you." Tim looked alarmed as Jared fanned his purple face. "Let me flag down a waiter."

"No need. I believe he is leaving," John said, looking over at Estelle, who nodded in approval. "Just tell me before you go—how was the golf vacation? Or should I ask about the trip to Mexico? Maybe that visit to your mother's house in Florida?"

The room shifted under Dylan's feet, and she put a steadying hand on a nearby dining chair to make sure she didn't topple over.

The massive reports she should have written with a team. Jared's cagey behavior. Everything clicked. Was he that stupid? Had he really gone on vacation and tried to fire her before anyone could figure him out?

"I'd never," Jared said, the indignation in his tone bordering on ridiculous.

"Spare me. Steve called last week," Estelle said. Her voice was barely above a whisper, but it rang with the kind of threat that only a woman who'd built a company with nothing but her wits could lay out. "The only question is exactly how we fire you. It is in your best interest to come clean. Otherwise, there will be more consequences for you than there were for Bernie Madoff."

Shaking her head, Dylan let go of the chair so she could look Jared in the face. "I should have known."

"Don't you dare imply—"

"Tread carefully." Estelle's interruption was sharp. When Jared stopped speaking, she placed her hand on Dylan's shoulder and nodded for her to continue.

A slow smile crept across her face as Dylan recalled the threatening emails, the irate voice mails, and their conversation earlier. "Jared. I'll do you a favor. I'd hate to ruin your career, so I'll give you ten seconds to leave before I call security."

She smirked as Jared recoiled and opened his mouth to respond but couldn't. Instead he stood there shaking, clenching and unclenching his fists as if they might resolve this for him.

"You heard the lady," John said, stepping aside so he could pass.

The gesture seemed to jog Jared into speaking. "Surely you can't think—"

"One." Estelle began to count. "Two."

Jared yelped, "I refuse to be dismissed in this manner. I demand—"

"Three."

"Think of your career, Jared," Dylan said, a hint of a smile betraying her.

"Four."

"This ten count is for you to get yourself to the parking lot. It isn't a generous timeline to argue and then head for the door," Steve said, his forehead wrinkling with a scowl.

"Five."

Looking around the group one last time, Jared shouted, "I'll see you on Monday." He pointed a stubby finger directly at John and froze in a dramatic attempt at a stare-down.

"Six." Estelle sounded bored, as if she were waiting for her manicure to dry.

When John didn't respond, Jared let out an indignant huff. Pushing past Dylan, he marched toward the door in short, bitter strides, barking at waiters to get out of his way. The staff mostly ignored him, adding to the insult. With a howled curse, he cleared the blue carpet, leaving what was left of the group and several guests staring at the hallway he'd vanished down.

"Who says charity events are boring?" Steve said, his shoulders relaxing. Tim whistled.

"I think he took that rather well," Estelle cracked.

"What a joke. Going on a golf vacation, posting about it on an open social media account, and charging drinks to the company. The jerk just forwarded along your reports as if he did the work," John said, shaking his head.

"Is that what he was doing?" Tim asked, indignant.

"Yes. And we all kept wondering why the reports were so thorough and well structured. Usually, we just ask our junior partners to fill out a one-page form and turn up for a call once a week. He was probably using your work to make the calls," John said, gesturing to Dylan.

"Amateur hour," Tim said, sipping his cocktail, prompting Steve to give him a curious look.

"Well, I'm glad to be rid of him. He was difficult before the Technocore placement; it'll be nice to have someone more reasonable to report to," Dylan said.

"I heard rumors." Estelle smiled. "I just wanted to see it for myself."

"Wait, so you flew all the way up here just to fire someone?" Dylan laughed, switching her half-full glass to the other hand so she could push her hair away from her forehead.

"Not entirely." John shrugged. "We also flew up to get a closer look at our new junior partner."

"You've already hired someone to replace Jared? That was fast."

"Oh no. We didn't hire anyone. We're promoting someone. You, in fact," Estelle said.

For a moment, Dylan was silent, trying to process what was happening. She'd walked into this evening unsure of her fate beyond the next week. Now she was being offered the junior partnership she'd been working so hard to achieve. "Thank you so—"

"Really, John?" Steve interrupted, scowling at the mother-son duo, neither of whom looked particularly upset. "We talked about this last week, and I made it clear that we were working on an offer for Dylan as chief strategic officer."

"Well, it was your fault for showing your hand when you called to confirm that she was no longer employed with us. It turns out she was, and now she'll remain that way." Estelle shrugged, a small smile playing with the corners of her mouth.

Tim's mood flipped into agitation, and he began bouncing on his toes, only slowing down to take a sip of his drink so it did not slosh so precariously close to the rim of the glass. "We can do better than them," Tim declared, leaning conspiratorially toward Dylan.

Dylan felt surprise jolt her sluggish thoughts. Turning from Tim to Steve, she began, "You want me to stay in Seattle?"

"We do." Steve nodded. "Dylan, with us, you'll have stock options. A *junior* partner doesn't have equity." Steve cast a glance back at Estelle.

"I'm sorry, darling. You are a nice young man, but I can't stand to lose," Estelle purred. "Dylan, how do you feel about being a partner?"

"We can't do better than that," Tim gasped and elbowed Steve, who held up a silencing hand, smiling as he watched Dylan think.

"I don't understand. Jared was a junior partner. And this is my first big account. Don't I need more time or experience or something?" she said, giving her head a shake.

"Why would you need more time? Steve here will hire you out from under our noses, and your level of commitment is too valuable to let go," John said, nodding affably at Steve and Tim. "We can come to a happy medium. You stay with Kaplan, and Technocore keeps you on retainer."

"That's better for everyone! More drinks," Tim said, waving at Trent as if he hadn't just lost a bidding war.

The offer was slowly sinking in, and Dylan felt the first tingles of excitement. Looking from Estelle to John, she said, "Thank you. I'm excited about this opportunity. Just one question."

"I'd be worried if you didn't have a few," Estelle said gently. "After all, this is big news."

"Do you mean full partner or, like, I get the title of partner, but I'm secretly a junior partner in all but name . . . that type of thing?"

"Oh no. We mean partner. It's clear there are opportunities for Kaplan in Seattle, but we need an office here to dig into the business. In order to do that, we need a new partner. That is, assuming you are willing to move back to Seattle." John's tone matched the kindness of his mother's.

"I . . . wow. This is a lot."

Estelle chuckled at her response. "Your work here has gone above and beyond what we usually see from our consultants. I flatter myself, but your commitment reminds me of when I first started. I'd roll up my sleeves and shovel shit if the client needed it." Laughing at the surprise on Dylan's face, she added, "Literally. My first client was a provider of septic tank systems."

"I'm honored. Really. Thank you for the offer."

"What do you say?" John asked, his arms spread wide.

Just over Estelle's shoulder, Dylan could see her family and friends, chatting animatedly and pointing at the pack of camels that had begun to cross the newly transitioned desert. They were loud and messy and constantly in her business. But they were also loving, and as much as she needed order, she also needed their chaos.

And then there was Mike.

He had stopped to talk to yet another donor, his posture slightly stooped as he spoke to a small excitable-looking man. He must have felt her gaze, because he glanced up, catching her eye. Dylan couldn't tell if the smile and nod were for the man bubbling in front of him or for her, but she knew for a fact that the flutter she felt was for him. She forced herself not to back away from the feeling. He had been kind, funny, and open with her. Thoughtful to a fault. Mike couldn't be a reason to stay, but he certainly wasn't a reason to go.

Taking a deep breath, she turned her attention back to the group. Her old highly ordered self was back in Texas. She had changed, and her new self belonged in the place she had left long ago.

"My answer is unequivocally yes. I'd be delighted to take on this new challenge."

"Fantastic," John shouted, extending his hand.

"Knew you could do it." Tim raised his glass. Dylan wanted to point out that he'd known no such thing given the circumstances but decided a smile was a better answer. Next to him, Steve grinned and patted her on the shoulder.

"We need to send out press releases and get everything settled, so you'll be split between two offices for a while," Estelle said, extending her hand. Looking Dylan in the eye, she said, "I'm delighted to have you on board."

"Thank you! I'm excited about this opportunity." Dylan's smile widened. Just over Estelle's shoulder, she could see Mike finish his conversation with the bubbling man. He met her eye and nodded. This time, there wasn't any question who the nod was for.

"I have every confidence you will rise to the occasion," Estelle said, glancing over her shoulder at what had caught Dylan's eye. "Looks like that handsome young man wants to talk to you."

"Oh no." She stumbled over her words, her face heating up as Tim, Steve, and John turned their heads to look. "That's not anyone. I mean, it is someone, obviously. But not to me. Not right now, anyway," Dylan finished, her words a flustered tumble as the group turned their attention back to her.

"Then that's a real shame for both of you." Estelle's answer was direct but kind. Turning to the gentlemen with her, she said, "Boys, let's go to the bar. Give Dylan a chance to talk with"—she coughed in a gesture so lacking in slyness that any member of the Delacroix family would have been proud—"no one."

"Really, you don't need to go," Dylan said, laughing at John's thumbs-up.

"Have fun tonight." Estelle winked at her, then looped her arm through Steve's and sashayed away with more speed and style than her sparkly dress betrayed.

John raised his empty glass and said, "See you soon," before turning to catch up to his mother.

"See you Monday, partner," Tim said as he walked by.

Dylan laughed. Remembering Stacy, she shot out a hand and caught Tim's arm. "Wait."

"What's up?" Tim asked, still looking over at the bar.

"About those 'calls' that you made for my friend Stacy," Dylan said, wrapping the word *calls* in air quotes. She now had the full weight of Tim's attention.

"What about them?" Tim said, feigning nonchalance with a poker face so awful that she would have to discourage him from entering even a charity tournament in the future.

"She was over the moon. Beyond grateful. Thank you."

Tim relaxed. "Calls are easy. It was no big deal. Really."

"Well, it's a big deal to her. And to me."

"I know I'm difficult at times, and after all you did for me, it seemed like the least I could do."

"Stacy is running around here somewhere. Short. Gold dress. Tall heels," Dylan said, looking around the crowded room. When she caught Tim gazing up at the rising sun on the walls, she gave up and said, "When I find her, I'll make sure to bring her over. I know she'll want to say thank you herself."

"Sounds good. Congratulations. Tonight is a real win for all of us."

"Thank you," Dylan said.

Watching Tim walk away, Dylan was suddenly aware of her alone-ness and the light touch of Mike's gaze. She took one more sip of champagne before lifting her head to meet it. Mike's entire posture was relaxed, as if he was completely at ease with himself and where the night was heading. Dylan felt her heart squeeze as she thought about how comforting that easy demeanor had once seemed to her and how alien it felt to be away from it so suddenly. Mike had been a calm in the storm of her own making, and without him, she felt unmoored.

Dylan exhaled, as if she were blowing out a birthday candle, then took her first step toward what she hoped was still a safe harbor. She attempted to slow down and match Mike's mellow saunter toward her, like the Hollywood dress was meant to imply. She closed the gap between them until she was close enough to see the delicate pinstripes on Mike's suit.

"All of this," Mike said, one hand still in his pocket, the other ges-turing around the room, "is incredible."

He had stopped about two feet away from her. A safe distance if he needed to run for cover. She couldn't say she blamed him.

"Thank you. It was a team effort. Deep and Brandt did a lot of the work," Dylan said, looking around the room, grasping for something to say. "And Susan from your office. She is great."

Mike wrinkled his nose at the mention of Susan's name.

"What's that face for?" Dylan asked, unable to stop herself.

"I have a confession about that." Mike shrugged, placing both his hands into his pockets. "I was at a conference in Lexington, and I was mad, so I dumped you off on Susan and told her to make whatever Technocore wanted happen. She isn't a fundraiser or even an educator. She is a mail room coordinator."

Dylan blinked at him. "Mail room coordinator?"

Mike grimaced. "I thought you were going to mail in a pity check and all she'd have to do was tell you the address."

She couldn't help it. Dylan busted up. "Seems like Susan is in the wrong role, my friend."

"I've been saying that for months, but no one would give her a shot. So I did," Mike said, relaxing as he watched Dylan shake her head. "Accidentally."

"That was a massive shot."

"In my defense, I had no idea. And none of the actual fundraisers would help me after"—he paused, choosing his words with care—"the first pass didn't work out."

Dylan tried not to let his delicate phrasing sting.

"About that." The band started a big up-tempo number, and she took a half step closer to him. She wanted to be sure he heard her the first time, because she wasn't positive she would be able to work up the courage to repeat herself. "I'm so sorry."

Mike looked momentarily surprised, rocking back on his heels and studying her. For a beat it looked like he might head for the door; then he dropped his shoulders, coming back to his relaxed stance. "It's okay. Given that guy's outburst just now, it looks like you had a lot going on."

"I mean, yes. But that is no excuse. I was wrong. And I knew I was wrong when I called you, but instead of giving you the apology you deserved, I was mean to you."

"You were kinda mean," Mike said, humor playing in his eyes.

"Kinda?" Dylan laughed. "I was so mean. Like, I was possessed kind of mean."

"You basically ate me alive. I low-key wanted to cry when I got off the phone."

"I'm surprised you didn't. I did, and I was the demon on the other end of the line."

Mike pursed his lips and shrugged. Dylan squinted up at him as his shoulders shook.

"Are you laughing at me?"

"It's just the mental image of your head spinning and vomit flying everywhere."

"Nice. Now I'm the possessed girl from *The Exorcist* in your mind. Very sexy."

"It's better than toe emojis."

"Low blow, man. Don't make me regret being nice to you."

"I noticed your toes are no longer smiling at me." Mike grinned as Dylan chuckled and shook her head. "All right. I'm sorry I made fun of your poor taste in pedicures. Continue."

"Anyway. It's . . ." Dylan trailed off, letting the last of her laughter fall away as she collected confidence from every corner of her body. He stepped a few inches into her sphere. His expression betraying his intent, as if listening to her were the only thing he needed to do for the rest of his life. "It's funny. When you weren't around, you were on my mind."

"How do you mean?" Mike asked, a tender confusion on his face.

Dylan paused to take the last sip of her champagne before setting the glass on a nearby table. "I used to need lists to get by. And you were at the very top of my no-go list."

The turn caught Mike off guard, and she rushed to make sense of herself, her words messy and fast. "But all my careful organizing let me down. I wanted to be different from my family so badly that I missed the good things in front of me. You were the bridge between chaos and the order I was looking for." She circled her hands in front of her to help her think, then added, "The feud, my family, your family. They are all easier to navigate when you are around. Everything is just easier."

Mike's confusion lessened into something sweeter. He smiled with one half of his mouth, showing off a dimple in his cheek.

"That is a lot for me, being with someone who doesn't feel like a safety item on a checklist. I wasn't sure that I could trust the feeling. Or you. But you didn't spend time with me in order to make my parents stop howling at the moon. I can just be with you and have no plan. I know that nothing will explode, or you won't forget and leave me at Costco if we improvise. It's new to me, but I think I like it," she said, feeling apprehension take root in her shoulders. "Does any of this make sense?"

"Dylan Delacroix, are you saying you like me?" Mike's half smile transformed into something bigger and more reassuring.

"I guess I am." Dylan felt herself settle into the warmth of his presence. Taking one step closer, she looked up at him.

"It's funny, because I noticed something similar." He looked up for a moment, watching the ceiling transition from the desert sun to a moonlit sky before looking back down at her. "I resolved to just leave you across the street where I found you. I didn't want that spontaneity in my life. One minute it was all tuneless karaoke and emoji toes. And the next, I was getting yelled at. Then I missed you. And I couldn't bring myself to cut you off. Hence Susan."

Dylan groaned, dropping her head to her chest.

"Hey." Mike gently placed a hand under her chin and tilted her face upward. "That is not where this is going."

He moved his hand to her arm, the touch sending shivers up and down her back. She risked looking up at his face, surprised to find contentment where she expected pain.

"Here is the thing about your lists. You bring a kind of creative energy to them. I mean, I thought I was ambitious. But this . . ." He shook his head, watching the sky overhead, then continued, "You put this together in two weeks with nothing but willpower, a lot of organization, and a few highly motivated friends."

"And Susan."

Mike laughed, gesturing around the room before letting his hand come to rest on her other arm. "It's what I missed about you. Why I didn't cuss you out and leave you across the street. Sure, aspects of your life are hectic, but you seem to have a system all your own for the disarray."

Joy pulsed through her as he spoke, and she instinctively leaned toward him, closing the gap between them without her mind asking her body to. She'd spent so long trying to put barriers between them, pretending her emotions were a product of chaos and his feelings some sort of mystery that was bound to dissipate. But here he was, and she couldn't rationalize or explain him away.

"Dylan, you are brave. It takes guts to be different from the people who raised you. But you being brave makes everyone around you bolder, including me. When you are around, people dream as big as you do, and they work just a little harder because they see you going after it. I was ready to give up on this dream. I wouldn't have been this brave or creative enough to chase this without you."

Mike slid his arms around her. Looking down at her, he said in a voice so low only she could hear him, "And, I think your lists are sexy. That is the honest truth."

Dylan laid her head against the solid muscle of his chest and laughed, the warmth of him seeping into her body as she returned his embrace. As the laughter slowed, Dylan turned her head back toward him, her neck elongating with the angle of her chin.

"So what do you say? Want to give it another try?" His question seemed simple; despite everything that had happened between them, there was no hesitation in his voice.

The idea coaxed a smile from her. "I sure hope you know a couple other slow-jam-and-sushi spots in town."

"I'm sure I can think of a few."

Her smile spread as the perfection of the moment sank in. Sliding her hands up Mike's chest, she felt the fine texture of his suit glide under her palms until she could clasp her fingers around his neck. Stretching up, she could practically taste the champagne on him as he drew her up to him.

Out of the corner of her eye, a flash of gold caught her attention, and she paused, turning her head slightly to the left.

Mike's patient sigh fell on her neck. "What is it? That yelling guy back?"

"Worse," Dylan said, dropping from her tiptoes. "We are being watched. By our families."

Mike laughed. "Are they waving or filming?"

Dylan peeked around his shoulder. "No cameras. Technically, only Stacy is waving, but Neale is giving me finger guns, which I think also counts."

"Let me guess: my moms are there clutching each other, *it's adorable* glued to their faces?"

"Pretty much," Dylan said, peeking around his shoulder one more time. "How did you know?"

Tilting his head back, Mike chuckled. "Neale is the worst secret keeper ever."

Dylan groaned, leaning against him, his shirt muffling her words. "She'd make a terrible spy."

"You're telling me. Mom and Ma have literally been asking about it for days. I knew the moment they walked in they'd be watching all night."

"And you were going to kiss me anyway?" Dylan said, smiling up at him.

"Well, yeah. They are already working on a seating chart for the wedding," he said, smirking and leaning in close to her.

Dylan tensed as the band shifted to a lush number, the night sky twinkling overhead. Mike bent close enough that she could smell his aftershave and whispered, "Joking."

Rising up on her toes so she was near enough to brush his lips, she said, "As long as they don't need me to organize anything, they can arrange all they like."

If smiles had a taste, this kiss was it. Whether it was the end of old habits or the promise of new things, Dylan could have sworn that this kiss felt like the first she had ever received. In that moment, she knew that wherever the person on the other end of that kiss went, as long as she was near him, she would be just fine.

She could check the perfect kiss off her list.

ACKNOWLEDGMENTS

This book belongs to my ancestors, for whom reading was an illicit act. Thank you for lending me your name, carrying me when I was afraid, teaching me how to hold my head up, and giving me a story. I hope I've made each of you proud.

My first big thank-you goes to agent extraordinaire Nalini Akolekar for seeing this book's potential, answering roughly 943 questions, and enduring an onslaught of emojis and Beyoncé GIFs throughout this process. You are wonderful!

I'm lucky to be supported by a fantastic team at Montlake, including Lauren, Jessica, Riam, Sylvia, and so many others. Thank you all for your hard work and support bringing this book into the world. Similarly, I am particularly grateful to Liz Casal Goodhue for my lovely cover. Another big thank-you goes to my editors Maria Gomez, who took a chance on a new author, and Selina McLemore, who shaped this into a real book. I'm still shocked you two were willing to work with me even after I admitted to spelling my name wrong on the SATs. Y'all are the best editors a bubble-challenged girl could ask for.

I'm equally grateful to my writer friends, including my Los Angeles coven, who are owed a tremendous debt of gratitude. I wouldn't have started writing without each of you. Another debt is owed to my Bay Area romance-writing friends. Y'all took me from baby author to published baby author. Your thoughtful guidance taught me how to pitch and what a writing community means and literally kept me in the room when it mattered most—a thousand times, thank you.

All of my family deserves a shout-out, but a special one goes to Joslyn for inspiring our bedtime stories and being my favorite lawyer. And to GAP, who gave me some of my first books and who, at ninety-five, still has a great book recommendation waiting every time I call.

A *forever fight on* to my day-ones, Angie and Ashley. Thank you for finding the grungy eighteen-year-old Seattle version of me worthy of your time and friendship. You two talked me out of (almost) all my bad ideas, supported me through my mediocre ones, and convinced me to chase every dream. Love you both!

Finally, my eternal gratitude to my dad, Randy, for helping me select outfits and delivering practical advice just when I'm about to freak out; my brother, Marshall, for following his heart and writing the first truly publishable piece in the family—that essay should have been laminated; my sister, CoCo, for every reassuring text and translating feedback into my idea of sexy; and finally, my mom, Kit, for having more faith in the family than any of us deserve. Also, she did, in fact, tell me so. Thank you all, because *we are a family and we love each other!*

ABOUT THE AUTHOR

Photo © 2020 Natasha Beale

Born and raised outside Seattle, Washington, Addie Woolridge is a classically trained opera singer with a degree in music from the University of Southern California, and she holds a master's degree in public administration from Indiana University. Woolridge's well-developed characters are a result of her love for diverse people, cultures, and experiences.

Woolridge currently lives in Northern California. When she isn't writing or singing, Woolridge can be found baking; training for her sixth race in the Seven Continents Marathon Challenge; or taking advantage of the region's signature beverage, wine.